THE FAKE FIANCÉE PROPOSITION

VIVIAN WOOD

ONE

RIVER

It's a lovely Georgia spring afternoon, chill and crisp, but beautiful nonetheless. Down here on the coast, the weather stays cooler for longer. One day soon, the oppressive summer heat will descend. But not today. Today, tender grasses unfurl. Young, still-green buds get the signal that they should soon bloom. The world seems to slough off its heavy winter mantle and worship the sun.

It's a day full of possibilities. It smells like business deals waiting to be made.

Cape Bistro bar and winery is absolutely humming right now, because it is packed to the gills with a who's who of Cape Simon families.

I take it all in with a jaundiced eye. The soft rustle of elegantly dressed guests mingling among tables adorned with crystal glassware and silver cutlery makes me feel restless.

Blush pink silk ribbons adorn the backs of chairs. The fragrant pink flowers that are gathered as centerpieces give the air a heavy, perfumed scent.

Instead of spending the day finalizing another million-dollar proposal, I'm here at Cole and Savannah's engagement party, gritting my teeth.

These parties are not exactly to my taste. They're meant to be a celebration of things to come... but the things to come are marriage and babies. Everyone knows those things aren't exciting to me.

In fact, I would say that the signs of commitment and settling down make me a little nauseated.

Not that I would say any of that to anyone here. I sip the glass of whiskey I'm holding and try to assess the party.

Are there deals to be made here?

"Beautiful, isn't it?" Savannah sidles up beside me. Her voice is quiet and sweet. Somehow it pairs perfectly with the clingy blush pink silk dress hugging her curves. The fabric catches the sunlight and casts a glow on her skin that makes her look like a fairy princess.

She seems like the perfect woman to pair with my brother Cole. Together, they are a replica of the bride and groom you'd find atop a wedding cake. It's nice, if you can stand how sugary sweet their whole *deal* is.

"Sure," I reply, adjusting my suit jacket. "If I was looking to throw an engagement party, which I am definitely not, I hope that I'd have half as much taste in silk hangings."

She grins at me. She's a sweet girl that can go toe-to-toe with my brother and my nephew. I'm glad that I talked Cole into kissing her feet and begging her to take him back. I might not need a partner in my life but Cole does. And he's infinitely better for it.

"River, don't be such a cynic. It's a party. Lighten up," she chides gently. She flicks a fingertip at my blush pink silk tie. Her fingers graze my chest briefly.

I sigh. Lightening up isn't exactly my forte.

I'm more the guy who stands back and observes. That is, unless I am given a risky business venture. I'm willing to roll the dice all day long when I'm dealing with properties and investments. Love, however, doesn't make my blood run hotter or my heart race. There is nothing so good as closing a deal that no one else could ever make.

I like to make mental notes of the dynamics at play in every situation. Just like right now, at this party. And the dynamics in play here are heavy and opulent enough to make anyone gag. Savannah may not be marrying my brother for his money. But my parents are celebrating this engagement with as many symbols of wealth as my no-nonsense brother will allow.

Speaking of the devil himself, Cole strides through the crowd. His suit is tailored to perfection. He's the physical embodiment of coolness.

"River, come join us," he calls out, waving a hand in my direction. His smile is practiced, but it's genuine enough to draw a few happy glances from the surrounding guests.

"Be right there," I respond. As I watch, as he turns back to a cluster of well-wishers, doling out firm handshakes and charming smiles.

I move through the throng of people, each step measured and precise. I can't help but feel like a wolf in a field of sheep. I'm different than most of these people. I don't want their cheesy good tidings or need their sentimental happily-ever-afters. Having a new bride on my arm has simply never been a part of my plan.

I usually don't think about it this much, but this party is practically bashing me over the head with Cole and Savannah's pre-marital bliss. I hate every second of it that I'm forced to endure. But I do it with a pleasant smile.

"Congratulations," I tell Cole as I approach him. The words feel foreign on my tongue. "You two seem... happy. Aren't you glad you listened to me?"

"Thanks, River," he replies, clapping a hand on my shoulder. "I'll try not to take it as a 'told you so'."

I straighten my lapels. "You asked, I answered. So I'm here with bells on. Until at least... what do you think? Eight?"

"You aren't getting out of here any time soon." He pins me with a look. "I don't care how much you hate wedding culture."

I raise my hands. "You won't hear a peep from me about why it's a huge waste of money and pretty insulting to women."

"Insulting to women?" He shakes his head a little. "Look I know that all this wedding mumbo jumbo isn't really your scene. I promise, there are only six thousand more bridal events before the actual wedding. Then you can relax."

"Sounds *amazing*." I lift a shoulder in a casual shrug. "I admit you and Savannah make a pretty cute couple. Just promise me there will be no funny business about setting me up with a bridesmaid or anything. It's the last thing I want."

"Relax, will you? Everybody who knows you, knows that you're against marriage."

I give Cole a look. "It's a sham. No offense. It's the old world desperately trying to reach into modern day relationships, just to fuck with them. Why should any of us have to do the whole swoony proposal schtick and promise our partners forever?"

Cole's look hovers on serious. I squint around at the room. This is not the place to be airing my personal feelings about the wedding industrial complex.

"Sorry, I got a little long winded there, even for a lawyer. I just have strong feelings. I swear to you that it's the last rant you're going to hear from me. At least today."

Cole squeezes my shoulder and offers me a wan smile. "You've made your views clear. Often. And loudly."

Wrinkling up my face, I sigh. I shouldn't go off on him about this on today of all days. Let him have his delusion.

"Today's about you, though. And I know that all the hearts and flowers and diamond rings are your idea of happily ever after. So... congratulations."

He shakes his head with a wry smile. "Thanks, I think."

When Cole gets distracted by another well-wisher coming up to shake his hand, I take a leisurely stroll through the sea of guests. Each one seemingly more enamored with the spectacle than the last. My eyes skim over smiling faces, all drunk on love.

Or maybe that's just the open bar.

Either way, their blissful ignorance grates on me. But I hide it well. After all, I'm River.

All I care about is when my next million is going to be earned.

Lost in thought, I round a table adorned with more pink petals than a florist's shop and nearly collide with a vision in...

Well, would you look at that, more blush pink silk. Pearl Brown nearly topples over. I grab her, trying to right her. And in doing so, my hands grab her taut ass.

She's all soft curves wrapped in that peasant blouse. Her light pink skirt rustles gently, a stark contrast to the rigid structure of the party around us. With her dark hair in neat braids, her sable skin looking dewy and perfect, and her flawless cheekbones, she's a freaking knockout.

"Sorry, didn't see you there," I say, steadying Pearl by her shoulders.

Pearl is a waitress at Gem's Diner. She also happens to be very close friends with Savannah and my little sister Lucy. Which I suppose is why she's here.

And did I happen to mention that she's absolutely stunning?

She makes my withered, frozen husk of a heart skip a beat.

"River," she breathes out. A hint of surprise in her voice suggests she wasn't expecting to be swept up off her feet today. "You're excused. This place is as crowded as a public bus."

"Seems like it," I agree. I take a step back, but I'm not able to peel my gaze away from Pearl's face quite yet. Or the hint of cleavage that she's showing off. "You look like you're about to bolt for the nearest exit."

She offers a small laugh, her fingers nervously smoothing down her skirt. "Is it that obvious? I guess these kinds of parties aren't really my scene."

"Join the club." I lift my glass in a mock toast. "But hey, at least we're dressed for the occasion. Your blouse and my tie match the decor to a T."

"Yeah." Pearl rolls her eyes but there's mirth dancing in them. "I swear, Savannah must have sent a memo to the whole town about the dress code."

"It was a thousand percent my mom's doing. She's been on cloud nine ever since Cole and Savannah announced that they were getting married," I reply. "She's been trying to convince them to get married at our family's home, La Ville Coralle."

"Hah! I think Savannah is nice enough that she would just let Sarah bulldoze her way into planning the entire wedding without her input." She looks mildly exasperated, but her voice hints at a fondness for Savannah.

I smirk. "That sounds like my mom's dream come true. I'm glad that someone in the family is going to let her fulfill her wedding planning dreams. The rest of the family is definitely not on the same track as Cole and Savannah."

Her lips twitch. "So, you're not interested in the whole 'for better or for worse' thing?"

I laugh. "Not even vaguely interested. At this rate, even Rex will be married before I go down. And Rex hasn't spent two consecutive nights with the same woman... well, ever."

"Honestly? I'm not really interested in dating anyone either. I just got out of a serious relationship last year. Now I'm like... allergic to anything other than light and fun." She wrinkles her nose and sighs. She looks around the room. "I should probably try to mingle."

Her reluctance is as clear as the day is long.

"Or," I suggest, leaning in with a conspiratorial whisper. "You could hide out with me. I'm thinking about sneaking out onto the patio with a bottle of whiskey."

"Is that so?" She quirks an eyebrow, amusement flickering across her features. "You know I love whiskey. How would you feel about making that a bottle of cinnamon whiskey?"

"Gross," I say, feeling a smirk tugging at my lips. "Cinnamon whiskey tastes like chugging those little heart-shaped candies. Bleh."

"I can just find somebody else to talk to," she fires back.

"Hey now, there's no need for threats. If cinnamon whiskey is a requirement, I can procure the supplies. I think I saw a bottle behind the bar."

"Oh, it's on." Pearl flashes me a naughty grin.

That grin goes down as smooth as a shot of real, un-cinnamon-flavored whiskey. I've chatted with her before, but this flirtation is a new thing, and I could get used to it.

I smirk at her. "Who knew dodging forced social interactions could lead to a secret whiskey mission?"

"I'll be Mata-Hari. You be Jason Bourne. Let's rendezvous on the terrace at 18:30 hours." Pearl gestures with a flourish. Her hand lands on her hip and her eyes issue a challenge.

Strangely, I'm looking forward to rising to that very mild provocation.

Moving separately but making a lot of silly faces, we navigate through the throng of guests. The DJ is starting to spin an old disco tune and we have to side step a few overzealous dancers.

We reach the fully stocked bar, an oasis in a desert of social niceties. The Cape Winery not only has every wine under the sun, but a selection of top shelf liquor too. The bottles are arranged in precise lines and the bottle of cinnamon whiskey is very close to the door.

I wait until the bartender turns away, then filch the bottle I want, leaving fifty dollars in its place. "Looks like we found the treasure," I whisper to Pearl.

"Definitely worth the expedition," she agrees. She gives me a cheeky grin that I can't help but like.

I might actually be having fun at this engagement party. Who knew? Pearl follows me out of the overcrowded bar and onto the patio.

It's the end of March, and still quite crisp outside despite the sun shining down on us. I sweep my jacket off and offer it to her.

We make eye contact. I'd never noticed before, but her darkened amber eyes are the same color of a very expensive shot of whiskey.

Our eye contact holds for a few seconds too long. Pearl blushes and accepts the coat, pulling it on. "Thanks."

I open the bottle of cinnamon whiskey, and take a couple of gulps. It burns as it goes down my gullet and I wince. It's so sweet that I'm pretty sure my gut is going to rot out on contact.

I make a disgusted sound. Pearl eyes me, but I just raise my hands in surrender. "It was an honest reaction."

"Uh huh." She takes the bottle and sips from it, wiping daintily at her lips when she's done.

I find myself wanting to stretch out the moment that we find ourselves reveling in. Her glossy lips keep catching my eye.

The last thing I want is for Pearl to catch me staring at her lips. Our flirtation is still very much in the silly phase. Being caught lusting after her would move us firmly to the 'should we do this already?' phase. And I don't think we're ready for that just yet. Still, I'm already at half-mast just standing here.

Imagine if she actually touched me with those lips. I would likely not survive the fallout from the explosion. I clear my throat.

"So, Pearl," I say. "How's life treating you?"

She hesitates, taking another sip from the bottle before passing it back. "Actually, things are terrible." Her voice trails off as glances toward the beach in the distance.

"Sounds serious." I take a shot of the whiskey and prod her, nudging her gently with my shoulder.

She takes the bottle back but doesn't make any move to drink more just yet. She bites her lip in this way that's somehow both cute and hot. Then her shoulders slump a little bit. Her mouth puckers.

Did I just misread her mood? Maybe I need to stop staring at her mouth and actually pay attention to her expression.

"My great aunt Delta's land," she finally says. Her whiskey-colored gaze returns to mine and I find it tinged with worry. "The property tax bill came. Land assessors were just out. They assessed an amount for the property taxes that's astronomical. That's on top of the several years of taxes already owed! We could lose everything if we don't figure something out."

"Shit." I try not to wince. "I'm really sorry, Pearl. Your family has had that land for a while, hasn't it?"

"A few generations." She blows out a breath.

"How much does she owe?" I ask. I like having all the facts. And dollars and cents are my specialty.

Pearl turns up her hands in a questioning posture. "Who knows? More than ten thousand dollars. Less than a hundred thousand. That's my best guess and I have *asked*."

She looks sad. I'd like to kiss her downturned lips until she smiles again.

But somewhere, in the back of my mind, gears begin turning. Ten thousand dollars is a pretty meager amount of money. Anybody can scrounge up that much if they really had to. Less than a hundred thousand is not something that anyone should wring their hands over.

I close deals bigger than that in my sleep. My tongue darts out of my mouth as I think it over.

Her aunt Delta is ancient and she's not exactly friendly. Especially not to people like me, who happen to own real estate brokerage firms. She has snapped at me several times and accused me of trying to take her land.

But I might be the solution to this whole problem. I sure as hell wasn't trying to steal her land then, but I might be now.

Well, not steal. *Sell for an ungodly profit* is more like it.

"Damn, that's rough." My brow furrows as I process Pearl's predicament. "Is the property all one piece?"

Pearl gives me a look out of the corner of her eye. "Yeah..."

Aunt Delta's estate is an important piece of history and it's woven into this town's tapestry. Located just south of South Shore, it's almost priceless. The land has fifty miles of shoreline and it is in pristine condition. I would be lying if I said the real estate lawyer in me didn't perk up at the mere mention of the land becoming *distressed*.

By distressed, I mean possibly underwater on property taxes.

Pearl... she doesn't deserve this stress. Plus, she would find herself in an endless sea of dollars if she *maybe* helped me sell her land.

And *maybe* I would receive a small finder's fee. Or better yet, *maybe* I could help the right company buy her property and then help them build something on it.

My brain is seriously chugging so hard it's about to catch fire.

"Have you considered any options?" I ask, trying to sound helpful rather than like the vulture I am.

"Not yet. I just don't want to have to sell any of it." The mischief and fire in her eyes during our whiskey mission is draining away. "I'm at my wit's end, honestly."

I lean back against the linen-covered table, watching the light play across her face, casting shadows that shouldn't be there on such a bright day. A plan begins to form in my mind.

Her problem is the land. Mine is that I am bored and need a new deal.

"Maybe..." I venture, drawing her attention. "I might have a way to help."

"Really?" Surprise lights up her features. But just as quickly, the bright expression dims and is replaced by skepticism. "What kind of help are we talking about?"

"Let's just say," I pause, the thrill of the gamble running through my veins. I lean into it because it is literally my favorite feeling. "It would be a mutually beneficial arrangement."

Her eyes narrow slightly, intrigued and cautious all at once. But behind that caution, I see it.

The spark of hope.

The possibility of a deal hangs in the air between us. Pearl's gaze, now a perfect blend of hope and skepticism, pins me in place.

I lick my lips. What else might come of us doing a deal together?

Pearl looks at me, her gorgeous mahogany-colored eyes like twin pools of molten amber. Her breath seems to catch. I lean in.

My brain has suddenly stopped working. A minute ago, I saw nothing but the cold hard dollar signs that could be made from this deal. But now I find myself wondering just what Pearl might like to get out of this scheme.

Would it involve me kissing her senseless? Maybe spending the night stripping her naked and burying my face between her legs?

"Pearl?"

She edges closer to me. "Yeah, River?"

"Would you—"

The whirlwind that is Savannah sweeps out of the winery, her satin dress fluttering behind her like a superhero's cape. She bangs open the patio door and looks between us with some surprise. We both jump apart and suddenly become quite interested in making sure our clothes are free of wrinkles.

As if Savannah can somehow tell that we almost kissed simply by being in our presence.

"Oh, there you are!" Savannah tells Pearl. "I was looking all over for you."

Pearl hands me the bottle of whiskey, grinning sheepishly. She looks at Savannah. "Busted! Please don't tell anyone that we decided to sneak off for some cinnamon whiskey. I don't really understand why anyone drinks wine."

"Well, I'm sorry to interrupt," Savannah chirps. She loops an arm through Pearl's. "But I need you to come settle an argument. You don't mind, do you?"

The attention slides to me. I shake my head and raise the bottle at them.

I hate to lose my only ally at this function, but I'm not the type to make a fuss. The bride asks for Pearl, so the bride gets to pull her attention away.

I'm a little disappointed. But I push a smile to my lips.

"Of course not," I say. "Pearl is quite popular today."

"Thanks, River," Sav says. "Don't stay out here too long. It's frigging cold!"

Pearl throws me an apologetic look over her shoulder. She starts to take off my jacket, but I shake my head. "Keep it. It looks better on you."

"You're ridiculous."

I cup my hand to my ear. "What's that? Ridiculously handsome, you said?"

"You're awful. We'll talk later, though?"

Oh, you can bet on that.

Savannah starts pulling her through the patio door.

"Definitely." I flash her a reassuring smile, already plotting how I can turn our potential deal into something concrete.

Something... mutually beneficial.

Something that I'm certain Pearl will enjoy as much as I will.

Two

The air buzzes with the kind of electricity that only money and an impeccable reputation can buy. Sav and I weave through clusters of guests. River's jacket is still around my shoulders, and I keep smelling faint notes of cedar and hints of tobacco rising from this elegant dinner jacket.

Which means it's River's scent. *Yum*.

Sav needs me to settle an argument over the wedding menu. For some reason, Sav likes to ask me questions about which wines pair with which courses. I know approximately nothing about wine, but I am the only one of our friends who works at a restaurant.

It's not a reason that anyone should ask for my opinions. But I still try to be helpful as much as I can.

"I think you want—" I hiccup. I might be a little tipsy from those shots. "Sorry. I think you want to move from the lightest wine to the heaviest. Then, of course, you would move to champagne and port after dinner. Those are things that I've heard, anyway. You really should talk to my boss, Gem if you want a foodie's opinion."

Sav nods eagerly. "That's exactly what I needed to know. I was telling Cole's mom we would need a lot more champagne than anything else."

I open my mouth to respond, but Sav is almost immediately pulled away by an older woman in a sterling silver dress. It's Cole's mom, I think. "Savannah! Come meet your new great aunt Beulah. She's over in the corner."

Savannah throws me a helpless glance over her shoulder as she is hustled away. I figure that's to be expected at her engagement party. Can't be mad at her for that.

I sweep my gaze over the room. The thought of returning to the patio to rejoin River is awfully tempting. Maybe if I move quickly, I might still find him out there.

I can't believe I just opened my mouth and let whole drama with Aunt Delta come tumbling out. But River seemed to take it in stride. He actually seemed interested in what I was saying.

Actually, he might've just been trying to get close enough to me to kiss me. I flush.

Am I glad that Sav interrupted us?

I'm not sure. We could've had a lot of fun together tonight. In fact, there's nothing saying we still can't.

I just have to find River.

Everyone around me is dressed to the nines and sipping on champagne that probably costs more than my weekly paycheck. The chime of the bartenders pouring expensive wine into crystal glassware lets me know just what this is.

The engagement party is nothing short of a *spectacle*. It's an explosion of blush pink and sparkling lights. Cape Bistro, the fanciest restaurant in town, has completely closed for the entire day just for this private event.

I work in a diner, a place way less nice than this. We've closed for Gem's family events. And we closed for Mr. Anderson's retirement party once; he was the local grade school janitor for fifty years. I know the faculty and his family paid Gem almost ten thousand dollars to close down the diner for a Friday night.

So, extrapolating from experience: the groom's family must have paid through the nose for this dedicated staff and the event space. On a *Saturday*, no less. I can't even begin to add up the chocolate fountain, the oyster buffet, the prime rib carving station. The cost must be in the tens of thousands, easily. Maybe almost fifty.

I tug at the lapels of River's oversized black dinner jacket. It's made of this almost gauzy, lightweight wool. Checking the pockets, I find a woman's phone number neatly scrawled in lipstick on a black cocktail napkin. It's probably not from here.

But it does remind me that River is very much a hot commodity. I bite my lip and search the room for him.

One of his brothers swans by in a blush pink tie and a dark suit. That's another cost: the bride and groom paid to have matching pink ties and skirts delivered to each of their bridal party members.

So rachet that cost up by another ten thousand. Gulp. I am not used to being in a room with this much money being spent in such a casual and cavalier way.

"Can you believe this?" I murmur to no one in particular. As a waiter sweeps by bearing a tray of champagne. I shake my head. "This is insane."

Champagne at the ready, mine for the taking. It's like being in a fairytale. If the fairy godmother wielded a platinum credit card instead of a magic wand, that is.

I sense eyes on my back and turn. It's him, of course. River Bennett, with his piercing gaze that seems to cut right through the crowd.

He's found me again.

I struggle to suck in a breath. How he does that to me with eyes cut from living sapphire, I don't quite understand.

My cheeks heat up with a telltale blush as our eyes lock again. It's involuntary. It's also embarrassing. I have graduated both high school and college. And yet I feel like I'm a little girl about to have her pigtails pulled every time River smirks at me.

I roll my eyes. I can't react to him like this. Especially not when I am a guest at his family's fancy celebration. I'm just here to enjoy myself.

Not give in to my impulses and stick my tongue down River's throat like I want to. *Badly.* I just barely escaped acting on my impulses when Sav interrupted River and I circling each other.

I know how that will end. I'll be momentarily satisfied and then I won't be able to make eye contact with River at the many, many wedding-related activities that I know are planned for me as a bridesmaid.

"Stop staring," I chastise myself. It's about as effective as using a glass of tap water to put out a forest fire. I shake my head, trying to clear the fog that River's smoldering looks seem to summon in my brain.

A tinkling laugh bubbles up beside me. I turn to see Savannah, her eyes dancing with glee.

"Girl, you're not fooling anyone." She nudges me with her elbow.

"What do you mean?" I go for innocence.

"Sorry. Wedding planning is going to be the death of me." Savannah sneaks a glance at me. "I meant to ask you about something. What on earth is going on with you and Cole's brother?"

"River? Nothing. We both just needed some air."

Sav looks down her nose at me, pinning me. "Those

little glances back and forth between you two? That's some major flirtation happening."

Her giggle fills the space between us. It's light and carefree, like Savannah herself. With her blonde hair and bubbly personality, I've often said that Sav is sunshine *personified*.

"Flirtation? Please." I roll my eyes even as I fight down the flutter in my belly. "We were just being delinquents. Besides, he's a man, isn't he? All men are a flimsy, two-dimensional sham." I hold up a hand to stop her before she can argue. "Except Cole. He's perfect. But River? He's only interested in hooking up with me."

Her expression softens, a sisterly concern seeping through her festive facade. "Pearl, you've got to stop thinking like that. You're amazing. Any guy would be lucky to have you."

"Saaaaaaavvvvv." I pretend to stomp my feet. "You are way nicer than any boy I've ever met. Are you sure you won't leave Cole and run away with me to be my platonic wifey? I'll treat you real good." I wink at her.

"Please." Savannah laughs and rolls her eyes so hard I'm surprised they don't get stuck. "You could have any guy here eating out of your hand. Besides, I really love Cole. He's the one for me, Pearl."

Nudging her shoulder with mine, I nod. "I get it. You two look like the dictionary definition of marital bliss. Like when I look up 'happily engaged,' I see a photo of you and Cole. It's gross."

"The point I'm trying to make is that maybe you should get gross with someone new. Not necessarily one of Cole's brothers, mind you. But—" She turns her head and looks over to catch River gazing at us. As soon as Savannah catches him, he turns away. She turns back to me and wiggles her eyebrows. "River seems primed for action."

"Hardly." A laugh bubbles up, bitter and sharp. "I'm just

a diner waitress, Sav. There's no way I could actually catch the attention of one of the Billion Dollar Bennetts. I know that you come from humble beginnings too, but you're all sunshine and warmth. Whereas I'm just... me."

"That's ridiculous. You're a diamond, shining in a world of dumb, dirty rocks."

She's so sweet that I want to pinch her.

"Stop it. Besides, even if I could grab the attention of one of the Bennetts, why would I want to? You know I don't date anymore."

She plants her hands on her hips, the universal sign that I've just said something particularly stupid. "You're crazy, Pearl. The Bennetts might be rolling in dough, but they are good people. Trust me." Her voice softens. "And after the nightmare with he-who-shall-not-be-named, you deserve someone who treats you right."

I look at her flatly. "I have a useless fine arts degree, and twenty-nine hundred dollars shoved in a shoe box under my bed. I'm pretty sure that, with student loans, I'm worth a negative number of dollars. The Bennetts might as well be royalty compared to me."

"You are gorgeous and smart and extremely funny," she insists. Her hands are planted firmly on her hips. "Money isn't everything. You're selling yourself short."

"Easy for you to say. You're marrying Cole Bennett," I counter with a sigh. "I'm just..." I get exhausted before finishing my sentence. "Me."

"Exactly!" she proclaims. "That's what I'm saying! You're you. You are wonderful. That's more than enough."

Savannah's voice is firm. Her belief in me is so *pure*. It's both comforting and frustrating how she refuses to see the world through my jaded eyes.

"River's a man." I shoot a scowl over my shoulder at him. "He's a flirt. He will run off and disappear the second that I start to actually look his way. After Bishop, I don't want to try to find anyone. Being with nobody is better than being heartbroken."

"Love will surprise you," she says softly, squeezing my arm. "It'll happen when you least expect it."

"Right now, all I *expect* is to survive this party without spilling anything on this dress."

Before Savannah can respond, someone calls her name again. Probably a distant cousin or another friend she's managed to charm without even trying. She gives me yet another apologetic look before she's once more whisked away into the sea of guests. I take a deep breath.

For a second, I enjoy the rare spot of solitude amidst the boisterousness of the engagement party. The wine has indeed been flowing and the crowd seems on the brink of becoming rowdy. Checking my watch, I note that it's already seven.

I have to work early tomorrow. So, if I'm smart, I'll leave before too long.

"Excuse me?" A hesitant voice pulls my head up. A young woman, barely out of her teens by the looks of it, cradles a bundle in her arms. She's a vision of new motherhood with red hair, tired eyes, and a hopeful smile.

"Hi, I'm Jenn. I'm a friend of the groom's family." Her gaze flits around, as if she's looking for an escape route. "Could you... would you mind holding my baby for a minute? I just need to use the restroom really quickly. My mom is here somewhere and she could take Amy, but I can't find her. I am embarrassed to say that I really can't hold it--"

"Of course," I cut her off. "You go! I will stay right here and make friends with Amy."

I extend my arms to take the baby. Amy doesn't make a sound, although she looks up at me with wide blue eyes.

She's teeny tiny, adorable perfection at what I would guess is two months old.

"Thanks so much. I'll hurry back!" Jenn says, pressing a kiss to her fingertips and then lovingly to Amy's cherubic face.

"Take your time. I'm here all night!" I try not to be too needy. But I *love* babies.

Okay, I *might* be a little baby crazy.

As her baby settles into my arms, Jenn gives me a grateful nod and hurries off. I look again at the tiny face peeking up at me. Her eyes are so wide and curious.

There's something about holding a baby that makes the world feel simpler, quieter.

Her innocent weight in my arms roots me to the spot. For a moment, everything else fades away.

The thumping music, the clinking glasses, even River's electric glances from across the room? *Poof*. Gone.

"Hey there, little one." She coos. I can't help but chuckle. "Looks like you and I are on babysitting duty, huh?"

I lean close and I catch a whiff of Amy's scalp. That unique newborn scent hits me. It's pure and sweet, like the promise of new beginnings. It stirs something deep inside me. I sway gently, making soft shushing sounds.

"I want a baby just like you someday," I can't help but coo at her. "Yes I do! Yes. Yes I do!"

I shift my weight, adjusting her onto my hip as I bounce gently. Amy makes a face that looks like a wide, gummy smile. It's a shot of sunshine straight to my heart. "You like that, huh?" I grin. I tickle her under her neck with gentle fingertips. Her eyes crinkle in response. She's feeling pure joy without reservation.

"Wow, you're a natural with her," Jenn says, returning

from her brief escape to the restroom. She watches me for a moment, a smile touching her lips.

"Thanks," I reply, feeling a swell of pride. The pride also comes with a pang of longing. I've always thought I had a knack for babies. But hearing it from a new mother is unexpectedly validating. My heart seizes with a fierce, desperate *want* for a moment, before I get it under control. "I can hold onto her for a while if you want."

I hope that isn't a weird thing to blurt out.

"You don't mind if I grab a plate?" Jenn asks, eyes going wide.

"Seriously, go nuts. I mean, don't leave Amy with me until midnight. But definitely go enjoy yourself."

Amy stretches and babbles. I find myself paying more attention to her than to her mom, who promises that she'll be back in just a few minutes.

"What are you thinking about, I wonder?" I ask the little one. "Astrophysics? The true nature of man? Something like that, I bet."

"Whose baby is this?!" Savannah's voice cuts through the hum of party chatter. I turn to see her approaching, with Grace in tow.

"Friend of a friend." As I say it, someone calls Sav's name. She flashes me a smile and an apologetic glance that seems to be becoming a habit, then turns away.

I look to Grace, who's left looking mildly panicked. I assume it's because she is an introvert by nature and has been since day one of our freshman year of college. She was clinging to Savannah like she was a life raft coming from a ship wreck.

"This is a lot of *peopling*," I tell her sympathetically. "I know that if I'm feeling partied out, you must be about to lose your fricking mind. Just hug the wall like me."

Grace offers a small, grateful smile. "Thanks, Pearl. You're too nice. Who's your buddy?"

"Friend of the groom's family," I explain, still swaying Amy in my arms. "Just helping out for a sec. You know how I feel about kids."

"Looks good on you," Grace observes. Her gaze softens as she watches me interact with the child. "You should definitely have a family."

"Some day soon," I say. The words are out of my mouth before I even really think about what I am saying. They surprise me.

"Really?" Grace's eyebrows rise.

"Really," I confirm. The conviction settles over me like a brand-new coat. "I mean, maybe. You know. We'll see how things go."

Grace chuckles, then shifts her gaze to me. Her eyes narrow with concern. "How's Aunt Delta? I haven't seen her at the hospital since her last fall."

I hesitate. I shift the baby's weight to my other arm. Until Amy landed in my hands, I hadn't been able to think about much else than my family's matriarch.

"She's okay, health-wise. Thanks in no small part to you, Miss Doctor Lady. But there's some trouble brewing, financially speaking. Times are tough."

As I just told River on the patio, I need to be careful about not turning this engagement celebration into a pity party.

Grace winces, sympathy etching lines around her eyes. "I'm really sorry to hear that, Pearl. I hope things look up for her soon."

"Thanks. Life just loves to throw curveballs, doesn't it?"

The baby seems to sense my upset and begins to fuss. Instinctively, I bounce her lightly. I whisper soothing sounds until her tiny features relax into a smile.

I sway gently on my heels, her head nestled against my chest. Her soft hair brushes my nose, and I breathe in that sweet, powdery baby scent. My heart does a somersault before squeezing painfully in my chest.

"She settled right down. How'd you do that?" Grace asks.

"I don't know," I shrug. "It's just instinct, I guess."

I look at baby Amy. She looks back at me and then yawns, waving her arms, and... I want this.

I want a baby.

Without all the muss and fuss of finding the right guy and settling down.

I don't have to have some guy's ring on my finger to be a good mom. My mom raised us by herself after my dad died. And I turned out well enough, didn't I?

"Okay, then." I bounce the baby a bit higher. Amy's cooing sounds punctate the air again. "It's settled. I'm gonna start tracking my cycle. I'm going to figure out the next steps to having a baby and being the hottest single mom on the planet."

"Wait... what?" Grace looks a little shocked. "I didn't even realize you were thinking about having a baby now!"

"Why not now?" I ask. I raise a challenging brow.

"I didn't say it was a bad idea. I'm just taken aback. I guess good for you, Pearl." Grace grins. She's always the supporter, even in my most impulsive moments. "You're taking control. That's what matters."

I nod, feeling empowered. This is me, grabbing life by the reins.

THREE

RIVER

Don't be a coward. Just get out of the damn truck and go inside. It won't be as bad as all that, I tell myself.

I'm sitting in my truck, parked along the winding private driveway of my parents' white beachfront mansion, trying to amp myself up.

Empty cars and trucks sit between me and the marble front steps. My brothers and sisters are already inside. The clock on the dash says I'm a half an hour late.

The thing is, I already know what I'm going to get when I head inside. My brothers will chuck me on the arm. My sisters will tell me they've missed me lately, and politely inquire about my dating life. My stepdad, Sam, will make small talk about business. My mom will tell me about her friends' eligible daughters.

I know all of this, because I've done this before. Sure, it's Cole's engagement brunch instead of a graduation party or a beach barbecue. But I'm still asked the same questions.

Have you met someone special? Are you settling down? Getting married? Having babies?

Now that Cole, the least emotional and most businesslike one of the bunch, has successfully found himself a fiancée, the pressure for me to find my soulmate has only increased.

If I'm being perfectly honest, my family is great, but they are *a lot*.

Sighing, I force myself out of my truck and up the sandy driveway. It's just turning to spring on the Georgia coast, and the sky overhead is miles and miles of unbroken gray steel. I feel the light patter of raindrops as I bound up to the front door. The raucous sound of laughter immediately washes over me as I elbow my way inside.

See? I tell myself. *It's not so bad.*

I enter the high-ceilinged entryway and spot my mother. Holding Charlie on one hip, she turns and breaks into a huge grin when she spots me.

"River!" she crows. "I was wondering where you were. We've been waiting on you to start eating."

"Sorry," I say. I rub my hand on my khakis and smile as I bend down to kiss her on the cheek. "Glad to be here, Mom."

"Uncle River!" Charlie bleats. He slides down my mom's hip. I kneel down and throw my arms out. Charlie runs into my embrace and hugs me hard.

"Hey, little man. What's up with you today?" I sweep his shaggy mop of dark hair away from his face.

He grins at me like I'm paying him to show me as many teeth as he can. "I'm going to science camp this summer!"

"That's exciting. You'll learn about dinosaurs, I bet."

Excitement lights his grin. "And sharks! It's gonna be cool."

"I bet." Before I can say another word, Cole calls Charlie's name. Charlie races off toward him, and I shake my head. "That kid is so excited about anything science related.

Plus, he's smart. He's probably going to be a nuclear physicist or something."

My mom gives me another side hug. "Undoubtedly. Now come on into the living room. Eden is here visiting from New Orleans. You didn't get to see her much because she left the engagement party so early."

"Really?" My sister's presence is a surprise. "I thought Mark had her under some kind of spell that prevented her from visiting," I joke.

My mom gives me a tart look, and warns me in a low voice. "Be nice. I don't want you offending her, or Mark, with your razor-sharp sense of humor. He could be your brother-in-law someday."

"Come on, Mom. Even you can't want Eden to settle down with Mark. He's so completely *dull*." I make a face as we step into the living room to join the rest of the family. Mom's jaw tightens and I stop her, leaning in close to whisper. "I promise I'll play nice."

The words are something to ease Mom's mind. I fully do not mean a word of my promise.

She gives my shoulder a quick squeeze before Charlie calls her away with a squeal. "Mimi! Mimi! Come see!"

My gaze slides around the room. Eden catches my eye first and gives me a little wave. She's wearing a light pink dress with a puff decoration on one sleeve that's the size of her head. Typical Eden; no matter what everybody else is wearing, she'll be dressed to the nines in something ostentatious.

I make a beeline for her, and give a hug while trying not to crush the delicate pink pouf on her dress.

She pulls back with a soft smile. "You're looking like a million, zillion bucks."

I grin. "I take that as a huge compliment from the girl

that always looks like she just wandered off a runway in Milan, and may be very lost."

She wrinkles her nose and elbows me, then turns to her boyfriend beside her. "You know Mark, of course."

Even though he is a good six inches shorter than me, Mark somehow manages to look down the bridge of his nose at me. His tweed coat and his black slacks are somewhere between not quite matching and clashing atrociously. He looks as if every exam proctor I ever had was smashed together to create a single, exceedingly dour, adjunct professor.

"How could I ever forget Mark?" I ask, offering a handshake. "The man, the myth, the legend." Apparently, if I can't be sarcastic, I'm overly complimentary to the point that it becomes trite.

Mark takes my hand with an expression bordering on distaste. "Hello again, Brooks."

I cough into my hand to hide my surprise at Mark casually mixing me up with my younger brother. My family went to Big Sur for a week, five years ago, and invited Mark along. It not like he's never met me. It's also not like Eden and Mark weren't at same damn party as I was at *last night*.

Then again, there are a lot of faces in our family. "Err..."

Eden grabs Mark's hand and squeezes it. "You mean River, honey. Brooks is over there."

"Hah! River and Brooks. I get it." Mark squints at me and shrugs. "Sorry. You Bennetts are confusing sometimes."

"There's nothing to get. Brooks' given name is—"

"No!" yells Brooks. I thought he was far enough away not to hear, but I guess I was wrong.

I cup my hands around my mouth to be heard. "Sorry!"

"Brooks is sensitive about his first name," Eden fills in. "It's best not to antagonize him."

"Anyway, as you were saying." I give Mark a cool smile.

"Bennett isn't actually my last name. I'm one of the Taylor clan. When my mom married Sam, she hyphenated her last name. But Brooks and I still have our father's name."

I am totally sick of telling people this. Not to mention the fact that Eden should be handling her boyfriend's questions.

Mark furrows his brow like he's trying to balance a goddamned algebraic equation. "Huh."

"I've explained this to you before," Eden murmurs to Mark. She doesn't seem upset in the least as she smiles and brushes a speck of lint from the shoulder of his jacket. "We're a blended family."

"Ah. Right." He looks bored. "Sorry, sugar dumpling."

Sugar dumpling? Ugh. Dude is the absolute worst. I hide my reaction behind a stiff smile. Throwing Eden a look that says 'Are you kidding me???' I take a step back. "I'm going to say hi to everyone else."

I veer away from them and swerve over to the next group. Savannah and Cole are there, beaming at each other. *Gross.* Beside them is my brother Brooks, who is dressed like a lost member of Nirvana in a black T-shirt, loose fitting blue jeans, and a red flannel shirt tied around his waist.

Brooks is staring daggers at Eden and Mark. My lips twitch. I secretly love that Brooks and Mark get along like cats and dogs. Seeing Brooks glaring in Mark's direction tickles me.

"What, I don't even get a hello?" I complain to Brooks and Cole.

Brooks meets my gaze, and he jerks his chin upward in greeting. "Hey." Then he immediately goes back to scowling at Mark.

"River!" Savannah chirps. "Thanks for coming last night. I didn't really expect you to stay until the place closed!"

The back of my neck heats. I definitely stayed because Pearl was still there and I thought there was a chance that I might get some more alone time with her. Unfortunately, I didn't.

"I did stay kind of late. And then I had a work meeting super early today." I see a chance to change topics and launch into it whole-heartedly. "You know, I've been slammed at work lately. The real estate brokerage is super busy. Plus, since Rex and Cole have been working together on the baseball training camp, I'm trying to get a resort community built to accommodate the guests that the camp will draw in."

Cole scratches his chin. "Did you get the South Shore planning board on board with the schematics yet? You'd think they'd be all over this resort idea."

Cole asking about the idea I have for Delta Jackson's property gets me excited.

I nod. "Not just any resort. I want a luxurious five-star hotel, a high end eighteen-hole golf course, twenty upscale private bungalows, and a brand-new boardwalk where resort guests can find the designer brands they love. I am putting in a ton of hours to make a presentation that will knock the socks off potential investors. You and Rex are planning on raking it in with the training camp. I want to position our family at the other end to make massive amounts of money after the resort is built."

"You mean you want to position *yourself*." Cole pins me with a steely gaze. "It's all well and good to talk a big game about how our family will profit. Just do me a favor and save that bullshit for Dad. You aren't selling us on jack squat."

He reaches out an arm and rubs Savannah's lower back. Being that close with another person isn't one of my life goals, but I am a bit jealous of how free and easy the engaged couple is with each other. It must be nice.

Savannah smiles gently, and fidgets with her huge engagement ring. "Well, I think your resort sounds fun. If Cole and I weren't already so busy with building the training camp, I'd say that we should team up."

"Don't forget that we're planning a wedding, too," Cole chips in.

I haven't exactly forgotten. Not only are Cole and Savannah engaged, but they are getting special treatment from my mom and Sam because they are settling down.

I've heard through the family grapevine that Cole is even getting his trust fund early because Sam approves of Cole settling down with Savannah. It's extremely unfair because everyone in the family knows that our trust funds aren't supposed to kick in until we're forty years old. Damn. If I only had access to that trust, I would have more than enough money to play real estate roulette for a hundred years.

How do I get a piece of that action? I wonder.

"Yeah, well. Maybe I need to recruit you two to join the project. Then Sam would actually start taking it seriously."

"What does that mean?" Cole asks.

Before I can answer, my mom's voice cuts through the party like a hot knife through butter. "Lunch is served!" she calls, clapping her hands to call the family's attention. "Everyone, find your seats in the dining room, please."

I move toward the dining room slowly, letting my family filter around me to find their seats. When I get in the dining room, I move slowly. Everyone else hurries toward food.

Not me, though. I don't know if it's dread or avoiding the conversation that is undoubtedly about wedding planning, but my footsteps are glacially paced. As I wait for everyone else to sit, it's almost like I'm watching a movie. I decide it's called *Happy Family Eats Meal Together: Now*

With Awkward Additional Brother Who Does Not Believe In Their Values System At All.

Because I am last to the table, I end up sandwiched between Mark and my mother. I don't mind. My mom is busy fawning over the newly betrothed, and Mark is, as ever, only interested in Eden.

I slip into my chair, and my youngest sister, Lucy, grins across the table at me, wiggling her eyebrows. She's the sibling I always connected with the most. She's also the baby so I can't help but indulge her. Being seated across from her is actually a relief.

I smile at her. "I heard you were at college all week on some kind of studying lockdown."

She shrugs a shoulder and toys with her place setting, moving the heavy pewter fork around and shifting the precise placement of her ornate crystal water glass. Lucy is always moving objects around, either out of boredom or some personal sense of feng shui that no one else gets. I think it's part of being an artist. Some innate need to make things slightly more beautiful than they are handed to her.

She doesn't meet my eyes as she says, "I needed a break. Dad sent the family private jet to pick me up since I'm just down from the city for the day."

Lucy is acting evasive, which is kind of strange. But she has to know that I don't care what her reasons are for doing any damn thing that she pleases. My being nonjudgmental is one of the reasons we stay close.

I give a low whistle. "Now that's how you travel in style."

Lucy gives me a mischievous smile. "I know. It's totally gauche. But it's way more luxurious than driving four and a half hours just to be here for lunch."

The kitchen staff appears with plates of food. I snag my napkin off my plate and sit back as a spring salad is laid before me. A woman comes around offering dinner rolls, while a third server pours me a glass of white wine.

I sigh silently. This is my parents' normal level of pomp and circumstance for any family gathering. Fine china, crystal goblets, a full coterie of maids, and servants, and butlers, and chefs.

Me? I own a huge house with nothing set up in it but my bed and a book case. My parents are maximalists. It's how they show love.

My mother leans over to me. "The wine is a Chablis that Sam and I found in France on our little winter getaway. It's very delicious."

I smile and taste the wine to appease her. I have to mask my immediate response, which is to spit it out like a child might a forkful of peas. The wine is so dry that it tastes almost astringent.

"It's nice," I mumble. "Seems very French."

My mom beams at me. "I'm glad you like it. Sam says that he doesn't care for this particular Chablis. I keep telling him that he just needs to expand his palate more."

I spear a huge forkful of salad and give her a look. "I'm sure that he loved being told that he isn't refined enough to enjoy something."

Mom darts a look at her husband and gives me a wink. Then she pulls out her phone. "While I've got you here, River, I wanted to show you a couple of girls that are single and ready to mingle, as they say. These are the daughters of my friends Elen and Christine."

I scowl. "I don't need you to set me up on dates, Mom."

She waves a dismissive hand. "Oh, I know that! And I know that you aren't interested in getting married right away. But that doesn't mean you shouldn't meet people!"

She hands her phone to me, and I can see that she's pulled up the Instagram account of a reedy blonde girl in yoga pants. If you added a mini-bouffant, she'd look exactly like my mom. *Gross.*

I frown and pass the phone back to her. "She's very nice. But I'm not interested in the daughters of your friends. I don't need a matchmaker."

"Oh, River." Mom screws up her face and releases a tremendous sigh. "I just want you to be happy."

"I'll be happy when I figure out the financing for the resort I'm going to build near South Shore."

And when I rescue the damsel in distress that presented me with this opportunity. I have no time for distractions. But Pearl may just be worthwhile.

Just thinking about her warm body pressed against mine while she gazes up at me, just a little breathless? I suck in a breath and cough into a hand.

Yeah, when I secure the financing for this deal, I'm definitely taking Pearl out to celebrate. Possibly the party can take place with both of us buck ass naked and Pearl moaning my name...

"River," my mom says. "Hello, earth to River."

My neck heats. "I'm listening, Mom."

Sam, who until now has just been listening to our conversation, clears his throat. "That resort is a pipe dream, son. Even if you had a concrete plan in place and investors lined up, you would still have to buy the land out from Delta Jackson. And Ms. Jackson is never going to sell. That land has been in their family for over a hundred years. There is no way that she willingly lets it out of her hands."

I try not to let my annoyance with my stepdad's words show on my face.

"Delta's niece, Pearl, already told me that her great aunt had a big property tax bill that she didn't know how to pay." I set my fork down and eye Sam, vindication rising inside my chest. "One way or another, that land is going to be distressed. The only question is whether it's our real estate firm that gets it, or whether some huge, out of town conglomerate scoops it up and starts building god knows what on the land. At least with my plan, the family will get enough money to start over somewhere else."

I cross my arms and give him a defiant stare.

Sam pushes his plate away from himself, plants his elbows on the table, and leans forward. He points a meaty finger at me. "You don't go celebrating someone else's downfall. There aren't a lot of Black landowners, period. Much less ones who own such a large swathe of land, or ones who've owned the land for a century."

His voice booms out, drawing the attention of my siblings. Everyone falls quiet and turns toward him.

I clench a fist but otherwise try to keep my true feelings out of my voice. I can't have it seem like I'm an unhinged madman screaming at an old man. "And I respect that. But if the property taxes on Ms. Jackson's land go unpaid for long enough, it will be auctioned off by the government for pennies on the dollar. I'm talking about helping her out, and keeping control of the land in the community. Otherwise, some corporate landlord will just gobble it up."

A vein stands out in Sam's forehead. "If Ms. Jackson needs money to keep her land, I'd rather pay her taxes out of my own pocket than see anyone take advantage of her plight."

I feel my neck heat. "Nobody said anything about taking advantage of her. I plan to write her a huge check."

Fuck. There goes that dream. Now if I don't get my trust fund, I'm going to be without capital for this project. And I can't have that...

"My point still stands." He glares at me as though spoiling for a fight. "Let the members of the Jackson family decide what should be done with their own land. Keep out of it."

"Daddy." Lucy puts her hand on Sam's shoulder, her tone cajoling. "Please, don't let your blood pressure spike. I'm sure that River didn't mean to upset you." She gives me a pointed stare. "Right, River?"

The only thing I hate about Lucy is her steadfast obsession with Sam. I've never understood it, but Lucy has always been Daddy's little girl. This is, unfortunately, pretty typical behavior for her.

When Lucy calls me out like this, I feel like I really have no other option but to back down. No matter how I may silently seethe in rage.

I shake my head. "I didn't mean to raise your ire, Sam. I'm just–"

"River!" Lucy pleads, cutting me off. "Read the room."

I look around at my siblings. Cole coughs to cover a chuckle. Brooks has a smirk that he's trying rather unsuccessfully to cover with his hand. Eden is glaring at me.

Oh, that's right. I forgot for one goddamned minute that I am the black sheep of this otherwise happy little family. My lips twist in a sneer. I toss my napkin down as a precursor to standing up and getting the fuck out of here.

When my mom cuts in, her voice is no-nonsense. "Everybody just needs to cool off. No more business talk at my table. It gets you all so heated!"

"But—" Lucy starts.

My mom gives her a quelling look. "Please, everyone. Can't we all be civil? Just one more hour and then I promise to release you out back like a pack of wild wolves."

I drum my fingertips. Lucy glares at Mom. Brooks manages to look stoic. Eden is whispering something in Mark's ear.

My mom gives us all a strained smile and pats Sam's arm.

She turns to look at one of the servers stationed by the doorway. "Miss Delphine, would you please clear our plates? We're ready for y'all to bring in the main course."

The rest of the meal is filled with my mom asking all of us questions about things that are coming up in the future. I tune out for most of it. All I can think of is my half-cocked plan to secure the rights to build on Delta Jackson's land, and the linchpin of my plot.

Pretty Pearl Brown. She of the sharp dark eyes and megawatt smile. Lover of cinnamon whiskey and blush pink skirts. Waitress and the only relative that Ms. Jackson seems to listen to. When Pearl told me about her quandary, I didn't have an answer. But now, I do.

Clearly the solution is to talk to Pearl... and probably kiss her too. Then if I can get Pearl to agree to talk to her great aunt on my behalf, I feel like my resort project will have a real chance at success.

Once we finish eating, the family begins to drift outdoors toward the beach. Before Lucy can follow, I pull her into the living room. "You know Pearl pretty well, right?" I ask her.

Yes, I know that Lucy was my enemy only moments ago. But she's the most solid of my sibling relationships.

And there's the fact that she happens to be good friends with Pearl too.

She narrows her eyes at me. "Yes. She was a senior at Agnes Glen when I was an incoming freshman. Why are you asking?"

"Don't you worry about that." I cross my arms and offer her a mischievous smile. "Do you happen to know where she'll be in the next few days? I might like to stage a run-in. But I don't want it to seem creepy."

Lucy cocks her hip. "Do you want to run into Pearl because you're going to rope her into your latest scheme?"

Scheme. Sounds a lot like Lucy's general attitude toward my ventures.

"Nah. I just want to see her." It's not exactly the truth. More like... truth-adjacent. But I do find Pearl appealing, in a girl next door kind of a way.

Okay, that's not exactly correct either. Pearl is an absolute knockout. Anyone with eyes can see that she's easily the most beautiful girl in the room. Literally wherever she goes, she fucking lights up the people around her.

So I choose to lean into that now.

Lucy studies me for a moment and then sighs, shaking her head. She pulls out her phone. "I know where she'll be tomorrow night, the first Thursday of the month. But you have to promise to show up with an open mind."

"What does that mean? Am I going to be weirded out? She's not a member of a cult, is she? Because I have been there, done that for a date. And the Regentologists do not want me back in their temple. I've been banned for life."

Lucy's lips turn up at the corners as she sends me the info. "It's definitely not church. Bring a snack and a blanket."

That gives me pause. "What? Why would I need those things?"

"Trust me." Lucy grins and jerks her head towards the huge plate glass door. "Now can I please go outside with everyone else?"

"Of course." I catch her hand and pull her into a hug. "Thanks sis."

"Remember, you promised an open mind..." She squeezes me and then pulls me toward the door.

Her smirk makes my stomach flip flop. But I'm set on this idea now, and I'm not going to let anything get in my way.

Four
Pearl

Driving down the rutted dirt road between the highway in South Shore and the Vintages trailer resort is like entering a liminal space for me. It's leaving behind work and the hustle bustle of the day and stepping into the quietude of home. Thick stripes of red-orange Georgia clay mixes with a sandier soil. A light thicket of pine trees rise up, dark against the blue sky.

You can't see the ocean from here. But I know that if I drove just another two minutes, the clay would give over to sand and the land would slope downward to meet the endless sea.

But since I'm just heading home, I take the final hairpin turn on the winding road driving away from the beach. My mind goes blank. My senses numb, but not unpleasantly so. It's a bit like stepping through a magical portal without any knowledge of what awaits me on the other side.

In the distance, the Altamaha River snakes away from my car and carries its silt-loaded, brackish backwater toward the ocean. I slow down as I pass the huge sign that reads 'The Vintages,' and enter the trailer resort. The sign depicts a gleaming Airstream trailer next to a kidney shaped pool and a few pine trees. My great aunt Delta had the logo made in the 80s, and keeps the sign nice and clean with weekly polishing.

The actual campground is just beyond, and is nowhere near as nice. There's a flock of worn plastic flamingos scattered through the expansive clearing. A dozen battered Airstream trailers sit in a broad semicircle around the proffered kidney-shaped pool. The pool is kept spic-and-span, like everything that my family owns, but it is missing a few tiles from the decorative border that lines it, and has clearly seen better days.

I swing wide, avoiding the campground, and bump down the very narrow path to the right. I pass three more Airstream trailers, each surrounded by pine trees, until I pull into the very last driveaway at the end of the lane. The clearing is just big enough for my battered but otherwise well-maintained Airstream, and a couple of pink plastic lounge chairs. And of course, my own lawn ornaments. A pair of classic-looking blue alien spaceships, each emitting a plastic picture of a green swath of light.

I got a kick out of them when I found them at a yard sale. My aunt Delta does not find their whimsy endearing. But she doesn't find much that pleases her. She's a Scrooge.

I get out of my car and pat the lawn ornaments as I pass by them, then run up the last few steps to my front door. It was an incredibly long day waitressing at Gem's Diner. I look forward to shedding my uniform – a blue dress and a matching apron – and watching All About Aliens.

I fling open the door, only to find my little brother sitting in my breakfast nook. His long-ass legs are stretched to rest on the corner by my stove and he watches my tiny TV set.

"Hey, Pearl," he says. His eyes never leave the TV.

"Watch this part. Coyote's about to get scammed, big time." I hear the cartoonish sounds of BONK and a scream. Malik laughs and shakes his head. "Dude is always in trouble. And he tries to fix it literally the dumbest way possible. It's great."

The analysis of the cartoon makes me smile. "Sounds like every cartoon I know."

This is very much a Malik thing to notice. He's been watching the same cartoons since we were kids. On any given day, Malik can be found here in this exact position, watching cartoons and eating Cheetos.

It's comforting to me and I hope that it never changes.

Malik lowers his legs and lets me by so I can get to my bedroom. "Sometimes, I just like to imagine if I actually knew someone who'd use an anvil as a weapon. Like... what is an anvil anyway? And how could a tiny ass little bird always be making them fall out of the sky?"

I snort. "I think anvils were used in blacksmithing. Like to make horseshoes and stuff."

"Well, okay, Ms. College." He rolls his eyes with an easy smile as I pull out the partition between the rest of the small space and my bedroom. Malik lives in the next Airstream over and has almost the same model as me, so he's used to the sounds of me rummaging through drawers and grunting as I change clothes. He calls casually to me. "You're gonna want some clothes that can get dirty. Mom is at a doctor's appointment this afternoon, so Aunt Delta needs us to turn over three trailers for new arrivals tomorrow."

I groan internally. I started work before dawn, and right now, my feet are straight up killing me. All I want to do is sit down for a few minutes.

"Ah, damn. Are we at least swapping days? Mom promised when we moved to the camp full time that we wouldn't be responsible for all the work." I grit my teeth, and drop the light blue peasant dress that I was planning on wearing back across my bed. Instead, I pick a pair of black leggings and pair them with a worn 'Jackson Family Reunion 1999' T-shirt. It's one of my Mom's shirts that I love. I put my work shoes away and quickly hang my waitress's uniform. I slip into a pair of boring black clogs, eying my pair of big, fluffy slippers with little green aliens printed all over them.

Later, I promise myself. *I'm going to put my slippers on, kick my feet up, and do absolutely nothing for an hour.*

I tidy away my shoes with efficient motions and roll the closet door closed. Living in an Airstream has made me appreciate organization; everything in my trailer has a place. There can be nothing that's extraneous when you live in such a small space.

I emerge at last and find Malik has shut off the TV and is typing something into his phone. From the goofy grin on his face, it's pretty safe to assume what's he's doing.

Malik and his boyfriend have been hot and heavy for two years now. I like Crisanto a lot and think they're a cute couple. But I do worry about Malik leaning on him.

He is a man, after all. He is probably going to let my little brother down at some point. So I keep my guard up with Crisanto, because he will eventually break Malik's heart. And Malik is my baby brother, so I have to watch out for him.

All men are disappointing in the long run. Ask my mom. Ask my aunts. Hell. Considering how things went with Bishop, ask *me*.

I give Malik a tart smile. "How is Crisanto? Still being an amazing boyfriend, I hope."

Malik glances up at me with a shy smile. "He's great. He's coming home from a work trip in a couple of days, and I can't wait."

I pull a kombucha from the tiny fridge and shoo my brother over to make room for me to sit. He is tall and lanky, with that physique that only twenty-year-olds have, so it's a squeeze for us both to sit comfortably in here. "You've been spending a lot of nights at his place in Cape Simon. Do you two ever talk about moving in together?"

Malik's lower lip protrudes. "We've talked about it. But we are taking things slow."

I nod and slip my arm around his shoulder for a quick hug. "That's smart. And you know you're my favorite person in the whole damn world. So basically, take all the time in the whole entire world. The longer you're here, the better it is for me."

Malik grins. "When I move, that means you're going to have to pick up the slack."

I laugh. "Shoot. No way am I working any more than I am already. Between Gem's Diner and here, I work all the damn time."

I complain about my schedule, but I'm okay with it. Working constantly is a good way to keep myself busy. And since I broke things off with my ex-boyfriend, I don't want to let anyone fill that space.

The Vintages can be my new beau.

Malik shrugs. "You don't have to. You can move out and stop helping around here. If you stopped, it would be a death blow. I think it would be a less painful way to go than the Vintages drifting toward oblivion at such a glacial pace."

Shaking the bottle, I screw up my face. I sort of agree, but I'm not going to be the reason that the Vintages ceases to operate. "Aunt Delta loves this place."

He cuts me a look. "Then Aunt Delta should figure out how to pay the back taxes on this place."

I take a sip and sigh. "Yep. That's tough. The last I heard, she was trying to get some bird-watching charity to pay what she owes for the right to use our land once a year. I think that sounds like a good idea, but it's unlikely to help our financial situation enough."

"That doesn't sound like a good deal. But you never know, I imagine those folks have a lot of white guilt." Malik eases himself up, moving carefully. "Let's get started on these turnovers. I want to go lie down and turn the air conditioner on full blast."

I follow him out of the trailer, watching his slight limp. He's favoring his right leg. My tone is a little more aggressive than I mean it to be. "Are you having a sickle cell flare up?"

"A little one." Malik waves my question away. "It's not that bad. Honest. This new medication is so expensive, but it really works."

"Malik Brown, you stop right there." I move around him, and stand in his path. "Why didn't you tell me? I can take care of the housekeeping on my own."

He flicks me an annoyed look. "I don't need you to do that. Last month you took care of the whole resort for two weeks. That's plenty."

I cross my arms and play the big sister card. "I'm your big sister. That means I'm in charge. Get your ass to bed, Malik."

"I'll make you a deal." He moves around me and slowly lopes toward the resort. "I'll help with the Airstreams, but I'll let you do the cabins on your own."

"There aren't any cabins on Auntie Delta's list!" My mouth bunches up. I trail after him up the little path that's a shortcut through the woods to the trailers.

He limps into the big clearing and heads toward the semicircle of Airstream trailers. "Good. We shouldn't have much to do, then."

I roll my eyes at him. He's not really respecting my authority and I don't like it at all.

First, I stop by the discreet housekeeping shed along the tree line to grab a bundle of sheets, and the mop bucket full of cleaning supplies. Then I head to see where my brother is.

He's flung open the front door, and all the windows, of trailer number 4 and is currently shaking out the narrow strip of frayed carpet that runs from the door to the bedroom.

I leave the mop bucket out front, and head to the back with the new sheets. Malik scoots into the tiny bedroom with me, and takes the other side of the bed without saying a word. Stripping the bed is so ingrained in my muscle memory that I do it without a thought.

"I saw Lucy Bennett-Taylor yesterday evening," I say, making conversation because the next part is so dull. "She was down from Atlanta to see her parents. She says hi."

"Oh yeah? I love that girl. She said that she's going to come talk to me about graffiti when she does her next art installation."

I dump the old sheets on the floor and shake out the fresh ones. "Yeah, she seemed really frazzled. I guess it's midterms right about now."

Malik shakes his head. "Don't remind me. I still have shell shock from college and I didn't even graduate."

I pin him with a look. "Yet. You haven't graduated yet. There is still plenty of time for you to go back and get a degree."

"True. I'm pretty happy with this found fashion thing, though. I post pictures of me looking super fly in my found fashion of the day. Two minutes later, my Insta blows up with fashionistas outbidding each other for the pieces. I make bank."

"I know. I'm just saying that college will be there waiting for you when you're ready."

Malik purses his lips and shrugs. "All right. Speaking of Lucy, you heard anything from her hot brother?"

A laugh bubbles to my lips. "You're going to have to be more specific than that. Which one? She has a ton of brothers and every single one of them is hotter than the last."

He gives a shake of his head, probably because of Lucy's past antics.

"Lord, I know that's right." He fans himself. "Those Billion Dollar Bennetts are so damn hot." He sucks his teeth and picks up the old sheet. "But I was talking about the one you got flirty with at Savannah's engagement party. River, right? You told me that you thought there was a spark between you."

I make a face. "I think I imagined it. I've seen neither hide nor hair of him since then."

"That's too bad. I thought maybe you'd zeroed in on a sperm donor. His whole family is hot so you know it runs in the family."

"I'm going to have to roll the dice with whatever the sperm bank in Chatahatchee has on offer. I told you I stopped by there before my afternoon shift, right?" I shake my head and head outside. "As soon as I get together enough scratch to go that route. Hopefully I'll be able to do it sooner than later, because there is a clock on my eggs. Women in this family stop being fertile as early as forty."

Malik winces. "I love you, but please don't start talking about menopause. You can vent to literally anybody else in the family about it. Aside from me, there's nothing but women as far as the eye can see."

I laugh. "Okay. I guess I can spare you."

We spend the next few minutes speed-cleaning the bathroom, kitchen, and dining room. As I prep the mop bucket, I point at the banquette seat. "Sit down, take a load off. Let me finish this part since it's easier for one person to do it anyway."

"Thanks." He slumps onto the red vinyl banquette and gives me a considering look. "You ever think about what your life would be like if our family didn't have the resort to run?"

I run the kitchen tap to fill the mop bucket, and add a squeeze of lemony soap. "All the time."

"Yeah?" he asks, sitting up a little. He looks like my answer surprises him.

"Definitely. The resort is a lot of work. Some days, I'm pretty sure even Auntie Delta would agree with that. And we both know that she doesn't agree with pretty much anything, purely out of spite."

Malik scratches the patchy five o'clock shadow that's beginning to form on his face. "Don't tell her I said so, but I've definitely noticed that almost all of the day-to-day duties of keeping the resort up fall to you and me."

I wrinkle my lips. "I've noticed it too. And I wouldn't say boo about it to anyone if Auntie Delta didn't owe almost twenty grand in back taxes on this property. I don't care about the money that the resort brings in, as long as we don't owe the government anything. But by not paying her property taxes, Delta is risking the whole piece of land being auctioned off."

Malik straightens, his eyes bulging comically. "How do you know all of this? Auntie is such a grouch when you so much as hint at asking about the family finances."

I add water to the bucket and give him a tired look. "I happened to be in her trailer when Auntie Glory came charging in waving a bunch of papers she said were from the IRS. Glory's the only one that Delta even remotely listens to, you know. They had it out over the back taxes. Auntie Glory said Delta was putting the family at risk by not paying. Delta muttered something about how the state of Georgia needs to pay us reparations and then left."

Malik gives a low whistle. "Auntie Delta ain't wrong, but I don't think the feds care about the fact that we've had this land for a century."

"Nope. They certainly don't care about how we're the only Black family in the state that owns such a large piece of coastal land."

Plunging the mop in the bucket, I clean the Airstream's floors in smooth, practiced sweeps. Then I roll the bucket to the front door and shoo Malik outside.

I grab the handle of the sloshing mop bucket and lift it. Focusing on the next trailer, I'm not even paying attention when a blurry toddler streaks across the yard toward me. I hear a joyous shriek of laughter just before the kid barrels right into my legs. It takes all my strength not to let the mop bucket tip over onto him. He has sandy brown hair, bright red cheeks, and wears the cutest bright-yellow fleece onesie that I've ever laid eyes on.

Malik jumps in and lifts the boy up and out of danger. The kid laughs and bends backward. Malik grips the kid and gapes.

"Ethan!" A harried-looking young woman wearing an oversized white T-shirt and teeny black shorts appears. She sees her son in Malik's arms and flushes. "Oh my goodness. Ethan, what kind of trouble did you get into now?" She hurries to scoop her kid out of Malik's arms, looking apologetic. "Sorry. He's a handful."

Ethan drops his red sneaker on the ground. My stomach twists as I bend down to retrieve it. It's so tiny!

"Oh, shoot." Ethan's mom holds out her hand expectantly. "Thanks for grabbing that."

I drop it onto her waiting palm. Sucking in a huge

breath, I give her a tight-lipped smile. "He's adorable. How old is he?"

She jiggles Ethan on her hip and puts the little shoe back onto his bare foot. "Eighteen months. I love him, but god, he's always into something these days. They don't tell you about that in sex ed class. They just tell you about having a little angel baby," she jokes. "Ethan is always moving around, always getting in something. But he's cute." She touches her baby on his nose. He laughs and puts his thumb in his mouth.

"He sure is. If you ever feel like you want a night alone, come knock on my door. I live just over there." I gesture to the trees behind us. "I love kids!" My eyes connect with Ethan's. I think of how much I mean what I just said and hot tears prick my eyes.

Ethan's mom gives me a strange look and mutters her thanks. Then she turns and hurries back to her rented trailer.

Wrinkling my nose, I sigh. "I just freaked her out, didn't I?"

"Yup." Malik rocks on his heels. "You have baby fever something fierce. You better get on CupidsArrow and find yourself a man to father your kids."

I heave a sigh. "Can I tell you a secret?"

"Of course." Malik slides me a sneaky grin. "I love a secret."

"Malik, I want a baby so damn bad. Did I tell you how much the sperm bank quoted me?"

His eyebrows lift. "No... Dare I ask?"

I give a humorless chuckle.

"It's pretty damn expensive for the sperm bank to match me with a sperm donor. Like fifty thousand dollars for them to match me and get me pregnant."

"Whoa! I went into the wrong line of work."

"Yeah, seriously. And get this. I asked if they have donors that would not be sickle cell carriers, since I already know that I'm a carrier. And the doctor told me that they could do it, but the bank's fees would almost double. Can you imagine?"

Malik sucks his teeth. "I'm telling you. You just get drunk one night with those Billion Dollar Bennetts and see if you don't get yourself knocked up. I'm betting that River's got real good genetic material."

I roll my eyes, turning away from my little brother. "Yeah right. Like River is just going to sleep around without using protection. Not very likely."

"I think it's more likely than you think."

I slip my arm around Malik's waist. "You're crazy. Now come on. You sit and keep me company while I do the other trailers. I want to hear about how your art is going."

Malik gives me a squeeze and grabs the mop bucket. We start walking toward the next rental.

FIVE

RIVER

At ten minutes to ten, I pull my truck into a grass clearing off the little two-lane highway tucked in the flat stretch of land below South Shore. I park next to a dozen other vehicles, most in varying states of old and decrepit. The beach sits on my left, looking peaceful in the night air. To my right, the ground rises steeply and then levels out, leaving a natural bluff.

The first thing I notice as I get out of my car is how clear and radiant the stars seem. They are scattered across the velvety night sky like faintly twinkling diamonds.

We're far from the light pollution of the city out here. Far from everything. I have to admit, this is a perfect spot for admiring the night sky.

But will it be good for spotting aliens? Lucy told me that I could find Pearl at a gathering of alien enthusiasts.

I grin to myself. Lucy also told me to keep an open mind. But in truth, my mind is about as open as an old metal trap that rusted closed. That's not really the point, anyway.

I'm just here to see Pearl.

I put on my black and red Atlanta Kings jacket to guard against the cool night air. Two older women are unpacking heavy looking telescopes from the back of a yellow hatchback car. Both women wear neon green hoodies that say I SURVIVED THE ALIEN INVASION. I nod at them as I walk toward the steep slope that leads up to the bluff.

The wind grows stronger as I reach the top. The grass is high and thick up here, whipping wildly, beaten back to form a path to the farthest end of the bluff. There's a wide, clear-cut swath of land here.

I walk down to the end facing the ocean. There are about twenty people loosely gathered around five pretty impressive telescope setups. They all wear the same bright green hoodies as the women in the yellow hatchback. A tall, stooped man faces away from me and points at something in the night sky. I read the back of his jacket. The totally incomprehensible letters GCUFOE are emblazoned across the back of it, in black block letters.

GCUFOE? What is this, an eye doctor's appointment?

I sweep my gaze over the gathering, furrowing my brow. I spot Pearl at the furthest tip of the land. *Bingo*. She's standing by one of the telescopes, grinning at an older man who is telling her a very animated story.

I make my way over to her, noting just how close the telescopes are to the edge of the bluff. It seems dangerous. Peeking over the edge, I'm relieved to see that it's only a six-foot drop down to the red clay ground below.

Pearl's laugh floats to me from a few feet away.

It's a throaty sound, the timbre medium-deep. For some reason, it causes a strange prickle at the nape of my neck. It's certainly distinctive.

Pearl's laugh rings in my ears as I step into her line of sight. My intention is to neatly skirt past the expensive telescope that stands between us.

But I knock the telescope's dark tripod leg, and the whole thing wobbles precariously.

Pearl's tawny face has the perfect look of sheer alarm. She stumbles as she tries to steady the telescope and begins to fall forward, her mahogany eyes widening. She lets out a low moan. "No!"

Moving quickly, I grab her by the waist and drag her body against mine. Catching her and dipping her backward probably looks more dramatic than it actually is, BUT my heart is in my throat anyway.

She clutches at the telescope, and it takes a few seconds of balancing for her to make sure it stays upright. Meanwhile I'm staring down into Pearl's luminous face. Pearl is an absolute knockout. When she steadies the telescope and looks at me, she flushes and two dusky red spots appear in her cheeks. Her full lips twitch.

I think she is going to be upset. But instead, she does the oddest thing. She grins at me, her wide nose wrinkling. "Hey there. I didn't expect to see you here."

The cadence of Pearl's voice sends a thrill racing up my spine. I smirk down at her, unable to resist her invitation for humor. "Hello, Pearl."

"Hey, River." She chuckles. "Would you be a darling and set me upright?"

I hold her for a second longer, looking in her eyes to judge her reaction. Her hitched breath is the reaction that I want. I swing her upright and step back. She plucks at the brown corduroy skirt that she wears with her oversized neon green GCUFOS hoodie. Then she runs her hand over her long hair.

It's only now that I realize she is wearing a headband with a pair of bright green springs attached to it like antennae.

What the hell is this girl into?

A young man in a stylish black wool jacket and jeans walks over. He has chestnut skin, dark brown eyes, and reddish-black hair that's shaved on the sides with curls on the top. There is no mistaking him for anyone other than a relative of Pearl's.

"Everything okay over here?" he asks Pearl.

Pearl is busy resettling the tripod legs. "Yep. All good. Malik, this is River. River, this is my little brother, Malik."

I stick out my hand to shake. Malik gives me a cool look and offers me a fist bump. I immediately switch over and tap his fist with my own.

"What's up, River. You're Rex Bennett's brother, right?"

A lot of people know me as Rex's brother. He's a famous baseball player, so I'm not even fazed. Instead, I shove my hands into my pockets and nod. "That's me. And like four other guys. We come from a big family."

"The Billion Dollar Bennetts." Malik grins. "Word gets around."

I slide him a tight smile. That nickname for our family is pretty unfair to me, being that I'm not named Bennett. But Malik doesn't need to know that I hate it. "My last name is actually Taylor. But Rex *is* my brother. And no, I don't carry any autographed photos. That's usually the next question."

Pearl looks at me skeptically. "He didn't ask you for anything, River."

"It's cool. I get it. You probably get asked that a lot." Malik splays his hands. "I'm going to make a run to the QuickTrip. Does anyone need anything?"

Pearl stops fidgeting with the telescope and pulls a small, pink wallet out of her hoodie pocket. She offers Malik twenty dollars. "Here's a little money for snacks. Get me a pack of chewy fruit candies, will you?"

"Yes ma'am. River, you good?"

I hold up a hand. "I'm fine. Thanks."

"Okay. I'll be back." He retreats down the hill into the darkness.

I look around, searching for something to comment on. Her aunt's property is all that I want to ask Pearl about. But it seems rude to launch into asking her to help me convince her aunt to sell me her property right away. I need something else to talk about first, to ease me into the part of the conversation where I ask Pearl for help.

While my wheels are spinning, Pearl cocks her head to the side and beats me to the punch. "What are you doing here, River?"

I rub the back of my neck. I'm embarrassed. "Well, to be perfectly honest, I came here looking for you. Lucy told me that you would be here. But she didn't tell me about... whatever GCUFOS is."

"I love me some Lucy." Her eyes light up. "She sent you in here blind? How devious."

"She's a handful all right."

Pearl steps over to me and puts her arm through mine as casually as you please. "Well, you're in luck. GCUFOS is meeting for the first time this season. And you probably aren't going to be the only newcomer to the meeting."

I look down into her face, thinking how perfectly sculpted her cheekbones are. I see a smattering of freckles over the bridge of her nose that probably grow darker with the summer sun.

This close, she's stunning. Her beauty empties my brain for a moment, and it takes me a few more to remember what we were talking about.

"What exactly is this group?"

She beams at me. "Investigators that believe in extraterrestrial beings."

The woman's T-shirt. The telescopes. The antennae headband. Several things click into place for me. I've made a grave mistake.

"Ohhh." I cast a look around the gathering. "I see."

"You're also here at the right time, because I just got this telescope." She gives me a gentle push toward it. "Check it out."

I lean down, shutting one eye while I peer through the eyepiece. The night sky unfolds before me, a series of dark purples swirled with pinks and faint blues, like the palette of some unseen artist. Laid among all the brush strokes are bursts of twinkling lights, the softly glinting stars.

I'm impressed. "Wow. You really have some definition here. It's so clear."

I look at Pearl as I step back. Her smile is so excited that it is radiant. "I saved up for ages to get a MagTek 3600. No more begging to look in other people's telescopes for me. See Mitch and Jenny over there?"

I look where she's pointing and see an older couple wearing the bright green GCUFOS hoodies and taking turns peering through the viewfinder of their large telescope. Mitch sees Jenny's phone hanging out as she bends over, and tucks it into her pocket.

Bleh. Mitch was probably his own person once, but now he and Jenny share the same clothes and energy. Gross.

"Yeah," I say, biting my tongue. "I see them."

"Well, they were nice enough to share their telescope for the first couple of years that I was a part of the GCUFOS. But now I'm bona fide."

Pearl says it with such pride and enthusiasm that it's impossible not to smile at her joyfulness.

"That's pretty exciting," I tell her.

"Uh, yeah. It's awesome." She fusses with a piece of silky

cloth, wiping her lens. "So why did you come here to find me?"

Right, the property. The whole reason I'm here. I forgot for a minute.

"I actually wanted to talk to you about your great aunt. When we were at Cole and Savannah's engagement party, you told me that your aunt–"

An elbow shoves me right in the middle of my back. Whipping around, I see a massive man with hazelnut skin and wearing a white puffy jacket, looming right behind me. I'm tall and broad, but this guy is built like a tank. There's not an ounce of fat on him, and he obviously spends a lot of time at the gym.

He smirks at me and says, "Watch your feet. Me and my fiancée are trying to set up our telescope here."

I narrow my eyes, but I step back because I was raised to default to politeness. I look over at Pearl, and see that the smile has been completely wiped from her expression. In its place is a wary look.

"How you doin', Pearl?" the man says, nodding to her. "You don't mind me and Anitta setting up here, do you? I thought since you two are kin, you'd want to be close to each other."

As if on cue, a pretty Black girl wearing a white fur coat, big gold hoops, and high heeled boots appears on the slope leading down to the parking lot. She carefully steps through the tall grass, and pats her long, straight hair. When she sees Pearl, she gets a feline grin on her face. "Hey, cuz. Long time, no see," she purrs.

"Anitta. You're massively overdressed for the occasion, as usual." Pearl clears her throat and gives the man a thin-lipped smile. "I don't care where you set up, Bishop."

Bishop's self-satisfied smile makes him look ugly. He

holds out a hand to Anitta and she hugs him. They proceed to kiss for a few seconds, and Bishop bites Anitta's lip.

Ew. I look at Pearl, lifting an eyebrow. She can't be okay with her cousin acting like this.

She flashes me a tiny smile and introduces me. "Bishop, Anitta. This is River. River, meet my ex-boyfriend and my traitorous cousin. I have no idea why they're here. I used to bring Bishop to these meetings, but now he's here with his new flame for absolutely no reason that I can see."

My eyes widen, but I just give them both a slow nod. You could cut the tension between them all with a steak knife.

"I can be wherever I want. You don't own the skies." Bishop releases Anitta from his grasp and wipes his mouth. "Who are you supposed to be?" he asks me.

I don't like this guy at all. Somewhere in the back of my head, alarm bells are going off. I open my mouth, and out rolls a lie that I can't fully explain. "I'm Pearl's date." I level him with a smug look as I step over to grab Pearl's hand. Pearl looks at me, her expression nervous, but I barrel on. "I've heard so much about you two. I can't believe that this is the first time we're meeting."

Bishop's eyebrows jump so high they disappear into his hair. "Pearl is single. Right, Pearl?"

Pearl gives my hand a squeeze as she catches up to the conversation. "Uh... no. This is my date."

She's a piss poor liar. But I tug on her hand and pull her against my body, face to face. She comes easily, but I can tell that she's hesitant. Tilting her head back with a finger, I kiss her lips. Nothing crazy, just a little more than a peck.

But the immense relief that has been building inside my chest and is now let go from just this simple brushing of my lips on hers is instantaneous. Her lips are warm and luscious. They invite me to linger.

But Pearl puts her hand on my chest, ever so gently pushing me away. And I let her.

She shoots me a rueful little smile. "River, you bad boy."

Bishop glares at both of us. "Anitta, why don't we set up on the other side of the clearing? I think there is a better view over there."

Anitta looks at us all skeptically. But then she smiles. "Of course, baby. Let's move now, before the meeting starts."

Bishop bumps my arm with his shoulder as he wrests his telescope from the ground and folds up the tripod. "Be seeing you, Pearl."

Pearl watches him go, and then eases out of my grip. She blushes and shakes her head. "Sorry about that. You really didn't have to step in."

"Are you kidding? I don't even know that guy, but I loved sticking it to him. I think I hate him. I just hope I didn't overstep by kissing you."

She blushes and shakes her head. "Not at all."

"Your ex seems like a tool."

"Yeah. Bishop makes it pretty easy to dislike him. Especially when he got engaged to my cousin a week after we broke up." She shakes her head and looks sad. "We were together for two years. I never had any idea that he could be such a snake. Thanks for covering for me, I guess."

I smile at her. "It was easy. We make a good team."

"Hah!" She chuckles. "I'm not much of a team player."

"Pearl." I catch her hand and look into her face. "We should talk about–"

"I saw one!!" Jenny howls from a few paces away. She points up at the sky. "I saw a UFO! Look!"

My words are lost as Pearl hurries back to her telescope, holding her breath. It's like she has completely forgotten about everything else.

I can kind of see now why Pearl likes UFOs. Her life as she explained it, with her aunt revealing a huge amount of tax debt for the land they both live on, sounds hopelessly complicated. But when she's looking through her telescope, I imagine it all fades away. I envy her that.

"Where?" she calls out. "I can't see it!"

I stand back, watching Pearl and her telescope. There are a lot of things I don't like about her. She's wearing antennae and looking for UFOs, for one thing. And she's in these beat up looking jeans and a GFUFOS hoodie. My type of girl is polished and sophisticated, two things that Pearl definitely is not.

But damn if I don't think she's pretty and cute anyway.

The voices all around me burble on. But I'm left thinking that I might need to arrange a way to see Pearl again soon. To talk to her about her aunt's property, that is...

SIX

PEARL

I pop my head into the chrome kitchen of Gem's Diner. Gem Cruz is waving a wooden spoon at Diego Garcia, a teasing expression on her wizened face. She unleashes a string of taunts at Diego in rapid-fire Spanish. The young cook unties his white apron strings and sighs in exasperation. "Don't lecture me about what young people do, mami."

"Do you care if I head out early?" I yell.

Gem and Diego look at me. Diego's expression is apologetic. "Sorry, Pearl. I already asked to leave. My boyfriend is on the couch, sick as a dog, and he needs some cold medicine. Any other day, I would be glad to stay."

I give Diego a conciliatory smile. "Of course. I hope Jared feels better."

He whips his apron into the drawstring bag of dirty kitchen laundry, and walks down the kitchen toward me. "Gracias, hermana," he says as he takes his leave.

Gem sighs once he's gone. "If things don't pick up in half an hour, we'll close early. I could use the extra sleep."

I step out of the kitchen, calling to her over my shoulder, "And yet, you look as fresh and young as the day you started this place, Gem."

"I know that's right!" she yells back.

I check my watch. It's almost ten thirty at night, and I've worked a grueling double today. But I'm patient as always. Gem counts on me to work all the weird shifts that no one wants to work. And I will gladly take them, even if I'm only earning minimum wage. What else would I be doing if I wasn't here?

Having sex dreams about River, probably. Although Auntie Delta would no doubt have me cleaning trailers.

A blush creeps up into my cheeks as I grab a rag to make sure every table is wiped down. I haven't been on a date since I broke up with Bishop, and it shows. River showed me thirty minutes of attention and now I regularly dream about him. Mostly about how I imagine his tall, toned body looks in the buff. River getting into the shower, River waking up early in the morning, River coming back from a run... YUM.

The bells on the diner door chime, jolting me out of my reverie. Sam Bennett, the gray-haired patriarch of the Billion Dollar Bennetts, pokes his head in the door. "Are y'all still serving food, darlin'?"

I straighten, feeling like I've been caught. "Of course! We're still open and ready to serve you."

"Thanks, doll. We need to soak up some of the beer we drank while watching the Atlanta Kings obliterate the New Orleans Pelicans."

"Wiped the floors with those Pelicans!" comes an all-too-familiar voice from behind Sam. My stomach drops and my heart gives a little flutter.

It sounds like River.

Sam winks at me as he parades into the diner. The man is as tall as an oak tree. Behind him march his sons, every bit as tall and handsome. There's boyish-looking Brooks, somber Rhett, and gorgeous River.

"Hey, Pearl," River says with a secret smile. "What's going on?"

I duck my head. Hottie Walker Harrison is the last to enter, and he comes up to clap Rhett on the back. I know Walker is best friends with twins Rhett and Rex; the town gossip mill is strong when whispering about the Bennett boys and their exploits.

They join the drunk, noisy pack as they head to their usual corner of the diner and sink into two booths. River makes eye contact with me from across the room, a flirtatious smile on his face.

Oh boy. This isn't my first time serving the Bennetts. Going by the last few times I've waited on them, I'm about to walk into a fat cash tip. I'm suddenly inordinately happy that I didn't leave after all.

But these guys can also be a handful.

I gather up five menus and head over to hand them out. Brooks and River are in the closer booth. Sam, Rhett, and Walker are in the one by the window. I turn on my brightest smile while I take their drink orders. Water and coffee all around, except for Rhett. Rhett orders a green tea.

I go to fill them as quickly as I can. From my vantage spot by the soda machine, I catch River looking at me once again. He breaks into a broad grin, like he's unashamed of being caught staring. This is different from how he acted before the UFO party. Like somehow, I am complicit. I gulp.

Is River a player? Because he's putting the moves on me without even trying. He showed up unannounced to the GCUFOS viewing last night. Then he pretended to be my boyfriend and even kissed me in front of Bishop.

I bite my lips as I consider how this affects me. I want to know more about River, that's for sure.

After dropping off their drinks, I take their food orders. I do Sam's booth first. Two waffles, three orders of eggs, and five hashbrowns.

Then I nonchalantly sidle over to River's table. I flip a page in my notepad and try to play it cool, but inside I'm as skittish as a possum caught by floodlights while on a stealthy midnight stroll. Resting my hip on the edge of their table, I lift my notepad. "What can I get you two?"

"It's nice to see you again." River's blue eyes flash.

I'm not sure how to respond to that. I just flush and tuck my hair behind my ear.

"I'll have three orders of hashbrowns, scattered, smothered, and covered. And can I get a cheeseburger with that?" Brooks asks, his eyes on his menu. He looks up. "Can I get a milkshake, too?"

My lips twitch. He's clearly been drinking and his antics are that of a child's. "Yup. Vanilla, chocolate, or butter pecan?"

"Pecan!" he says, pushing his menu away.

Act businesslike. You can do it. "Got it. And you, hon?"

River spreads out, taking up all the space in the booth and not looking exactly bothered by it. Of course he wouldn't be bothered. He's a big guy. He's wearing a long-sleeved Atlanta Kings T-shirt, an Atlanta Kings championship hat, a sexy black motorcycle jacket, and black jeans that are snug in the butt and thighs. Every piece of clothing fits like a glove.

That's something I really admire about River.

He looks at me dead in the eye, smirking a little. "I have a question."

"What?" Tossing my hair, I hold my notepad up.

He looks me up and down and asks, "Can I order one of you? You're the most appetizing thing in this whole place."

I feel my cheeks flush. "Exactly how much beer did y'all have when you were watching the game?"

Brooks snorts and tries to cover his reaction by chugging ice water. River seems completely unbothered.

"No beer. Only whiskey." He wiggles his eyebrows. "But my question stands. Are you on the menu?"

Rolling my eyes, I dodge his question. "You're making your whole family wait, River."

"Dude, just order already. I'm starving!" Brooks moans.

"Fine." River slides his menu to me. "I want the all-star special with my eggs over easy.

"Bacon or sausage?" I ask.

"I already have all the sausage a girl could want." He gives me a mischievous grin. "But I'll always take a side of bacon."

"You're ridiculous." My tone is flirty as I stuff their menus under my arm. "I'll get your order in. Try to behave yourself while I'm gone."

"Not a chance," he shoots back.

My heart beats a little faster. It's not often that I have someone as good looking as River being so flirtatious and bold with me. I can usually fend off any advances that customers make... but what if I don't want River to behave?

God, I really need to get laid.

I shoot River a quelling look and hurry to the kitchen window. Calling out the order is quick work. I can hear Gem firing up the grill as I dart around, blending a milkshake and perking up a new batch of coffee.

Throwing myself into my work is easy. I've been practicing this for years at this point. Keeping my hands busy and my feet moving is almost second nature.

In fact, it only barely keeps my mind from drifting back

to River. When I add the ice cream and milk to the blender and turn it on, I look over at him. He flashes me a smirk as he says something to Brooks that I can't hear over the noise of the machine.

River showed up unexpectedly at the GCUFOS meeting the other night. Where he kissed me, I might add. And now he's here at my work, being all sexy and tempting. And he clearly thinks I'm hot, so–

"Pearl!" Gem yells from the kitchen. "You're going to burn the blender's motor out!"

Shaking myself out of it, I turn the blender off and go through the motions of serving up the shake. Gem starts putting up plates and ringing the bell for service.

I'm busy carrying plates to the tables for the next ten minutes and then running around getting the Billion Dollar Bennetts whatever condiments they need for the foreseeable future.

When I'm finished with that, I need a break. I check my watch. It's now past eleven. Heading into the kitchen, I find Gem washing dishes. "Hey Gem? Do you mind if I take five?"

Gem nods and stops spraying dishes. "Go ahead. Take ten if you want."

"You are awesome and the best boss of all time, ever." I pull my apron off, and brush a few crumbs off of my antique-blue diner waitress's uniform skirt. Grabbing a white cable-knit sweater, I head out the back door and walk ten feet to the aging picnic table.

When I get outside, I take a deep breath, inhaling the night air.

There's nothing outside here but the long, silver back wall of the restaurant to my left and the gorgeous, moonlit beach much further off in the distance to my right. It's cold out here. The moon and stars are impossibly brilliant against the black backdrop of the night sky. I sit down on the edge of the table and wrap my sweater tighter, looking up.

Before I can even begin to relax, I hear the crunch of footsteps on the gravel of the parking lot. I tense up. The restaurant's boxy shape casts a deep shadow over the parking lot, obscuring the approaching figure. Who is coming to intrude on my quiet moment?

But I already know who, even before River's shape coalesces out of the darkness. He has his hands shoved in the pockets of his impossibly snug jeans. And the look on his face is far hungrier than the flirtatious one he'd given me inside the diner.

When I see his blue eyes, a ripple of unnamed emotion runs through me. Maybe I'm just horny. Or perhaps lonely.

He walks over to me, eyeing me like a cat creeping up to a mouse. "It's cold out here, Pearl."

"I like it," I say, just babbling as an excuse to fill the space between us.

My heart rate increases with each step he takes. He comes to a stop mere inches away from me. My tongue feels too big for my mouth.

River is so damn hot. He cocks one eyebrow, and his eyes glint a soft blue in the shadows. The way he is looking at me right now, like I'm a whole damn snack, makes my knees weak.

"Do you need more syrup or something?" I joke.

A dimple flashes in his cheek. "I need something, all right."

Gulp.

I ball up my fists in my sweater and try to play it cool. This is not even close to the first time a customer has hit on me. But River is the man I've been obsessing about since his lips touched mine last night. The blossoming burst of butterflies in my belly is a novel experience.

Just like spending the night with River would be, a naughty little voice in the back of my head whispers.

He doesn't beat around the bush with me at all. "I want to take you out on a date."

Double gulp.

I give my head a gentle shake. "You're drunk, River."

He reaches out to me, making eye contact with me the whole while. Asking for my permission to touch me without saying a word. I swallow, and offer no resistance as he slides his hands around my waist and pulls me against his body. My hands land on the lapels on his motorcycle jacket. I bite my lip and look up at him.

He flashes me a smile. "I think you're gorgeous, Pearl. Go out with me."

My heart leaps into my throat. I'm equal parts excited and afraid. I grip his jacket. "You don't seem like the type to like diner waitresses."

"You don't know me well enough to know what I like." He catches a few strands of my hair and tucks them behind my ear. "I'm not crazy. There's a pull between us. Why shouldn't we explore it?"

I open my mouth, but I don't have an answer to his question. Instead, I ask, "How drunk are you, exactly?"

"I wouldn't have come out here if I was drunk. Do you think that I didn't suggest coming here to my family? This was very much planned, darlin'."

Oh. He wanted to see me? A chill races down my spine.

River nudges my chin up, angling my face just so. My heart is galloping when he lowers his head. My eyes sink closed and I press up on my tiptoes to meet him halfway.

Our lips touch, hot and wet. Distantly, fireworks explode in my head. River kisses me surprisingly hard, his hands on my waist pulling at me as if he can get more of me that way.

I press my thighs together. The need I feel surges. A trickle of wetness blooms in the dampness between my legs.

Yes, is the only thing running through my head. *More.*

River presses my ass back against the table. I let him lean me back, feeling his lips as they press kisses into the sensitive skin of my neck. His hand slips down to cup my breast through my shirt, shaping my nipple.

My mouth opens up toward the night sky and I release a jagged moan. I shift against the pressure rising inside me and wrap my legs around him. His denim-covered cock settles along the seam of my pussy, thick and heavy. My eyes bug out a little as he sucks at a spot just under my collarbone.

Digging my fingers into River's hair, I bring his mouth to meet mine again. His fingers dance along the top of my thigh and I writhe against him.

Here, I thought I was never going to want another man to touch me after Bishop treated me so poorly and left me heartbroken. But now I'm gasping and pressing again River like I'll die if he doesn't keep touching me.

River's fingers skate up my thigh, grazing the front of my panties. I'm aroused so there is a sizable wet spot there. He groans when he feels it.

"Fuck, darlin'. Is that all for me?"

I just kiss him because I am too embarrassed to talk about it. His fingers brush my panties again, teasing me.

What if... what if I went home with River? What if River got me pregnant?

The idea honestly leaves me breathless. A baby with River's tall frame and ocean blue eyes would be stunning. And I would know that he's not a Sickle Cell carrier.

I imagine holding a baby with bright blue eyes, snuggled

and warm and held close to my chest. My heart *hurts* with how badly I want that.

River moves to deepen the kiss, which snaps me out of my thoughts. I push against his chest. And he instantly pulls back.

He doesn't let me out of his arms, though.

"I'm not in town forever," he says. "Eventually, I'll have to move back to Atlanta for my career. But while I am, it would be crazy for us not to date."

My brow furrows. My swoony moment begins to disintegrate. "Are you asking me to have a one-night stand?"

"No." River's lips twitch. "I think we both know that it would be difficult to stop after just one night. What I'm suggesting is more... sex with no strings attached. And maybe we go on dates sometimes."

"Oh." My excitement gutters and dies. He's looking for a fuck buddy. I don't have a lot of time to devote to that.

"Did I say the wrong thing?" River asks.

I shake my head. "No. I just don't think we want the same thing."

"I like you, Pearl." He grips my hips. "I'm not going around trying to seduce every woman I see. When we're dating, you'll be the only woman I want. I know a gem when I uncover it."

I recoil.

Good *lord*. What a bunch of bullshit. Men are all the same. They all flatter you and make you feel good for a minute... and then let you down the second things get hard.

River tries to pull me closer. The scent of whiskey is strong on his breath. I push him away and put a few inches between us, pinning him with a serious look.

"You're drunk, River," I remind him.

"I told you already. I'm very much not." He pushes a hand through his hair and gives me an easy smile. "Just think about my offer. I'll give you multiple orgasms. You'll have control. We can go on dates... or I can just be a late-night booty call on speed dial."

"It kinda sound like you're just drunk, horny, and full of yourself." I screw up my face, and he laughs.

"Oh, Pearl. Just you wait. We could even pretend that we're in a serious relationship and rub it in Bishop's face."

I roll my eyes. "I have to go inside, River."

River's eyes glint. "Wear pretty panties the next few days. Because I am going to be back here in the light of day. And I'm going to rip them off and eat that pretty pussy, Pearl."

A ripple of electricity shoots through my body, and heat floods to my cheeks. River doesn't know this, but explicit dirty talk really turns me on.

That dimple in his cheek flashes again as he grins. "Think about it."

He raises his hands and backs away, turning around and heading back into the shadows. I press my hand to my heart and swallow. I said I don't want a one-night stand, but what if I look at this from a different angle?

River is hot. He's not planning on staying in town forever.

Maybe I should ask him to be my sperm donor. No strings attached, of course. Then we would both get what we want.

SEVEN
RIVER

Pulling my truck to a stop near the little pod of food carts, I grab aspirin from a bottle I keep in the cab. I wasn't drunk last night but damn if I don't feel hungover today. I guess I didn't get enough water in my system before I went to sleep. I chase the pills down with a bottle of water as I get out on the street.

From here, I can see downtown South Shore and the silhouettes of two construction cranes. That would be where my brother Cole is building a hotel to service the training camp that he's building with Rex.

I keep an eye on the construction as I head toward the food carts. That's the origin of my planned resort. If the town is already going to be getting a huge boost in tourism, the next step is to capitalize on it by adding a resort.

I wince as I hear a heavy saw whirring in the distance. I'm usually used to the bangs and high-pitched whines that are the sounds of construction. But my hangover is pretty dire by now.

Thus, the agreement to meet Lucy for lunch here, at my

favorite pho cart. It's my go-to after I've spent the preceding night making not the greatest decisions.

The carts are arranged in a loose circle, with shaded picnic tables in the middle. As I walk through the circle, I shade my eyes against the bright midday light, looking for Lucy. It's pretty packed here at lunch time, and nearly every one of the fifteen tables is occupied by hungry townspeople.

I make a note of how full the pod is. When the resort is complete, we will draw a lot of this lunch hour traffic away from it. But Pho Queen will have a permanent spot at the resort.

They just don't realize it yet.

"River!" Lucy waves at me from a crowded table. "Over here!"

The most amazing pho I've ever had in my life will have to wait a few minutes. Diligently, I head over to Lucy's table. She's eating a big bowl of pho already and she slurps up a noodle as I approach. My soon-to-be sister-in-law sits across from her, looking as blonde, bubbly, and lovely as ever. Next to Lucy is a young woman with thick black hair and warm brown eyes tilted at a sharp angle. She is getting up to leave as I arrive. Savannah rushes to make the introduction.

"River, this is Grace. Grace, this is Lucy's brother, River."

"Hello. I think I saw you at Savannah's engagement party." She checks her watch before giving me a hurried smile. "Sorry to run, but I'm due for a shift at the hospital. Lucy, text me about that philosophy project if you want."

Savannah stands up with a smile and picks up a tray. "I should get moving too. Charlie has a half day at school today, and I'm supposed to pick him up soon. River, nice to see you."

She gives Lucy a little hug and then the two women hurry off, whispering to each other.

A smile tugs Lucy's lips as she watches them go. "Pearl's going to be disappointed that she missed them."

I squint. "I know she's friends with Savannah, but that's all I know about Grace."

Lucy slurps another noodle. "She's another Agnes Glen grad. We're all in a coven together, pretty much."

I snort at Lucy's joking reference to being a witch. Being witchy is cool these days, I guess.

But the mention of Pearl has me sitting up and eagerly looking around. "You said Pearl's going to be here, right?"

Lucy nods and jerks her head toward the line for Pho Queen. "Turn around. She's in line already. She just walked over here after doing the breakfast shift."

My head whips around and I lay eyes on Pearl. She's wearing a billowy white dress and clutching a stylishly over-sized brown purse.

I want to lift up her skirts and see what's underneath. If she is trying to look extremely fuckable, well damn. Mission successful.

I may have been less than sober last night, but I remember every word I said. I meant them too. Including my hope that she is wearing nice underwear.

"Excuse me while I go woo a woman," I tell my sister. Her eyebrows fly up but I don't stick around to hear her response.

I steal around behind Pearl, feeling like I'm on the hunt. My little mouse doesn't seem to realize I am here until I get right up behind her and whisper in her ear. "Have you been a good girl since last night?""

Pearl's shoulders jump toward her ears. Then she whips around and glares at me. "You scared the bejeezus out of me!" she shrieks.

I wince at her high-pitched protest. "A little softer, if you don't mind."

Her face softens and her lips twitch as she looks me over. "You do look a bit like a run over possum."

"I could be your run over possum if you'd let me."

She smirks. "And here I thought you were just having lunch with your baby sister."

"A man knows how to multitask."

"Uh huh." Pearl turns around as the only person ahead of her in line moves out of her way. "You're persistent. I'll give you that much."

I look at her figure in that dress. My persistence has a very important reason. I can't see her ass, but the dress does bare her shoulders and give a hint of cleavage. Damn, I must be hard up for a date if I'm practically salivating over Pearl's body in such a modest dress.

When I finally get a tray with hot soup and sit down, Lucy is getting up. "I'm going to go get some ice cream," she says, looking distracted.

I look over my shoulder and spot Walker Harrison waiting in line behind a few customers at the ice cream van. Walker hit the whiskey bottle really hard yesterday. He's almost definitely way more hungover than me, though I can't see his face from here.

"I have to go. Um... over there." Lucy's eyes are glued on Walker as she gets up.

Catching glances with Pearl, I manage to wait until Lucy wanders away from the table before I chuckle.

Pearl smiles and turns to watch her walk away. She wrinkles her nose and gives a sympathetic shrug. "She's got to know that following that guy around like a puppy is not going to work."

Squirting hoisin sauce into my soup, I smile slyly. "I don't know exactly what her plans are concerning Walker. But seeing as how he's Rhett and Rex's best friend, I don't think he's going to do anything so stupid as kiss her anytime soon. When you ask him about Lucy, he mumbles and avoids the question."

Pearl puts fresh basil in her soup and stirs it with chopsticks. "Smart man. I wouldn't want Rex Bennett mad at me."

I pick up my oversized soup bowl and carefully take a sip of the salty brown liquid. It's burning hot as it slides down my gullet and I ease the burn with a gulp and a frosty lemon-lime sports drink.

"Ah." I sit back, my initial itch in the process of being scratched. "This is the best pho in the state."

"It's pretty good. I like International Delight in Decatur."

That gives me pause. For some reason, I didn't expect her to list some place in Atlanta as her favorite pho restaurant. It trips me up for a second. "That's near where you went to college, right?"

"Yep. It was right up the corner from Agnes Glen and it hit the spot every time, without fail." She slurps up some noodles and taps her lips with her napkin.

"Interesting." I eye her, thinking that there are probably a lot of things about her that I don't know. Things I'd like to discover.

My mouth curls up at the corners when I start thinking about stripping her down and discovering her body with my lips.

I turned things decidedly sexual between us last night. But that's just a precursor to the big ask. See, I need to be taken seriously as a committed adult before I can use my trust fund.

So the real question is will Pearl pretend to be my fake fiancée so that my stepfather will take me seriously?

I'm thinking that if I date Pearl, that puts me first in line when her aunt is looking for a way out of financial straits. It just leaves me with one big question.

How do you ask someone to be your fake fiancée without sounding insane?

Pearl's expression pinches as she looks over my shoulder. She sighs. "Great. The gang's all here."

I turn to look and spot Bishop helping her cousin Anitta down from a big red truck. Anitta is wearing a clingy blue bodycon dress and a white wool cloak. Bishop is dressed casually in jeans and a pair of Timberland boots, but it only seems to highlight the fact that Anitta is wearing a pair of dainty heels.

Bishop keeps putting his hand over Anitta's stomach in a protective gesture. His eyes dart around, glinting, as if daring someone to ask about it.

They head into the circle of food trucks. Bishop hasn't even noticed Pearl yet, but he smirks at the world around him. The guy has got to have one of the most punchable faces I've ever seen.

"Is Bishop trying to announce that he's going to be a daddy?" I ask Pearl, turning back to her.

Pearl's shoulders droop. She gasps and then clenches her jaw. "I don't know. I try not to hear about his life, if at all possible."

I take another sip of my soup and chew some glass noodles while I try to think of how to respond to that. She looks so sad.

Is it possible that Pearl didn't know before now? If so, I want to punch Bishop in the face.

Pearl glances over my shoulder and mutters, "Damn. He spotted me. Shit, he's coming over."

I raise my brows. "Want me to tell him to fuck off? It would truly be my pleasure."

"No. Bishop walks around just looking for a fight. Don't give him the satisfaction."

Then Pearl's expression goes completely blank. Bishop and Anitta walk up to our table, hand in hand. Bishop rubs his open palm over Anitta's flat stomach.

"Hey, Pearl. Did you hear my amazing news?" Anitta purrs.

Bishop doesn't give Pearl time to reply. "We're just starting to tell people today. Since you're family, Anitta wanted me to make sure that we told you that she's going to make me a daddy."

"Oh." Pearl blinks languidly. "Congratulations."

"I would expect more excitement for your cousin. I know that babies are a pretty big occasion for your family. It's been, what? Five years since Felicia had little Zami?"

Pearl looks at Anitta. She shrugs noncommittally. "Mmhm. Maybe."

Bishop swings his gaze to me, obviously frustrated that he's not getting the rise out of Pearl that he expected. "You still dating this fool?" He sucks his teeth. "It's a pity that a beautiful Black woman needs to run around with some White boy. That's diluting the bloodlines."

I stand up casually, my gaze hard on Bishop. Shooting Bishop and Anitta my most threatening smile, I spread my hands. "Pearl doesn't seem interested in your news. Now I suggest you go on about your day."

Bishop sneers. "You don't tell me what to do."

"Stop it!" Pearl pleads, standing up. "I'm serious."

Heads are turning our way. The people gathered seem to notice the tension. Bishop's gaze slides to the watchers, then back to me.

"This isn't over," he hisses. "The next time I see you, I'm going to teach you a lesson about being rude."

I'm a fighter by nature. Pearl is standing right here and

I'm not looking to cause her problems, but I am usually the first one to throw a punch in any altercation.

"Bring it on." A malevolent grin spreads across my face. "You name the place and time."

Bishop's jaw tenses. His hands ball into fists. He eyes me, sizing me up, weighing his chances of getting his ass beat if he decides to throw down right now.

I lean forward, inviting him to throw the first punch. Begging him to be the spark that leads to the firestorm and ends with me laying this motherfucker out.

Anitta pulls on Bishop's arm. "Come on, baby. You promised me you were going to get me a cheesesteak."

"All right, all right," Bishop mutters. He points at me. "I'm going to see you around. Make no mistake."

As he turns away, I call, "Can't wait!"

He fires back, "Can't wait to see you at our baby shower, Pearl!"

I flex my fists and sneer at him. "Motherfucker."

Pearl swallows, her eyes shiny. Having grown up with two sisters, I know the signs of incoming tears when I see them. She needs help right now.

I put my arm around her shoulders and lead us out of the circle of food trucks with her sheltered against me, shielded away from the curious gazes of the still hushed onlookers.

We make it as far as my truck before she really begins to cry.

I open the driver's side door wide and lift her up into the seat. She wipes at the tears that stream down both sides of her face but doesn't make a sound other than the gentle shuddering of her breath.

She also looks away into the distance, as if my presence isn't helping.

I can't stand her tears and I am itching with the need to put a stop to them, however I can.

At length, she says, "I knew that Bishop and Anitta were going to announce something sooner or later. They've been trying to conceive since they got together."

"You handled it well, if it makes any difference." I screw up my face. "Bishop is way too excited about getting to tell people. We get it dude, you had sex. Not that you can tell from looking at Anitta. If he wasn't acting like an idiot, no one would know."

"He's trying to rub it in my face." Pearl sighs. "I guess you don't know the whole story. I broke up with Bishop for a lot of reasons. He was a liar and a cheater. I caught him sexting half the town. God knows who he actually met up with in the three years we were together."

"He deserved to be dumped by you. You're *magic*. He's trash."

She looks guilty for a second. "That's actually not why I broke it off. My family liked him. I would have stayed with him, I think. The bigger issue that we couldn't tackle was that he is sickle cell carrier."

I squint. I think she's talking about some disease, but I don't really know that much about it. "Sickle cell? That sounds vaguely familiar."

Pearl chuckles humorlessly. "Sickle cell anemia. It's a horrible disease and it causes sufferers a lot of pain. My mom and Malik both have it."

Whoa. That's a lot of information. It takes me a minute to let it sink in.

"But not you?" I ask.

She shakes her head. "For someone to have the disease, both their parents have to be carriers. I've been tested and I'm a carrier. When I was with Bishop, I wanted to get pregnant. Because the disease mostly runs in Black families, I asked Bishop to get tested for the gene." She blows out a breath. "It turns out that he is a carrier too. And he wouldn't hear anything about adopting or using a sperm donor. So... I broke up with him."

She turns away and wipes a tear from her face. This took a toll on her.

"Ahh." Things suddenly click into place. "And because Bishop is a fucking asshole, he couldn't wait to tell you that he'd gotten his girl pregnant."

Pearl looks at me, swiping away a tear from her big brown eyes. "Not any girl. My cousin. A girl that could very well be a carrier too. They have both decided not to get tested. It makes me want to *scream*. I would say that they deserve each other... but I don't wish sickle cell on anybody."

"I see."

Pearl's lips twist. "Do you?"

I think, anyway. Pearl has more valid reasons than most for her breakup. And now her recent ex has knocked up her cousin instead. It's a two-fer.

"I do," I reassure her. Taking her hand, I give it a squeeze.

She licks her lips. "I doubt it. Having a family is all I've ever wanted. And if I want to have more than one kid, I have to get pregnant in the next year. Basically..." She looks at me, flushing. "I need a sperm donor ASAP."

She grabs my hand and bites her lip. She arches a brow. Is... is Pearl asking me to be her sperm donor?

"Are you asking me what I think you're asking me?"

She looks nervous. It takes a few seconds for her to answer. "Maybe."

A slow smile spreads across my face. A sperm donor? Well, this sure makes *will you be my fake fiancée* sound a lot less wild.

"We should talk about it." I slide my hand up to Pearl's face and cup her chin. "Somewhere private."

Pearl's cheeks flush. But at the same time, I can see a glint in her eyes. We both have something we need from each other. And when that happens in business, it's time to make a deal.

EIGHT

PEARL

"*Are you asking me what I think you're asking me?*"

As River drives me home to talk in private, I can't get his words out my head. They replay and replay every time I sneak a peek at him.

He's still tall, dark-haired, and *very* handsome. Swoon City, if you ask me.

When River pulls into my front drive and looks out the window, I can see him look at my Airstream trailer with a calculating expression. It makes me worry that he's wondering if he underestimated our class differences.

If he is like every other man in my life, he'll let me down soon. Every single man I've ever known has eventually proved a disappointment. Except my loving little brother, that is.

But I don't need River in my bed forever.

I just need him for a few months.

Without waiting for his reaction, I fling open the truck's passenger side door and bail out of the cab. I'm nervous and I might be mildly running away from the entire situation.

As River hurries to catch up with me, I zoom up to my front steps and push the front door open.

It's never locked, because who would bother to come all the way out here to steal something?

Nervous energy is driving me as I step inside the Airstream. I hang my keys up by the front door and shed my coat, placing it carefully on the dinette bench.

River has to duck his head as he steps inside the trailer. He looks comically large in here, where the fridge and bathroom door are two-thirds the size of normal ones. He looks around with a curious expression.

God, what must he be thinking? Nothing good. I'm not ashamed of having less than he does. It's just a fact of life.

Not all of us were born with a silver spoon in our mouth.

"Welcome to Chez Moi," I say. I shoot him a nervous smile.

River zeroes in on the tiled kitchen backsplash, which feature hand-painted UFOs. His lips twitch.

"Alien-themed kitchen?" he asks.

"Actually, the whole place has a UFO theme." I flush and spin around to point at the little green men-shaped pillows resting on the banquette of the dining area. There are pictures of UFOs hanging on the walls, a fun alien themed shower curtain and bath mat in the bathroom, and tiny UFOs hanging in the corners of the bedroom.

"Interesting." He looks around, taking it all in. "It fits you."

"I suppose." I smooth my hands over the front of my dress. Why are my hands shaking ever so slightly? I need to do something comforting right now, something familiar. Given the option of places to go, I blurted out that he should come home with me.

Was it the best choice? Maybe not. But it puts me at ease knowing I hold a lot of power here.

"Why don't you sit?" I wave to the banquette. "I'll make us some tea."

River studies me for a moment, his sapphire blue eyes intent. Then he takes a seat next to the twee UFO pillows. He seems to weigh his words carefully before speaking. "I didn't know that you lived in a... what do they call these trailers again?"

"Airstreams." I fill the kettle out of my small kitchen sink. "You've never been out here, have you? It's a trailer resort. Aunt Delta has a whole bunch of them for the hotel, but she set a few aside for family members." I grab two mugs and drop teabags in. "I've lived here since I graduated college."

River digests that as he sweeps his gaze around the trailer again. "Your aunt Delta is the one that you told me about, right? You said that she hadn't paid the taxes on this land for a number of years?"

Blushing, I shoot him a look. "Yes. We are pretty close to getting a notice from the IRS at this point. But I'm still having a devil of a time getting her to listen to me. She's so damn stubborn. I asked her who she can go to for a loan. She says she is tapped out. I tried to work out a payment plan with the IRS, but Delta won't sign off on it. She says she shouldn't have to pay taxes."

"She sounds... spirited."

I laugh. "That's certainly one way to put it. She would have a heart attack if she knew that I was flirting with one of the Billion Dollar Bennetts. She says that your family thinks they are so high and might just because y'all are rich."

He snorts. "Billion Dollar Bennetts."

I sit down across from him, dunking my tea bag in my

mug to stir it. "Sorry. I know that you hate that nickname. I won't use it again."

River shrugs the topic off and sniffs his tea. "This smells horrible."

"First the cinnamon whiskey. Then ginger tea. I just saw you down a bunch of pho. You can't tell me you don't like strong flavors. Maybe you just don't like spices??"

"I like things that taste good. Point blank. And judging by the smell alone, that tea is not going to taste good."

"It has medicinal effects," I reply tartly. "Try it. It's great."

I sip the zesty tea, watching his face as he tastes it then pulls a face. He slides his mug away a few inches.

"It's not for me." River trains those probing blue eyes of his on my face. "You were telling me about your Aunt Delta."

My eyebrows rise. "What else is there to say? She's determined to lose this land to the IRS before I ever inherit it."

He puts his arm up on the back of the banquette, his fingers brushing my shoulder. "You are supposed to inherit it someday?"

I sip and then nod. "Yup. With Aunt Delta making the calls, I have no say in financial matters. In fact, Aunt Delta has told me to butt out repeatedly."

"She doesn't have anybody that she goes to for financial advice?"

I snort. "No. She keeps her own counsel. Aunt Delta really doesn't even like anybody other than me, my mom, my Aunt Glory, and Malik. She won't even consider taking our advice."

"I gotcha." River looks thoughtful. He flexes his outstretched fingertips, intentionally stroking my shoulder. I shiver, swiping my tongue over my lips, and imagine the feeling of those two fingers flicking my clit.

Heat gathers between my thighs.

"So?" he intones.

Gulp. River's eyes are like two deep oceans, begging me to scoot closer and take a dip.

"So?" I try to keep my tone light, despite the almost painful flip-flopping of my stomach. "You want to talk about... the deal?"

He smirks and his dimples flash. Suddenly, I realize my kid could have his dimples, and go all tongue-tied. Pressing my thighs tighter together, I pray that I can keep my shit together in front of him.

"Now that we're somewhere that we won't be interrupted." He slips his warm hand around my waist and pulls me closer to him. "I very much want to talk about the deal." His fingers touch the bare skin of my shoulder, tracing a pattern into my flesh. "It sounds like you need a baby daddy."

Swallowing, I give my head a tight shake.

"I need someone willing to donate sperm. But I don't want them around forever, taking my kid away for visitation or thinking they have a say in how I raise my kid. I don't want or need that."

One of River's eyebrows rises. "Oh? So you're just looking for someone to knock you up?"

It feels like every ounce of blood leaves my lower body and circles in my cheeks.

"Yes." My eyes are steady on his. "But I don't want it to be unequal. If you agree to this deal, I'd want you to get something you'd want, too."

His smile turns brilliant.

"It just so happens that I already know what you could give me."

My heart pounds against my chest. "What?"

His eyes slide away for a moment. "I want you to pretend to be my fiancée."

I give my head a shake, worried that I heard him wrong. "Wait... what?"

"I need a girl to pose as my fiancée." His grin widens and mischief sparkles in his eyes. "For a few months. You would have to pretend that we'd had been carrying on in secret for a while. I already told Bishop that we were dating, so that should help. You'd have to come meet my family as my fake fiancée. You'd probably have to do a few pre-wedding events by my side, too." He squints, tallying. "I guess you would have to let people in town think that we were engaged."

My stomach sinks. "That sounds like a lot of lying. I'm a bad liar."

River looks amused. "Yeah, you're too honest to be any good at it. But you won't be put on the spot. I'll do all the massaging of the truth. You'll just be next to me." He skates his fingers around to the back of my neck, dropping his voice to a purr. "And in exchange, I'll get you pregnant. I'll have to draw up a contract to protect my interests. I don't want to be medically or financially obligated for anything. But..."

"I would never ask that of you!" I blurt out. "My baby's parentage would be a secret forever. I would carry your name to my grave."

He leans down and whispers. "It sounds like we have a deal, darlin'."

His lips brush my ear. My mouth falls open. A shiver runs down my spine. A part of me is very ready to tear his clothes off and fuck his brains out. I have to grip handfuls of my skirt to still my hands. "River..." I protest. "We have way more to talk about."

He slides closer, settling his big body against my thigh. He walks two fingers up my neck and turns my head, angling it so he can place a burning kiss right where the line of my jaw meets the slender column of my neck.

"Do we need to talk first?" His voice is hushed and harsh. "Or do you just want to fuck? I can't wait to lick that hot, sweet pussy. At the diner, I never did get a chance to taste you on my tongue."

Every muscle in my body clenches at his explicit whisper. It takes me a second to rein myself in.

The protest leaves my lips anyway before I can stop myself. "River! I didn't mean you should actually get me pregnant the old-fashioned way! I thought you were agreeing to go with me to the clinic and jerk off into a cup."

He bites his lip, amused. "Why should we do that? It sounds like a lot of bullshit. I want you. You want me. Let's just fuck until we reach the desired result."

River tips my head up with two fingers. He looks at me for a moment before closing his eyes and kissing me on the lips. His mouth is hot and demanding, and he immediately deepens the kiss. I open my mouth, helpless under his onslaught, my fingers gripping his leather lapel like I'm clinging to a lifeline.

In this moment, I am ready for him. Prepared to rip my dress up off of my body and shred his jeans. Primed to mount his cock and ride him until I can't move anymore.

He sinks his hand in my hair and tugs it back to expose more of my neck. Then he runs a line of fire-hot kisses down it. I am paralyzed with need.

"Your neck tastes as sweet as I thought," he husks. "Makes me think your pussy is as sweet as muscadine wine. How about you take off your clothes and sit on my face, darlin'?"

I'm speechless. God help me. Give me a handsome man and a little dirty talk and I'll fall to my knees.

I need River to follow his dirty talk with filthy actions.

But I suddenly realize that I haven't trimmed or shaved my bikini area... like, at all. My bedroom is still a little messy.

I haven't prepared for sex... and I'm not ready for River, period.

Cursing myself for my cowardice, I gently push him back.

He stops his trail of kisses, breathing hard, and looks at me with concern. "What do you need, darlin'?" he asks, his silky voice gone to gravel.

"Protection."

He arches a brow at me. "Pardon?"

I clear my throat, flushing. "Legal protection. To keep us both safe."

River eases back, not seeming remotely upset. "Okay." He licks his lips, looking at me carefully. "As you say. I'll draw the contracts up."

"Shouldn't we get a lawyer to do it?"

He rolls his eyes. "I am a lawyer. I specialized in real estate and contract law. My day-to-day job just doesn't call for those skills very much."

My eyebrows jump up. "Oh! Sorry."

He gives me a small smile, pulling a fancy pen and a piece of paper from his jacket pocket. "Let's get down to the nitty gritty." He starts making a list in neat block letters. "Two orgasms guaranteed every single time we fuck. We keep it up for six months, or until you're pregnant, whichever comes first. And in exchange..." He writes it down quickly. "Four pre-wedding events. Dinner with my family once per month for the length of the agreement. And I can tell anyone that I deem important that we are engaged."

I swallow, my pulse still racing from his touch. "Can I add something?"

River looks up. "Of course. Anything."

"Flowers. Once a week, you'll bring me flowers. Just so that it doesn't feel so transactional between us."

I feel a little stupid for saying it, but I don't want him to become a task to be checked off. I don't need romance, but I do want pizzaz.

He smiles and nods, then adds that. "Flowers once a week. You got it. I think that we'll keep the exchange going for as long as it takes you to get pregnant... or six months maximum, at the outside. Sound good?"

My lips twitch. I hold out my hand. River takes it without hesitation.

"It's a pleasure doing business with you, Mr. Taylor."

His eyes shine with promise. "It will be, Ms. Brown."

NINE
RIVER

I stand in my living room and cast my gaze around at the tall piles of blue plastic moving crates crammed with books and art that dominate the space. There is a soft, brown leather couch that is pushed into the far corner. Unsurprisingly, there are more crates stacked haphazardly atop it, poised to cascade to the floor at any moment.

Every room in my house is crowded with randomly placed towers of crates. All except the spartan bedroom and the bare bones office. The two rooms I use the most.

You would think that I had just moved in yesterday, given the state of the house. But in reality, I've lived here for going on eighteen months now. My maid service comes in once a week and diligently dusts and vacuums around the crates. They've never said a thing, though I'm sure that they have some opinions.

The thing is, I don't really care about where I live. This multimillion-dollar beach house serves as a place to sleep and occasionally work. That's it.

But right now, as I'm waiting for Pearl to get here, I wish

like anything that I had at least a couch for both of us to sit on.

She texted me this morning with, *I'm ready to meet and talk more. Your place this time?* And I quickly agreed.

But as I tried to prepare for Pearl's arrival, I realized that I was feeling a bit unprepared.

What will Pearl think when she walks into my house? At best, she'll be unimpressed with how I live. That thought unsettles me for some reason.

I spend about five minutes clearing the plastic crates off the couch and stacking them against one wall. After dragging the hulking leather sofa into the middle of the room, I look around.

Sad? Yes. But maybe Pearl will overlook the sadness of the sofa in favor of the big bay windows that look out onto the beach.

The doorbell startles me. I dust myself off as I jog to the back door. I'm nervous, but I can't figure out why. It's the first time I've seen her since the trailer. My last couple of days were Pearl-less, but I admit to having dreams about today.

I'd present her with the contract. She'd sign it. Then we'd fuck on top of the pages and smear the ink everywhere.

It's just Pearl, I tell myself. *Chill out.*

I fling open the door. There she is, looking as pretty as a picture in a gray wool coat, and a blue and white striped shirt dress. My very first instinct is to look down at her cleavage, where I can see the edges of a lacy white bra.

Holy shit. This woman is so fucking hot. She has that girl next door thing going on and it's driving me wild. I grip the door hard and try to compose my face into anything but a grimace. "You made it," I manage to say.

Her wavy hair is coiled up into a bun. She tucks a strand

of the black silk behind one ear as she greets me with a shy smile. "Hey, River. Thanks for sending a car for me."

A smile tugs at my lips. Pearl always seems to have a teasing tone going on. I bow low, making her laugh.

"Of course. You are my fake fiancée, after all. I don't need tongues wagging about how I treat you before we even get the chance to introduce ourselves as a couple."

I step back, waving her inside. She sails past me, head held high and back straight. But she only makes it a few steps before she's come to a full stop in my living room. "Did you just move in?"

She went right for the question that I was hoping we'd avoid. I wrinkle up my face and sigh. "Does two years ago count?"

She snorts, walking straight to the bay window and peering out at the beach. "Wow. Talk about a million-dollar view."

"It's why I bought this house. In five years, when my brothers have their baseball training camp built, I'll sell this house for four or five times what I paid for it to some chump with too much money to spend." I flop down on one end of the couch, watching her closely.

She studies the view, walking to the doorway of the adjoining room. It's just an empty room with another pile of crates in the corner. There's a set of French doors that lead outside onto the deck. From there, it's just a short flight of stairs down and then you're on the beach.

"I would keep this place," Pearl says softly. I'm not even sure if her words are intended for me. "Imagine having such a view from your living room." She turns around and pins me with a stare. "This room seems unused! You need to put your couch in this room here and face the view."

I shrug. "I'll think about it."

Pearl takes my noncommittal answer as the blow off it is.

She comes over to me, sitting down on the other end of the couch and putting aside her oversized purse.

"So." Pearl crooks a brow at me. "What should we talk about?"

"We could go ahead and fuck." I splay out over my end of the couch and smirk. "Or we could talk about how I am going to use this fake engagement to get what I want."

She ducks her head. "And what do you want?"

"I want my stepfather to let me have access to all of my trust fund. Right now, I'm only getting a small part of it. But when I get engaged, the vault opens." I pause, my eyes narrowing. "Or so Sam says."

She doesn't need to know what the trust fund will buy me. Namely, a stake in her family's land once it's developed into a resort.

"And you're not going to wait around to meet Mrs. Right, I would guess."

"Correct." I wiggle my eyebrows. "Who has the time to meet someone? Not me."

Pearl pops her jaw beneath her hand and leans on the couch, pursing her lips. "We'll have to be very convincing to fool your family."

I nod. "We'll have to be comfortable with physical closeness. I guess it will only help matters that we'll also be fucking regularly."

"Oh." Her cheeks glow pink. "I wish you wouldn't say it like that."

"What? That we're fucking?" I reach out two fingers and brush them over the exposed skin at her knee. Her eyes widen and I can tell she is trying not to jerk away.

"Relax." I smooth her dress back down over her knee. "I won't bite. And I won't push you to do anything you don't want to do. If you're not enjoying yourself, then I'm not either. I want you to want me."

Pearl nods, not quite meeting my gaze. "It's a little hard for me. I know that you're just supposed to be my sperm donor, but I don't want the story of my pregnancy to start with, yeah, so I was fucking this stranger..." She shifts and sighs. "*'My fiancé got me pregnant and then we broke up'* isn't perfect, but it's more understandable."

I give her a knowing smile. "I can understand that." The last thing in the world I want is for Pearl to feel awkward around me. I pat the seat beside me. "Why don't you come over here and sit with me while we chat? Get used to me. That's the first part of getting comfortable with someone."

She bites her lip for a second. Her steady gaze bores into mine. Just when I think she's going to refuse, she moves down toward me and sits an inch away.

Looking at her stiff posture, I can see Pearl is going to need some help relaxing. I slip an arm around her waist and pull her knee up to cross over my own. She goes along with it and takes my big hand, wrapping her smaller one in it.

"There we go," I say. "Nice and easy."

A bark of laughter escapes her. "Feels weird."

"It'll get better. I promise." I look straight ahead. If I'd had the foresight to move the couch to face the window, we could've stayed there for a bit. But after a minute of being in my grasp, Pearl starts to shift and wiggle.

"Can you not be still?" I ask.

She scrunches her face. "Sorry. It's not really in my nature."

"Thankfully, your nature isn't really what we are relying on. Being still won't get you pregnant," I tease.

Her nose wrinkles. "What... what if I get pregnant immediately? Like the first time we have sex?"

"I will high five myself for a job well done."

She lightly elbows me in the ribs. "I'm serious."

I consider her question. "We should stop fucking as soon as you get pregnant. It's the best policy."

"Yeah?" Her lips twitch.

"I mean it. It'll help keep either of us from catching feelings for the other." I feel strangely defensive about my stance.

"Oh, I won't catch feelings for you. You're way too strait-laced."

My eyebrows jump up. "Me? Strait-laced?"

Pearl stares at me. "I'm a diner waitress who loves chasing UFOs. Most people are too dull for me."

"Ouch." I put my hand over my heart. "Well, I can't catch feelings for you either."

"No?"

"Nope. I already have a good idea of what my someday-fiancée will be like. She's sleek, cosmopolitan, and worldly. In twenty years, I'll be ready for her. You... you're soft, a little country, and... well, I can't think of a better description than to say otherworldly."

Pearl's eyes narrow on my face and her humor seems to die down. "Good to know."

Ah. I seem to have put my foot in it. I try to play it off. "You're too good for me, Pearl. You know it as well as I do."

"That's for damn sure." She scoots away from me, standing up from the couch altogether. When she speaks, her voice is cool and aloof. "Do we need to do any more talking? Or are we ready to trade contracts?"

"One second." I hop up and walk to my office, grabbing the few sheets of paper and the beige file folder with the blank check inside. I return and hand the file folder to a nonplussed looking Pearl. "Here's what I want you to sign. It basically says that you agree to be my fake fiancée for up to six months in exchange for consideration. By that, I mean my genetic contributions." I give her a lazy smile. "I need you to have it looked over by your own lawyer. And I have included a check in there to pay for the lawyer's time."

She opens the file and immediately hands me the check. "I'll get my cousin Patricia to look at it for free. She went to Georgia State, and has a family law practice in Alpharetta."

I nod. "Sounds good."

She reaches down to her purse and pulls out a printed set of forms titled 'Consent to Termination of Parental Rights.' I take the papers and jog them.

"I'll look these over and get them back to you the next time I see you. Hopefully that'll be in two days? My mom's throwing a gala for whatever new pediatric charity Rhett has turned her onto now. It's going to be at the Grand Ole Maison."

"Really? The Maison is fancy with a capital F. I've been to two weddings there and both of them were really chichi affairs."

Spreading my hands wide, I offer her a smile. "Mom is on the board of executives for the Grand Ole Maison. Sam's the vice president of the Coastal Golf Club. My family is really ridiculously fancy. These ritzy-ass people are about to be your fake in-laws for a while, so get ready for that. If you don't know it now, I think you'll find out soon enough."

She presses her knuckles against her lips for a moment. "I'll try to keep up as best I know how."

My lips twitch. "You're going to knock 'em dead."

Drawing a big breath, she lets it out in a rush. "How can you be so sure?"

"Because." Stepping close to her, I take her hand and give it a squeeze. Then I pull her body against mine. "You're going to be with me. There's no way this can go wrong. I won't let it."

My sudden burst of protectiveness takes me by surprise. It's brand new, but it feels like a welcome emotion.

Pearl gives me a shy smile. "You're awfully cocky."

"I only boast about things that I can follow through on." I wink at her, just to make her blush. "Have I mentioned today how fucking beautiful you are? My cock's been hard for days, thinking of when I'm finally going to strip you naked and run my tongue over every inch of you."

"River!" she protests. But even as the words leave her lips, she grins.

Fuck, she really is gorgeous. I make teasing eye contact with her for a few more seconds and then jerk my head toward my bedroom. "Ready for today's last surprise?"

Pearl wets her lips and dashes a glance at the hallway. Toward where I assume she thinks my bedroom is located. "Can I keep my clothes on?" she asks cautiously.

I roll my eyes. "Relax, darlin'. You can keep your panties on."

Steering her by touching her shoulders, I walk her ahead of me into the bright, airy kitchen. This room is in pretty much the same condition as the living room was this morning. Several piles of blue plastic crates are stacked high where a dining room table should be. There is a high-end coffee pot and a bean grinder on the white marble counter to my left. To my right is a wide, white marble island with a single gray steel bar stool.

And right in front of the stool is a folded piece of black velvet measuring six inches by twelve inches.

Ushering Pearl to the seat, I pull it out. She sits down, her eyes roving around the kitchen. "God, this room is insane. I can't believe that you still have boxes piled everywhere. Such a waste."

"Shh," I tell her, pointing to the velvet. "I'm trying to propose to you, Pearl."

She looks down and points to the fabric. "You want me

to look here?" She picks it up carelessly, as if there weren't millions of dollars of jewels just below her fingertips.

"Easy!" I say, clamping my hands over hers. I stand right behind her and pull back the top layer of black velvet to reveal ten glittering, gleaming engagement rings. The metals vary, the gemstones differ slightly, and of course the styles do too. There is everything from a huge, square cut diamond with two dozen pave diamonds fanning out both sides, to a circular cut yellow diamond in an ornate gold setting.

Pearl's mouth drops open.

Something about her total shock makes me grin. It's nice to get a rise out of her.

"Oh my god," she whispers. She looks at me with wide eyes. "These aren't real, are they?"

"Very real. All worth at least thirty thousand dollars. I had our very discreet family jeweler stop by and leave you a selection. I'll let you choose."

Her brows furrow. "Oh, River. You can't leave me in charge of a ring like this. What if I lose it?"

Smiling playfully, I pluck one of the rings up and offer it to her. "Don't worry. It'll be insured."

Making firm eye contact with me, Pearl says, "Are you sure?"

Taking her left hand, I slide the ring onto her fourth finger. She watches, her facial expression completely unreadable. Her other hand clutching the marble countertop tells me more than I can read in her face.

I hold her hand up, admiring it in the light. The ring is on the gaudy end, a big diamond surrounded by pearls. Not to my taste at all. Then again, what does my taste matter here?

"It's sparkly," Pearl murmurs. But she's soon slipping it off.

Whew. That's a relief.

She skips over the huge diamond solitaire, and the biggest yellow diamond set in white gold. Instead, she traces her fingers over a ring that I had to look at twice because it was so unusual. A large, round salt-and-pepper diamond set in a frame on a delicate, rose-gold band decorated with leaves.

She doesn't quite pick it up, merely running her finger around the inside. "This one is so beautiful."

I hold it up. "Let's see how it looks on your finger."

Her head dips and I'm certain she's flushed. "Okay."

I slide the ring on her finger. It's a little snug, but the diamond rests against her hand. The rose gold looks good with her skin color. And when I check her face for a reaction, I see it in her eyes. She's totally taken with it. Not because it's the largest or most expensive one. But just because it suits her best.

Pearl doesn't operate by the same rules as other women I've known. She's playing a different game. What the rules of it are, I don't yet know.

TEN
PEARL

"Whoa." River spots me as I get out of my Uber in front of the Grand Ole Maison. He lets out a low whistle. "Holy shit, Pearl. You are really something else."

His eyes travel down, drinking in every inch of my body in the clingy, full-length, champagne-colored velvet dress he had sent to my house. With the tall gold heels, I feel like Frankenstein's monster stomping around.

That isn't how he makes me feel, though. His eyes glitter with a mix of lust and admiration as he catches up to me at the curb of the venue.

"Thanks," I say. I flash him a small smile. "I feel ridiculous. This dress is definitely not my style."

River eyes me up and nods. "Yeah, it's more form-fitting than what I've seen you in so far. But damn, girl. You're going to be the sexiest woman in there."

He jerks his head behind him to the Grand Ole Maison. An old but impeccably kept up antebellum mansion, it's built out of gray stone and glass, with two floors of huge floor-to-ceiling windows. At four stories high, it is easily the tallest building for fifty miles in every direction.

But I'm not even looking at the venue. My eyes are fixed on River's tuxedo. It's immaculately tailored, the lines long and lean, making his muscular arms, chest, and thighs stand out.

Dayum.

"I know what you're thinking." River sees me staring and grins. He offers me his arm. "You can't wait to jump my bones. I can see it in your face."

My lips twitch even as I flush. I take his elbow, and allow him to usher me toward the building. "I'm just looking at you like that because I'm imagining the genetic contributions you're going to make," I tease. "I'm not even thinking of myself."

That is a bald-faced lie. It's written all over my expression and it makes him laugh.

"No?" He cocks a brow at me as he walks me inside, leaning his head close to mine. "Just for that, I'm going to make you beg me to make you come when I feast on your pussy."

My eyes widen and my cheeks feel hot.

But I can't whisper anything back to him, because there is a red-vested greeter rushing toward us. She pulls out an iPad and holds it at the ready. "How y'all doing?" she asks. "Can I have y'alls names?"

"We're great." River gives the woman a polite smile. "River Taylor. And this is my plus-one."

He slides his arm around my waist as the woman looks at her tablet for his name. I bite my lip and shiver at his touch. He shoots me a smirk and winks.

Be cool. Act like you've been on a date with a hot guy before.

But if I'm honest with myself, I've never been on a date

with anyone as hunky as River before. I mean… I can't even think about how great he looks in his tux or I might get all tongue-tied.

It's fake. Remember that it's all fake.

Steeling myself, I try to calm my nerves. When the greeter waves us through toward the ballroom, River whispers in my ear. " I'm going to introduce you as my secret girlfriend. We can quote-unquote 'get engaged' later. Okay?"

I give a stiff nod as he propels me through the main door. For a second, I'm overwhelmed by the sheer opulence of our surroundings. Baroque gold touches on the walls, and dusty pink velvet drapes, surround the massive ballroom. The crowd is glitzy, the women wearing floor-length dresses in every color of the rainbow, the men in expensive tuxedos. The smell of perfume wafts through the air, mixing with the soft jazz notes of the live string quartet.

If it were raising money for a cause, I would die to do it in this ballroom, with these fancy rich people.

River uses my arm to steer me to the left, using a free hand to make enough room in a little circle of people.

"Scuse us," he says. He jostles people to the side. Then he looks at a glamorous older couple. The silver haired man is tall and broad, the tiny blonde is in a silver sequined number that shows just a hint of cleavage.

She was introduced to me ever so briefly at the engagement party, but now she beams at me like I'm a precious diamond.

"River!" the woman says, her expression jubilant. She never looks away from me. "You came!"

"As promised. Mom, Sam, this is my girlfriend, Pearl. Pearl, this is my mom, Sarah and my stepdad, Sam."

At the word girlfriend, Sarah looks shocked. "Girlfriend?!"

Sam's creased face turns toward me. He thinks for a second, probably trying to remember where he knows me from. Then a lightbulb switches on and he smiles.

"Pearl. It's nice to meetcha. You work at Gem's, right?"

I swallow tightly and nod. "Yes sir, Mr. Bennett."

"Call me Sam," he replies. His smile is easygoing, but I don't miss the questioning glance he aims at River.

Sarah cuts him off by flinging herself at me. I flinch, but she hugs me so hard that I can't breathe for a second. She seems to be over the moon.

"Pearl!" She releases me but grips my upper arms, beaming up into my face. "I'm so happy you're here! River has never brought a girlfriend to meet me. You're the only one."

"Mom. Please. Let Pearl go," River says. There's a slight edge to his voice.

Sarah immediately drops her hand and steps back. She wraps her arms around her waist and bites her lip. Sam eases over to her, comforting her with an arm around her waist. "Why are you suddenly interested in introducing us to your dates, River?"

Sam pins River with a look. I have to give him credit because he doesn't even miss a beat. "I just felt like it was time." He drapes his arm over my shoulders, casually. "We just celebrated our two-year anniversary."

Sarah's jaw drops. Sam narrows his eyes.

"River!" his mother cries. "You've been dating for two years? Where have you been keeping her?"

"You sat at the dinner table and complained about the monogamy mindset way too many times for me to believe that, son." Sam looks disbelieving.

My heart rate soars. I see River stiffen. His jaw clenches and something in his eyes hardens. "When have you ever given me the benefit of the doubt, Sam?" he tosses off.

Sarah jumps in, putting herself between the two men.

"Boys, please. We aren't going to rehash old grievances here and now. This is a benefit for kids, for god's sake." She smiles gently at me. "I hope River will bring you around again. I would love to get to know you better when it's a little quieter."

I smile nervously at her and tip my head. "Yes ma'am. I'd like that."

A tall man with dark hair and dashing good looks elbows his way into the circle. "Dad, can you give me your car keys? I forgot the cue cards for my speech in the car."

River's arm tightens around my waist.

"Pearl, this is my brother Rhett. Rhett, this is Pearl." His lips form a thin smile. "My girlfriend. Rhett's the doctor of the family."

Rhett shoves a hand through his hair, squinting his eyes at the pair of us. His examination of me is a little longer, his eyes traveling down my figure. His lips part, surprised. "Girlfriend?" He offers me a handshake and the hint of a smile. "I think I recognize you from Gem's, right? You must be amazing for River to bring you to meet our parents."

Stiffening, I force a smile. "Nice to meet you, too."

Rhett chuckles. "Sorry. I was just caught off guard. It really is a pleasure."

He rumbles the last bit, looking contrite. He's very attractive, as are all River's brothers that I've met. But add a sparkling pair of light blue eyes and a white doctor's coat to the mix?

Yeah, I can see that Rhett is probably a lady killer. He turns back to Sam and holds his hand out.

"Keys?" he prompts.

Sam hands them over just as a bunch of middle-aged ladies in their silk gowns and rustling crinolines inject themselves into our circle. The circle is demolished, quickly turning into small cliques of two and three.

"Sarah, darling!" crows one of the ladies. "This is such a lovely soiree. Thank you for inviting me. Have you met Loretta Haines?"

River looks down at me, his lips quirking. "I think this is our chance to escape."

He pulls me away from the group, heading for the bar. I let out a huge breath and roll my shoulders a few times.

"That went better than I expected," I admit. "Your family was nice." I pause, wincing slightly. "Well, your mom and brother were, anyway. It seems like your dad wasn't really convinced by our playacting."

"Sam's my stepdad," River corrects me. "And you were perfect. He's just really skeptical of me. There's a lot of history there. It's a long story, honestly. Too much for tonight."

With that, he steers me forward to the full bar.

"What can I get for you?" the bartender asks.

"What kind of whiskey are y'all serving?" River asks.

"Buffalo Trace, High West, and Blanton's."

"I'll have a double of Blanton's with a little ice." He looks at me. "What do you want?"

"Do you have cinnamon whiskey?" I ask the bartender.

The bartender shakes her head. I purse my lips. "Just your fruitiest red wine, please."

"You got it." She starts uncorking a bottle of wine.

I reach in my purse to pull out my money, but River frowns and stills my hand. "Everything is paid for."

"I can still tip, can't I?"

"Nuh-uh." He pulls a money clip from his pocket and drops a twenty-dollar bill in the overflowing tip jar. "If you were my real fiancée, I wouldn't let you reach for your wallet. We are trying to be as real as possible... while we are here, at least. Keep your money in your purse."

I give him a tart look and then accept the glass of wine from the bartender.

After we get our drinks, River leads me over near the string quartet. A few couples are dancing slowly to the tinkly sounds the musicians are playing. River pulls me into his arms, swaying. I have to bite my lip to keep from laughing.

"What?" he asks, pulling me closer. "Am I amusing?"

"This is just a strange event. Everyone is so quiet. There's no buffet. Cupid Shuffle and the new Beyoncé album aren't playing on repeat. If my family were in charge, it would be way less..." I search for the right word. "Subdued. Black folks like to have a good time whenever they get together."

River smirks. "I'd rather go to that event. It sounds more fun."

"You know it."

I gaze up into his handsome face, pressing myself against him as we sway to the music. One of his hands presses against my lower back. He presses his hips against my belly in a gentle motion. Heat fills my cheeks and a shy smile spreads across my face.

Yeah, this relationship is fake as a Barbie doll's hair. But the promise that River is making with that intense look on his face is all too real.

We're going to bang, he's saying. *You're going to love it.*

He cocks a brow. "You know–"

"What the hell are you two doing together?"

I look to my right and see Bishop nudging an older couple aside to get to us. He's dragging Anitta behind him by her hand. She's dressed like Glinda the Good Witch in a glittery pink ball gown.

My blood pressure skyrockets. I can hear my heart beating in my ears. I wasn't expecting a face-off with Bishop. Or needing to defend my fake relationship. Not here, not yet.

But luckily, River seems born to play the role of my defender.

"Bishop!" he calls out. "So nice to see you here. You know, I didn't have you pegged as the charitable type."

Bishop grimaces and turns to me, as if River hadn't spoken. "Pearl, why are you slumming it with this guy?"

The laugh that bursts past my lips is genuine. "Slumming it?" I shake my head, perplexed. "Why are you so worried about who I'm here with, anyway? We are clearly quite broken up."

I nod at Anitta, who scowls at me. She wraps her arm around Bishop's bicep possessively. "Pearl's just jealous," she hisses. "She wishes she was in my place."

"Uhh, dream on. If anything, I need to thank you, Anitta. You pulled a snake out of my garden. Now my life's all roses."

Anitta's expression darkens. "You need to watch how you're talking to me."

"Don't you worry about Pearl, baby. She's going to regret falling into bed with just any old man."

"Are you kidding? You're one to talk. You're dating your ex's cousin!" River cries, getting heated.

I place my hand on his bicep and squeeze it to draw his attention to me. "Calm down, honey."

Bishop points at River. "We have a problem. If we weren't surrounded by all these fancy people, I'd beat your ass."

River gives Bishop a feral grin. "I would love to see you try."

"River!" I hiss. "Look around you! You're drawing a lot

of attention to us. This is not the time nor the place for a fight."

He looks around to the gathering crowd of onlookers and his mouth thins. "Sorry, darlin. You're right."

Bishop sneers. Anitta pulls at his arm. "Let's go, baby. I see some people that I want to talk to," she says. She shoots me a murderous glare as Bishop shakes his head and walks away.

As soon as they are swallowed up in the crowd, River slides his gaze back to me. "Where's your engagement ring?"

"Uhh..." I stammer. "In a Ziploc inside my purse. Why?"

He gives me a smug look. "Because. It's time that we told the whole town just how serious we are."

River gestures for me to hand it to him, his eyes on the crowd. Feeling my stomach drop, I juggle my wine and look in my purse. "What are you going to do?" I whisper. I sneak the ring into his hand and he puts it in his pocket.

"You'll see." A malicious grin breaks out across his face. "Stay put."

Draining the contents of his whiskey glass, River wades through the crowd. I'm left alone with my glass of wine, nervously clutching it. I don't even take a sip but feeling it in my hand grounds me somehow. My eyes dart around the ballroom.

What is River planning? I can't guess, but I don't think I'm going to like it.

Before me, the sea of brightly-colored ball gowns and black tuxedos ebbs and flows. I empty my wineglass and turn toward the bar for a refill. A second glass is definitely something I've earned tonight.

I'm almost to the bar when I hear someone tap a microphone. Freezing in place, my eyes widen.

He wouldn't.

"Hello, everyone," River says.

I squeeze my eyes closed for the briefest moment. My heart pounds. I turn ever so slowly, looking for River.

"Everyone having a good time? Be sure to open your hearts –and your checkbooks – for this event. My mom, Mrs. Sarah Bennett-Taylor, would kill me if I didn't mention her charity first. Thank you all for supporting the Bennett Foundation for Pediatric Health."

I finally find him. He's standing across the room on the small stage that was set up for the jazz quartet. I see him scanning the crowd. "Where is my girlfriend?" he says. "Pearl, come up here, if you will."

A sudden buzz ripples through the crowd. As if by magic, the crowd steps back from me, leaving me standing alone.

Oh god. Am I dead? Is this a nightmare?

River catches my gaze and smiles encouragingly. "Pearl is shy. Come on, darlin'."

I shoot him a pleading look, but start moving toward him, feeling as though I'm slogging through wet sand. My cheeks are on fire. My head dips down.

Why didn't I tell River that being called out in public like this is the very last thing I'd ever want?

The crowd parts like the Red Sea, forming a narrow path up to the stage. I plod along it until I find myself being helped onstage by my friendly fake fiancé.

His sapphire eyes twinkle as he grips my cold fingers. "Hello, darlin'."

I look at him, kicking myself for not being able to just play along. If he has any idea how nervous I am, he doesn't show it.

"For those of you who don't know, Pearl here has been my loving, supportive girlfriend for over two wonderful years. Pearl, I am honored and awestruck every single day we are together. Your smile lights up my world, baby." River pauses for dramatic effect, wiggling his eyebrows. "I want everyone to know that you are my world."

My stomach flip-flops. I could die at this moment. And I do not mean in a fun, happy way.

"I... love you too?" I say. It comes out as more of a question.

River stares down at me, seeming enraptured. "You complete me. If soul mates exist, you're definitely mine."

Gag. His playacting is way over the top.

I nod, forcing myself to speak. "You too, baby. You're... my other half."

River looks to the audience for support. "Isn't she great? How about a round of applause for my lovely girlfriend?"

The crowd breaks into gentle cheers and whistles. Before I can respond in the slightest way, River pulls me in his arms, dips me backward, and kisses me.

His lips are hot and sweet. He molds me against his body. For a moment, I fall under his spell. I kiss him back.

I forget, for just a second, that we're deceiving everyone.

River breaks the kiss and smirks down at me.

"Well done," he whispers in my ear. "I think it's fooling everyone."

I swallow and give him a tight smile. "Think so?"

Maybe I'm fooling myself. But I feel like maybe... just maybe, it means something.

ELEVEN
RIVER

I'm standing by my desk at the offices of the Bennett-Taylor Real Estate, peering down at a set of blueprints. My office is at the front of the building, and light pours in through a large picture window. From here, I have a decent view of Cape Simon's quaint downtown strip. Beyond that is the sandy strip of seashore. But I can't really see that unless I press my face against the window just so.

Trust me, I've tried.

Leaning over to the intercom on my desk, I press the discreetly-placed button. "Hey Wesley? Could you bring in the remaining proposals for the Jackson land?"

I hear my assistant rummaging about in the other room. Then he taps the intercom. "Yep!"

Wesley comes in with an armful of rolled up blueprints. He is dressed to the nines in dark slacks, a yellow silk button-up shirt, and stylish black suspenders. He's dark skinned. He keeps his head shaved smooth on the sides, and gathers the neat dreads along his crown into a topknot. Today, he sports a gold chain around one wrist and a matching gold pinky ring on the other hand.

My part-time assistant is always the *peak* of style.

He lays the blueprints down on my desk and purses his lips. He starts tidying the stack of blueprints that are on the desk, then glances at my drafting table. I'm not an architect, but having a drafting table does make it easier to make notes on the actual blueprints themselves. On the table, several file folders are open, and dozens of loose contracts lay there in disarray.

"What have you been doing in here?" Wesley asks. His voice chides me as he walks over to the table. Wesley is the only one that gets to talk to me like I'm a kid.

I sigh and throw up my hands. "I haven't seen a single proposal for the Jackson property that I like. When I met with these contractors, I described exactly the style of resort that I'm looking for, and exactly how big it needs to be. I even gave the businesses a rough sketch of the property." I pick up a blueprint, frowning. "But most of them completely ignored my ideas. They just sent me blueprints for buildings that are on flat land. I guess they expect me to bulldoze the land."

Wesley stacks all the contracts and jogs them. "Maybe you can pick and choose from a few of the proposals. Maybe one has a great main lodge. Another has a great overall layout. Like that."

Squinting, I rub my eyes. "I feel like I've been staring at them forever," I sigh. I stretch my arms up over my head and walk toward the front window. I lean one arm against the glass and let my head hit it with a thunk. "You're probably right. At the very least, I'll have to go back to all the contractors and have them deliver a second draft."

Wesley places the contracts in a neat stack on my drafting table. Then he turns and glances at me. "I'm supposed to leave in an hour to lead a class on personal expression at the community center. But I can be a little late if you think you'll need me."

"You've done plenty." I pull a face. "Go ahead and get out of here a little early. Nothing groundbreaking is going to happen today."

He flashes me a quick smile. "Peace. I'll be in tomorrow."

Groaning, I turn back to the window. Two older women, decked out in expensive yoga gear, walk down the street toward Tranquility Yoga. Maybe I should go get Zen with them.

Or I could finally fuck my beautiful fake fiancée. That would go a long way toward relieving some of my stress. My lips turn up at the corners as I ponder the possibilities.

"Yo! River!" My brother Rex calls to me from the front office.

I'm not expecting to see him today. This is an unexpected, but not unwelcome, visit.

I walk out into the lush, couch-lined waiting area. Wesley's desk sits to my right with the chair pushed in, the PC turned off, and the desktop as neat as a pin.

Rex and Cole are just sitting down on the plush leather couches. Rex is dressed in a dark Atlanta Kings hoodie and black track pants. Cole is wearing jeans and a white button-down.

"I didn't expect to see y'all until the Kings game next weekend!" I say. I grab a seat in the matching leather chair. "Rex, you look like you're slumming it, as usual. Cole, I'm surprised to see you in jeans."

Cole cuts me a droll look. "Savannah won't come into the office unless I wear jeans to work. It's a whole thing, that I can't really get into."

"Sounds like you let your woman run your whole life." I

reach out, grinning, and tap his knee. "I'm kidding. I like Savannah."

"You're such a little kid." He shakes his head at me.

"Which is why I was so surprised to hear the news," Rex cuts in with a sneaky smile. "Dude, you picked a very splashy way to announce that you have a girlfriend."

"Ah." I'm not going to pretend that lying to my brothers doesn't feel a little weird. I shift in my seat and wrinkle my brow. "Y'all heard about that, huh?"

"Uh, yeah. We heard. Not only is your relationship the only gossip the whole town's talking about," Cole smirks and pulls out his phone, showing me the screen, "but your little public announcement is up on Cape Simon Around Town. It already has three thousand likes."

I snatch the phone from his hand and hit play. It's a shaky video, but Pearl and I are in front of a crowd of people. I'm talking to her. She looks like she's about to shit a brick. Which is not exactly my memory of how it went down.

"Fuuuck," I sigh. "Everybody knows, huh?"

I make it sound like I'm against it, even though it was my plan all along.

"Oh yeah. You two are all anyone is talking about. Savannah is driving me up the wall, demanding to know if I knew you were a couple." Cole cocks a brow. "I was under the impression that you were staunchly opposed to being monogamous. You were a total prick about the whole 'marriage' thing when I got engaged to Savannah."

Wincing, I nod. "Yeah. I'm sorry. I have no defense. Pearl's the one that changed my mind."

"Two years into your secret relationship?" Rex asks, his tone skeptical. "Yeah right. What are you getting out of this?"

I lick my teeth. "Nothing," I insist. "I'm just taking the

next step. Right? Isn't that what y'all keep parroting back to me? First you find a girl. Then you ask her to marry you. Then you have a baby. Those are the steps."

I really need to convince Rex and Cole. Together with Rhett, they are the three brothers that the rest of the family follows. Once I get them on board, my parents will be much easier to ensnare.

"Whoa. First you introduce this girl out of nowhere. Now you're talking about marriage? You are moving with lightning speed, little brother."

"Mom says that when you know, you know," I say. Yeah, I feel a twinge in my chest for misleading my brothers. But they will understand. I think when I explain that I faked my engagement for money, they will roll their eyes and mutter about how that is something I would do.

"I love her," I say, finishing strong.

The words feel strange in my mouth. But I try to tell myself that my brothers would do the same thing in my position. At least Rex would; I have no doubt that in my shoes, my brothers would do the same thing. It's just Cole that is too truthful for his own good.

Rex slaps his knees. "Can we continue this argument over lunch? I'm starving."

Saved by the bell. Or Rex's rumbling stomach, I guess.

I spring to my feet, eager to change the subject. "Where should we eat? Mari Macs? The Cape Bistro?"

Cole rises and looks at Rex. "You're the one on a strict diet."

"Can we hit the salad bar at the Cape Market? I love to load up on a big salad and a grilled chicken breast."

"That sounds good," I agree. "I'll race you to the Market."

Rex is off like a shot, elbowing us in his fight to get out of the door the fastest. Cole is right on his tail, giving him zero slack. I have to lock the office up so I trail behind by almost a minute.

The Cape Market shares a patio with the Cape Bistro and Winery. We grab trays and load them up with our salads. I opt for a huge turkey and brie sandwich, a salad, and I snag a pack of Sandy's Sweets Salted Butter Pecan Shortbread Cookies. Paired with a cold hibiscus iced tea, it's a balanced meal.

Paying on the way out, I find my brothers already on the patio. They are settled in at the corner table, overlooking the ocean.

I put my tray down on the wrought-iron table and sit in a lightweight aluminum chair. Rex stabs his fork into his huge green salad. He's also got three grilled chicken breasts on a side plate. Cole sips a plastic cup of hibiscus iced tea with a contented look on his face. He has a salad and a side of cheesy baked mac.

"Oooh, I didn't see that," I say, pointing at the macaroni.

"Too bad. You know I don't share," Cole says.

"No? Not even for a trade?"

I crinkle the pack of cookies to open them and then set them on the table before my tray. Helping himself to a crumbly shortbread, Cole sits back.

"I'm going to eat this cookie. But it doesn't excuse your sneaking around with Pearl for two years," he says. "And I'm still not sharing my food."

Rex snorts and raises his fork, pointing it at me. "Seriously. Explain yourself. Why did you spring this relationship on the family? You know that you gave Sarah and Dad an absolute melt down."

I wince. My mom probably did blow a gasket.

"I don't know what more there is to say." Ignoring the look of disgust that Rex aim at me, I dump a whole packet of ranch dressing on top of my salad. "Pearl is the hottest, sweetest girl I've ever met. I like her. She likes me. She wants a baby, so..." I shrug. "The timing just makes sense."

Cole chokes on a bite of his salad. "A baby???!" he manages. "You got her pregnant?"

I flush and scowl. "No. I said she wanted to have a baby. Not that we are having a baby. Get your ears checked."

"Jesus," Rex wheezes. "Don't scare me like that. I can't think of anyone less suited to have a baby than you."

"Okay, slow down." Cole looks at Rex, chuckling. "I could think of a few candidates. You, for example."

Rex punches Cole on the arm. "Asshole."

"Dick." Cole hits him back.

Between the two, there isn't really a safe side to pick. Rex is a superstar athlete; everyone in our family and the entire town worships the ground he walks on. He can't be wrong, no matter how ridiculous and loud his boasts might be.

Cole, on the other hand, is measured and calm. Always calculating, never cutting loose. That's why he is Sam's go-to guy whenever he needs any business dealt with.

I lack their unique skillsets. At times, it makes me feel a bit like a boat in the middle of a storm, with the sea tossing me this way and that.

I guess my first line of defense is humor. "Y'all are so helpful," I mutter.

"I just never saw you being in a relationship. Or if you did, you'd be one of those horny eighty-year-olds who gets engaged a nubile young lady with huge..." Rex looks around the patio, then changes what he was going to say. "Potential."

Cole smirks at me. "I don't know. Now that I think about it, a hot woman steamrolling River into a big wedding, and a baby sounds, about right. He thinks he's so special. But really he's every bit as susceptible to a gorgeous woman as the rest of us."

"Speak for yourself," Rex grouses. "I'm never getting married. Too much commitment, you know?"

"See, that's what I thought." I take a big bite of my sandwich.

"But your mind changed?" Rex asks.

I shrug, chewing and swallowing. "I always thought that if I settled down, it would be with someone cosmopolitan. Someone from Atlanta, a girl who's on an upward trajectory in her life." *In twenty years from now, when I'm ready to settle down*, I add for my own benefit. This is, in fact, still what I believe in the core of my being. My brothers don't need to know that, though.

"Pearl doesn't really have any aspirations other than working at the diner, right?"

"There's nothing wrong with that." I cross my arms and shoot him an imperious gaze. "When I met Pearl, I realized what I thought I wanted, and what I really need, are two different things."

The thing is... love is fine, but this situation with Pearl is not love. It's a fully fake engagement for a marriage that neither of us wants. With a side of hot sex. Plus, she gets a baby in the bargain. Everyone wins. What more could I possibly want?

"Look who it is!"

I tense and my hands form fists even as I turn toward Bishop. I glower at him as he swaggers over to my table.

"What? Are you following me now?" I spit.

The smug look on Bishop's face always makes me want to clean his clock. And without Pearl here to keep me from trouncing him, it might finally happen today. I crack my knuckles.

"I'm just here getting some lunch with Anitta." He

gestures behind himself, though she isn't anywhere to be seen. "Where's my sloppy seconds? She sniffing around here, trying to pick up her next rich White dude?"

It takes a mere moment for the cruelty of his words to sink in. I'm up in a flash, seeing red. "What the fuck did you call my girlfriend?" I hiss.

Bishop's face splits wide in a grin. He gestures to me. "I know that you two started fucking before we were even broken up. I counted your timeline. The math ain't mathin."

"You can't trust a man so concerned about another man's girl." I lick my lips and edge toward him. "Why aren't you worried about your own woman?"

"Pearl is nothing more than a whore." He spits on the ground. "She's not worth the ground I walk on."

Rex stands up, putting his hand on me before I can lunge at Bishop. "You do not want to fuck with River," he growls at Bishop. "He's fast, he fights dirty, and right now... he's rolling three deep."

Cole springs to his feet, cracking his knuckles. I happen to know that Cole hasn't been in a fight since junior high. But he manages to sell it.

Maxine Parker, the Cape Market's owner who is a hundred years old if she's a day, hobbles out onto the patio. "Rex Bennett! Are these men bothering you?"

Rex jumps like he's seen a ghost. "No ma'am. Sorry. This gentleman was just leaving."

Bishop starts to snap back, but Maxine steps in front of him and starts herding him off the patio.

"G'won. G'won, get!" she says. "Messing with my customers. You aren't even pretending to carry a tray around. I know all about you, Bishop Jones."

"All right," Bishop says with a sneer on his lips. He points at me. "I'ma see you later. Count on it."

"Fucking asshole," I retort.

"I heard that!" Maxine turns her head back, expression pinched. "Rex, make your brother sit his ass down and cool off."

She and Bishop disappear inside the shop. Rex cracks his knuckles. Cole rubs the back of his neck and turns to me. "I get it now."

I sit down, my eyes still trained on the door where Bishop just disappears.

"Get what?" I ask. Honestly, I'm only half listening.

Cole sits and bumps my knee with his knuckles. "Pearl. I get why you're devoted to her."

Blowing out a long breath, I give him a long look. "What are you talking about?"

"I just put together why you're rubbing your relationship with Pearl in Bishop's face. You only have to meet the guy for half a second to realize that he's a bully."

Rex snorts. "You got that right. He probably only had to tease Pearl one time in front of River for him to lose his shit."

I fold my arms across my chest and lift my chin. "I have no idea what you're talking about."

"Mannnn." Rex rolls his eyes over to Cole. "Remember that kid that River had beef with when he was in middle school? What was his name...? Marbles...? Marxist...?"

Cole raises a finger, his lips twitching. "Marburg."

"That's right." Rex pounds his fist on the table at me. "You beat the crap out of him for bullying Brooks. You were almost kicked out of Bay Sands Private for that."

"Dad had to build and furnish a school computer room, I think," Cole adds.

I splay my hands. "What, I was supposed to just let Brooks get his ass kicked? I don't think so."

Cole laughs. "What about Mr. Lassiter? That college professor you almost had a fistfight with?"

"And of course, we can't forget when that lady. What was her name? She worked for your first law firm out of school?" Rex is barely able to contain his laughter. "You walked out of work and managed to take a few poor, stupid souls with you."

I glare at them both. "Her name was Mrs. Klebbe. And she held every first and second year in fear of their jobs. Now *she* was a bully."

"You see?" Cole kicks back and grabs his iced tea. "You have a thing about bullies."

"That has nothing to do with my relationship with Pearl." I wave the thought away.

"Uh huh." Rex elbows Cole. "Hey, everybody has a kink. You happen to get massive justice boners."

Cole looks gleeful. "He really does."

"Fuck off, both of you. Now either we change the subject or I get a to-go container and head back to the office."

"So touchy!" Rex jests. He rolls his neck. "In other news, have y'all seen Sarah's new car? It's got a driverless mode. And she is freaking out."

As the conversation shifts away from me and my possible kinks, I am left with one thought. Is it possible that I revealed just a little more of my feelings about Pearl than I meant to?

TWELVE
PEARL

I've just gotten back to my Airstream from a long shift and put on my fuzzy UFO slippers when there is an insistent banging on my trailer door. "Pearl Brown! You open this door right now!"

I open the door to find Aunt Delta. Her hands are on her hips and the expression she levels at me is angry.

Uh oh.

"Hi Aunt Delta." I step back, inviting her inside.

She struggles to climb up the steps; now that she's seventy-three, her aging hips bother her regularly. I hurry forward and grab her elbow to steady her as I guide her into the kitchen.

She shuffles over to the dinette and sits down heavily. Then she looks at me with a stern expression. "Is there anything you want to tell me?"

My heart starts to pound. I slide into the booth across from her. I look at her proud, chestnut-brown face and quaver. "Can you be more specific?" I try to keep my tone light.

She scrunches her face into a scowl and pulls out her

phone. Before she even pulls up the Instagram app, I already know what she's about to show me.

Whoever CapeSimonAroundTown is, they were present at the charity gala. Or maybe they got the video secondhand, I guess. Either way, they posted River's surprise relationship announcement for all their followers to see.

I stop her hand, putting my fingers over her phone screen. "I'm sorry. River wasn't supposed to spill the beans like that. He just got caught up in the moment."

Her lips thin. "This is not how I expect my grand-niece to behave. That young man said that you two have been sneaking around for almost two years! I can't believe that you didn't once bring him around to introduce him to your family." She clucks her tongue. "Your mom and your aunt Glory called me in a panic."

"Awww, shoot." I fidget, my face heating. "Mom knows too?"

"Yes indeed." Aunt Delta rocks back in her seat, pinning me with her brown-black gaze. "She is very hurt by the news. This does not make us look good, Pearl."

I bury my face in my hands. This was not the agreement that River and I settled on. I guess I didn't give a lot of thought as to how I would keep the news from my family. But it's too late for any attempts to save it now. "I wanted to talk to the family later. I didn't mean for y'all to find out this way."

"Mh-hmm." She shakes her head. "I found out from Beatrice Wilson and she just loved that she knew something about you that I didn't. Your daddy would have been livid if he had lived to see this, young lady."

My heart seizes up in my chest. The fact that my great aunt just invoked my father in this fight is brutal. My hand flutters up to cover my heart. "I'm sorry, Aunt Delta. I should have come to you first."

"Lord." Her mouth pinches together. "I need to meet your boyfriend. Before you get any more serious, I need to see for myself that he has good intentions. You're going to inherit all of my lands one of these days. And I have to know that you're not with a man who will use his connections to get it and then leave you high and dry."

"You will," I assure her. "I'll bring him out to meet y'all this week. I promise." I hesitate for a moment. "Have you reached a settlement with the IRS about the back taxes on this property?"

She snorts and waves her hand like a fan. "The details are still being ironed out."

I study her face and try to decide if she's being completely honest with me. It's hard to know with Aunt Delta. She plays her cards very close to her chest.

She leans in, her eyes intense. "Let me worry about that. All you need to know is that I expect you to keep our lands wild and free. I don't want you even entertaining the idea of selling it off. Business men often come to me with offers to buy and develop it. But I say no. I want our land to stand on its own, as it has for almost a hundred and fifty years."

"But Auntie, if you don't pay what the IRS is demanding–"

My aunt holds up both of her hands, quickly shaking her head. "Let me take care of that. I won't hear another word about it!" she insists.

I suck in a breath. "Okay. I will stop bothering you about it for a while."

My great aunt points at me. "And watch out for rich men who are only interested in you for your land. Why do you think I never married?" She pulls a face. "These men, especially White men, only want two things. One is in your pants. And the other is in your checkbook."

Dropping my gaze, I nod. I've heard this droning dirge

of hers for my entire life. But inside, I'm wondering at her words.

Is the type of man she's describing anything like River? I'm pretty sure he's not like that... but I don't know for certain.

She scoots out of the red pleather booth, leaning heavily on the table to get up. "Come on. Get dressed in something you don't care about. Cabin five has a leak coming in from the ceiling."

"Again?" I ask. Getting up, I head back toward my bedroom. "What are we going to do about that?"

"It's leaking in a different spot than last time. I'll just probably have you replace a couple of roof shingles and mop up the mess in the attic again. What the cabin needs is a whole new roof. But that's way more money than we have to spend."

I puff out my cheeks as I change into a pair of running leggings and a pink crop top. That sounds like a lot of work. I'm supposed to meet River in a few hours... but I'd better cancel.

"I'm just going to text River real quick," I call. "We have dinner plans. But a leaky roof sounds more vital than that."

"I'm going to go by my trailer. It's time to take my pills. Maybe sit and rest a while, just to get my breath back. I'll meet you down at the cabin in a little while. Okay?"

"Sure, sure. Go rest for a while. Get off your feet!"

Delta is already trundling away, fussing with her scarf as she goes.

I stand in the doorway of my trailer and stare blankly into the distance. Aunt Delta may be old as the red clay beneath our feet. But she does know a thing or two about life.

She has called out several times when I was about to be done wrong by a man. She's proved that she can tell things about men that I can't. Now I'm wondering if she can possibly know something about River that I don't.

It seems unfathomable to me that he would have some hidden motive. How could he possibly be so shady?

My shoulders slumped, I head to my bedroom and text River. *Not going to make it tonight. Sorry. There's an emergency at the trailer resort.*

My phone buzzes a few seconds later. He must have been waiting for me to call.

What kind of emergency? Is it something that you could use a big, tall guy for?

I tilt my head to the side and mull his offer over. On one hand, I just need to get my rear in gear. The sooner I start, the sooner I finish. Plus, I may have just learned something less than positive about River.

On the other hand, he is tall, like he said. And I do sort of want to see him...

Okay, I really want to see him. If nothing else, I know he can drown out my great aunt's pessimistic words still ringing in my head. River seems good at distracting me.

Sure, I text back. *I'll be at my place. Wear clothes you don't mind getting dirty.*

Be there before you know it.

I pocket my phone and put my Nikes on. When I stand up from my bed, I bump again the tiny bedside table. A framed photo of my dad, taken during one of his firehouse's training days, wobbles and falls. I throw myself onto the floor to catch it before I can even feel silly for saving a photo frame that probably cost less than five dollars.

I stand up, carefully replacing the picture in its place of honor on my bedside table. In the photo, my dad is only a little older than I am now. He's young, and strong, and running flat out with a fire hose over his shoulder. His face shows the dedication and concentration that I've long wished I had.

Malik got Dad's perspicacity. I just got his big ass feet.

He died when I was young. But at least I have my memories of him. Malik doesn't remember him at all.

I clear my throat, feeling strangely emotional. Determined to be in a good mood when River comes over, I spend a few minutes cleaning my bathroom and cleaning up this morning's rinsed-out-but-not-washed oatmeal bowl. River's knock comes just as I am drying my hands on a clean dishrag.

Dashing to the door of the trailer, I open it. There is River in his full glory. He's still dressed in dark jeans, and his shiny black motorcycle jacket. It's what I consider to be his regular outfit.

I raise a brow. "I thought I told you to wear your cast offs."

He smirks and his sapphire blue eyes flash. "I'm here. I'm in the dingiest clothes I own."

He points down to the cuff of his dark jeans. Squinting, I can make out a couple of lighter smudges.

"That's dirty to you?" I ask. I give him a funny look. "Never mind. I'm just glad you came."

He steps up into the doorway, more than filling it. I'm only steps away and his nearness is all it takes to make me flush.

Take it down a notch, girl. He's just here to help.

River has a smug little grin on his face when he considers me. "You don't look so bad, either. Those leggings are...." He puts his fingers against his mouth and pulls them away with an audible kissing noise. "Perfect."

"Ha ha ha." I give him an exaggerated, dry laugh. "Let me grab a scarf for my hair and then we'll go check out the leak."

He cocks his head. "Leak, huh?"

"Uh huh." I duck into my bedroom and grab a pretty white scarf, with tiny lavender laurels printed all over it. It takes me just a moment to pull up my hair and tie the scarf over it, tucking the ends in to protect my hair from any musty muck we might come across during this leak-fixing adventure.

When I come back out of the bedroom, I find River studying the large, framed photo that hangs in my kitchen. It's one of my immediate family, taken when I was six years old. I'm holding baby Malik on my lap. Mom is sitting beside me, beaming like a woman who's got the world on a string. And my father is standing behind us all. His grin is too honest for me to look at. He really loves his life and his family.

That's the last portrait we all got together. My dad died not long after that.

"That's a good-looking family, right there." River nods at the picture.

I give him a tight smile. "Thanks."

He reads my curtness as it's meant to be taken. "Should we go?"

"Yep. After you."

I lock my Airstream, and lead River through the little path in the woods. We pass the trailers and keep going to the older section of the resort park. The cabins are back here. They predate the trailers by a couple of decades. Each one is rustic, simple A-frame built of leaning, peeling logs. They've certainly seen better days. But they are far down on my personal list of things to spruce up around this place.

As I swing open the door to cabin five, I see that water is actively spilling down one of the walls. I swear up a storm while River jumps back. Water pools on the floor, and when I clear a pathway with the door, it begins to pour outside.

It's probably only three inches deep but there are signs of chaos everywhere. An old, wooden chair is overturned near the wall. Closer to where we stand, there is an electrical outlet with a huge sizzle pattern all around it. It looks as if it was connected to the toaster, but someone unplugged it recently. Maybe something to do with Aunt Delta cutting the power.

There are also a hundred tiny sugar packets that were knocked off the kitchen counter somehow. They are now floating and soaking in the pool.

The whole house smells like rotting wood.

I stand in the doorway, trying to take it all in. "What a mess!"

River splashes through the water to the wall. After looking at it for a second, he drags over one of the wooden chairs. He hops on it and removes the ceiling tile directly above him. With a quick, sure motion, he reaches in and fiddles with something in the darkness.

"I think there used to be a sprinkler system in here," he says. "Does that sound right?"

I screw up my face. "Yeah. I think so."

"Well, the line is backed up. It probably has been for a number of years. I'm surprised that this is the first leak you've had."

I shrug. "It may not be. I was away at college for four years. Who knows what's been broken and fixed while I was studying."

He smiles at me. "That's probably true." He hops down, rubbing his hands. "I shut the water off at the line up there. It should be okay until you can get someone out to take a look at it."

A laugh burbles to my lips.

"Get someone? We are someone. Delta is not about to pay for a handyman to come out here."

River squints at the hole in the ceiling. "I don't think a handman would do it. You need a plumber. And probably an electrician for that outlet." He does some quick calculations. "I'd say you have about three thousand dollars' worth of stuff to fix. And that's only for this one problem. If a licensed electrician came out and had a look at what I assume is the nightmare that is your wiring, I think he'd have no choice but to call the county and have this place condemned."

"What?" I yelp.

"I'm pretty sure that's why no professional has ever stepped foot in this place."

My mouth twists. My shoulders sag. "I don't have three thousand dollars lying around," I say. "I don't think Aunt Delta does, either."

River cocks his head, thinking for a moment. "I think I know an electrician and a plumber who can come out."

I sigh. "You're not listening. I can't pay for them. I guess we'll just have to close this cabin until we figure out a plan."

River shoots me a secretive little smile. "They both owe me a big favor. Trust me when I say that they'll do the work for free."

He fiddles with his phone, sending a text message. I pull a face. "Are you serious? You can't waste your favors on me."

"Why not? You need it. I have it. It's done."

I walk over to him and tug his hand holding his phone. "Seriously. Don't. I don't want to owe you anything."

River smirks. "Don't be so calculating. We have a relationship. I mean, the fiancée stuff might be fake. But that doesn't mean I'm heartless. Let me do this for you."

Looking into his eyes, I feel my heart beat race. I scan his face. Is he for real?

He reaches out, puts a hand to the small of my back, and draws me in. I press against his torso and tilt my face up.

He kisses me, his lips hot against mine. My eyes sink closed and my hands wind around his neck. He deepens the kiss and dips me backward. I clutch his neck, feeling heat slide through my body.

Oh yeah. He's about to get rewarded, big time.

River releases me and grins. "I'm dispatching the workers."

My cheeks feel hot and I feel as unsteady as a fresh born foal. I give him a grateful smile. "Thank you."

His lips twitch. "You're welcome."

Is it strange that I feel such a magnetic pull between us? I must admit that this is just supposed to be a getting pregnant romp. Nothing else. Hell, I haven't even had sex with River yet. And already, I can feel my brain attaching delicate strings to him.

It's a terrible idea. But I can't seem to help it.

I need to remember my reasons for not being interested in the false promise that River seems to offer.

"This doesn't mean anything," I blurt out.

River looks up from his phone. "Excuse me?"

"You helping me out. I just want to be as clear as possible. This doesn't mean we're in a real relationship. I'm not like... your girlfriend."

His brows rise. "I hardly think that this is payment for being my girlfriend. This is just me being nice." He purses his lips and gives me a considering look. "We're on the same page, Pearl. I still plan to move to Atlanta in less than a year. Not only that, but... you're not really my type. I like a career woman. You don't seem interested in that track."

"I'm not," I supply quickly. "I'm just looking for a sperm donor. Nothing else."

He slowly nods. "We're in agreement, then. Casual sex. Pretend engagement. Six months from now, we might never see each other again."

"Okay." I smile, relieved. "Just checking. It seemed like we were vibing for a minute there."

"We can vibe and still keep it casual. I promise."

"That's good. I'm not looking for my great love. Not now, not ever."

He gives me a lazy half-salute. "Aye aye, captain. I hear you loud and clear. Want me to kiss you again though?"

I can't suppress a grin. "Okay, sure. You win."

I open my arms to him and he scoops me up, carrying me off while I burst out laughing.

Thirteen

River

Pearl hasn't stopped clutching my arm since I picked her up this morning, with a cappuccino and a sleek black garment bag in hand. Even now, as we sit side-by-side in the helicopter, she acts as if she will blow away if she lets go of me.

I can't keep the smile off my face as I watch her. She is staring out the window as we draw closer and closer to the Atlanta skyline. She's glued to the window in the most uncomfortable position I can imagine.

"Jesus." Pearl turns around to me, her eyes wide. "I can't believe you're actually flying me into an Atlanta Kings game."

I grin at her awe. It's been a while since I brought a date to an event like this. I forgot how they react.

Pearl wasn't born into this family and the kind of wealth afforded to us all from the time my mother married Sam. I've grown accustomed to it, but it's refreshing to hear Pearl's awe.

"It's pretty nice," I agree. "I usually don't fly to games. But this is a special occasion. My family's rented out the

Kingdom sky box as another stop in Cole's month-long engagement party. And I figured you hadn't been taken anywhere in quite this way before."

Unable to tear herself away from the view for long, Pearl bites her lip and looks through the glass again.

"You got that right." She leans so close that her breath fogs the window. "Am I dreaming? I'm in a chopper, on the way to a private box at Kings Stadium, in a designer dress..." She tugs at the hem of her long, white babydoll dress. "You didn't have to do all this, you know."

I run my hand down her arm, enjoying her little shiver. "I wanted to. You're so damn beautiful. And you work so hard. You deserve to be a little spoiled."

Pearl tosses a shy smile over her shoulder. "You're going to ruin dates for me. Nothing will be able to live up to this."

"I'll see about that."

She's extremely cute right now, her long hair in twin French braids, her strappy, glorified sundress pale against the burnt umber of her skin. As the helicopter begins its descent toward the stadium, I settle back in my seat. Sure, Pearl may not be the real deal. But our chemistry is so natural that spending time with her is very pleasurable. My gaze skates down to her hips and snags there.

I won't lie. It's very hard not to pin Pearl against the seat and strip off her fancy dress. I'm extremely horny and she looks so damn good.

I swear that I'm going to go insane if I don't taste her soon.

The chopper lands. The door opens and I climb out, helping Pearl down. She looks around at the rooftop, her jaw dropping. We're in the middle of downtown Atlanta, in the midst of the perpetual rush hour. Everywhere I look below us, there are SUVs and cars honking their horns. The helipad is actually a perfect vantage point to take it all in, but we can't just hang out here.

"Come on." I coax Pearl to hurry toward the waiting elevator. She huddles against me to avoid the cold spring wind that's whipped up by the helicopter's blades.

We are escorted down a series of large concrete hallways. The Atlanta Kings' logo is proudly placed in every conceivable spot, and I start seeing fans wearing Atlanta Kings jerseys as soon as we get into the hallway that leads to all the skyboxes. Pearl looks around with a curious gaze.

"You've never been to the boxes before, huh?" I ask.

Pearl swipes her tongue over her lips. "I've never actually been to a baseball game here before. The closest I got was the baseball diamond at King Taylor high school."

"Seriously?" I slide my arm around her waist and hug her closer. "Then today's really going to be a treat for you."

We are ushered into the huge box. The large picture window on the wall straight ahead shows the quickly filling stadium seats just beyond it. Below us lies the court.

To our right is the classy bar, with a bartender fulfilling orders. Next to that are tables laden with pre-game snacks, and Atlanta Kings themed desserts. Near the window, there are a few rows of stadium seats. Most of my family is already here, talking excitedly amongst themselves. There are a few older couples that are probably my parents' friends seated with them.

As soon as my mom sees me, she squeals with delight. She's dressed in head-to-toe Atlanta Kings merch and makes a beeline straight to us. "River! And you brought Pearl!" She hugs my fake fiancée, hard. It goes on for a second too long. I have to put an arm around mom and gently wrest her away.

"Someone's in good spirits," I say, once I separate the two women.

My mom is a little flushed. I can tell she's been drinking, and she doesn't have much of a tolerance. I'm sure that we'll see her napping before the game is over.

"I'm so pleased that you are both here. Really." My mom gestures to the bar and the food. "Can I offer you anything? They have these cupcakes that have Rex's face on them."

"Thanks, but I am not really thirsty or hungry just now," Pearl says. She beams at my mom. "It's so nice to see you again, though."

My mom takes Pearl's elbow and points to Savannah. "Let me introduce you to my daughter-in-law."

"Savannah and I are old friends," Pearl says. Her eyes are wide, I imagine because she hasn't told Savannah that we have supposedly been secretly dating. Whoops. Pearl continues, "We went to Agnes Glen College together."

My mom is completely electrified by her response. "You went to Agnes Glen?"

Pearl gives her a funny look. "I was Lucy's college big sister."

My mom gapes at her. "You know Lucy? How have we not socialized before now?" She turns to me. "You should have brought Pearl to meet me right away."

I raise my hands. "Guilty."

Mom gently tugs on Pearl's elbow. "Let's go talk to Savannah."

Pearl shoots me a look over my mom's head, but I can't quite read what it is supposed to mean. I head over to find Sam, Brooks, and several of Sam's golf buddies standing together.

"And I said, 'that's not investing the way I do it!'" Sam howls. The whole circle around him breaks into laughter.

Brooks is the first of the group to spot me and he raises his pint of beer in celebration. "Look who's here?"

I slide into the circle, saying hi to everyone. Sam looks

around and sees my mom with Pearl. His expression tightens.

He's so suspicious of me. He's always been that way. Granted, this time I'm actually trying to pull the wool over his eyes.

But what about all the other times he hasn't trusted me?

Scenes flash through my head at lightning speed. Sam accusing me of stealing a candy bar from a gas station. The time a whole bunch of students in my high school biology class got caught cheating on a test and Sam just automatically grounded me with ever hearing my side. My senior year, Sam once thought I smoked pot because I avoided the living room full of my family members. But I actually just had a stomach ache and didn't want to tell everyone my business. Several times in college and right after, I went to Sam with a hot tip about what the stock market would do. He ignored every single one, where he could have made millions if he'd just listened.

I could go on and on.

"You brought Pearl," Sam says. "I was wondering if you'd drop her or if she'd make another appearance."

I give him a tight smile. "She's still here. Not going anywhere."

Sam's blue eyes burn into my face. "Mhm."

"Let's grab a beer," Brooks jumps in, throwing me a life preserver. "The game is about to start."

He's right. When we make our way over to the bar and order pints, the organ's opening chords play. One of the game's announcers says that some new country songstress will sing the national anthem.

Brooks leans over to me during the warbly singing and whispers, "You brought the waitress from the diner?"

I look at him coolly over the rim of my pint. "Yes. Is there some rule that says I can only date women who don't wait tables for a living?" I can't help it. My tone is downright ornery.

The national anthem finishes and the crowd goes wild. Brooks shakes his head. "I didn't mean it that way. I'm just surprised. Mom said that you've been dating Pearl in secret for two years? I have a hard time wrapping my head around that. Whenever anybody even mentions marriage around you, you usually have a lot to say about it. It doesn't jibe with you having a SERIOUS GIRLFRIEND."

I can hear the all caps in his voice.

"Well..." I scan the room, looking for a way out of this conversation. Brooks and I have been close our whole lives. I don't want to lie to his face, but he's not making it easy.

I spot Cole and Charlie entering the box. Cole is carrying an armful of Kings toys and merch. Charlie waves a plastic light up sword with the Atlanta Kings' logo on it. He runs over to Savannah, eager to show off his new treasure.

Cole puts all the swag down on a table and heads over to us. "Hey! You made it."

"Yep." I jerk my chin to Pearl, who is listening while Charlie tells Mom and Savannah about going down to the merch booth. "I brought Pearl."

"I can see that." Cole shoves his hand through his hair. "Before you know it, you'll be old and married. Then you can make Atlanta Kings' merchandise runs with your kids."

I roll my eyes. "One step at a time."

Brooks nudges me with his elbow. "Twenty bucks says that Mom is already planning your wedding. No, wait. A hundred."

Cole snorts. "There is not a doubt in my mind that Sarah has binders for each of us, full of wedding plans. She pulled out mine as soon as Sav and I announced our engagement. And it is detailed." He shakes his head, horrified. "Gotta put all that energy somewhere, I guess."

Rex's name is announced over the loud speakers and a cheer goes up, not just in our box, but the whole stadium. Mom takes Charlie up to look out over the field. I shoo my brothers toward the front. "Let's go stand near our significant others." I slide Brooks an arched brow. "You can come too."

He punches my bicep and I grin. Cole leads the way to where Pearl and Savannah are standing, looking out the big picture window. I look down onto the field. Rex and his teammates file out of the dugout and run onto the field.

"This is so cool!" Pearl says. "I rode in my first helicopter. Then I get to sit in the nicest box in the whole stadium? Jeez Louise."

"I know. It's a little surreal," Savannah replies. She looks at Pearl for a long second. "Much like finding out you're dating Cole's brother. I though we knew everything about each other."

Pearl looks embarrassed. "I'm sorry. River and I made a promise to each other... and then it kind of spiraled out of control. Before I knew it, it had been too long to come clean to anyone without someone getting offended."

Savannah narrows her eyes at Pearl as if she doesn't quite believe her. She gives her a strained smile. "We can talk about it in private. Now isn't the time or place."

I sidle up behind Pearl and slip my arms around her waist. "So, you're in the best suite in the whole stadium. Is it as good as you hoped?"

Pearl throws her head back and belly laughs, which makes me feel good. "It's something, all right."

I can feel Cole and Brooks staring at us. So I move to kiss the column of her neck, just above her shoulder. Her fine baby hairs get in the way. I smooth them back and she shivers, clenching her hands over mine. It's not a natural gesture but I think Pearl's bright laugh afterward sells it.

"You're so bad," she says, grinning.

"You don't even know the half of it."

I press against the small of her back, half aroused. Her lovely peach and vanilla scent teases my nose. She half-turns, her eyes flashing, and schools her expression. "Behave yourself."

I know that she's just pretending. But it's a hell of a performance. I am almost fooled. I wink and enjoy her cheeks coloring. "Not a chance in hell."

Cole slides an arm around Savannah's shoulders and studies us. He purses his lips. "How's your resort project going?"

For a second, I freeze. I swing my gaze to him, shooing him the tiniest glare. "Fine."

Pearl glances back at me, as if trying to discern why my body language just changed. Her brown eyes scan my face.

Cole squints at me. "Have you found a new site yet?"

I force myself to smile and relax. "No, not yet. I'm looking at a number of properties."

He raises a brow. "No leads you're willing to talk about?"

"What, are you looking for another big project? I would think that you have plenty on your plate as it is." To Pearl, I say, "He's working on building the new training camp that's going in north of the Cape."

"And we're renovating downtown South Shore," Savannah adds. She smiles at Pearl. "You probably know this already, but the project is how Cole and I met last year."

"Right, of course. That makes more sense," Pearl says. "Are you in real estate law too?"

The group falls silent. Everyone exchanges glances. I realize that Pearl just messed up my job title a little. While I am technically a real estate lawyer, I am actually the CEO of our family real estate group.

"Pearl just likes calling me a lawyer," I cut in. I squeeze her waist. "Because she never hears the end of any argument. Sorry, darlin'."

Pearl's smile is forced. "It's true! He is always snapping back, just when I think I've won. It's infuriating."

"You love it," I add.

Pearl blushes. "I guess I do."

"River, don't you think that's a big liability in a relationship? I would hate to be part of one of those couples that always nitpick at each other." Cole looks a little too smug as he kisses the top of his fiancée's head. "That's why I know that Sav and I are meant to be. It's always very harmonious around our house."

Pearl's expression hardens and she gives Cole a look.

"No offense to either of you. But Sav is your second fiancée, Cole. I think River is doing just fine without your advice."

Sav's face goes red and Cole grimaces.

"Sorry," he grits out. "I think I'm going to go check on Charlie. Sav, you want to come with?"

Sav nods and hurries after him. Brooks looks at Pearl with a chuckle. "Damn, Pearl. You didn't need to absolutely wreck him like that."

Pearl swallows and looks at me, seeking my validation. "Was that bad? I was just trying to get him to back off."

"You did fine, darlin'. I promise. Sometimes you gotta show the world that you have fangs. I bet Cole will think twice before crossing you again."

She presses her hand to her heart. "I hope he's not offended."

"Cole's easy to offend. But equally easy to forgive and forget. I wouldn't worry about it."

She pulls a face. "I will definitely wake up in the middle of the night, worried that Cole hates me."

Pulling her close, I drop a kiss on the crown of her head. "You do you."

The next few hours fly by. With Savannah stationed at her side, Pearl seems to relax just a bit. My mom and Charlie pull the girls into their little circle. For the most part, I just keep an eye on her from across the skybox. By the time we reach the sixth inning, she's laughing and comfortable.

Good timing for what I have planned.

I slide over to Pearl and touch her waist. "Want to go down and see the field? We can while the teams have their seventh inning stretch."

Pearl arches a brow. "We won't be chased off?"

"The Bennett-Taylors do it almost every game." I turn to Mom. "Hey! Are you guys going down to see Rex?"

"I think we are staying put this time. But definitely take Pearl down and give her the red carpet treatment. It's nice to know people." She winks.

Brooks coughs into his hand and mumbles, "It's even nicer to be part of a family of billionaires."

I grin. "Let her believe whatever she wants."

Taking Pearl by the hand, I lead her out of the skybox and down the long, concrete hallway. Once we make a turn, we enter the throngs of fans queueing in the lines for food. Pearl lets out a big gust of breath, giving her body a shake.

"Ahh!" she says. "That was longer than I thought I'd have to act like your fiancée. It's kind of tough to be so friendly while I'm lying through my teeth."

"You were a rock star in there," I praise her. "Seriously. Such good work."

She gives me a little smile. "Thanks. It's actually harder than I thought it would be."

"You're still in, though. Right?"

She wrinkles her nose at me. "I'm still in."

"Good. Because I want you to prepare yourself for the next step."

Pearl smirks at me. "The part where you announce that we are secretly engaged?"

We head down some stairs, Pearl's high heels clicking with every step. "Something like that."

I usher her through a security checkpoint and down another long concrete hallway. When we get to the end, a suited man greets me. "Hello, Mr. Taylor. Nice to see you."

"This is my girlfriend, Pearl," I say by way of introduction. "Pearl, this is Dave Fourtier. He's going to show us onto the field as soon as the players clear off for their break."

"Nice to meet you," she says. She grabs my hand, taking me by surprise. I give her a quiet smile.

"The teams are clearing off now," Dave says, looking out at the field. "Let's give them one more minute before we head out."

Pearl squints at him, frowning. She can sense that something is off. She just doesn't know what.

"Okay. Now you can go out to the pitcher's mound for a photo if you'd like to," Dave offers.

I raise my brows at Pearl, tugging her hand. "Maybe we'll just head out to the dugout for our photo op? I don't want you to trip and die in those heels."

She laughs and nods. "I would appreciate that."

Making sure that she has a good grip on my arm, I walk Pearl out onto the field. There are a few other people on the field too: two maintenance workers groom the grass, a group of Japanese tourists looks at the whole stadium with wide eyes, and an elderly couple are escorted by a young player from the opposing team.

I walk Pearl to the home plate and then stand back, looking up at the sea of fans. It's pretty overwhelming if I spend too much time thinking about it.

Dave follows dutifully, holding a large camera. He snaps a few candid pictures and then calls to us. "Are you ready?"

A lump forms in my throat. I grab Pearl's hand, stand back, and sink down on one knee.

She looks at me, as still as petrified wood.

"Pearl. Will you do me the honor of being my wife?"

Every ounce of blood floods into her face. She locks eyes with me, her expression hard and terrified. "Y-yes?" she squeaks.

I slide the ring from my pocket, put it on her finger, and then stand up. I raise her hand, showing it to the stadium. A cheer rises and the speakers blare the first few notes of the wedding march. "Ladies and gentlemen, she said yes!"

I pull her into my grasp and then kiss her passionately.

When I pull back, she is staring daggers at me.

"What the hell was that!" she demands in a rough whisper.

Putting her hand on my arm and waving to the crowd like a politician, I say, "That was putting on a show. Trust me, my parents definitely saw."

Pearl digs her fingers into my arms and forces a bright smile to her lips.

"So did everybody else. That includes my family." She leans her head down to my shoulder, hugging me, and whispers, "You should have told me about your plan!"

My heart skips a beat. Is Pearl actually mad? I didn't really consider her when I put this plan in motion. "Can we talk about this when we're alone?" I hiss.

"Oh, you bet your ass we will." She looks up at me, smiling brightly but with eyes like daggers. "Count on it."

Fourteen

River and I aren't fully alone again until many hours later, when the limousine finally drops us off at his beach house. I am still miffed at the lack of thought that River put into his marriage proposal. It didn't even occur to him to give me a heads up so that my mom, brother, and my aunts wouldn't find out my big news secondhand.

That lack of foresight on his part is frankly astounding to me.

River slides me a gaze as he opens the door. "Are you brooding over there?"

I give him a look. "You fucked up, River." I kick off my heels and head straight to the couch, which is the only piece of furniture in this empty museum he calls a living room. "I'm going to have to do some serious damage control tomorrow. My whole family is going to be furious with me."

He pulls a face. "I'm sorry, Pearl. I guess I thought that you would be more surprised and pull off the whole fake fiancée thing a lot better if I didn't tell you. It was a mistake." He sinks onto the couch beside me and looks me right in the eye, his gaze unwavering. "I'll make it up to you," he promises. "I'll even explain to your family that it was a spur of the moment decision. I'll tell them you didn't know."

"That won't be a lie, at least." I exhale a huge gust of breath. "I just thought we were spending more time with your family. And Aunt Delta wants to meet you. If I hadn't already agreed to this little deception, I would have to go along with it now. Or face public embarrassment, I guess."

River's eyes flash. He leans closer to me, a smile playing on his lips. "Forgive me?"

I am caught in his sapphire blue gaze. He takes my hand and kisses the back of my hand. Then he places a kiss at the pulse point of my wrist.

My lips part. Between my thighs, my core heats. I swallow and press my legs together.

God, am I really going to forgive him so easily just because I find him so irresistible? I bite my lip, hating myself for it even as I lean into his beckoning posture.

"Promise me that you won't do it again." My voice comes out breathy. "There can't be any secrets between us, River. Or surprises. This is a contract."

He moves closer so that there is no space between the hard line of his body and the softer one of mine. Shifting his weight, he sinks his hand into my hair and tugs back, exposing my neck. "I promise, Pearl. No more secrets," he utters. "And I intend to seal the promise with much more than a kiss."

Even though I am desperate for him to touch me, some unnamed alarm bells go off in the back of my head and I stiffen in his hold. "What do you mean?"

He chuckles and lowers his lips to my throat, placing a single burning kiss to my flesh.

"It means that we are long overdue for my half of this

baby bargain to be paid," he whispers. "I've kept myself in check around you because I respect you. But I've wanted you ever since I laid eyes on you, Pearl."

He kisses my neck again and I can't help but release a moan that's been building inside me for weeks now.

"Tell me what you're going to do me, River. I love when you talk dirty to me."

He tugs my head back further and trails kisses down my neck into my cleavage. My adrenaline shoots through the roof and pleasure drips from my breasts to my pussy. He's barely even touched me and I can tell that my panties are ruined already.

"I'm going to strip you naked," River says, his voice ragged. "I'm going to rub your clit, make you come, and then fuck you so hard you won't be able to see straight." He pauses, then shakes his head. "God, Pearl, you have no idea how much I want you. Do you know how often I fantasize about you when you're not around?"

His voice wraps around me, husky and laced with desire. It's all I can do not to visibly shudder. I shake my head.

"River..." His name escapes my lips on a breathy exhale.

I watch as his eyes darken. His pupils dilate with the same hunger that's burning up my insides.

"Every time I see you, it's like I'm drowning in this... this *need*." He's closer now. I can feel the heat radiating from his body. "It's not just your body, Pearl. It's your spark, your essence. It's all of you."

A tremor runs through me. His words are like fingers trailing down my back, setting every nerve ending alight. The anticipation builds within me, coiling tighter and tighter until I think I might snap from the tension.

"River," I whisper. It's both a warning and an invitation.

"God, Pearl..." His voice is strained, almost a growl. It's as if he's holding onto his control by his fingernails.

I can feel the muscles of his torso through his crisp shirt. The firmness of his muscular body contrasts with the softness of my curves. It's as if we're two puzzle pieces clicking together. We're made to fit in this exact embrace.

His large hands are suddenly on my waist, fingers splaying wide as if claiming their territory. They pull me in closer, leaving no space, no air between us. There's a dominance in his grip, a silent assertion of *you're mine*. It doesn't scare me.

His possessiveness *thrills* me. With River, I never feel overpowered. I feel empowered. Like his strength is bolstering my own.

"Tell me what you want," he commands softly. His breath is hot against my cheek.

"More," I breathe out. I barely recognize my own voice, grown husky with desire. "I want more. I *need* more. I want you to take control of my body."

"That's what I fucking want to hear," River says. "I always want to give you what you need, darlin.'"

I grip his shirt, biting my lower lip. "I'm starving for you, River."

His lips graze the shell of my ear. In a flash of lightning, my world narrows to the husky timbre of his voice.

"I'm going to make you feel things you've never imagined, Pearl."

Every whispered word is like a spark to dry tinder, sending a lick of flame through my veins. My breath catches, hitching in my throat. Suddenly I've forgotten how to do something as simple as breathe.

My knees tremble. My body threatens to betray me by buckling under the weight of his promises. But it's not just his words that set me on fire.

It's the certainty behind them, the raw edge of need that reflects the deep well of hunger I have inside.

"River," I manage. "Please?"

He pulls back, just enough for me to feel the loss of his heat but not the magnetic pull of his gaze. His eyes dance with a mischievous glint that tells me he knows exactly what he's doing to me. Slowly, deliberately, his fingers move to the top button of his crisp white shirt. The click of each button releasing seems to echo in the quiet emptiness of his beach house.

One button. Two. Then three. Each reveals more of that chiseled chest I've spent hours staring at. He's honed from years of strict discipline.

"Like what you see?" he teases. The corner of his mouth quirks up in a devilish grin that does unfair things to my stomach.

"Maybe." The word tumbles out. It sounds coy, and bolder than I feel as I drink in the sight of him. His skin is a canvas of smooth planes and hard edges, begging for my touch. My eyes trace the path down from his collarbone to where the fabric still clings to him.

My fingers itch to touch him. I reach out, but he steps back playfully.

"Only maybe?"

"Definitely," I correct myself. "I think my pussy is getting damp."

My heart races at my own audacity. River's eyebrows rise. The air between us crackles with anticipation and the promise of what's to come.

I reach out, my hand trembling. My fingers brush against River's newly-bare chest, tracing the hard lines of his pectoral muscles. They are hot to the touch.

His hands encircle my wrists, gentle yet unyielding. There's a look in his eyes. It's a glint of raw, primal control that sends a shiver down my spine. He holds up a finger.

"I think we should go into the bedroom."

Just like that, he picks me up, carrying me as if I weigh nothing at all. He puts me down in his bedroom right in the middle of a big white bed. It looks like a hermit lives in here. Aside from the bed, the only furniture is a bedside table, an ivory-shaded floor lamp, and a half-filled bookcase.

"Your décor style leaves something to be desired," I say.

"Don't worry about my room." River's lips twitch. He motions to me. "It's time for me to get you out of that dress, darlin.'"

I blush. Getting to my knees, I turn so that the long zipper on the back of my dress faces him. "Unzip me?"

"With pleasure." He unzips the dress then pulls the straps down. Then he tugs the entire garment free, casting it aside.

I look at it, narrowing my gaze. "River, that is a five thousand dollar dress."

"It can stand to lie there for a while." His eyes dip to where my breasts are barely covered by a lacy black bra. "God damn, woman. You're trying to kill me with those matching bra and panties."

I giggle. "I knew you'd like them."

"I more than like them." He lifts my hands, guiding my wrists together with an ease that speaks of practice. Then he opens a drawer on his bedside table and pulls out a long strip of red satin. "Now be a good girl for me. Let me tie you up."

"Oh!" I say. But it's not a protest, exactly. More of an inquisitive sound than anything.

With deft movements, River binds my wrists together, the silk knotting with a soft rustle. The fabric is cool against my hot skin. But the sensation is quickly replaced by the warmth emanating from his closeness.

River knots the binding securely. The silk is taut enough to remind me of my position. Of the fact that he's the one dominating me here. But it doesn't pinch or chafe. He pushes me back on the bed and then raises my hands over my head.

I am very aware of my own vulnerability in this position. My lacy strapless bra digs into my sides and my tits are a quarter inch away from bursting free. I squirm and River clucks his tongue at me.

A rush of anticipation floods through me. I'm exposed, open to his gaze, to his touch. My heart hammers against my ribcage.

"Perfect," he murmurs. He back to admire his work.

My breath is shallow, a silent symphony of nerves and need vibrating through me. I press my knees together because I'm feeling moisture slipping from my pussy.

It's arousal and the awareness of what's to come.

He comes to kneel on the bed. River's breath ghosts over my skin as he lowers his head to my neck. Goosebumps break out over my skin. The first touch of his lips is a stroke of heat that blooms and spreads.

"River..."

It's all I manage before he responds with his mouth. He traces the column of my throat with kisses that promise so much more. He alternates between nipping and soothing with kisses. My legs tremble and my hips rise toward him.

This is an ache that only he can satisfy.

"Stay still for me, Pearl." His command is harshly spoken.

I force myself to relax and fight to obey his wishes. My instinct to arch into him is nearly overwhelming. But I clench my teeth and hold still. I'm held in place by the silk at my wrists and the intoxicating trail of his lips moving lower.

Each burning kiss teasing the sensitive skin at my collarbone.

"Please," I whisper. I'm enthralled by the sweet agony of

his teasing. There's laughter in his next kiss. The feel of him chuckling against my skin that tells me he enjoys this.

"Patience," he murmurs. "Let me savor what's mine, darlin."

I'm his? But of course I am.

His for now, a voice says in the back of my head. I push it away.

A surge of heat courses through me as River's hands glide over the contours of my naked skin. My skin tingles under his touch. I'm so alive and his caress reminds me of that. His fingers trail a path of fire down my hips.

It feels so good. I can't help but arch into him, seeking more of that exquisite sensation.

"River..."

His touch intensifies. His fingers play over my skin with a skill that borders on reverence. It's a dance of push and pull, each caress expertly bringing me closer to the brink.

"Tell me what you want," he demands, his voice a husky whisper. "I want to hear it, Pearl."

I bite my lip. "Please, I need—"

"Need what?" His words are velvet against my raw need.

"More," I say on an exhale. "You know just what I like."

River's hand skates across the gentle curve of my belly. He teases the pair of lacy panties I'm wearing there. I tense, all my muscles flexing.

"Say it, Pearl. Tell me where to touch you. Beg for me."

River places a kiss just above my belly button and then looks at me. There's a gleam in his eyes. It's a mischievous spark that speaks of his confidence and control.

"River, please," I plead, my restraint crumbling. Every stroke of his hand fans the flames higher. My body trembles and burns with urgency. "Rub my clit. Put your cock in my pussy. Make me come. *Please*."

"Good girl," he murmurs. His approval sends a fresh

wave of desire coursing through me. I can feel moisture seeping from my pussy, spreading across the wet spot at the front of my panties.

River parts my thighs and touches the wet spot ever so gently. I almost come off the bed. I've been teased and tormented quite a bit, so I'm shaking, already on the edge.

He strips my panties down my legs and pushes my knees apart. He looks at me while he casually skims a finger against my pussy. When I shudder, he kisses my knee.

"You're so sensitive, darlin."

Parting my lips, he runs his fingertips around the entrance to my pussy. I stifle a moan and shift my hips toward him. He shows me his glistening fingertips, wet from my excitement. Then he rubs his fingertips against my lips.

My mouth opens and my tongue catches his fingers, tasting my own essence eagerly. He chuckles and pops his fingertips in his own mouth. His eyelids flutter closed.

"So fucking sweet," he concludes. "I love your taste, Pearl."

He uses his fingertips to find my clit. My intake of breath is sharp and sudden. He swirls lazy circles over my clit and watches me squirm.

"You want to come?" he asks.

I grit my teeth. "Please," I pant.

"Close your eyes, baby." My eyelids shut. All I can feel now is him circling my clit, picking up speed. If he doesn't make me come in a second, I'm pretty sure I will actually *die*.

The world narrows to the heartbeat thundering in my ears. The heat of River's body against mine. The relentless movement of his hand. A deluge of sensation washes over me.

I'm drowning, sinking deeper into the abyss of desire

with every calculated stroke. Or burning, destined to become cinder.

"Let go," he commands. His words are laced with a raw edge that leaves no room for doubt. "Surrender, Pearl."

And I do. I shatter the walls I've built, brick by painstaking brick, all my practicality crumbling under the weight of what I feel for him. What he does to my body.

It's terrifying and exhilarating. A freefall into the unknown.

I never want it to stop.

While my pussy is still spasming, he unzips his slacks and positions his big cock at my entrance. He pushes inside with one hard thrust. We both cry out.

"Fuck," I whisper. I pull him down on top of me, rocking my hips.

He looks at me with such a reverent expression that it takes my breath away. "You're fucking perfect, darlin. So fucking perfect."

"River," I breathe out, a desperate chant.

He starts moving, thrusting my cock into my tight pussy. I mirror his movements. Our bodies sync up, a perfect rhythm that echoes the pounding in my chest. We move together in a seamless choreography of need and fulfillment.

"Look at me," he demands. Our eyes lock. There's a fierceness in his gaze. A reflection of the possessive desire that he feels.

He grabs one of my hips and moves his hips faster than a piston. Just looking at the way he brings our bodies together and hearing the slap of hips upon hips makes me groan.

Oh god, I'm going to come again.

My moans crescendo. They mingle with his low groans as we spiral upward, chasing sheer sensation. The air crackles with the energy we generate. Each gasp and shudder a testament to the power he wields over me.

"River, I'm—" The words dissolve on my tongue as the dam breaks.

A cataclysmic wave of pleasure crashes over me. I'm ablaze, consumed by the fire he's stoked within me. Each pulse of ecstasy radiates outward until I'm lost in pure feeling.

"Pearl!" His voice is hoarse. "Fuck, I'm coming..."

His fingers dig into my hips as he brutally thrusting into my pussy, stretching it, coming very close to hurting me. He shudders as he comes, four great thrusts and four intense lashes of semen. I can feel the burning hot liquid as it heats my pussy walls, coating them.

He closes his eyes and struggles for breath, his cock still twitching inside me.

My breath slowly returns to a regular rhythm. The frenzied beat of my heart steadies as I float back down to reality. His eyes open, still the same sapphire blue, and he reluctantly slips his cock from my pussy.

River's fingers work deftly at my wrists and the smooth silk scarf slips away. It liberates my skin from its gentle restraint.

"Better?" River's voice is soft, the rough edge of desire smoothed into tender concern.

"Much," I reply, my voice barely above a whisper as I flex my wrists, relishing the freedom yet missing the delicious pressure.

He gathers me into his arms, his chest still damp with the exertion of our passion. Our bodies meld together. His heartbeat against mine is a soothing drum.

"Stay with me," he murmurs. His lips graze my forehead.

I nod, not trusting my voice as emotion swells within

me. I don't want to ask the only question that seems relevant right now.

Why would I want to leave?

When we resurface, our breathing beginning to slow, I look over at River. He rolls onto his side facing me and presses a kiss to my temple.

"Fucking hell," he says, trying to catch his breath. "That was... incredible."

A laugh burst out of my throat, unbidden. "It was."

I grab a pillow, wiggling around to wedge it under my butt and tilt my hips skyward. River watches me with vague amusement.

"What are you doing?"

"Helping your swimmers swim in the right direction."

He arches a brow. "Does that actually make a difference?"

I shrug my shoulders. "Maybe it will just make me feel better. Anything I can do to help the process is going to get done, period."

"No rush." River wiggles his eyebrows. "The sooner that I get you pregnant, the sooner we have to stop fucking each other's brains out."

The thought gives me pause. "Have you thought that far in advance?"

He looks at me a little skeptically. "Yeah. Haven't you?"

"Definitely not. I guess it's pretty obvious, but I swear it didn't enter my head even once. I'm a little ashamed of myself right now."

He pushes his mouth to the side of his face. "I think we'd be crazy to keep having sex if you're already pregnant. I like you. Don't get me wrong. But... I'm not looking to get serious."

"Neither am I!" I say, defensive. "I'm just looking to start my family."

River relaxes. "Just making sure we're still on the same page. You're smart and pretty and a definite catch. But I'm not looking for that right now. I have plans for the future."

"Like moving away," I say.

"Exactly. I want to relocate to Atlanta and eventually get myself an ambitious, career-oriented girlfriend. That's what this whole fake fiancée ruse is supposed to help achieve."

Putting aside the fact that we just had some of the hottest sex ever, I am in agreement.

"Like I said, I was just surprised that you'd thought it through that far. We are on the same team."

"Team knock you up and get my family to release my trust fund early."

"That's the gist of it, yup."

Silence stretches between us for half a minute.

"Since we're already naked, do you mind me asking why you decided that you have to have a family right now? You're pretty young. You still have plenty of time to meet someone and have kids."

"Because in my family, women go through menopause really early. My mom had her change of life at thirty-six."

He's quiet for a beat. "That's still twelve years from now."

I shake my head vehemently.

"I've done the math. Say I want to have three kids, with a year in between. That's well over ten years. And what if I struggle to get pregnant? I can't take chances with my fertility."

"You could always adopt..."

I look at him, gesturing to my face. "And miss out on seeing a baby with this adorable face? I don't think so. Besides, assuming that Aunt Delta doesn't lose the family land to the IRS, I have to have somebody to pass it on to." I give him side eye. "Our land is worth a lot, you know."

River looks at me, his eyes widening. And then he clears his throat and looks away. "I think I heard something to that effect."

"Well, whatever you heard is true. In order for me to have a baby to inherit the land, you have to do your job and knock me up."

His lips twitch. "Yeah, well. Speaking of the deal... I think we'll have to bring your family into the wedding planning that will no doubt be occurring starting tomorrow."

I wince. "I hate that my mom and Malik have probably already found out."

"Well, if you don't tell them, Instagram will. CapeSimonAroundTown will definitely know by tomorrow. Which means that the gossip will spread like wildfire."

I squeeze my eyes shut with a groan. "You got that right. I always kind of liked reading CSAT's posts about our town gossip. But now that I'm the subject, I'm starting to rethink my admiration."

'"Yeah, well. Be on alert from here on out. We both have to be fully invested in order not to get caught out by CSAT. So, like... no screwing around with anyone else until our deal is complete."

I roll my eyes. "I wouldn't do that. I don't just have sex with every guy I meet, River."

"I never thought you did." He smirks. "I have to say, Pearl. Given our explosive chemistry tonight, I am glad that you picked me."

My cheeks feel hot. I bite my lip and reach out to run my hand down River's bicep. "You know, if you want, we could explore our chemistry again--"

He stops me with a kiss on the lips, dragging me back down into the depths.

Fifteen

River

When Pearl finally pulls into the parking lot of La Petite Boulangerie, it's almost twenty minutes after our reservation time. I glance at my watch as she hurries over to my truck with an anxious look on her face.

"Sorry! Sorry, I got stuck at work. The girl that was supposed to relieve me called out and--" She stops, her cheeks glowing a dusky pink. "And you are not interested in all that."

I give her a tight smile. "Maybe save it for later. Right now, I need you to change out of your uniform and into the dress I brought for you."

Pearl looks down and runs her fingers up the apron skirt, where a dark brown stain has taken hold. "It's soda," she explains when she catches me noticing it. "The soda machine broke and I had to climb up on the counter to reach the instrument panel."

Suppressing a sigh, I open the door to my truck. "Gem is lucky to have you."

"Trust me, she knows that." She shoots me a quick smile

and climbs in. She turns in the seat and starts to unzip the back of her dress.

She doesn't seem to know or care that anyone walking by might see her changing. Just another reminder that Pearl is totally different from the other girls I have dated. They would pout and simper when anything was the least bit hard, or wrong.

I unzip the garment bag that I brought and hand her the designer gown with pink and gold sequins. Then I partially close the door for privacy, although I don't think Pearl really cares all that much. She pushes on the door to be let out and looks down at her sneakers. "You didn't happen to bring shoes, did you?"

"As long as you don't mind recycling, I can give you the ones that you wore to the Kings game." I check in the truck's back seat, which resembles a mobile closet for Pearl. The personal shopper I paid to pick out fancy dresses for my fiancée just came by this morning, and I haven't had time to move the clothes into the house yet.

I make a note to get the shopper to order more shoes.

Once I hand the gold heels over, Pearl turns away from me, showing me her spine in the unzipped dress. The flash surprises me; most girls I know would definitely care if I saw them half-naked, even after we'd had sex.

There is something almost erotic about the sight. I clamp down my raging libido, reminding myself that we are late.

There's always later tonight for seeing Pearl's incredible body buck naked. I take a deep breath and try to calm my suddenly-racing heart.

Pearl gathers her hair at her nape and says, "Can you zip me?"

I can't help brushing my fingertips along her spine. She

giggles and looks back at me. I zip the dress up and help her to step away from the truck.

My eyes rove down her figure, snagging at her shapely ass. The dress fits her like a glove, and stops midthigh so her toned legs are on display.

Pearl looks like a whole-ass treat, and I'm a man who's been starved for a thousand years. I open my mouth to suggest that we just ditch the dinner.

But Brooks sticks his head out the restaurant door and calls to me. "There you are! Can you come inside so we can order already? I'm famished!!"

I press a kiss to Pearl's knuckles. Leaning my head close to hers, I whisper, "You look like a million bucks, darlin'."

She laughs and catches my hand. "Stop blowing air up my skirt."

Brooks holds the door open and points us toward the private dining room. Beau Rivage is the fanciest restaurant for miles around, and its interior reflects that. All the furniture is sleek and black. The tables are lit by candlelight and the uniformed waiters rush to and fro in front of the big windows overlooking the beach, carrying drinks and plates on giant black serving trays. We bypass tables full of couples whispering to each other over their menus and step into the large room just off the reception area.

I stop as I take in the long table, and the faces of my family and Pearl's sitting around it. No one looks particularly thrilled to see us, which isn't exactly the way I wanted to start things off.

An older Black woman gets to her feet as soon as we enter. "Pearl!"

Pearl puts her hands over her mouth and looks at me with wide eyes. "You invited my family?! River! We talked about this!!"

My mom jumps up, hustling around the table to hug

Pearl. "Come in! Come in, sit down. We saved you two these seats right in the middle."

Pearl smiles and greets her, and then heads around the table to hug her Aunt Delta, her mother, and Malik. I see that Cole, Brooks, and Rex are here, in addition to Sam. After a minute of greeting everybody, I pull out Pearl's chair and wait for her to hurry over to it and sit down.

I sit down and look to my right. Pearl's Aunt Delta glowers at me.

"Hello," I say. I force a smile. "You must be Aunt Delta."

She looks like she's sucking on a lemon. She picks a piece of lint from her black dress and gives me a calculating look. "And you must be the boy that my niece has been sneaking around with. I don't know what Pearl was thinking, hiding a relationship from her family. Makes me wonder if the engagement is even real."

My heart rate rises and I feel my face get hot. "Err..."

"Delta, we talked about this in the car. Nobody wants your crackpot theories, okay?" Pearl's mom is quick to fire back. She levels an apologetic smile at me. "I'm Flo. And you probably know Malik, Pearl's brother."

I nod to Flo and offer Malik a quick handshake. "Pearl talks about you guys nonstop."

That's a direct lie, but it is out of my mouth before I have time to consider it. Delta arches a brow at me. "Is that so?"

My mom, who has strategically seated herself across the table from me, jumps in the conversation to rescue me.

"Miss Jackson, I was thinking of hosting my sorority sisters for a weekend at a hotel. Your resort would actually be the perfect place. What do you think about having a group of Kappa Alphas and a lot of wine? It sounds fun."

Delta smiles at my mother. "We would love to have you.

Here, let me give you my card so that you can call me when you have your calendar in front of you."

She hands my mom a slick business card. Mom looks at it carefully. "Do you guys have a website?" she asks. "To share with the girls, before I book."

Malik clears his throat. "We have an Instagram. We're The Vintages Coastal."

Delta pats Malik's hand. "My nephew is very good with the internet."

Pearl looks over to our half of the table with a timid smile. "Is everyone playing nice over here?"

"Nice enough," Flo says. "We were just about to ask your fiancé a lot of personal questions. See if he's good enough for you, Pearl."

Delta coughs into her hand. I swear that I hear a low, *'not a chance in hell'*.

"River, what do you do for a living? How are you going to support my daughter? And your kids, I assume."

"Mom," Pearl squeaks. "Please. This is the man I love."

She puts her hand on my neck, caressing it. I lean into her touch just a little more than is necessary.

"I am the CEO of our family's real estate company. And if it helps at all, I have a law degree from Emory University."

Her mom purses her lips. "That's a good school."

"It is," Malik adds. "My boyfriend wants to go there."

"Definitely let me know if I can give a reference. Emory is nuts about students that know alumni."

"Sounds pretty nepotistic," Delta says, frowning.

"Aunt Delta!" Malik scolds. "Come on. Be polite. We're guests here."

"Oh look!" my mom calls, desperately waving the waiter over. "I think we could all use a nice glass of wine. Anyone else?"

"I'll take a glass," Flo says. She's staring daggers at Delta.

"So what does a CEO of a real estate company do?" Delta asks, complete unperturbed.

"River is basically a project manager. Our family has a lot of construction projects going on at any one time. So River manages those and does anything that an architect doesn't do. Isn't that right, baby?" Mom answers.

I try not to sound sulky as I answer. "That's right."

"Uh huh." Delta looks unimpressed as a nervous waiter fills her wine glass with some expensive white wine. "Just to be clear, though. You're not looking for property to develop, right?"

"No," I say, cutting off any other answers. "The family just took on a large project north of Cape Simon. That's what the family is focused on right now."

I can feel Cole's eyes on my and I see his brows knit together.

"Y'all are doing a big renovation in downtown South Shore too. Right? My sister Glory said she worked with one of you Bennetts on that," Flo says.

I point to Cole. "That would be Cole. He told me that Glory made him jump through hoops to get that construction permitted."

Delta sniffs. "She's just doing her job as an elected representative of her community."

Pearl smiles at Delta. "Everyone agrees with you, Auntie."

"Oh, they're bringing the food," Malik announces. "Thank god. I'm starving."

The next ten minutes are taken up by waiters arriving with steaming platters of coq au vin, sausage cassoulet, duck confit, salad, and various bowls of tarte tatin, bouillabaisse, baked Brie, and giant piles of crusty sliced French bread.

After we have all filled our plates, but before I manage to tuck into the first mouthwatering bite, Delta stands up.

"Let us pray," she announces. She glares around the table, especially at Brooks, who'd stuffed half a slice of French bread in his mouth already. He swallows convulsively.

"Go ahead, Miss Delta," Sam calls. "Remind us why we need to give thanks."

Delta frowns around at the table. "Bless us, oh Lord, and these, Thy gifts, which we are about to receive from Thy bounty. Give us this day our daily bread. Deliver us from trespassing, as we may forgive those who trespass against us. May the Lord God almighty bless these two children, who have gathered us all here to discuss their engagement. Pearl and River, let the Lord shine his light through you both. Let you both practice abstinence and chastity until you are wed, as God commands. In the name of the Father, the Son, and the Holy Ghost..." Delta draws the moment out, making me want to squirm. "Amen."

"Amen!" my mother calls. "That was the best blessing I've ever heard. Hear that, River?"

"It was definitely... good..." I mumble.

Pearl presses her lips together, her eyes full of mirth. I reach under the table and squeeze her thigh. She jumps at my touch and squeals. "River!" she protests.

I flash her a wide smile. "What?"

Pearl leans close and scolds me. "Behave."

"Not a chance in hell," I whisper back.

She's just taken a sip of water, but she spits it back into her glass. Her shoulders are shaking with laughter. "You're terrible," she accuses.

"And you are an angel, descended from heaven, made to walk among us mere mortals for eternity." I splay my hands. "But what are you gonna do?"

Pearl's grin is wide and genuine. "I couldn't possibly say."

At this exact moment, it's easy to forget that we are not a real couple. In fact, I struggle to recall my perfect career-minded female counterpart at all.

All I can see right now is Pearl. I drop a quick kiss to her shoulder, making her shiver. She's so damn responsive to my every touch.

It's even tougher to remember that this is temporary. She will go her own way, and I will go mine. There is nothing that will keep us together after the next few months.

"River?"

I blink, breaking the reverie. I turn to find that Sam is talking to me.

"What's that?" I ask.

Sam spoons sauce onto his chicken from a nearby platter.

"I asked when Pearl was moving in with you. I assume that you two will do it sooner than later."

"Uhh..." I stammer. I look to Pearl, as if she has the answer I'm seeking. "I don't know."

Sam pauses, his fork in midair. "Is there some reason that you don't want to take that next step?"

I feel my face heat. "No. Pearl and I just haven't decided on the details. We've talked about it, obviously."

"Maybe they shouldn't move in together until they are a married couple," Delta says, her expression tart.

"No, no," I correct her. I don't want Delta to go into the religious speech that I feel is building up in her throat. "What do you think, Pearl?"

Pearl gives me a wide-eyed look. "I don't know, honey."

"I think y'all should go ahead and move in," my mom chips in. "Just to make sure that y'all don't drive each other crazy when you're married. You know, he leaves his socks on the floor, she spits toothpaste in the sink without rinsing it. Get the kinks worked out."

I tense. My mom's words immediately put a filthy image of me, naked as a jaybird, standing over a kneeling Pearl. She's wearing nothing but a white silk blindfold and a white silk binding on her wrists. I'm brandishing a fully erect cock and a cat-o-nine tails.

Kinky, indeed.

"Yes," Pearl blurts out. "Let's do it, baby. Let's move in together."

Now I'm the one who has a wide-eyed look.

"Okay..." I say hesitantly. "Whatever you want..."

I shovel a giant forkful of duck confit into my mouth, trying to figure out just what I have gotten myself into this time.

SIXTEEN

PEARL

The trees thicken once I turn off the highway, and I swear that I can breathe a little better than before. Today was a really challenging day at work and I desperately need to turn my brain off.

My old car doesn't have autopilot. But I have driven this bumpy back road so many times that I steer by muscle memory alone. When I turn the final corner to my Airstream, and more importantly my bed, I see a huge box truck parked beside my trailer. It has the words Red Carpet White Glove Moving Service emblazoned on the side.

What the hell is this truck doing here?

River stands up from one of my patio chairs and waves me over. "Hey. I was expecting you earlier."

"Well hello to you too," I reply tartly. "We were slammed at the diner and I had to stay late. Apparently, it's a school holiday today. Your brother Cole and his mini-me stopped by."

He shoves his hands in the pockets of his dark jeans. He's not wearing his usual black leather jacket, and his biceps in that soft-looking gray T-shirt make him look like a model. I'm not sure what River is selling, exactly, but I want to buy it.

I giggle, feeling loopy after a long day of work. River smiles, but his eyes are concerned. "Are you okay?"

I wave his apprehension away. "Fine. Just tired." I turn around to jerk my thumb at the truck. "What's up with the truck?"

"They're here to move your stuff. I think the crew got bored and went to check out the rest of the property. But as soon as they get back, they're ready to work."

I look at River like he's grown a second head.

"I'm sorry. Did we decide that I would be moving into your house? I must have missed the memo."

Digging my keys out of my purse, I open the Airstream's front door and head inside. I leave the door open for River and hear him enter behind me a second later.

Heading down the hallway, I throw my purse on the kitchen counter and make a beeline for my bed. I collapse on it with a groan. The king-sized bed was the main selling point of this place; if I hadn't moved in here after college, I'd probably still be at my mom's house in South Shore. My bedroom there is cramped and certainly wouldn't fit a bed this big.

Then again, considering that the whole room is taken up by the bed, maybe the Airstream isn't much better. But at least it's private.

"We need to talk about you moving," River says. He's right behind me, and the unexpected closeness of his body causes goosebumps to break out over the back of my neck.

I groan again and roll over, patting the bed beside me. "Sit down."

He does, his big frame eating up more space than I thought he would. He glances back to the headboard, his eyes sparkling with amusement when he sees the felted little green men that I placed there. He picks one up and turns it this way and that.

"Where did you get this?" he asks.

"I made it." I tease the doll from his fingers and place it back against the pillow. "It's one of the first UFO-themed crafts I ever made."

"Oh." River pauses, squinting. "That's... cool."

I harrumph. "Did you just come here to insult my felting abilities?"

He shakes his head. "No. I came here to move you to my house, like I said."

I sit up and give him a frank look. "Moving to your place in the Cape would mean I would be driving back and forth between here and your place a lot. It would double or triple my drive time."

River looks at me, confusion written plain across his face. "I just assumed that you would jump at the chance to get out of here. It's so cramped."

"It's not cramped," I snap back. "I'm economical with how I use my space. Besides, after your little announcement at dinner the other night, Aunt Delta has been muttering about renting my trailer out if I move. When the fake fiancée facade is over, I would have to find a new place to live. Do you have any idea how expensive rent is these days?"

He gives me a rueful little smile. "I do, actually. That's part of my job."

"Then hopefully you know that I've got a good deal here."

He studies me for several beats. "You can't expect to stay here with a baby."

"That is none of your business. And may I add, beside the point."

"But I already told both our families that we're moving in together."

He's like a frigging dog with a bone. I squint at him, leaning in to whisper to him. "If you want to move in so bad, move in here."

"Here!" River looks gobsmacked. "You can't be serious. Two people living in… three hundred square feet?"

"It's two hundred and seventy-two square feet." I cross my arms. "Don't act like you really live so differently. I've seen your house. You have your bed, a couch, and a kitchen counter that's way more cluttered than mine. You basically live in an Airstream already. Your space is just contained within a zillion-dollar beach house."

He blinks a few times, absorbing that thought.

"People will think I'm crazy for moving here."

"Well, love makes you do crazy things, right? Besides, if you need space, you can always stay at your place."

He blows out a breath. "That's true. Plus, there's the fact that… you know… this is all a sham. We are friends with benefits, nothing more."

"The benefit being… a baby," I agree. "If you don't want to do my plan, come up with a solution that won't cause me to drive all over the damn place."

River snakes his hand out and touches my face. I look at him, frowning. "We can stay here until I come up with a better solution. Okay?" he sighs.

Under his sapphire gaze, I melt a little. "Okay."

He stands up, hitting his head on the sloped ceiling with a thunk. "Ow."

I stand up and gently rub the side of his head where it hit the ceiling. "Sorry. I promise, you'll get used to it."

He looks at me with a smirk. "I'd better. I can't wait to fuck you again, darlin'. I've been dreaming about it."

I blush and drop my hand. He's not the only one having sex dreams every night of the week. "We'll see about that."

He jerks his head toward the door. "I'm going to go tell the guys that we won't need them today."

Then he turns and lumbers out of the trailer. I fall backward on my bed, arms out. Mostly I'm wondering just what the hell I have signed myself up for. Can we peacefully co-exist in this small of a space?

River comes back in the Airstream. I hear his footsteps slow in the kitchen. When he finally comes back into the bedroom, he holds a piece of paper between his fingers. "Is this your list of potential baby names?"

River shows me the list and I feel my face heat. "Yeah." I sit up again, feeling a surge of awkward energy wash over me.

He sits down and studies the list. "Selene, Lyra, Astrid, Mariam…" He purses his lips and looks up at me. "Going for a celestial theme, I see."

I pluck the list from River's fingers and smooth it out against the bed, my touch tender. This list means a lot to me. I'm not going to let River or anyone else spoil my heart-felt excitement.

"Nothing personal, River. But you don't get any input in what I plan to name my baby. You may be giving me your sperm, but I am the one with the final say in the kid's life."

He raises his hands to wave an imaginary white flag. "I never thought I had a say. But right here," he says, pointing to the boy names. "Draco? Sirius? Have a heart. Don't give him a name that's in Harry Potter."

That was not what I was expecting him to say at all. I tip my head back and laugh. "And what would you suggest?" I ask.

He snags the list and turns it around, studying it.

"Sterling is a good, strong name. And Kepler is good, too. After Johannes Kepler, I assume."

"That's right!" I beam at River. "He used math and

observation to figure out that the planets orbit in ellipses, not in circles. He studied the skies before there were even telescopes."

"That's extremely cool. Kepler isn't as good of a name as Sterling, though."

"Yeah, well. It's just a list of names I like." I grab the list and head back into the kitchen. I place it on the fridge, with a magnet to keep it in place. When I return, I take off my shoes, putting them in the shoe caddy I keep under the bed. I swap them for a soft pair of alien head-shaped slippers.

River lies back on the bed, looking comfortable. I don't know if it's just his confidence or what, but River seems like he is able to relax anywhere. He looks at ease in almost any situation.

Not like me. I'm a fish out of water nearly everywhere I go.

River eyes me with a smug smile.

"So now that we live together... how about you take off that dress and come over here?"

Blushing, I can't keep a smile off my face. I slip the dress off, but keep my fuzzy alien slippers on, ready to pounce on River.

SEVENTEEN
RIVER

Pearl scrunches up her face when I pull my truck into a spot at the Cape Simon Marina. She looks out of the sea, where expensive yachts and priceless sport boats bob gently in the water.

"You have a slip here?" she asks.

I nod, opening my truck door. The salty sea air hits me and I grin. "This is my favorite place in the world."

She gets out of the truck, clapping her hand against her oversized sun hat to keep it from blowing away. I grab a large knapsack, my tackle box, and the rolling cooler. "Got everything?" I ask.

She pats her large woven bag. "I think so. Like I said earlier, I don't really know what I need. I haven't spent that much time on boats."

"Oh, darlin'." I point her in the direction of the pier and we start to walk. "That changes today. I fucking love being on the water."

We trundle down to the boat. Pearl keeps a watchful eye on the water, as if she doesn't fully trust it. I walk to my prized possession, eager to show it off to her.

"Here she is," I say, dropping the cooler next to my luxury fishing boat. It's thirty-seven feet long, and it has an enclosed cabin with a roof that overhangs the back deck. Below the main deck is a smaller cabin with a leather couch and a lavatory.

If I could be on the sea every damn day, I would. I love my real estate business, but it's really only a distraction from boating all day.

Pearl shades her eyes, her sunglasses making her face hard to read. "Uh, cool."

I give my head a tiny shake and hustle her on board. Setting the cooler down in the large upper cabin, I unload my knapsack and tackle box. Pearl stands, gripping the side of the boat, swaying slightly.

I turn to look at her. "Are you okay?"

Pearl lifts her chin, swallowing. "I'm fine. I haven't ever been on a boat like this before."

I walk back to her and offer my arm. "Come on. Lean on me. You'll appreciate sitting in the cabin."

She clings to me, stepping uncertainly. I don't really understand what is going through her head, because the boat isn't listing or anything. We are in the marina and there isn't much wake at all. I help her into the cabin and sit her down. She flops into the leather bucket seat and clutches both sides. I give her a look as I move around to the captain's chair.

"Have you been on a boat before?" Pearl glares at me. "Of course I have. Just not this big. My cousin has a catamaran and we've been out in that a few times."

I touch her arm, trying to reassure her. "This boat is a lot safer than a catamaran. Nothing bad will happen to you. I promise. You can stop gripping the seat like that."

Pearl gulps. "I'll stay right here, thanks."

"Suit yourself. I'm going to start the engine." I screw up my face. "It's going to be loud."

Pearl sits back, looking straight ahead, and nods her head somberly. "Do what you have to."

If I didn't think she was really scared of this boat, I'd laugh at her. But honestly, I feel really protective of Pearl and concerned for her right now. I am starting to be able to read her mood; that quick scan tells me that a joke is not what is needed right now.

I caress her thigh and give her an encouraging smile. I need to play this one differently.

"I'll cast off. Be right back." I duck out of the cabin, untie the boat from its moorings, and do a quick check that everything is in order. Then I head back to my seat and start the motor.

Pearl doesn't flinch, but I can tell that she struggles to keep her face blank and expressionless. I back out of the dock and turn us toward the open sea.

Pearl seems to relax more as we pick up speed. At this velocity, there is less rolling of the waves under the boat, and more of the constant whirr of the engine against the water underneath. When we make it past the marina and I ease the throttle up to full speed, I glance over at Pearl.

Her eyes are glued on the sea ahead of us. But she has loosened her death grip on her seat. The color is incrementally returning to her face.

"Are you doing okay?" I ask. I brush a strand of her hair back behind her ear.

I feel a little useless in the face of her seasickness. I want her to be comfortable, yet just being on this boat makes her ill.

"Yep." She flashes me a quick smile. "I think I just needed to adjust."

"Fair enough. We're not going far. My plan was to go up

to Wolf's Head Island. There are a few deep pockets near there where I always have a lot of luck fishing."

She frowns and glances behind us. "This is probably a stupid question. But... you have fishing rods, right?"

"Yup. I keep my rods in a storage case just downstairs. Don't worry about that part. I'll bait your rod. You just have to hold it."

She cranes her neck toward the rear deck. "I'm guessing that we'll sit back there in those two chairs?"

You got it." I grin at her. "It's just about a ten-minute ride up the coast."

Pearl pushes out a long breath. "Okay. I'll be fine."

I don't know if she's trying to reassure herself or me, but I can't help the little grin that blooms on my face. "I believe you, darlin'."

As I drive the boat, I keep looking over at her to make sure she's okay. Her posture seems less rigid than it was before, but her eyes are still cemented on the sea. I guess I'll take what I can get.

I get a text and I pull my phone from my pocket. It's my mom.

Be a dear and pick a date for your official engagement party. Also if you could find out what Pearl's dietary restrictions are, that would be amazing. Oh, and ask her for a date that works for her family, too!

"Yes!" I cheer. I put my phone away and look at Pearl. "My mom just texted, asking to throw us an engagement party. This is a really good sign. If my mom gets behind us, Sam's not far behind."

Pearl frowns. "And you need Sam's approval, right?"

"Less his approval and more my trust fund. I'm not supposed to get it until I'm forty. But I want access to it now."

"Right. To invest in some real estate venture, I think you said. It's got to be hard to lie to your mom, though..."

My eyebrows fly up. "I'm not lying to her."

There is a moment of silence. "Do we have a fundamental misunderstanding of what you have told your family?" Pearl bites out. "Because I was under the impression that you were telling them that I was your fiancée."

"Well, I am." My face grows hot. "I don't see it as lying to my mom. When I get the project funded and finished, then I can turn my focus to dating and procreation. So I see it more as delaying the truth by a few years. I might say that it's *embroidering* the authenticity of my life."

"Hah!" She laughs, but there is no humor in her tone. "That is straight up crazy. You know that, right?"

I direct my glare straight ahead. "It's my life."

Pearl's tone softens. "You're right. It is. I just don't want you to ever 'embroider the authenticity' of the facts you tell me. With me, I want you to shoot straight."

"Of course." I feel tongue-tied, as if she actually caught me in a lie. "I am only misleading my parents because they have this old-fashioned mindset. They think that being married equates to being settled down in life. If they hadn't tied my trust to a sham institution, none of this would be happening."

A flicker of some emotion passes over Pearl's face, there and gone before I can even name it. But I think it might have been disappointment.

I feel a hollow pang in my stomach. She's right to feel disappointed in me. More right than she realizes. But of course, she has no idea that the real estate venture I want to invest in is her family's property.

Guilt fills the hollow pit of my stomach. Her face is so expressive; I know the exact face she's going to make when she realizes what I've done. And it's not one I want to see from her.

Deftly pushing that aside in my head, I steer the conversation neatly away from that topic. "Right. My mom is asking if you have any dietary needs. She's probably planning a big celebration."

"None that I can think of." She sighs. "My family will probably throw us a barbecue." She goes quiet, looking off as though lost in thought.

My tone is reassuring. "My mom will invite your family to whatever she decides on. Don't worry about that."

Pearl's brow furrows. "I'm not worried exactly. I just feel bad. I didn't realize that you were going to propose so publicly. I thought... I thought that I could keep my family out of this. Now my family is deeply involved. It's gonna be a whole thing when we break up."

"What do you mean?" I slow the boat down a little, looking at the shoreline. We're almost there.

"My family is not going to take you leaving very well. Even if I say it's my decision, they're probably going to ice you out."

I look at her, confused. "What does that mean?"

"My cousin Ashley broke up with her fiancé a couple of years ago. My aunt Glory denied him a permit when he applied for a liquor license in downtown South Shore. My mom told everybody with ears what a bad guy he was. Aunt Delta put a hex on him." She shivers. "He got so fed up with the badmouthing that he moved to Savannah."

I snort. "Don't worry about that with me. I'm unhexable. I'll be okay."

She makes a noncommittal little 'hmm' and looks away. I feel another pang. Our engagement was perfect from my standpoint. But I guess I didn't really take Pearl's feelings into consideration. "I'm sorry," I say at last. "I guess I didn't think it through."

Pearl shrugs a shoulder. "What's done is done."

I slow the boat down further, drifting closer to shore before cutting the engine completely. All the while, I'm kicking myself. Also wondering what other things Pearl might not be thrilled about, but won't complain about.

I drop anchor and stand up. Now that we're not moving, the boat is very much at the mercy of the rolling waves once more.

I offer her my hand. "Come on. Walk to the back of the boat with me. If you decide you hate it, we can head back."

She forces a small smile to her lips. "You're very chivalrous."

I bow to her. "My lady."

That earns me a laugh. I help her up and she clings to my arm as I walk her back toward the rear-facing stationary chairs. As soon as Pearl grabs onto the seat, she collapses into it. Her face has gone eerily bloodless again.

I stand right beside her, wordlessly supporting her. She breathes in and out a few times, gulping. Just when I'm about to throw in the towel and ask if she wants me to take her home, she waves me down. "I think I'm fine." She turns around and casts an angry glare at the deck. "As long as I'm not walking, I guess."

"Can you wait here while I fetch the rods?"

She nods quickly. "Yeah."

I practically race down to the cabin to fetch the rods. I'm feeling like a complete tool for not even bothering to ask her if she liked boats or got seasick. What kind of idiot plans a date on a boat and doesn't think about an alternative just in case their date doesn't like boats? I'm a *fuckhead*.

Shaking my head at myself, I grab the cooler, the tacklebox, and my knapsack. Armed with everything we need, I return to the end of the boat.

Pearl's color has returned. She offers me a weak smile. "I think... I think I can stand up and move around."

Before I can stop her, she pushes out of her seat. She doesn't walk anywhere, but stands in the same spot, swaying with the gentle movement of the boat. In her pink floral sundress and oversized straw hat, she looks like summer incarnate. She looks at me, pleased with herself. "I stood up!" She laughs. "That sounds incredibly stupid, doesn't it?"

Abandoning the rods, I move over to her, shaking my head. "It doesn't sound stupid."

Her good attitude about my terrible date is amazing. She laughs again, throwing her head back. God, she is radiant. Not to mention sexy.

I want to kiss her. But she has only just found her feet. I don't want to interfere with anything. I jerk my head toward the fishing rods instead. "How about I set up our lines?"

She nods. "You'll have to. I don't know the first thing about catching fish."

It's the work of a couple of minutes for me to set up her fishing pole and attach a live cricket to the hook. She watches with interest, but she makes a face when I slide the barb of the hook through the cricket's body.

"Gross," she sniffs.

"Fishing is pretty gross. Just wait until you actually catch a fish."

She makes a gagging expression. "If I catch a fish, you'd better believe I'm not touching it. I like my fish one way, and that is breaded and deep fried. That's the extent of it."

"You only have to touch it with one finger. Just to know what it's like. I'll do the rest," I promise.

She raises a brow. "We'll see."

I hand her the rod. Then I quickly step in behind her,

putting my arms around her shoulders and my hands over hers. She looks at me, pausing. It's hard for me to tell because of her dark sunglasses, but I think she's remembering how well our bodies fit together.

I move my hands down to her hips. "Spread your legs to give yourself a nice, strong base."

She complies, giggling. I put my hands back over hers and start to explain the very basics of casting. I only get a few steps in before she pulls her glasses down with a finger. "Are you being serious right now? Why don't you just show me? I can learn about the ins and outs later."

I shake my head, but a grin bursts across my face. "Was I mansplaining too much for you?"

"A little," she admits. She pushes her sunglasses back on.

I help her cast. She laughs when her first attempt falls in the water only feet from the boat.

As a guy that's had a boat for a long time, Pearl is definitely not the first woman I brought on board. Heck, she's not even the first girl I've brought to Wolf's Head Island to fish.

But hearing her laugh, feeling her warm body press against me, watching the way she looks to me for feedback... I have to admit that it feels different.

Special, somehow.

I know that I'm not exactly her ideal man. Not for dating purposes, anyway. But it does feel nice being so intimate with her. Not exactly sexual, but... deeper than that.

Pearl Brown might just have me hooked and be reeling the line in without even realizing it.

EIGHTEEN

PEARL

I'm at the diner, scrubbing the long counter that is perpetually greasy, no matter how many times I clean it. It was busy, up until 12:45. Now the diner is vacant, silent except for the hum of the running dishwasher, and the whoosh of the dish sprayer being used to prepare another load of dishes. Diego is listening to some Cuban big band music in the back. Gem is here too, probably out chain-smoking on the patio while she calls vendors.

I give up on trying to remove a stubborn stain, and grab a silverware basket and a pile of cheap white napkins from the kitchen. I start mindlessly rolling up silverware, placing a knife, fork, and spoon together and covering it with one end of the napkin. I roll in quick motions. Doing silverware as side work has an almost-pleasing mindlessness to it. My body knows how to do it without much thinking at all.

As I stare out the window, my mind wanders. I'm thinking about whether I should go to the GCUFOs gathering tonight. God, GCUFOS meets once a month. I can't believe all that's happened between me and River since the last meetup.

Bishop will probably be there, dragging Anitta around like he's at an amusement park and she's the huge stuffed bear he won. *Boo.*

Bishop seems to bring out River's worst side. And because River now technically lives with me, it would be rude to go to the meetup and not invite him along.

The doorbell chimes, saving me from my thoughts. I look up, ready to greet the customer coming in the door. To my surprise, Lucy and Savannah enter.

"Hey girlie!" Lucy says, grinning and launching herself at me.

"You're skinny!" I chastise her. "Are they feeding you at Agnes?"

"Like you wouldn't believe," she assures me.

Sav gives us a tired look and gives me a half a hug. "Hey, Pearl. Sorry, it's been kind of a day."

Her expression is withdrawn. I suspect that she is tired. I also suspect that her tiredness will soon be revealed to be baby-related. But since she hasn't told me anything, I don't ask.

She might be worried about announcing her pregnancy too early and then miscarrying. I know it's a fear of mine, anyway.

Instead, I pivot to Lucy. "I'm so excited to see you both!"

"I know. It's been a while since it was just us hens in the henhouse." Lucy looks around and sees that there are no other customers. "Do you think we can visit for a minute?"

I grin and point to two barstools at the counter. "Grab a seat. Are you eating?"

"Nah," says Sav. She sits down. "We're just coming from that little farmer's market that sets up at the end of the main strip."

"You didn't find anything? Not a single asparagus stalk or a solitary tangerine?"

Sav laughs and shakes her head. "Nope. I think we were both just getting a little stir crazy and wanted to enjoy the weather."

"It is beautiful outside," I agree. "What'll you guys have to drink? I just made sweet tea. Or you could try some hot ginger tea. I finally talked Gem into carrying it."

"How about a coffee? With a little creamer and a pound of sugar, please?" Lucy asks.

"You got it. Sav?"

Sav wrinkles her nose. "I'll have a cup of ginger tea."

"No problem." Their drinks take less than a minute to gather together. I set the coffee and tea down, then I push a large glass sugar shaker across the counter to Lucy.

She proceeds to pour a ton in her coffee, snaking a spoon from the basket of clean silverware.

"So, what's been going on with y'all?" I ask. I start rolling silver as I talk, but I look at them attentively.

Lucy slurps her coffee. Sav smiles and rolls her eyes.

"Not too much over here. Charlie learned that rocket ships exist. So our whole house is full of model rockets now. It's..." She pressed her lips together. "A lot."

"And you?" I ask Lucy. "How's Agnes Glen?"

"Did you have Dr. Blatt for English Comp?"

I squint. "I don't think so. I remember Dr. Hensu running that department with an iron fist."

She sighs. "Dr. Hensu retired, I think. Dr. Blatt just assigned me so much reading that I'm about to be buried in textbooks."

"I remember that feeling," Sav sighs. "This too shall pass."

"We came here to talk to you about the wedding planning," Lucy says. "Not for you guys to tell me that my reading crisis isn't a big deal."

"Sorry, Luce." Sav's lips twitch with humor. "Pearl, tell

us about your wedding! I've done so much planning for my own that I think I'm planned out."

I point a roll of silverware at them both. "Y'all are cute, thinking that I have anything planned yet. I didn't even know that River was going to propose."

Sav looks at me with a concerned expression. "Are you two okay? I mean, if Cole had proposed to me without us talking through our plans for the future first, I would be livid."

Lucy snorts. "Yeah, that would be a bonehead move. But it's something River would pull though."

I swallow, trying to control my expression. I'm immediately transported to the conversation I had with River about lying to his mom.

What did he call it? Embroidering the truth?

I do not want to do that. So I am very careful about what I say to my friends.

"River and I are totally fine. But again... I haven't thought about wedding plans. It wasn't completely out of left field. But I am not really super interested in having a big wedding."

"Uhhh... you'd better tell my mom that," Lucy says. "She is fully losing her mind over getting to plan another wedding."

"Sarah's planned like seventy percent of ours," Savannah chips in. "She was on cloud nine. If she hasn't called you personally yet, I bet River is blocking all of her wedding planning energy from you."

"Wedding planning energy is like big dick energy, but wayyyy more gay," Lucy cracks.

"You two are a regular Abbott and Costello over here. You should start charging for tickets."

Sav laughs but Lucy just screws up her face. "Who?"

I wave away her confusion. "Sweet summer child. They were a comedy duo from the 1940s."

"Oh." She shrugs. "Okay. You know, I'm not that much younger than you."

"Don't tell me. Tell Abbot and Costello," I say, grinning.

"Y'all are too much." Sav checks the time on her phone and slurps her tea. "We have to get going, Lucy. I promised your mom I would be back to take Charlie by 1:30."

Lucy holds up a finger and guzzles her coffee. I laugh and shake my head.

"I'll get you a to-go cup," I offer.

"Nah. This was the perfect amount." She pulls out her wallet and drops two twenty-dollar bills on the counter.

I immediately grab the cash, take her hand, and force the money into it. "No way am I ever taking money from you for a cup of Gem's coffee."

Sav pushes herself up from the counter with a smile. "Especially considering that y'all aren't just Agnes Glen sisters anymore. You're about to be literal sisters-in-law."

That thought hadn't occurred to me. But I find myself nodding. "Plus, I know how expensive living in the city is. Agnes Glen makes you live on campus, but you still have to pay for almost everything else."

Lucy makes a face. "My parents pay for almost everything. Let's not get carried away."

I hurry around the counter to hug them both. On the way out, we make vague plans to hang out in the future. Sav waves as she ushers Lucy out, and I see the two of them head off in the direction of the family mansion.

Twenty minutes later, I cut the last lemon wedge. Gem comes out from the back and looks around the empty diner. "Has it been like this for a while?"

"Yeah. I had side work to do, but it's all done now. Do you think I can go early?"

Gem jerks her chin out at the parking lot. "Looks like you're just in time. Your husband-to-be is here."

I turn and spot River climbing out of his big truck. He's dressed up in a light blue button-down, and dark slacks. His top button is undone, revealing a perfect triangle of tanned throat and sparse dark hair.

For some reason, that little triangle does something to me.

Specifically, it makes me horny. I bite my lower lip and imagine the crazy sex we're probably about to have.

God, I'm like a teenage girl, waiting on her crush.

"Pearl?" Gem says.

I look at her, flushing. "Oh, yeah. Uhh... what were you saying?"

Gem shakes her head and sighs theatrically. "Go, honey. I'll handle the midday lull."

I am ashamed to admit that as soon as my brain processes her command, I turn back to River. "I'll see you soon..." I utter, completely distracted by his approach.

"Don't forget your tips. And your jacket. And your freaking purse, for God's sake."

I quickly grab the aforementioned things and rush to the door, putting on my warm jacket as I step outside.

River immediately grins at me. "I was just coming to see you."

"Well, here I am," I say, striking an awkward pose. "Gem told me to am-scray."

"Good. I was planning on sitting down and ordering some food, because that way I could tip you. But it's so nice outside. I'm glad you got sent home early."

I shove my hands into my jacket pockets to keep myself

from reaching out to touch him. There's no one looking right now. Therefore no need to act like we're in love. "Do you want to go walk on the beach with me?"

"I'd love to."

We walk down to the beach, making small talk and enjoying the feeling of the sunshine on our faces. Winter is really over and the sunny, hot days are right around the corner. Today is the best of both worlds, sunny without the heat biting at its heels.

"How was work?" I ask, looking at River out of the corner of my eye.

He stops and takes his shoes and socks off, sinking his feet in the mix of sand and soil. As the treeline breaks, the soil disappears and leaves nothing but sand under our feet as we walk out onto the mini sand dunes. It's low tide now and the beach is gloriously huge and empty.

"It was okay." River looks toward the sun as I take my shoes off. We leave our shoes there and start to meander down the beach.

"Do you care to elaborate?" I ask. "I actually don't know what you do all day."

"I should take you by the office on the way back. It's on the pier near the lighthouse." He spots a piece of sea glass and picks it up carefully, avoiding any edges it might have. It's perfectly blue-green, just a few shades lighter than his eyes. I have to bite my tongue to keep from blurting out some drivel about how they match.

When I don't say anything, he continues, "I spend most of my days looking at blueprints and construction contracts. It's pretty boring to outsiders."

"I don't think it's boring. Or at least, not any more boring than rolling silverware and carrying plates for a living."

River stuffs his hands in his pockets. "Can I ask you something that might sound a bit rude?"

My eyebrows rise. "Now you have to ask, because I am curious."

"Why are you waiting tables? You have a fucking college degree. You could be doing so many other things."

I prickle, feeling defensive. It's a question that I often ask myself, but coming from River it sounds haughty. Sighing, I consider his question for a beat.

"Gem hired me when I was still in college to work part-time in the summer. When I graduated with a poli-sci degree, I didn't know what my next step would be. Gem offered to hire me full time.... and I just sort of fell into it that way." I pause, deciding my next words. "Plus, it pays pretty well. Better than any of the other opportunities that I had in front of me. On a good night, I make four or five hundred dollars."

He glances back toward Gem's. "And what about the less good nights?"

I shrug. "There's only one a week. Some weeks, I pull in three thousand dollars."

"God. That's more than I thought," River admits. "But that's it. There's no chance to make more, is there?"

"Not without starting my own restaurant. Which I have no real desire to do."

"Gotcha." He looks at me, as if appraising my value. "I was just curious. You don't have any secret ambitions?"

"Going to college and graduating with a poli-sci degree was the ambition. Now I've set my sights to the future. I want to start a family. Having kids and carrying on my family line will really fulfill my soul." I suck in a breath. "It sounds like you don't approve of that."

River holds his hands up in surrender. "I'm just trying to get to know you better. That's all."

"So you're not secretly judging me and thinking how unworthy I am to have a Bennett-Taylor baby?"

He stops cold. "I thought we were clear on the point of you not needing my financial assistance or last name. You signed a contract--"

"Whoa. Whoa, now. I was just kidding. I just meant that you were trying to figure out if I was dating material or not. Aren't you? And I thought we were both very much in the 'no thanks' camp."

His eyes narrow on my face but he doesn't say anything for a long moment. "We're on the same page."

I choose this very moment to step on something sharp. Yelping, I lunge forward to keep from cutting my foot any deeper. Before I know it, I'm tumbling forward....

And River, the dashing man that he is, actually catches me.

He hauls me to him, and I'm suddenly staring into his gorgeous sapphire eyes. There is warmth there, a playful twinkle. I step forward again, pressing my hips against his. He surprises me then, because he's half-erect. I know all too well what his long, proud cock looks like.

I've only fantasized about it every night since I saw it.

Looking into River's eyes, there is a moment of connection. He seems to know what is on my mind.

I press up on my toes to meet his lips. He makes a muffled sound of surprise but he responds, his warm, soft lips against mine.

Then he pulls away and looks down at my foot. "You're bleeding," he says gently. "I think you stepped on something that cut your foot."

I pick my foot up. Sure enough, there is a decent amount of blood seeping out of a gash just below my toes. Now that I am focused on it, there's a very mild burning sensation. "Fuck." I grimace.

In the next second, River shocks me by sweeping me up in his arms and carrying me back toward where we left our shoes. He leans down and whispers in my ear, "Now I'm going to take care of you. Just hold on and enjoy it, Pearl."

So I take his advice and try to feel cared for.

Nineteen

RIVER

I sit on the patio of Pearl's Airstream trailer, my mind wandering. I left work early and came back here, but Pearl's not home yet. I brush the pine needles off the table and kick my feet up.

I look at Pearl's yard. It's evident that she has put in some time here. There are several bright pink flamingo lawn ornaments set up on the lawn, and around each of them Pearl has planted several concentric circles of pink and blue pansies. The decorative shrubs next to her trailer have been carefully trimmed. The mailbox at the end of the gravel driveway is freshly painted. The little white picket fence that runs around the Airstream is in pristine condition.

I have some misgivings about living here, even temporarily. But I will say this: it might be a trailer, but it's a well-loved home.

Pursing my lips, I pull out my phone. Speaking of my arrangement with Pearl being temporary, I need to pull the trigger on the next phase of my plan. It's that, or I have to get used to living in this damn trailer forever.

I compose a text to Sam.

Since I am engaged now, will I gain access to my trust? Cole said that he did when he got engaged.

I put my phone down on the table and fold my hands on my stomach. Looking around the wooded area, I wonder if I should be worried about ticks. Especially because I am going to have to go for a run in these woods very soon. I usually run on my name brand treadmill and lift weights in my home gym, also known as my home office.

But there is no room for a treadmill in Pearl's trailer. No room for most of my things, even though I live relatively simply.

My phone buzzes. It's a text from Sam.

Sam's text messages always end as though he were writing a letter. I'm pretty sure that he programmed his phone that way fifteen years ago and never thought about it again.

Hello River. I am not convinced that your engagement is real. However, your mother has told me to get the stick out of my ass. So I will call the trust fund manager and start the process of thawing your trust. Yours in Christ, Sam Bennett.

I pump my fist triumphantly and hiss, "Yes!"

Gravel crunches on the road, alerting me to Pearl's return. I sit up, dusting my jeans off to remove the clinging pine straw from the pines all around the trailer.

Pearl pulls her car up along the yard, and huffs as she gets out. She glares at my big truck in the driveway. "River," she scolds. "It's not right for you to park in my driveway."

Getting to my feet, I spread my hands. "Why? I live here now."

She balls her mouth up and marches up the steps to her trailer. "It has been a long day already." She unlocks the door and steps back, waving me inside. "I still have a lot to do today. Please don't make my life harder."

I feel a pang of guilt. Here I was, thinking about me. Now that I look at her, Pearl does look quite tired. "Give me your keys. I'll go move my truck and park your car in the driveway." I put my hand out.

Her expression is pained. She shakes her head. "No, thanks. I just want to move on. It's nice of you to offer, though." She gives me a look as she points in the trailer door. "Are you coming?"

Feeling off-kilter, I rush up the steps and inside the Airstream. I have to duck my head when I get inside. Sitting down at the little red-checked table, I try to retain some semblance of coolness. It's pretty hard to do in here, where I'm perpetually cramped.

Pearl shuts the door and hangs her purse on a hook. A place for everything, and everything in its place. This tiny trailer takes that idea to the extreme.

She starts toward the bedroom. I get up and follow her, noting that I already know her routine. She kicks off her work sneakers. and puts them in their little cubby in the closet. She sits down, her eyelids fluttering shut. She rubs at a knot in her neck.

I join her on the bed and reach over to sweep her hair back from her neck. The fine hairs on her nape prickle as I touch her neck and begin to knead her shoulder. An involuntary groan slips from her lips, loud enough to make her eyes pop open. "Oops."

I smile. "I'll take that as a compliment."

She chuckles, but she groans when I hit the right spot. "Ohh. Oh, yeah. Right there," she purrs.

I'm always semi-hard whenever she's around. But her gasps and little words of encouragement are like catnip to me. My cock stiffens, and I become painfully aware of how horny I am. It doesn't help that I'm massaging Pearl's shoulders. If I angle myself just so, I'm looking right down her shirt. My eyes lock onto her cleavage. The lacy pink bra she's wearing peeks out occasionally.

I want to destroy that bra and obliterate her clothing. That's all that's going through my mind when Pearl sighs.

"I hate to tell you to stop." She wrinkles her nose. "But I have a lot more to do before I can relax tonight."

I drop a kiss on her neck. "Are you sure? I could strip you naked, rub your whole body down, and eat your pussy like there's no tomorrow."

Pearl turns to me, a half-smile on her face. "Can you do that after I do my work?"

I smirk. "Anytime. That's a promise. The second you say you want sex, my pants are off."

She turns around, kissing my lips softly. Her hand gently touches my ribs then trails down to caress my cock through my jeans. Her fingers dance lightly over the denim, taunting me.

Hot damn, the woman knows how to tease.

She breaks off the kiss, licks her lips, and pins me with her burnt umber-hued eyes. "Just a little taste."

I bite my lips and thrust up against her hand. Her eyes take on a devilish gleam as she grabs my package through my jeans. "I want to ride you later." She pulls her hand away and scrunches up her face. "But first I have to do chores."

"That idea is terrible and boring."

She stands up, a sigh on her lips. "I know. But if I don't do the room cleaning, it won't get done. And if it's not done for a few days, then we won't be able to rent rooms out anymore. It's a fragile system."

Pearl grabs a pair of leggings and a T-shirt out of the closet, then shoos me out of the bedroom. To my surprise, she pulls a small accordion room divider out from the wall; it's a built-in feature, it seems.

When she reappears, sliding the divider back in its slot, she's moving slow.

"What are we doing?" I ask.

"We?"

"Well, yeah. You're not going to just leave me here, are you?"

She shakes her head. "I'm supposed to turn over a few cabins. You know – change the sheets, clean the kitchen, mop the floors. Aunt Delta is going to swing by in the morning and refill the fresh coffee and place a new complimentary gift basket in each cabin."

"Okay. Maybe you can show me how you clean the first cabin. And then we can split them between us."

She looks at me like I'm crazy. "And you're just volunteering to help?"

I shrug. "I've got time. You need help. The sooner you finish your chores, the sooner I can have you all to myself. Preferably in bed, naked, and moaning."

Flushing, Pearl gives me the same smile she would a crazy man with a gun. "Okay…"

As we walk down to the cabins, I glance at her, and finally ask the question that's been on my mind. "Have you thought about who is going to do all this work when you're pregnant?"

She snorts. "Every woman in this family has worked a physical job right up until the day they gave birth. I'm going to be exactly the same."

"And after the birth? I don't know a ton about having babies. But I know enough that I think you need to rest for a while. Isn't that the whole point of paid family leave?"

"You've got to be crazy if you think that everybody gets paid leave just because they had a baby. This is not some progressive state. This is Georgia. There are no social safety nets for moms. Not even if there are complications, like a botched C-section. That happened to my aunt Shayla, and the family pulled together to help while she recovered enough to hold her baby. Then," she mimes wiping her hands. "Shayla was back working at her factory job the next week."

It takes me a few moments to absorb that. "That's fucked up."

"That's the way everybody around here lives. Most of us don't have the same kind of help that Billion-Dollar Bennetts probably have."

My head whips around so I can look at her. "Are you saying that a week is an acceptable amount of time to recover from having a baby? Because that seems nuts."

She purses her lips and doesn't look at me. She shrugs a shoulder. "That's just how things are in most of the world."

Pearl starts jogging toward the cabins, clearly signaling that she doesn't want to talk about this anymore. I follow her around while she cleans the first cabin in silence.

I hear chirping. Curious, I head back onto the porch. It looks like the gutters haven't been cleaned in over a year, allowing pine straw to build up at the corners of the roof. Nestled in the pine straw are a family of birds.

I'm going to have to clear that out at some point. Otherwise, one of these days it will rain and the water will back up until it weighs too much. At that point, it'll find a weak point in the roof and leak into the cabin.

Pearl's cleaning strategy is nothing if not efficient. She replaces the linens first. Next, she cleans the tiny kitchen and bathroom. Then she mops all the cement floors. In, out, done and dusted in little more that fifteen minutes.

I'm much slower when I start my own cabin. Fumbling with the sheets takes a few minutes. I notice that the top sheet that I'm putting on the bed is so old and worn that it has several sewn-up holes in it.

The kitchen also shows extreme signs of wear and tear. The laminate countertop is chipped and stained. The sheet pan that I wash is rusted. The ancient stovetop is peeling and cracking in patches, and spots of rust dapple the surface.

Cleaning the bathroom is much the same. A large chunk of the laminate counter in the bathroom is missing; you can see straight through to the cabinet underneath.

As I scrub the stained bathtub, I realize that I will not feel bad when I buy Pearl's family out. They have taken care of these cabins, but even carefully maintained spaces eventually show their age.

Sure, I will feel guilty for embroidering the truth when I talk to Pearl. But this place? I will not lose a single night's sleep knowing that it has been knocked down.

Mostly I'm wondering who chooses to stay in a cabin so decrepit. How does Pearl's family continue to rent them out?

"Are you done yet?"

I jump at the sound of Pearl's voice. Turning around, I find her standing in the doorway with her hands on her hips.

"Just finished."

"Good. Let's go." She walks out the front door.

"Do you want me to start the next cabin?"

Pearl reaches out and touches my arm, softening. "No, River. I already cleaned three more cabins while you were finishing this one."

I look at my watch and realize that it took me almost forty-five minutes to clean the cabin. Tapping my watch and feeling as though I somehow time warped, I shake my head. "Where did the time go?"

She comes close, twining my arm with hers and taking my hand. "Where it always goes. Into the past."

Pulling on my hand, she tugs me back toward her trailer. I let her guide me; I would probably follow Pearl off the edge of a cliff if she batted her lashes and smiled at me while we tumbled to our deaths.

Even knowing that, I still allow her to lead me, hoping that eventually the trail will end at her bed.

Twenty

PEARL

River's soft breaths against my neck stir me from slumber before the morning has fully begun. With eyes still heavy with sleep, I feel his lips graze my shoulder.

It's a tender kiss that sends a ripple of warmth down my spine.

"Morning, beautiful," he murmurs. His voice is husky with sleep and something more primal.

I roll onto my back, meeting those piercing eyes of his that always seem to see right through me. "Is it morning already?"

My words come out thick and lazy. They belie the tingle in my body that is waking up fast.

"Early enough," River replies. He props himself on one elbow to look down at me. He's got that half-smile that makes my stomach flip-flop. Especially when he's this close.

I stretch beneath him, aware of the heat building between us. The sheets are tangled around our legs, evidence of last night's activities.

We've been trying for a baby. My bathroom cabinet is

full of ovulation kits and I have nothing against banging on schedule. Not that we need it, exactly. We haven't been able to keep our hands off each other for long enough to need to schedule sex.

But right now, seeing River's eyes darken with desire, I know I'm not actively ovulating. There's no chance of getting pregnant today.

But I still want him.

A pang of guilt twinges in my chest. This isn't part of the plan.

Wanting River Taylor is decidedly not part of the plan.

"Should we be doing this?" I ask. Even as the words leave my mouth, my body arches towards him. I *crave* his touch. "Don't you want some time to recharge?"

River leans down, his mouth hovering just above mine. "Do you want me to stop?"

His breath mixes with mine as he lays down a challenge. He knows perfectly well what he's asking.

My heart races. I reach up to thread my fingers through his tousled hair.

"Don't you dare," I breathe.

That's all the invitation he needs. His mouth captures mine in a kiss that obliterates any lingering doubts. The practical side of me might be screaming about schedules and optimal times. But the rest of me drowns in the sheer intensity of wanting him, here and now, consequences be damned.

"God, Pearl, you feel so good," River groans against my lips.

I can't help but press closer, wanting to melt into him. I want to breathe him in, to drink him down. I'll take him any way I can get him into my veins.

"Keep making me feel good, then," I whisper back,

giving myself over to the moment, to the rush of heat that only River can ignite.

My pulse hammers in my ears. My heart has its own heady rhythm that syncs with the urgency of River's kisses. With a sudden boldness, I wrap my legs around his waist. I need to bring him even closer, if that's possible.

His desire is a palpable force. I can feel his thick cock where it presses against my belly. It excites me and fans the flames of my own desire.

"River," I gasp between the press of our lips. I can feel his cock hardening against me. I rock my hips against his. "I need you, baby."

His whispered words are laced with lust. They speak of a dirty promise that sends shivers down my spine. "I want to stretch you out, Pearl. I'm ready to fill you up with come until you can't take any more."

A wave of butterflies erupts in my stomach. Oh, this is *definitely* happening.

"Please," I murmur. My fingers explore the contours of his back. His muscles shift like taut cords under his skin. "Fuck, River. You make me crazy."

River's hands glide over my body, his touch both gentle and reverent. There's an ownership in his caress, but also an adoration that warms me from the inside out. He pauses, hovering above me. His gaze traces the lines of my face before drifting downwards.

"Your skin," he murmurs. "It's so soft, so perfect."

His fingertips wander across the mahogany canvas of my body, igniting tiny fires wherever his touch goes.

"Every inch of you is exquisite," he continues. He leans down to place a kiss in the valley between my breasts. "I intend to taste every single part."

I arch into him. I'm offering myself up to the sensation, to the anticipation that builds with each word, each touch.

"Then what are you waiting for?" I challenge, tilting my chin up. My lips are a hair's breadth from his. "Taste me, River. All of me."

The grin that spreads across his face is devilish, promising a pleasure that's both torturous and sublime.

I'm fully in his world now, the one where every breath is a silent plea for more. River's gaze locks onto mine, dark and commanding—a look that speaks of raw possession. My heart races, my body aching for his touch.

I'm on fire, every nerve in my body screaming for River's touch. I barely register the shift as he turns me over, positioning me onto my knees. My breath catches. The cool air of the room contrasts sharply with my heated skin.

The feeling of exposure sends an electric thrill through me. He spreads my knees wide.

I'm acutely aware of how vulnerable I am, displayed for him like a feast. He stands, leans over my body, and draws both my hands up to the edge of the bed.

"Keep your hands together," River's voice is low, commanding. It's a delicious tone that promises untold pleasures. "If you move them, I'll stop touching you."

His words are a velvet threat that wraps around my consciousness, binding me to his will.

The anticipation is a tangible thing, coiling inside me. I nod in agreement. My heart beats wildly as my hands lie where he put them, obediently minding his words.

I want this. The heady mix of excitement and surrender is the best drug I've ever had. I can almost taste the control he has over me right now. And it's intoxicating.

His fingers trace a line. It's light and teasing, heading down my spine, sending shivers skittering across my skin. He finds the warmth between my legs, circling my clit. My eyes sink closed. I can't help but push back against his fingers, craving more.

But the moment I do, the tantalizing pressure vanishes.

"That's not what we talked about, darlin. You promised to stay still."

"River, please," I beg, the words spilling out of me without thought. I need his touch like I need air. The ache for release growing stronger with each second he denies me.

"Patience, Pearl," he chuckles softly.

There's a hint of something darker in his amusement. Then, slowly, oh so torturously slowly, his fingers return. They slide over the slick folds of my pussy. A moan escapes my lips as he circles my clit with practiced precision, drawing out the pleasure until it's all I can think about.

"You're so hot, Pearl. So tight and wet," he murmurs. The raw approval in his voice is another kind of caress. "I can see how excited you are. Your pussy is dripping with honey."

"River," I gasp. I swear, trying to keep still under his masterful touch, I know that any movement might rob me of this ecstasy. His fingers move faster. I'm lost to the sensation, to the quick circles that promise a world of pleasure just within reach. "Don't stop."

"Wouldn't dream of it," he replies, as casually as you please.

The heat of River's breath fans over the curves of my backside before his tongue sweeps a bold path across my sensitized skin. I tremble, fighting the urge to rock back against the tantalizing caress that promises so much more. His hands grip my hips, steadying me as he explores my pussy with his tongue. He flicks it inside my pussy and I make a strangled sound.

Then he glides his tongue over my clit. My nails dig into the mattress. Surely, this is torture.

"River, please," I whimper.

He increases the speed, then slows it. My pleasure mounts to an unbearable pitch. He stops.

"Stay still, Pearl," he commands. "Be a good girl."

His voice is a dark caress against the charged silence of the room. But the next flick of his tongue against my throbbing clit sends a spasm through my body. I jolt forward involuntarily.

Instantly, the divine pressure of his mouth is gone, leaving me bereft. Tears prick the corners of my eyes

"No movement," he reminds me. I can hear the smile in his voice. It's a game to him, this push and pull. I nod frantically. I'm desperate for him to continue.

"Good girl," he murmurs, before sliding two fingers inside my pussy, slick with my own arousal. They move in a rhythm that leaves me panting, while his other hand trails up to tease the puckered entrance of my ass. The sensation is both foreign and intoxicating.

"River!" I cry out, as he presses a wet finger against that untried boundary, circling gently. He sucks hard on my clit then. The world narrows down to the overwhelming burst of pleasure that racks my body. My orgasm crashes over me like a wave. It's fierce and almost painful in its intensity.

"Beautiful," he breathes.

But he doesn't give me a moment to recover. My pussy is still twitching like it's been possessed when he starts touching me again. His hand remains firmly between my thighs, fingers drawing lazy circles around my overstimulated clit. My hips jerk reflexively. I'm trying to escape the onslaught of sensation more than anything.

"Baby..." I whine.

"Trust me?" River asks. "I only want to make you feel good, darlin."

"Yes, of course," I gasp out.

But in truth, I'm clinging to the last shreds of my control.

"Then relax," he instructs. His touch becomes firmer, coaxing yet another crest of pleasure from within me. "I know it feels like too much, but you can take it, Pearl. Let go."

I bite my lip and wince. But his words are both a command and a promise.

Just have to relax, I remind myself.

Something inside me unwinds. Right now, River is control personified. He'll guide me to heights I never imagined. I just have to trust in surrender.

"Let go," he repeats.

I do.

Heat coils low in my belly. A simmering promise builds with each of River's deliberate strokes. The pleasure is maddening, teetering on the edge of unbearable. I'm close again. So damn close to tumbling over into that abyss of ecstasy for the second time.

"River," I pant. "Make me feel good."

Suddenly, his fingers still against my throbbing flesh.

"Darlin," he says, his tone laced with that intoxicating blend of command and concern. "Let me take you a little further. Let me fuck your ass."

His words are honeyed filth. They send a shudder of anticipation through me.

"M-my ass?" It's a dirty idea. But not one that I haven't considered...

River kisses my lower back. "Yes. I promise, you'll come harder than you ever have before. You just have to trust me."

I feel the blush scorch my cheeks. The taboo ignites an unfamiliar thrill within me.

"Yes," I breathe out. "I trust you, River."

"It's going to be a different kind of climax," he promises.

His voice is deep and dark with the promise of pleasures unknown.

With a slick sound, he coats himself with lubricant, the clear gel glistening as he prepares himself. I watch him, biting my lip. Watch him stroke his thick cock with lube is stimulating all on its own.

His hand returns to my pussy, two fingers circling my clit. They reignite the fire that had barely begun to wane. A moan escapes me, unbidden, as his touch fans the flames.

"Relax for me, baby," he murmurs. "If you're tense, it won't feel as good."

His fingers press insistently against my sensitive bud. I close my eyes and do my best to make myself relax. He rubs my clit and I focus on that pleasure.

As I melt under his ministrations, I feel his cock nudging at my ass, pressing gently at the entrance at first. Inch by inch, he eases into me, the sensation of fullness growing exponentially. It's foreign, intense, and utterly consuming.

I catch my breath, my heart hammering against my ribs as I adjust to the invasion.

"Good girl," he praises. "That's it. Feels better than you thought, doesn't it?"

I can only nod, words lost in the whirlwind of sensation. The way his cock stretches me out, the fullness I feel. It's *overwhelming*.

Yet there's a thread of pleasure weaving through the tightness.

"Move with me, Pearl," River coaxes, his hands guiding my hips back to meet his slow thrusts. "Come on, darlin. Touch your clit and fuck my cock."

A chorus of gasps and groans from deep within us both as I do what he says. Each careful movement drives me higher. I rub my clit as the pressure builds like a storm surge within me.

"River," I whimper. "Baby..."

The pressure builds inside me. An insatiable need that gnaws at my core. I'm teetering on the edge, every touch sending electric shocks through my body.

"Fuck, Pearl. Your ass is so tight. And the way you fuck me..."

He groans as my hips move faster.

"River, please," I beg between panting breaths. "I'm ready."

His chuckle is a low rumble against my skin. I can feel the smirk in his voice. "You're so beautiful when you beg, Pearl. So ready to let go."

I shudder, embracing the role he's carved out for me. A submissive to his dominant.

"Then give it to me," I plead. I shove my hips back against him, seeking friction, craving the thrust of his cock deep inside me.

He complies, starting slowly. But soon he's really fucking me, going hard and deep. With each powerful stroke, I'm propelled further into a realm of sensation. I revel in the fullness, the stretch, the sheer intensity of being filled to the brim. It's dirty, it's illicit, and it's utterly divine.

"God, yes... River! River, fuck, just like that," I moan, my nails digging into the sheets as I brace myself against the onslaught of pleasure. "Don't you dare stop."

"Never," he grunts. His movements become more forceful, more insistent. He's a man possessed, consumed by our connection, driven by our shared lust.

The sound of our bodies coming together fills the room, a rhythmic symphony of flesh meeting flesh. I lose myself in the moment, in the feeling of him moving within me, staking his claim with every thrust. I reach down and rub my clit in quick circles.

"River," I gasp. "River, I'm going to come. I'm going to come."

The world narrows to the point where he and I merge. His name is a mantra on my lips, a plea and a declaration all at once.

"Come for me, Pearl. Let go." His voice commands and soothes, guiding me to the precipice.

I'm close—so close. The pleasure coils tighter, a spring ready to snap.

"Touch yourself for me, Pearl." River's voice is a low growl behind me, laden with authority. An edge of raw desire that I hear sends shivers down my spine.

I can't help the soft whimper that escapes my lips.

"Fuck, yes... just like that," he encourages. "God, that feels so good, darlin. Show me how much you want my cock."

I circle my clit with practiced ease. The pleasure builds rapidly as he continues to drive into me from behind. His pace is relentless, each thrust pushing me closer to the brink. My body responds to his words, to the delicious filth spilling from his lips. He's painting vivid images that only fuel my arousal.

"Does that feel good? You like playing with your pretty pussy while I fuck your tight little ass?" he taunts.

I can hear the smirk in his voice.

"More than you know," I pant. My movements grow more desperate, more frenzied. He's always been able to draw out this wild side of me, the one that craves the raw and unpolished facets of pleasure.

"Come on, baby. Come for me. I want to feel you clench around me when you do," he commands.

I'm powerless to resist.

The orgasm hits me like a tidal wave, overwhelming and all-consuming. My vision blurs. I cry out, the world narrowing to the pulsing ecstasy that radiates from the epicenter of my climax.

"River!" His name is both exclamation and benediction. My body shakes with the force of my release.

I barely register the warmth flooding inside me as River follows, his own groan of satisfaction mingling with the aftershocks rippling through me. He fills me completely. The sensation of being full grounds me as I float back down from the dizzying heights.

"Christ, Pearl. You're incredible," he breathes out.

The awe in his voice matches the awe in my heart. His hands grip my hips, holding me close as we both catch our breath. We're basking in the afterglow of our shared decadence.

In the aftermath, we're a tangle of limbs and heavy breathing. Our connection is a tangible thing. It's a force that wraps around us like a cocoon. For these few moments, there's nothing else. Just us, and the undeniable truth that what we share is as inevitable as the sun's rise.

I collapse in a boneless pile. River lies on his back next to me, sucking in breaths. I can see the fine sheen of sweat on the muscles of his chest and abs. The tiny bedroom smells like lust and sex.

"God, Pearl. That was..." He searches for the right word. "Glorious."

I laugh and snuggle close to him. He wraps an arm around me, making me feel like I'm a precious object that he wants kept safe.

"It was pretty good," I say. "I don't want to say too much, because I don't want you getting a big head about it."

"I distinctly remember you like my big head," he teases. "You said, and I quote, 'Don't you ever stop, River'."

I slap his pec lightly. "You know what I mean."

"Always." He kisses me, long and slow.

I lay my head on his sweat-damped chest. If I could open him up like a sleeping bag and crawl inside, I probably would. I want to live right here in this moment forever.

River sighs and gently moves me off his chest. He sits up and looks around. "I need to shower. Do you have any towels?"

My abs hurt as I roll off the bed and open the closet. There are some towels at the very top shelf, and I have to stand on my tiptoes to reach them. When I pull a couple down, I turn to him.

He is looking at my ass with the most mischievous grin on his face. "Damn, Pearl. I'm not even an ass guy, but I'm ready to say fuck the shower. Why don't you come back to bed and sit on my face?"

He sticks his tongue out and wiggles his eyebrows. I'm pretty sure that if there was an actual devil, River would be it.

My face feels hot as I chuck the towels at him. "Surely you are worn out by now."

River cocks a brow and looks down, flexing the muscle that controls his cock. "I'm good to go again if you are."

I put my hands on my hips. "I have to eat dinner and do a million other things before we go to bed again."

He leans back and looks at me speculatively. "We can order pizza. Then while we wait, I can whet my appetite by eating your ass like a cupcake."

"River!" I say, my voice strangled. "Please. Just go shower. We can talk about sex again before we go to bed."

He pulls a face. "You're no fun."

"Who said I had to be fun?" I am ticked off now. Cocking my head, I put my fists on my hips. "I am just trying to be an adult and set myself up for success tomorrow."

"So I shouldn't suggest that you play hooky tomorrow?" he asks.

His teasing tone aggravates me. "No." I grab my robe out of the closet. "Listen up. You're here right now because I'm doing you a favor. I'm lying to everyone I love and letting the whole town think we're engaged. And yes, you're doing your part by trying to get me pregnant. But anybody could be my sperm donor. You just happen to be ruggedly good looking, and pretty good in bed."

River looks surprised. "I didn't mean to make you mad. Honest." He picks up my hand, turns it over, and places a kiss against my palm.

I have to resist the urge to melt like a snowflake near a furnace. "Is that your way of saying you're sorry?"

He looks up, his expression contrite. "I'm sorry, Pearl."

I'm not even sure he knows why I'm irked.

I sigh and run my fingers through his dark, silky hair. He rubs his head against my hand like a cat seeking affection. I cup his cheek and kneel on the bed, leaning down to kiss him. But before the kiss turns into more, I step back. "Go shower. You like seared chicken breast and green salad, I'm hoping?"

He stands up and flashes me a smile. "I like anything you feel like making, darlin'."

The way he calls me *darlin'* makes me weak in the knees. I clear my throat and hustle out of the bedroom, because there is not enough space in this bedroom for the light, airy feeling that fills my chest when he says that word.

Darlin'. I shiver and hurry out to the kitchen. I cook while he showers, and lay out a pile of fresh bread I brought home from Gem's on the table to accompany dinner.

River pads out of the bedroom, wearing nothing but a

pair of boxer briefs. When I look at him with a raised brow, he shrugs. "At home, I wouldn't be wearing anything at all."

We sit down to eat. I notice that I have several texts and read them while shoveling salad in my gullet. "Shit." I push the salad away, my appetite deserting me.

River glances over his half-eaten bowl, lifting a curious brow. "What?"

Exhaling a long second, I flip my phone face down on the table and shake my head. "Aunt Delta just texted me that this property is officially distressed. She sent me a bunch of pictures of the forms that the IRS sent her." I slap the table, frustrated. "I can't believe she let that happen. Now we'll have to pay a bunch of fines to the IRS for them to lift the designation. How are we going to pay for that??"

River's expression is sympathetic. "That's a tough situation to be in."

"No kidding." I scoot out of the booth and pick up my phone. "I should text my mom and my aunt Glory. If you'll excuse me." I hurry toward the bedroom, my head full of anxieties.

TWENTY-ONE
RIVER

"You've got to be kidding me." I give Cole a heavy side eye.

He holds his hand out over the conference table, palm down. A signal for me to shut up, I'm pretty sure.

Sitting across the table from us are several men dressed in plaid button ups, the universal uniform for men in the construction business trying to look dressed up. They represent the company that won the bid for the Jackson property by submitting the best blueprints and guaranteeing the best price.

But now that I've actually met them, I am ready to turn the whole deal down. They may have the best ideas, and the ability to execute them by the deadline I set. But that doesn't matter if I won't be able to stand the people I'm dealing with on a day-to-day basis.

I lock eyes with the man sitting furthest to the right. Bishop sits there looking perfectly innocent. But I can feel his smugness filling up the room.

"So you see," says Carson, the construction company's

CFO. "We'll be able to finish the work faster than any other company possibly could."

"And we have several architects who will be on call to handle any emergency changes in the blueprints," Bishop says. He smiles pleasantly at me, which makes me want to punch him in the face. "Coastal Construction is the only real choice for a project of this scale."

Act professional. Play it cool.

I smooth my tie down and lean forward, spreading my hands.

"I will be the primary point of contact for this project. And I'm not confident in your company's management team. To put it bluntly, I don't think I will work well with them."

Carson eyes me for a long moment. "I don't know what you mean."

Cole clears his throat and butts in. "I think what my brother is trying not to say, is that he's had several personal arguments with your construction manager, Bishop. They've almost broken into fistfights."

Carson turns to Bishop, surprised. "Bishop? Is that true?"

Bishop gives him a bland smile.

"Yes. But I'm a professional. I don't bring my personal beefs to work." He turns to me. "I assume that you are the same."

"Why would I agree to work with someone I actively dislike?" I answer. "That doesn't make sense."

Cole glares at me. "Just a moment, gentlemen. Do you mind if I talk to my brother privately?"

Dale pushes back from the table, eyeing Cole. "I hope we can come to an agreement. There is a lot of money at stake here."

Bishop stands up and follows him out of the room,

closing the glass door behind them. I watch Bishop as he leaves, loving how hard he has to work at pretending he doesn't want to beat my ass.

"I don't want to hear it," I say, raising a hand to Cole once they've left. "I brought you here to advise on the project, not to tell me who I have to work with."

Cole runs his tongue over his teeth and levels me with his gaze. "You're being shortsighted, River. You asked this company for a pitch. They returned with the closest blueprints to what you want. They returned under the budget that you set. And they can finish it months ahead of schedule. If you have to work with one asshole to get all of those things... I think you'd be crazy to refuse."

"I don't trust Bishop not to talk out of school about my plans for the Jackson land. It's not Pearl that I'm worried about finding out. Pearl is already on board. It's everyone else. Once word of this kind of earning opportunity leaks, we will be inundated with a million different companies and sales people. Everyone is looking out for themselves."

I narrow my eyes and cross my arms. That was some creative license I took with the truth. But I think I pulled it off.

He frowns. "You had them sign a non-disclosure agreement when they walked in here, didn't you?"

He has a point. "Yeah, but..."

Cole glares at me. "You have a multi-million-dollar project that you are letting be jeopardized by a personal beef. You wanted my advice? Here it is. Grow the fuck up and sign this deal."

I cough, mostly to cover my wince. Cole is a thousand percent right. I slowly let out a long sigh. "I guess you're right."

"Damn straight." Cole pushes himself up. "Now go shake Carson's hand."

I amble out to the waiting room of my office, pursing my lips. "As long as you can guarantee good behavior on your side of the table, you have a deal." I tell the waiting crew, "Let's sign a contract."

Signing the papers takes only a minute. This isn't the full contract, which will come later after our mutual lawyers haggle over all the details. I sign the letter of engagement, standard in our area and expertise.

Carson grins and offers me a handshake. "We're going to make a lot of money on this. You'll be glad once the project is complete."

I don't know about that but I shake hands with him anyway. "Thanks for coming in," I manage.

Cole and I walk the three men outside on the main strip of downtown Cape Simon. It's nice enough, the sky blue and with not a cloud to be seen. Dale and Carson climb into their SUV and leave.

Bishop watches them go, hands clasped behind his back. The second they are gone, his eyes roll to me. "I saw on CapeSimonAroundTown that you have asked Pearl to marry you."

I slowly nod. "Yep."

"I think that's a mistake," Bishop says, like he's giving me a tip I should be grateful for or something. "I'm trying to save you some heartache."

My fists bunch up at my sides. Cole steps in front of me, putting his hand up to stop me from firing back the insult that's on the tip of my tongue.

"I think we should lay some ground rules. No personal talk. No mention of Pearl. And you should leave as soon as your work is done every day. There's no reason to hang around," my brother says.

"No, let him run his mouth about my fiancée. See where that gets him," I growl.

Bishop tenses. I start pushing up my sleeves.

"I'm glad Pearl dumped you. She deserves so much better than you, Bishop."

Cole points a finger at me. "Go inside, River. And you," he points at Bishop. "Get lost."

Pearl comes from across the street, choosing exactly the wrong moment to walk up to us. Shit, I completely forgot that I said we'd have lunch together after her shift.

She looks at Bishop, then at me, her eyes widening. Cole makes a move toward Bishop, and the other man backs away, glaring at Pearl and me.

I gather Pearl under my arm, and steer us both into the office, shouting at Cole not to wait for me. As soon as we step inside, she hugs me. "What was that all about?"

I exhale a breath I didn't know I was holding, and wrap my arms around her. Closing my eyes, I kiss the crown of her head. "Nothing, Pearl. It was just Bishop blowing a bunch of hot air up my ass. The construction company he works for is bidding on one of my projects, that's all."

She peers up at me, smoothing my hair back from my forehead. "Are you okay?"

Her sweet question is like an arrow shot right through my heart. I just want to reassure her. How I do that without lying my ass off, I'm not entirely certain. "Now that you're here, I'm a little bit better." I toy with a stand of her hair. "And hey, he said that he saw us on CSAT. So we must be fooling someone."

"Right." Her mouth twists to the side. "We're just playacting."

"We're not faking everything." I pull her against me and press my hips into hers. My cock stirs, and desire blooms between us.

"River," she says, rolling her eyes. "What about your assistant?"

"He has the afternoon off." I brush her hair away from her neck, and place a single burning kiss to her throat.

She shudders and slides her arms around my neck. "Can we at least move this to your office?" she asks, her voice growing husky.

I pick her up and she wraps her legs around my waist. "Your wish is my command, darlin'."

I kiss her firmly as I carry her into my office.

TWENTY-TWO
RIVER

It takes less than a minute for me to carry Pearl inside my office and close the door behind us. I set her down by my desk. She skates her hands up my biceps and tilts her head back. I can feel my fingers tremble as I tuck a strand of her hair behind her ear,

"How do you always do this to me? I'm always so affected by you." My voice drops lower as I lean in, pressing a kiss to the soft curve of her shoulder. She smells like wildflowers and something richer, spicier.

Something so precious that it makes my mouth water.

A shiver runs through her. She puts her hand to my shirt and tugs me closer by the collar. I capture her lips with mine. The kiss acts as a spark that bursts into a full-blooded flame. I make a soft noise as I kiss her. She's all soft curves and warmth pressed against the hard lines of my body.

"River..." Her whisper is a mix of warning and invitation.

That's all I need to hear.

"Shh." I nudge her knees apart. My hands finding purchase on her waist as I draw her closer. She doesn't resist. Instead, her legs wrap around my waist, her white dress riding up to reveal more smooth skin than it conceals.

"Does this feel good?" I ask against her neck. Even as my hands roam with a mind of their own, I pray that her words urge me on.

Because I do not know if I can stop, now that I've started. She's alluring and her skin's so damn *warm*.

"God, y-yes." Her breath hitches as I pull her against me, eliciting a low groan from my throat.

God, I love when she looks at me like that. I feel like I'm the only man in the fucking universe.

My lips trail from hers, heading down the delicate line of her neck. I can feel the rapid pulse beneath my mouth. The taste of her skin is addictive, the scent of her skin intoxicating as I breathe it in.

She's an open goddamned flame. And I'm too close. I'm already being singed by her heat.

"River," she breathes out. She tilts her head to give me better access. Her fingers work deftly at my belt. In seconds, she has whipped it out of the belt loops of my pants. It clatters against the hardwood floor, discarded.

She wants me as badly as I want her. That knowledge drives me insane.

The zip of my slacks follows the clatter of the belt. It's a whisper of sound in the charged silence between us.

"God, Pearl..." My voice is rough with desire. "Where have you been all my life?"

She laughs. I bend her gently backward, my hands sliding up her thighs, bunching that white dress around her waist. I'm peeling away layers, barriers.

"God I want you," I murmur. It's more of a confession than a statement. My fingers glide over her mahogany skin, marveling at the softness. "Every inch. You make me crazy."

My words are laced with hunger. A promise of worship and pleasure.

She shivers, her breath catching. For a moment, we're suspended in time. Then she places a hand on my chest. It's a silent command. I freeze, anticipation coiling tight within me.

Surprise jolts through me when she stands, her movements graceful and sure. There's a fire in her eyes that matches my own.

What the hell is she doing?

It's all I can do to stand still as she sinks to her knees before me.

Oh. My. God.

I reach out to cup Pearl's cheek. She's bold and unashamed of her desires. It's a damn siren call to everything male in me.

"River," she says, her voice low and husky. Her fingers hook into the waistband of my pants and boxers. She pulls them down just enough, freeing my aching cock.

I can't help but groan at the sight of her on her knees, ready and willing. She licks her lips and my cock jumps.

"Fuck, Pearl..." My voice is strangled, every nerve ending screaming for her touch. She knows exactly what she wants.

And now? So do I. There's something about this woman. It's like she's under my skin. I'm itching for her. I just can't get enough.

"Show me what you like," she commands softly.

Her words aren't bossy. They're powerful. It's Pearl, knowing her worth and taking what she wants. And right now, she wants me.

All of me.

And I'm all too willing to be taken.

"Tease my cock with your lips. Don't suck my dick yet, just kiss and lick it. Worship my cock, darlin."

Her tongue flicks out, teasing the sensitive underside of my shaft. I can't hold back a low moan.

I smooth her hair back. "That feels so good."

Pearl's eyes lock onto mine, dark with desire and mischief. She knows exactly what she's doing to me. The exquisite torture she's inflicting as she brings me to the brink only to let me hang there.

"God, Pearl... You like driving me crazy, don't you?" My voice comes out rough, strained with need.

She hums against me, the vibration sending jolts of pleasure through my body. She doesn't look at me when she speaks.

"Talk to me, River. Tell me how much you want this," she murmurs. Her breath is hot against my skin.

"Darlin'--"

I groan as she wraps her lips around me, taking me in deeper than anyone ever has. The way she manages to take me almost completely is staggering. She uses a free hand to fondle my balls and I clench my teeth for a second.

Damn, she's got me ready to blow.

"You're incredible." Sinking my hands into her hair, I fight the urge to thrust into the warm haven of her mouth.

I'm supposed to be in control—the CEO, the one who calls the shots.

Somehow with Pearl, all that power feels like it's slipping through my fingers. She's got me by the balls, quite literally. And damn if I don't love it.

"Fuck, I want to bury myself in you," I confess, my voice laced with raw lust. "I want to feel how tight and wet you are. I love the way your greedy little pussy milks my cock."

She slides back down on me, her throat constricting around my length. She sucks hard, her cheeks hollowing.

God damn, her mouth is so fucking perfect.

I'm right there on the edge, a precipice I'm all too willing to leap off.

But then she stops, pulling away with a pop. She looks up at me, her lips swollen from sucking my cock.

"I love the idea of you filling my pussy with your cum. It turns me on." She licks her lips again, which almost kills me. "Would you rather come inside of me?"

The question hits me like a punch to the gut. Because yes, that's exactly what I want. I didn't even know it until she suggested it. But my cock jumps in anticipation.

"Fuck yes," I breathe out, my hands tightening in her hair.

She's read my mind. Or maybe we're just that in sync. It's a dangerous thought, one that hints at more than just physical compatibility. But I quickly shove it aside for now.

There are more important matters at hand.

"What are we waiting for?" she asks. She stands up and moves toward me.

I'm fucking crazy about this girl. It's insane, really.

Pearl has lived in the same sleepy town as me for years. And somehow, we've only tangled sheets once before today. My mind races with questions.

But my body isn't listening. It has a one-track agenda. Fucking Pearl is all I can focus on.

I spin her around so her ass hits the desk. Slipping my hand down her body, I rub her clit. She's already wet for me already.

A groan escapes my lips, deep and primal. I pop two fingers in my mouth and taste her on my fingers. I taste earth and the tart tang of cherries. She moans as soon as I touch her. Her fingers clasp my shirt.

God damn, she's the hottest thing I've ever known. She throws her head back. Right now, she's moaning my name like it's a prayer meant only for the confines of this room.

"River..." The way she says it, drawn out and breathy, sends shivers down my spine. She yanks at my shirt again. "Take this off. There can't be anything between us."

There's a frantic moment where we both strip off clothing. Our lips seek and find each other. She slips her hand between us and pumps my cock a few times. I groan. Each movement sends sparks of pleasure shooting through me.

With every flick of her wrist, my restraint frays a little more. She notches my cock at her entrance, teasing me with the promise of what's to come. The tip of my cock is already wet from a moment of contact with her pussy.

I swear I can feel the heat of her pussy even without the final union of our bodies. I can feel the beat of my heart, urging me onward.

"Ready for you," she whispers, and those three words are all it takes.

"Fuck, Pearl..." The rest of my thoughts scatter.

I slide into her with a deliberate slowness. My heart hammers against my chest as if trying to keep pace with the thrusts I'm holding back. She's tight, hot, and every inch I gain is a test of self-control.

Pearl's legs wrap around me. She flexes her leg muscles, pulling my body against hers. A silent plea.

"Be patient, darlin," I grit out.

"River..." Her voice is laced with a mixture of frustration and desire. I can feel her body encouraging me, urging me on. But still I go slow, letting her adjust to the fullness of my girth.

"God, if you don't start fucking me, I'm going to scream," she warns. Her eyes are blazing with that fiery spirit that drew me in from the moment I saw her.

Her words are the catalyst I need, shattering the last of my restraint. I lift her ass from the edge of the desk and splay her out so that her back is pressed flat against the cold wood.

A stack of papers and a heavy chunk of metal that I use as a paperweight are knocked to the floor.

It only heightens the moment for me.

I begin to drive into her with a fervor that matches the pulse of my heart. My fingers find her clit, circling it, teasing it. I amplify single every sensation until her moans fill the room.

"More, River, don't stop," she gasps. Each word punctuated by the hard thrusts that I deliver again and again. The sound of our bodies coming together is a rhythm that sings of raw, unbridled passion.

The sight of her beneath me, all flushed skin and tousled hair, is enough to drive any man insane. But it's the way she looks at me, like I'm the one she's been waiting for.

That's what's got me spiraling.

"Fuck, you're so tight," I groan, my breaths coming out in heavy pants as I watch her beneath me.

"River," Pearl cries. The way she calls my name, all breathy and desperate, sends a shiver down my spine. "Please, I need you to—"

"I know what you need," I cut her off, my voice low and rough with desire. I lean in closer, my lips grazing the shell of her ear as I whisper, "I'm going to make you come so hard, darlin'. Can you feel how hot your pussy is? How it's just milking my cock?"

A whimper escapes her. I can't help but smirk at the response I elicit. She's wild, untamed.

And yet here she is, unraveling beneath me.

"Fill me up," she gasps, her chest heaving. "I want to feel you come inside me."

"Baby, as soon as you come, I'll give you everything," I promise. Each word is punctuated by another deep thrust. The control I pride myself on is slipping. I'm struggling to maintain my calm façade.

But right now, I don't give a damn. All that matters is the way she clutches at me. How her body responds to mine.

Pearl's hands wander to her breasts, pinching her nipples into hardened peaks. The sight of it is almost too much to handle. I have to bite back a groan. Her hips rock up to meet my thrusts, creating a rhythm that has us both spiraling toward oblivion.

"Keep going," she urges, her voice tinged with a hunger that matches my own. "Just like that, River. Don't stop."

And I don't. I won't. With every slam of my hips against hers, I'm reminded why this woman has become a craving.

My muscles tense, the edge of no return looming dangerously close. Pearl's grip on my desk is white-knuckled. Her body is sweaty and coiled with a tension that mirrors my own. I watch her, every movement, every shudder under my touch.

"River," she breathes out. Her eyes locking onto mine. "Tell me I can come."

"Fuck yes, darlin'," I growl. The words barely escaping before they're drowned in the intensity of the moment. "Let go for me, Pearl. Come for me."

With my permission, she shatters. Her entire body spasms around me in waves of ecstasy that rip through her like a hurricane. Her nails dig into my back, likely leaving crescents etched as a reminder of this unbridled passion. The sight, the feel of her coming undone is the trigger I didn't know I was waiting for.

I'm powerless to fight it. I do what I just urged her to do: I let go.

For half a minute, I hammer my cock into her body so hard that my vision blurs. Then my breath halts and my toes curl so damn hard I fear they might cramp. With a guttural groan, I release inside her, hot jets of cum filling her as she commanded. She doesn't stop moving, her hips grinding against me, pulling every last drop from my cock until I'm completely drained.

Greedy fucking girl, milking my cock for all it is worth.

"God, Pearl..." The words are a husky whisper. A testament to the mind-numbing intensity of our climax.

Pearl's arms snake around my neck. Her lips find mine with a tenderness that belies the ferocity of moments ago. I can't help but chuckle against her mouth, the sound bubbling up from somewhere deep inside me. It's a laugh born of satisfaction and of disbelief at the intensity between us. "Jesus."

Gently, I brush a stray lock of hair from her forehead, still damp with the heat of our encounter.

"River," she murmurs. Her expression shifts into something almost childlike. Her bottom lip juts out slightly.

"Hey, what's this?" I tease. I use my fingers to brush away the pout as I ease back, slipping out of her warmth. The feeling of loss is immediate. Her eyes flicker with a playful annoyance.

"Sad to see me go?" I quip, snagging a box of tissues from my desk drawer.

I'm all about the aftercare, making sure we're both cleaned up and comfortable. Pearl watches me, her eyes tracking every movement.

She tilts her head. "Always. I love the way you make me feel, River."

My heart wobbles. I think I've always wanted someone to need me like that. Too bad we'll be over and done in a few months.

Maybe it'll take her a little longer than expected to get pregnant, I think to myself. *That'd be amazing.*

"Let me clean you up, darlin'," I say softly, brandishing a couple of tissues.

"Thanks," she whispers, her cheeks tinged with a rosy.

I step in and wipe the milky mess from her thighs, then gently swipe the tissues over her pussy. I make sure to look her dead in the eyes as I clean her.

There's something incredibly intimate about this. More so than the act itself. I watch her for a moment. I admire the way the light catches in her raven-black hair before turning my attention to myself.

When I'm done, Pearl digs through the scattered clothing on the floor and retrieves her panties. She grabs a lacy little number that didn't stand a chance earlier. They are tattered and she frowns at them.

I put my hand out for the panties. She stares at me for a few seconds before nodding and dropping them into my palm. I put them in the back of a drawer and lock it with a flourish.

There's absolutely no way that I'm not going to rub one out several more times with Pearl's ripped panties pressed against my face. This moment has been too damn hot to pretend otherwise.

"Sorry for being bossy," she says. Her voice is soft but not quite apologetic. She's looking anywhere but at me. I realize with a start that she's uncertain how I took her assertiveness.

"Bossy?" I arch an eyebrow, stepping closer to zip up my slacks. "Pearl, if that was bossy, then you've got an open invitation to be 'bossy' with me anytime." My voice dips lower. "I loved it."

"Really?" Her eyes lift to meet mine, searching for sincerity.

"Really," I confirm with a nod. I reach out to tilt her chin up, ensuring there's no doubt left in her mind. "It's so damn sexy."

"Good," she says. A sly smile plays on her lips as she

steps into her dress and starts wiggling into it. I can't resist; I lean in and steal another kiss.

This one is slow and languid, savoring the taste of her, the feel of her pressed against my chest.

"Next time, though, we take our time," I murmur against her lips, pulling back just enough to speak. "I'll be less greedy, I swear."

"Next time?" she exclaims, a hint of laughter in her voice. "Never apologize for worshipping my body, River."

My lips tip upward. "You are a goddamn work of art. I hope you know that."

"You remind me regularly." Light shines in her eyes. "Should we get going?"

I pick up her dress and slip it over her head. My hands trace her arms, her breasts, her hips as I smooth it out.

I do worship Pearl's body. I worship damn near everything about her.

And I hope to do so for several more months... until everything comes crashing down on our little bubble of happiness.

Twenty-Three
Pearl

River pulls the truck to a stop on the left side of his parents' long, gravel driveway. Cars line both sides, a snaking parade of parked luxury vehicles shining brightly in the brilliant April sunshine. The mansion itself is a series of sprawling white marble structures, like a coastal villa.

I expel a long breath and look at River. He's turned the engine off, but his hands still grip the wheel. The way he stares at the house, and the look of foreboding on his face, make the butterflies in my stomach feel more like angry bats.

"River," I prompt him after a few seconds. "This is our engagement party. And we're already late. My mom has been blowing up my phone asking when I'm going to get here. So... I think it would be rude not to go inside and rescue her. Like, soon."

He sighs. "Yeah."

I reach over to him, touching his forearm lightly. "Are you okay?"

He nods hesitantly. "I'm just preparing myself for battle. Usually when I step into my parents' house, I know I'm going to face a lot of questions about my business and my personal life. I can't say that I expect today to be any different."

I've never seen cool, confident River act nervous before. There must be more going on under the surface than I originally sensed. "One thing is very different this time." I touch his face with gentle fingers and turn him toward me. "You're going in with me. I'll have your back, no matter what."

My voice sounds more certain than I am. But bravado counts in this game. He swallows. For a second, a negative emotion flashes over his face. Guilt or anguish, maybe. But then it's gone, replaced with a tight smile.

He leans over and kisses my lips ever so lightly. His lips against mine cause a burst of butterflies in my stomach. I don't have time to examine exactly why. "You're right," he says. "Let's go."

He gets out of the truck. I climb out too, tugging at the short hemline of my pastel green dress with a Peter Pan collar. Grabbing my purse and my camel cardigan, I take the arm that River offers me. Together, we walk up to the house.

The massive oak door is standing three quarters of the way open. The babble of voices hits me as soon as I step inside.

River ushers me into a high-ceilinged living room, and my eyes widen. My family has turned out in full force. They stand in small clumps, socializing with each other. River's family is mostly the same.

Everybody is keeping to their own side. Black faces and white faces are not mingling in perfect harmony. It seems like it's easier to stick with the familiar than get to know anybody outside their family.

The exception, as it always is, is the kids. There are six kids causing a ruckus in here. Their excited voices and giggles fill the air. They run through the living room and out the back patio, heedless of the tension swirling around the adults.

Aunt Glory is the first to spot me. "Pearl!" She rushes over with a small smile on her face. "We were all placing bets on whether or not you'd gotten cold feet."

River slips his arm around my waist and gives Glory his most disarming smile. "Nope. Just running late."

My aunt jerks her thumb at me. "This one will be late to her own funeral. Drives me crazy."

I feel my face grow hot. "Auntie! I'm hardly ever late."

Glory squeezes my arm affectionately. "You know I love you."

Malik swoops into the conversation before Glory can start listing all my faults. He hustles into our little group and gives me a side hug. "Hey, sis."

"You made it!" I say. "I'm glad you're here."

"Where's Mom?" I ask Malik.

He slides Aunt Glory a look. "She's in the kitchen. Apparently, she brought food."

I scrunch my face up. "Was she supposed to bring food?" I look at River, who shakes his head.

"I don't think so. My folks have a five-course meal and a whole staff for days like today," he says.

"I told your mother that the food was taken care of," Glory says. "But she wouldn't hear it."

"Good lord," I sigh. "I should go check on her. See if there's any way to derail the crazy train."

"I'll show you the way," River is quick to add.

As we pass through the living room, we're stopped by my aunts, uncles and cousins, all wishing us a happy engagement. Most of them also make thinly veiled comments about how they've never been invited to an engagement party before. The subtext being, I guess, that this sort of event is not done in our family.

It makes the fact that there are several differences in class and race between the two families glaringly obvious.

River's brothers and sisters stop him, probably having the same semi-polite chit chat. I spot Sav and Lucy outside with the kids, but they don't see me.

It's too bad, because I could use some friendly faces right about now.

Eventually, River puts his arm around my shoulders and hurries me through to the kitchen. When he pushes the door open, steamy, spicy air hits me.

I immediately sneeze.

My mom and Aunt Delta both stand over the stove, stirring pots. River's mom, Sarah, stands a few feet behind them, her knuckles pressed to her lips. She's watching them with a guarded expression. A dozen white-uniformed chefs and caterers rush around, pulling loaves of bread from the double oven and plating huge platters of fried chicken.

My mom turns to one of the chefs. "This red rice is ready to be served. Delta's shrimp stew just needs a few more minutes."

"What kind of dish should I serve your food in?" the chef asks. He's polite, but looks strained.

Delta looks imperious. "This food had best be served in this pot, baby."

My mom turns to the chef and starts instructing him about moving the huge pot of spicy okra and shrimp stew to the table.

Sarah walks over to us, her hands clutched in front of her body. She's wearing a khaki-colored sheath dress and she has a nervous look on her face. "Hi, Pearl." She hugs me and then turns to River. "Pearl's family brought enough food to feed a hundred people."

I look at my mom with a skeptical gaze. "Let me guess. They just showed up with food."

Sarah looks embarrassed to say yes, so she doesn't answer my question directly.

"It's fine. Really." She smooths her hands down her dress.

"I'm sorry. I didn't really think about it. It's customary for the bride-to-be's family to host all the wedding events. But I am just so excited! I'm like this with all my kids." Sarah presses her knuckles against her lips. "I mean... I can share."

She seems deflated. I touch her arm and smile at her. "I'll go try to rein them in. They're just reacting to the engagement, I'm sure."

River slides a wide-eyed glance at me. But now is not the time. I start off toward my aunt and my mom. "Hello, hello," I say as I glide up behind them.

My aunt startles, and then her look turns haughty. "Well, look who finally showed up to her own party," she scolds.

"Here, taste this," Mom says. Without waiting, she thrusts a spoonful of red rice out at me.

I smile and accept the bite. As always, it is delicious and well-spiced. "Mmm." I nod, then put my arms around the two women. "Your food is excellent. Now can I ask a favor, since it's my party?"

My mom looks annoyed but nods. I've seen this before. Food used as a weapon. It's up to me to keep the peace between our two families. And talking my mom down is the first step.

"Can you step away and let the cooks finish this up?"

Delta looks over her shoulder at Sarah. "These people were going to serve veal cutlets and sauteed chicken breasts. The most boring meal imaginable! And they were going to have servants bring everybody individual dishes of every course. When I suggested a buffet, that chef snorted." She fixes her eyes on me. "I mean, can you imagine? I was cooking when he was in diapers."

Sneaking a look back at the chef she's talking about, I stifle a laugh. He's a young man with dark hair and light skin, probably around my age.

"You set him straight," I say. "Now, let's go and get out of their hair. Mom, I want you to sit by me while we eat. I feel like it's been ages since I have talked to you."

She turns to me and hugs me hard. Then she gives me a kiss on the cheek before releasing me. "I am excited for you, baby. I love you, Pearl. And I'll love that white man like a son if you tell me I should."

I clasp her hand in mine and tow her toward River and his mom. "Let's go out to join the rest of the family. What do you think?"

When we get out into the living room, River locks onto my mom and turns on the charm. "Thank you for coming to our engagement party. I know Pearl is kind of worried about our two families getting along. But I don't think it will be a problem. I thought maybe we could take some time to get to know one another." He flashes her a smile. "Maybe you have some pictures of Pearl as a baby?"

My mom looks at him for several seconds and then holds out her arm.

"I have albums full of photos. Let me get my phone."

For the next twenty minutes, the two families begin to thaw out and slowly mix. I stay with Glory, chatting about the South Shore's new community center. River acts enthralled as my mom monopolizes all his time showing him picture after picture of my childhood.

Sarah comes up and asks for drink orders, ever the hostess. "Can I fix you ladies anything to drink? Sweet tea? Sparkling lemonade?"

Delta peers at her. "I wouldn't mind a sweet tea."

Sarah practically runs to a discreet bar set up in the corner of the living room. My mom pulls her glasses down her nose, eyes the bar, and then heads off that way.

I release a breath. River grabs me by the waist and pulls me close to murmur in my ear. "Do you think everyone is buying it?"

"Buying what?" I ask. He looks at me funny and then the pieces click into place. He's talking about our engagement. I gesture to the crowded room. "I would say so."

He swings his gaze around, then sees his stepdad approaching.

"Watch out. I've been expecting Sam to put in an appearance with the newly engaged couple. Be ready." River's whole body tenses up.

I rub his back, whispering in his ear. "Don't let him scare you."

This might be the first time that I've seen this side of River around his stepdad. River is always scrupulous about masking whatever feelings he doesn't want anyone else to see. But I guess I've been around him long enough now that he has relaxed those walls enough for me to see over them. He has anxiety about Sam coming over here.

I really feel for River. Luckily, the lunch is announced before Sam actually arrives.

Sarah cups her hands around her mouth. "If everyone could start moving toward the dining room, that would be great! Start serving yourself. We're doing a buffet style brunch."

"Saved by the bell," says River. He sounds relieved.

We move through the line, which has red rice, crab cakes, and okra stew, in addition to veal cutlets, chicken breast, potato salad, baked yams, fresh fruit, and green salad. I grab a plate with a little bit of everything. River gets green salad, chicken breast, and a nearly overflowing bowl of okra stew. I raise a brow at his food selection and he flashes me a grin. "The stew smells better than anything else here."

Look at him going for strong flavors! I'll civilize this man yet.

"Damn straight." I follow him to the twenty-four-person dining room table, which has been elaborately set with glasses, silverware, and beautiful pink and white flowers in lavish gold vases.

I look around for my mom and wave her over. "Come sit by me!"

My mom frowns. "Aunt Glory and Aunt Delta are already sitting together outside."

I look around the room. Most of my family must be sitting outside together, because I see a sea of white faces here. I'm a little saddened by that fact. I know that I can't control people like they are chess pieces I can move around their board. But I would have encouraged any of my family to continue the social mixing that happened earlier.

"Okay." I wave Mom away, a little sad. "Have fun."

She's already out of the room by the time I'm finished speaking. I end up next to River, with River's step dad beside me and River's mother beside him.

"Thank you for throwing us an engagement party," I say as I sit down.

Sam's lips purse. "Of course. You're family. Isn't that what family's for?"

I laugh. "True."

He smiles a bit ruefully. "I was talking to Miss Glory for a minute. She said that y'all don't really do engagement parties."

I nod. "She's right."

"Can we pray?" Aunt Delta's voice cuts through the chatter from clear outside. "Everybody, bow your heads, please."

I do it instantly, closing my eyes. Aunt Delta leads us in the Lord's Prayer and then we all say 'Amen'. When I look back at Sam, he's giving me a calculating look. "Young lady. Do you believe in Jesus?"

River looks over quickly. "Sam."

"I just want to know," Sam defends himself.

"It's okay." I put a hand on River's arm. "I am spiritual. But I don't go to church. I try to live as close to the way I would imagine God wanted me to live as possible."

Sam nods his head slowly. "And if you brought up my grandbaby? Would you take her to church?"

I blink at him. "Uhh..."

River cuts in. "Don't answer that, darlin'. He's just trying to get your goat."

"Am not," Sam fires back. "I want to know."

I pick up my fork, swallowing. This is a man that's probably going to be pissed to find that not only did I raise River's kid without taking him or her to church, but that I raised their grandbaby without actually telling any of River's family about it. Honestly, until this very moment, I had simply never considered the possibility.

"That's something that we'll settle between ourselves," River says. "Now for everyone's sake, let's change the subject."

Sam looks at me, arching his brow. "I'm just trying to talk to Pearl. Make sure we have similar ideas when it comes to the important stuff."

I feel my face growing hot, but wrap my arm around River. "I care about the only thing that you want me to care about. River's happiness."

His brows lift. He seems unsure what to say for a second. "That is important, yes," he eventually allows.

I lean over to River, hugging him around the waist. "As

long as you know that, I think we can let everything else slide. Can't we, River?"

River pins Sam with his eyes and clears his throat. "That sounds about right."

Looking down at my hands, I notice I am trembling. Maybe an after-effect of lying through my damn teeth.

"Okay then!" I release River, and pick up my fork. "Did you try this red rice, Mr. Bennett? My mom makes the best you've ever had."

He looks at me, his gaze calculating. As if he's now having to take my measure once again because he got me wrong before. "You don't say." Sam picks up his fork and spears a veal cutlet. "Tell me about your family. Have they been here since before the Civil War?"

I brighten. Here is a topic I can talk about at length.

"I hope you're in for a long journey. Because my family actually came from what was then called West Central Africa..."

TWENTY-FOUR
PEARL

The ferry chugs along narrow waterways, on its way from the mainland to Sapelo Island. I'm seasick but doing my best to repress it. So I lean on the railing of the boat, wondering how old it is. At least forty or fifty years would be my guess.

Aunt Delta sits beside me on a bench, looking silently out at the sea.

"It's pretty today," I say. "Look at all the greenery coming to life."

It's true. Every massive oak tree that we sail past is dripping with dark green moss. Bountiful green grasses sprout from the shore to our left. Even the water that the ferry cuts through has a sheen of green algae on the surface.

Delta looks up at the sun with a frown. "At least it's not hot," she allows. "In a couple of weeks, we wouldn't be able to come out this way in the middle of the day like this."

The ferry slows, turning to make its final approach to the ferry terminal on the island. I can see the oversized shed that stores a bus and several golf carts beside the terminal.

An older man stretches, eyeing the ferry. He's probably leading tours of the island today.

"Thanks for coming out today," I tell Delta. "I wanted to come out here on a whim."

My aunt stands up, lifting a large basket on her forearm.

"I'm always glad to come here. This is where our people are from."

I purse my lip. It's no use to point out that two days ago, my aunt was railing about how Black people can't ever feel comfortable in the United States and we all need to go back to the motherland in Africa. Delta regularly flip flops on whether our home is Sapelo Island, our home is the Vintages Resort, or our home is Africa. I let her have her own feelings, because I haven't lived her life of struggle and heartache.

At seventy-three years old, Delta is an elder worth respecting.

I take her free elbow, guiding her off the ferry as soon as it docks. We rent a golf cart and start down the bumpy main road.

Everywhere I look, things are in bloom. As we drive away from the sea and toward the center of the island, houses begin to spring up. A row of storm-damaged houses wrapped in yellow and blue plastic tarps lean crookedly; two young guys work a band saw out front. One of the men lifts a hand in salute as we pass.

Ever the Southerner, I wave back as I navigate around a huge pothole. Delta points at the next structure, huffing. "I can't believe that big, empty house is sitting right in the middle of the island. You know, that's Jim Parsons's vacation house."

I eye Delta. "Who is Jim Parsons?"

As we drive past, the mini-mansion sticks out like a sore thumb, a three story monstrosity with white columns, and an Antebellum feel. It's all brand new and flawless, looking like a termite's dream.

"He's the only White face on the Sapelo Island Preservation Committee. He and a realtor teamed up to take over the committee and now they're okaying new construction left and right. They voted to allow construction of private residences up to thirty-five hundred square feet. Then they turned around and made it possible to turn already-built private residences into vacation rentals." Delta smacks her lips. "It's corruption, pure and simple."

I lift a brow. "I hadn't heard about that."

"You should pay more attention. It's your birthright that Jim Parsons is turning into a tourist trap."

I'm about to argue that she's exaggerating. After all, it's just one house. But then I see a whole new block of row houses has popped into view. Outside, an older White couple pushes a stroller down the newly laid sidewalk.

"Holy crap," I say. I have to do a double take. "It's only been six months since I've been here. But there's a new block of what looks an awful lot like rental homes."

Delta fans herself, looking like she smells a rotten egg. "It ain't right."

We head into the main drag of Sapelo Island, Hogs Hammock. The little strip contains a few historic houses, the post office, and the sky-blue general store, which is in an old trailer that's been recently painted.

Aunt Delta runs into the store with her basket full of jars of jam. She must be doing some visiting, because I'm left sitting in the shade of an oak tree for a while.

While I wait, I take stock of the changes. In the distance, I can just make out the outline of a large structure. The Acworth plantation house, I think. This island has a lot of history to the Black people for miles around. And even here, not all of it is necessarily good.

A school bus lumbers up, letting off a small group of tourists, cameras around their necks, snapping pictures of everything they see. They are Black, but not from the area, because they gawp at everything in sight.

"Will you look at this place!" an old man hoots. "It's untouched by time. Carla, come over and take a picture by the store with me."

It takes everything inside me to look away and not roll my eyes. He probably doesn't realize that treating Hogs Hammock like it's a historical curiosity rather than a living, breathing, vital community is kind of heartbreaking.

When Delta finally comes out of the store, I can't wait to start the golf cart's engine and pull away.

Aunt Delta clutches the metal railing and gives me a prying glance. "What got into you?"

I screw up my face and sigh. "Nothing. I was just thinking that I'm glad I know where I'm from, that's all. I just watched some tourist who acted like he was visiting Colonial Williamsburg or something."

"Ah." Delta puts a comforting hand on my arm. "I hate that the village relies on visitors to stay alive. If I had my way, the state would pay for the upkeep. Tourists ruin the experience of being here, sometimes."

I wait a beat. "I guess you get tired of tourists, hmm? Since you run the Vintages and our main source of income is tourism."

Delta grunts a laugh. "I know that's right. I've been running it for long enough to know that we butter our bread from tourist dollars."

I scrunch my face up. "And you don't get tired of that? Sometimes I feel like I live to serve."

"Look at me." Delta peers down her nose, pinning me with her gaze. "You are descended from strong Black folk. Our people worked the lands, tended the houses, and rose up when we had the chance to. They were warriors. They made us all but unbreakable. So don't you ever let other people make you feel small or less than. You stand tall, just like our ancestors. You hear me?"

A lump forms in my throat. "Loud and clear, Aunt Delta."

She purses her lips and looks off into the distance in a way that makes me giggle. We aren't here for much longer. Aunt Delta has a stop to call on someone from her church, an older lady that has been out sick for several weeks in a row.

I sit in the golf cart as they visit, fanning myself. I find myself chewing over Aunt Delta's words.

You stand tall.

I don't feel that tall working at Gem's. I like the job, but it doesn't exactly lean toward a lot of self-respect. Then again, what job would? I can't think of any job but being someone's mom.

And if I am going to be a good mom, I need to learn to communicate effectively about what's going on.

I think about the situation with Aunt Delta and her land. Chewing my lip, I already know what I'm going to have to do. I'm just going to bite the bullet and ask Aunt Delta what is going on.

I wait until we are back in the car, headed back home, to bring up the IRS predicament. "Have you had any luck talking the IRS into a payment plan?"

Delta's lips twist with a sour emotion. "The agent said that if I make a lump sum payment of fifty thousand dollars, then we can talk about payment plans."

"Fifty thousand?" I gasp. That is SO much more than I thought! "Auntie, how much money do we owe them?"

Delta shifts in her seat and looks out the passenger window. "A lot."

"Well, how long has it been since you haven't paid taxes?"

Delta's mouth draws together. "Six years."

I clutch the steering wheel so hard that my knuckles turn white. What the hell was she thinking?

"Where are you going to come up with that kind of money?" I ask.

She narrows her gaze. "I don't know. Maybe you could borrow it from your fiancé."

"River?" I ask, astounded. "Absolutely not. Even if he had that kind of money, I would never ask him to give it to me."

"Lend it," she corrects me. "You're not asking him to give you the money. It would just be a loan until... we work something else out."

I tighten my hands on the wheel. "No way. Between you, me, Mom, and Aunt Glory, we must be able to pull the money together."

Delta is quiet. Too quiet. I look at her as I pull the car up outside my trailer.

"No comeback?"

She huffs. "I already got your mom and your aunt to put in money the last time the IRS was calling. That well is tapped out."

I stare at her, jaw hanging slack. "What do you mean the last time? You mean this has happened before?"

She folds her hands in her lap and gives a tiny shrug. "Yes. A couple of times."

"A couple--" I cut myself off, because I am either about to blow a gasket or yell at Delta. Tightening my jaw, I point at her. "You didn't tell me that little fact. Aunt Delta, I need to sit down and look at the books."

She waves me off. "No, you don't."

Grabbing her hand, I force her to look at me. "I really

do. If I'm going to move heaven and earth to save my inheritance, I need to be sure that the inheritance is more than its mounting debts."

Delta looks at me for a long moment. Then she sighs. "If I promise to think about it, will you let me out of this car?"

Hitting the unlock button several times, I manage to unlock the doors. "There. But don't think that I'm not coming over tomorrow to see what you've got in the way of spreadsheets."

Delta climbs out of the car, already closing the door on me and my demands. I sit for a second, wondering if Delta has a long term plan, or if she's just winging it. An unpleasant pang in my stomach tells me she's managing this place like freestyle jazz.

Damn. It turns out that everybody is faking it a little when it comes to having life figured out.

When I check my phone an hour later from the relative comfort of my bed, I have a few texts from Aunt Delta.

Pearl, if your man won't lend you cash for something you need, I think you should rethink the engagement. I hope to high heaven you're on birth control. Otherwise you're likely to get baby trapped.

Don't be ridiculous, is all I text back. I know what River's game is.

But the thought stays with me all night, following me around like a dark shadow.

TWENTY-FIVE
RIVER

"Wow." I walk up to the gate of the festival with Pearl on my arm. "How much of the budget would you say they spent on that sign?"

Pearl gazes up at the big neon sign announcing that we are entering the Tri-City Interdependence Jamboree. Each letter is sculpted from a local source of agriculture income. Pecans, fish, sorghum, blueberries, cotton, peaches, and a weird white substance that I would guess is milk.

"It's definitely festive." Pearl tugs my arm, pointing toward the Ferris wheel. "I don't get why they won't just call it a carnival."

I point to a small cluster of educational booths sit near the front of the event. "That's why. I think the whole shebang is funded by lobbyists."

Pearl looks around at all the rides and food booths scattered between them. Almost everyone we know is here, and those people brought their relatives. The jamboree is pretty crowded for an early Saturday afternoon. The screams of excited kids on a neon green inversion ride cut through the babble of the crowd.

I slip my arm around Pearl's waist and pull her hip against mine. She gives me a wry smile. I can't suppress the desire to kiss her, tenderly and with plenty of lip smacking.

Pearl whispers to me. "Laying it on thick, aren't you?"

I squeeze her hip. "Whatever it takes."

Her eyes narrow on my face. "Everyone except you." She pauses. "Right?

Something dark deep in my core bares its teeth at her question. Just because it's true doesn't mean she needs to keep rubbing it in.

"Yeah, darlin'." I release her, keeping a smile on my face. "Not me. Just everyone else."

Pearl nods and looks away, clearing her throat. She's quick to change the subject. "Should we make a lap first? See who's here before we pick what to do?"

"Yup. You lead the way."

Pearl breaks away and heads off, elbowing her way through a group of teens. We check out the lines at the Scrambler and the Gravitron before I see my brother wave to me from a picnic table. "There's Rex. Let's go say hi."

Pearl takes my hand as I edge through the crowd. She's trusting me to lead her. Even though the stakes are not very high, it feels good. My ego purrs like a happy kitten every time independent, strong Pearl leans on me for support.

I make it to the picnic table and survey the scene. Rex is standing with one foot on the table, staking his claim. Several of Rex's fans hover around the table. By fans, I mean women who unabashedly think Rex is the hottest thing to walk on two legs. They fawn and simper over Rex in his blue jeans and tight white Atlanta Kings T-shirt. And sitting at the table to Rex's right, is a curvy blonde in jeans and a black tee, with a badge hanging from a lanyard that reads "PRESS". She's jotting something in a tiny notebook as I approach.

"What's going on here?" I ask. I wait for Pearl to join me and then usher her forward with my arm around her shoulders.

"I was just telling..." Rex pauses and turns back to a pretty young Latina wearing an Atlanta Kings jersey. Her eyes never leave Rex's face. "What was your name again, sweetheart?"

The girl flushes and smiles hopefully at Rex. "Elaina."

"Right. Uh, I was just telling Elaina here about the time I hit the winning homerun in the championship game."

The blonde sitting next to him snorts softly but doesn't interrupt. Rex glares at her then clears his throat. "Elaina, honey. Why don't you find me later? Give River and his fiancée a little room." He looks around, smiling benevolently as if all these women exist solely for him. "I'll see you all later."

Elaina and the other fans move away. Elaina blows a kiss, which Rex pretends to catch. I can't roll my eyes hard enough.

Rex catches my eye roll and shrugs in response. "What are you going to do? They asked for autographs." The blonde coughs. Rex glares at her. "What? They did!" he insists.

"Uh huh."

Pearl leans forward. "Aren't you Savannah's sister?"

The blonde straightens and beams. "I am! Do you know her?"

"I've heard about you!" Pearl clutches her hands to her heart. "Sav's one of my favorite people. I'm Pearl."

"Birdie." They shake hands and Birdie offers Pearl a seat. "Please! Any friend of Sav's is a friend of mine."

"Thanks." Pearl turns to me. "This is River. My fiancé."

"And my brother," Rex adds.

"Hi." I look her up and down. "Are you actually a reporter?"

She gives me a strained grin. "Yup. I work for *The Island Daily*. I'm doing an in-depth piece about Rex Bennett's life. People want to know where he hangs out, what he eats, who he spends time with."

"I can answer that. He hangs out at home. He eats nothing but egg whites, spinach, chicken breast, sweet potatoes, and brown rice. And he hangs out with..." I cut Rex a look. He glowers at me, making me grin. "His family, mostly."

Birdie is jotting down more notes. She pauses and gives me a blunt look. "Uh huh."

"Enough about me," Rex says, eager to change the subject. "What about you? Have you guys picked a wedding date yet?"

"Nope. We're... uh... trying to pick." I raise my brows at Pearl. "Isn't that right, darlin'?"

"Yep." Pearl bobs her head. "There are a lot of schedules to take into account."

Rex frowns. "No one asked for my schedule."

I resist the urge to roll my eyes so far back in my head that I go blind. "We already got your schedule from Mom."

"Oh." He nods, seeming satisfied with that answer. "Okay."

"Scuse me," a little boy says, approaching our group shyly. "Could I take a selfie with you, Mr. Rex?"

I didn't think it was possible for his smile to grow any bigger. But Rex grins as he leans down. "Of course. What's your name, kid?"

I look at Birdie. "Tell Rex we will swing back by. We're going to look for the best ride and eat some fair corn dogs."

Birdie gives me a firm smile. "Do I look like his secretary?"

Raising my hands, I shake my head. "Fair point."

"It was really nice to meet you, Birdie. I'm sure I'll see you around." Pearl clasps her hands, giving Birdie a warm smile.

It's like Pearl has flipped Birdie's switch. Sav's sister is suddenly all platitudes. "So nice to meet you. I'll tell Sav I ran into you. She's supposed to meet me here at some point. She's watching my son Dex for the afternoon."

"Please do."

With that, we step back, allowing the crowd to swallow us up. I let out a long sigh.

"What?" Pearl asks. She starts heading toward the back of the carnival. I follow her, rubbing my neck.

I shrug. "Rex just gets to me sometimes."

She slows down, peering at me. "What do you mean?"

"Ah." I scrunch my face up. "He's just hard to be around when he's around anyone outside our family. It's like he has to turn on the charm or something. It's exhausting just to watch."

"Yeah? Has he always been like that?"

"Yep. Pretty much. There is a huge people pleaser inside that mountain of smarmy good looks. I love him, and he'll always be my brother. But he's so incredibly tightly wound. He's going to explode one of these days."

Pearl takes my elbow as we give a couple with their toddler in full meltdown mode a wide berth. She puts her head on my shoulder and hugs my arm in a comforting gesture. "That must be hard."

I snort. In a sarcastic, singsong-y voice, I say, "It's just part of being one of the Billion Dollar Bennetts."

"Yeah? I have to imagine that growing up in Rex's shadow made you feel... less visible."

I make a face. "That's one way to put it."

"How would you say it, then?"

I look down at her, a trace of a smile on my face. "It wasn't that bad. I've lived a privileged life."

She pats my arm and purses her lips. "Just because Rex is too nice to be mad at doesn't mean that you're not still mad all the same. Like... when I was a kid, my dad died in a work accident. He was a firefighter and he died fighting a house fire."

"Whoa." I pull her to the side of the bumper cars, out of the relentless foot traffic. "Are you for real?"

She nods. "Yep. My dad died a hero. But just because he died heroically doesn't mean he didn't leave us behind. It didn't help me to know that he died saving lives. Just because you understand, or champion, someone's reasons for doing something, does not mean that action can't still hurt you."

I stare down at Pearl. Her brown eyes probe mine.

"Shit." I shake my head. "I'm sorry I even complained. My petty jealousy is dwarfed by your... your catastrophic loss.

She wrinkles her nose. "Thanks, I guess. But that's not really the point I was making."

I cup her face. "I feel sorry for your dad."

Her brows knit. "I've never heard anyone say it quite like that."

"Really? He didn't get to see you grow up into an independent, smart young woman. I think that merits some pity."

Pearl's look of shock would be comical if the moment weren't so serious. She looks away, clearing her throat. Tears shine in her eyes, but they don't dare fall. She has her emotions too well-controlled for that.

She clears her throat. "Uh, thanks. Though I'm not sure your opinion counts here."

"My opinion? Darlin', it's a fact. You are a beautiful, stubborn woman with an iron will."

She laughs, patting at the corners of her eyes. "I'm not sure if you're trying to make me laugh or cry."

"Either? Both?" I joke. "Just making conversation at this point."

Pearl points toward the Gravitron. "Should we take a gamble on that ride? It looks dangerous as hell, but we should at least try one of the rides first. You know, before I fill my stomach with carnival food."

My lips twitch. She just said gamble. And I love to roll the dice. "Lead the way, darlin'."

She grabs my hand and starts pulling me toward the ride. I follow her to the ticket window, getting a couple of tickets.

As we stand in line, I purse my lips. Something occurred to me late last night when I was thinking about my role in Pearl's life.

Am I just a baby maker to her? Or something more?

"Can I ask you something that you might potentially take the wrong way?"

Pearl pulls a face. "I guess?"

"You said you lost your dad when you were a kid. And I would guess that you really missed having him around for a lot of things. I mean like... holidays, birthdays, graduation, whatever."

She hesitates, then answers. "Yeah..."

"I guess I'm just wondering why you, a person who knows how hard not having a dad can be, are willing to sign away your future child's chance at having a dad."

Her eyes go wide. Her nostrils flare. My point is made, but I don't feel any satisfaction about it.

"I'm proof that a kid can turn out perfectly well without

a father around to raise them. Unless you're saying I'm somehow deficient?"

I put a calming hand on her wrist, which she shakes off. She glares at me, but I press on. "The thought hadn't occurred to you that you were... maybe repeating the cycle?"

"No." Pearl's cheeks flush. "And unless you really want to offend me, you'll stop asking me these questions."

"You know you've got me in the palm of your hand, Pearl. Your wish is my command, darlin'."

She plucks the twenty-dollar bill from my hand and moves ahead to the window, not saying a word. The whole time we stand in line, and even while riding the Gravitron, Pearl is silent. I let her stew for a little while.

Truth be told, I kind of thought that would be her reaction to my question. I guess we have reached the point where I'm able to predict her reactions.

Too bad that doesn't stop me from blurting out questions about her dad. I feel like an ass for even asking the question.

"I'm sorry," I say as we slow to a stop. "I shouldn't have asked you that."

She sighs. "No, you shouldn't have."

As we clank down the metal stairs off the ride, I offer Pearl my hand. "Friends?"

She rolls her eyes but takes my hand. "I guess."

That's the second reaction that I correctly guessed. "Let's go get corn dogs."

She holds up a finger. "Corn dogs, elephant ears, and deep-fried pickles."

I cock my head. "Are you sure you're not already pregnant?"

She elbows me in the ribs. "Deep fried pickles or no deal. I can go back to being mad at you."

I grab her, playfully pulling her in for a kiss. "Please, darlin'. Have mercy. I'll get you all the pickles you want."

While we wait in line for food, she checks her phone. Then she sighs, as if aggravated, and puts it away. "What?"

Pearl makes a face. "Aunt Delta."

"Oh yeah? What's she up to now?"

"She told me yesterday that the IRS is threatening a lien on our property for fifty thousand dollars. She also filled in some backstory." She screws her face up. "Apparently my mom and my aunt Glory have already bailed Aunt Delta out before this. She said they were unlikely to do it a third time."

"Bailed her out?"

"Gave her a bunch of money to pay taxes and upkeep on the land. We're talking about thirty or forty thousand dollars. Basically, Aunt Delta told me that she can't afford to keep the property. She just doesn't see it yet."

"Shit." I cringe. But inside, my heart rate picks up.

Delta can't afford the land. That means that I could swoop in and save everything. I'd be a hero.

Especially to Pearl. Suddenly, being her hero feels more important than anything.

And then maybe we could talk about me maintaining some kind of non-custodial relationship with my kid. You know, for my family's sake. My mom and Sam will go crazy if they find out I had a kid in secret and signed away my parental rights.

It's one hundred percent that and not at all because I'm starting to grow attached to Pearl and having a hard time imagining my future without her in it...

Twenty-Six
Pearl

iver's hands cover my eyes as he walks me slowly and carefully up the sidewalk. "Okay. Two more minutes. Then I'll let you look around."

"This is so ridiculous," I tell him. But I can't repress the giant grin on my face as we step into a blast of cool air.

A rush of excited voices washes over me. I can't quite tell where I am, but it sounds like I'm surrounded by a lot of people. River keeps walking me forward and I strain to listen to the world around me.

A woman yells, "This is awesome!"

I hear an electronic *zap zap zap*.

A man's voice very close to me says, "Hey, no aliens allowed back here!"

What the what?

"River. Please let me see," I beg him. "You made me wear a blindfold for half an hour. I got all excited when you said I could take it off, but now you are keeping my eyes closed! It's killing me."

He chuckles and pulls his hands away.

I am standing in a giant convention center and there are

what looks like a thousand booths set up. The booth to my left is selling a variety of laser toys. I look right and there's a booth hawking books about alien abductions and UFOs.

I wheel around to River, startled. "Is this... a space convention?"

River's grin stretches ear to ear.

"It's the Intergalactic Believers Encounters from Aliens. IBEA, for short."

I launch myself at him, throwing my arms around his neck and squealing.

"I can't believe you actually brought me to a UFO convention!!"

His big hands flatten across my lower back as he holds me close. "Of course. I looked into bringing you to Roswell, but that would require more coordination and planning with a lot of different people. I can't swing something like that without telling you about it."

I kiss River's lips and grin as I look around. The aisles between the booths are bustling with UFO enthusiasts and skeptics alike.

"God, I'm so surprised! You could about knock me over with a feather."

He flexes his hands, squeezing me closer for just a moment. Then he lets go and steps back, gesturing at the convention.

"Where do you want to start?"

I pucker my mouth, looking around. "I have no idea. Should we just pick a direction?"

River nods. "I am following your lead, darlin'."

My bones melt just a little at his pet name for me. Darlin'. That name always makes me feel some type of way when he purrs it at me.

Taking his elbow, I pull him straight down the row of booths. The fair seems to be set up with fifteen booths per row, and a seemingly endless number of rows. My attention is pulled in a thousand directions at once.

Alien and UFO themed bars of soap. Leather chaps that are supposedly good at repelling tractor beams. Cute alien dolls with giant heads, huge eyes, and tiny bodies. Alien themed kettle corn in spaceship tins.

It's a lot to look at.

The first booth that really pulls me in has a bunch of sleek black viewfinders, halfway between binoculars and the really sexy, tiny sunglasses you see on models. The walls of the booth are plastered with colorful galaxies.

"C'mon in! Try the GalaxyFinder3500!" a woman encourages me.

I look over my shoulder at River as I step forward, making a silly face to crack him up. He follows me closely, accepting the wraparound glasses when they're handed to him. I put on mine and look up, expecting to see cool galactic lights.

But all I see is the cement ceiling far above our heads.

"You can't see much because we're inside," the woman warns. "But you can look at the galaxies that I've picked out here."

I jerk when I feel her hands on my head. She guides me to look at the same galaxies I saw on the posters hanging on the booth's wall. Only this time, they seem to be moving. I hear something whirring in the glasses and then a rainbow sheen takes over my view, dancing and bright.

"Okay," I say, freeing myself from the viewfinder. I blink, trying to focus my eyes. River is doing the same thing, blinking rapidly at his glasses. "What the hell?"

"A little trouble focusing when removing the viewfinders is normal."

"God, you could've warned me," River grumbles.

"They're only ninety-nine ninety-nine each!" the woman chirps, not swayed by his complaint.

River grabs my hand and scowls at the salesperson.

"I'm usually not the first one to say this, but what a complete waste of money." He glances at me. "Are you okay?"

I twine my arm with his and nod. I feel a wave of disappointment. This is the booth that caught my eye first. But it turns out to be nothing more than plastic junk. How awful.

"Yup. Ready to go." I wave to the viewfinders. To the sales lady I say, "They're really... uh... different."

The woman beams at me, but I let myself be pulled along back into the crowd. We walk for a while, stopping to check out silly alien-themed sunglasses and a booth where a "live" alien autopsy is being conducted. Members of the audience are being called on to remove 'organs' from a quite realistic-looking alien corpse. The booth is selling full surgical autopsy kits, *'just like the researchers at Roswell used!'*.

River gives me a hard look but doesn't say anything until we're well away from that booth. "So do you believe in alien autopsies?"

I bark a laugh. "No. Thinking that aliens might be out in outer space is one thing. Believing that there is a vast conspiracy to cover up that aliens have been here on multiple occasions is something else entirely."

He pantomimes wiping sweat from his brow. "Whew. I wasn't sure how deep your belief in all things UFO goes."

I scrunch my nose. "It's more of a whimsical belief for me. Like... that famous poster of the flying saucer that says, 'I want to believe'. I want there to be more to this life than working all day and being exhausted at night. With UFOs, I think the world gets a lot wider."

He slides me a glance. "Have you been visited by little green men?"

I elbow him in the ribs. "No. But just because I haven't doesn't mean it doesn't happen to people every day."

River scratches his chin. "I guess that's true."

I lean my head against his shoulder for a moment. River's much taller than almost everyone else here, so the crowd just mills around us as we drift. He plants a kiss on the crown of my head and I smile.

I love the feeling of drifting around with River, lackadaisically examining weird UFO equipment and countless booths of freeze-dried astronaut food. It's like we are in a bubble, floating here and there, unbothered by the rest of the world.

"Can I tell you a secret?" River asks after a while. "You have to promise not to tell a soul."

My heart rate kicks up a notch. Swallowing I nod. "You can tell me anything, River."

His smile doesn't waver, though some of the light leaves his eyes. He takes a moment to compose his thoughts. The moment builds.

Is he... is he going to tell me he loves me?

It's a silly thought, a fantasy. And yet, I find a teeny tiny part of myself longing for it to be true. It's a dream: having a man like River, a man who is so vibrant and interesting and worldly, claim to love a diner waitress like me. And yet, it persists.

Damn, am I having feelings with a capital F for River? What a fantastically, spectacularly bad idea.

"I used to watch Star Trek when I was in middle school," River says.

I am yanked from my thoughts. "Uhh... what?"

He holds up a hand, shaking his head. "I know. It

doesn't really sound like me. But I really liked all the drama. Plus, they always had the coolest outfits."

I squint. "The uniforms that the crew wore?"

"Yep. I had dreams that I would meet a girl in a Lycra space outfit like that and we would run away together." He pauses, thoughtful. "I was going through a lot of puberty right then."

I laugh. "I'm sure if you look around, you'll see at least one sexy girl in a space suit at this convention."

River nuzzles my shoulder. "I think I'm all set for sexy girls. Though if you wore one of those Lycra leotards, I would not say no to that under any circumstances."

I playfully shove his arm. "Dream on."

"I will." He winks. "Don't think that I'm not storing away memories of exactly how you sound and taste every time we have sex. I'm preparing for the future."

That thought makes me sad for some reason. I look away, scanning the booths. "Hey, look!" I point. "UFO burgers. I'm starving."

We get two alien-themed burgers, which are encased in bread formed to look like a flying saucer. We follow that up with out-of-this-world milkshakes, which are just vanilla with little space themed chocolate candies in them.

We sit down at the packed food court and chow down. I didn't realize how hungry I was until I take my first bite. Then the beefy, cheesy goodness zings my tastebuds. "Ohmigod," I say, chewing slowly. "It's so good."

"It's definitely hot, at least." He goes for his milkshake and takes long pulls through his straw. "So there are panels tonight, I think. And a costume party."

I wolf down half the burger, nodding. "I saw. I think I'm okay on that. I don't really want to listen to people tell me about how I should feel. That's not what UFOs are about to me. Besides, I didn't even bring a costume."

He shrugs. "We can always cobble together costumes from things we find here."

"Nah." I sip my milkshake, which is delightfully creamy. "I'm having a ball just wandering around with you. Thanks for planning this, River."

"Anything that pleases you is all right by me. I may not believe in this stuff, but it's fun to see all the wild things that people are selling."

He stops for a second and a drop of milkshake lands on his lower lip. Without thinking about it, I lean forward, smudging my thumb across his lips. River catches my hand and yanks me closer, sinking a hand in my hair and kissing me so thoroughly that I swear hearts and stars explode like fireworks in my mind.

My heartbeat speeds up. My body craves his kisses, and I can't stand the thought that one day soon, I will be pregnant... but I won't have River here to kiss anymore.

Oh. Oh no.

I find myself in a place I never wanted to be in: wondering whether it is too late to change the terms of my contact or not.

TWENTY-SEVEN
RIVER

An entire plate of Mary Mac's fried chicken and baked mac and cheese sits in front of me, all but untouched. Dale Tribley, Coastal Construction's chief architect, suggested that we meet at Mary Mac's this time to talk about the construction project details.

But as I stare at Dale, and his right-hand man, Bishop, anger roils in my guts.

Bishop has been careful to keep his mouth shut while we've been at lunch. But he has a faint smirk all the time, and I want to rip the barbecue sparerib from his hand and stuff it up his ass.

Dale looks at Cole while he wipes chicken grease from his mouth with a paper napkin. "How do those deadlines sound?"

I lean forward, not letting Cole get a word in. "They're very impressive. But I'm worried that you can't possibly keep up with them. Your crew chief here has proven himself to be quite a hothead. So I would just like some assurance that if you fall behind, there is a plan in place to fix it. A plan that doesn't include Bruiser over there being a total dick."

Dale crosses his arms, sighs, and sits back. He glances at Bishop. "You aren't going to be unpleasant, are you?"

"Nah." Bishop looks bored. "I'm straight. I don't have to like you to do my job."

Dale raised his hands. "There you go. Straight from the horse's mouth."

Cole looks at me. "River, if this is going to be a problem, we need to know now. What's your plan for approaching Delta Jackson and telling Pearl that you are trying to buy her land out from under her?"

I pause for a few seconds. "It's not going to be a problem for me. But I was thinking about the buyers--"

The door to the restaurant opens and Rex comes in, brushing off raindrops from his coat. He sees us and makes a beeline for our table. "Sorry I'm late. What'd I miss?"

He grabs a chair and turns it around to sit down. I roll my eyes at his showmanship.

"I was just going to say that the property we are going to buy is vast. Hundreds of square miles. What would you all say if I offered to buy all but a small portion of it? We would take ninety eight percent and the original owners would keep the remaining two percent."

"Hah!" Bishop laughs. "I knew it was the Jackson property."

"Wait." Rex shakes his head, looking at me with concern. "It is? Pearl knows about this little scheme, right?"

"Not exactly," I hedge.

"Are you serious right now?" Cole breaks in. "I thought she knew. In that case, I would also be very interested in hearing how you plan to tell her she's evicted from the land her great grandfather struggled so hard for."

"River, you are really playing with fire here." Rex gives me long look. "Unless your whole engagement is fake and y'all don't care about each other."

"It's not fake," I say, clenching my teeth. "And can we please talk about this later?"

Rex looks at me, scratching his cheek. "Oh, you bet your ass we will."

"Maybe I should talk to Delta," Bishop offers. He spreads his hands magnanimously. "She always liked me."

Dale rebukes him without hesitation. "Bishop, that's enough. If you like your job, keep your damn mouth shut. I will remind you that you have signed a non-disclosure agreement for exactly this scenario."

"Yes sir. Just trying to be helpful."

"It's not, so cut it out," Dale says. He looks at me. "Get the rights. And not to part of the land. I'm talking about the whole thing. Any way you slice it, no one is going to want to invest in a property that might be tied up in court for years. Make sure that we can get the land free and clear. Then we will make our next move."

He stands up, checking his watch. Everyone else stands up and shakes hands, saying goodbye awkwardly.

When I'm left with my brothers, I sit back down. My brothers are both staring at me so hard my skin itches.

"What?" I ask.

Cole points his fork at me. "You're going to be in so much trouble."

Rex's eyes are on the kitchen. To keep from talking about Pearl's family, I ask him, "Do you want me to get the waiter?"

He shakes his head slowly. "I can't eat anything here. It's full of gluten and trans fats and god knows what else. If it tastes good, I probably can't have any."

"I feel bad for you," Cole says. "This corn pudding is the best thing I've ever eaten." He pauses. "With the exception of Savannah."

I smile, but my mind is still on the meeting with Coastal Construction.

"Hey, that's my line!" Rex complains. "I guess I should let you have it in this case, though."

"I know," Cole says dryly. "I could see it in your eyes."

"Can we focus please?" I ask, gritting my teeth.

"On which part?" Cole smiles ruefully. "The fact that you're selling Pearl's land out from under her?"

Rex scratches his chin. "Yeah, River. Is that true? Dad is going to fucking kill you. You know that, don't you?"

"Dad won't have the chance because Miss Delta will get to River long before Dad does. Miss Delta and Pearl are going to take this shit out of your hide," Cole says.

Rex spreads his hands on the table. "Wait, so how much of this does Pearl know?"

My neck is on fire as I answer my brother. "Almost none of it."

Cole slaps the table. Rex gives me a sorry shake of his head. For a long second, neither of them speak.

"And how much of your engagement is just for show? Does your fiancée realize that she's just a pawn?" Rex asks eventually.

I grit my teeth. "None of it is fake!"

My protests sound feeble even to my ears.

"Pearl is perfectly innocent in this whole scheme. And she's not a pawn, either. Just a bystander. But my relationship with her is very real."

Cole crosses his arms and slides a disbelieving look to Rex. "Are you buying this?"

"Hell no. I thought that it was suspicious when you announced that you'd been dating in secret for two years." He sucks his teeth. "Dad really is going to kill you."

"No, Dad's going to disinherit him." Cole squints at me. "That might mean we get a cut of your money instead of you, River. But you've made contingencies for that, I bet. You expect to get paid a lot of money when we secure investors."

Rex nods, slowly stringing it together. "How much? Fifty million?"

I lick my teeth, looking back and forth between them. "Something like that."

"That's a huge gamble, River. You could end up with nothing," Cole says.

"I think the odds are that my risk pays off." I screw up my face. "If Bishop doesn't rat me out to Delta Jackson."

Our table is quiet for a second. We're all doing the math of the likelihood that Bishop takes his NDA seriously. It's not favorable to me because if he violates it, I would have to get lawyers involved. And lawyers are expensive.

"I don't love it," Cole finally announces.

"You don't love most things," Rex says.

"Look." I smooth my hands out on the table. "Pearl will probably not be thrilled. But I swear, I'm doing her family a huge service by hooking them in with this deal. As it stands, Delta Jackson has not paid property taxes for years. The IRS is going to take their property and auction it off to the highest bidder. Some out of town player who won't care about how long the land has been in Pearl's family. They'll pay pennies on the dollar for every acre. And they won't hire locals to do the construction, either! They'll bring in a cheap crew to do cheap labor. As far as I can see, I'm doing Pearl, Delta, and the entire community a big favor."

Cole and Rex look at each other for a second. Then Rex sighs.

"I don't think anybody else is going to see it that way, River. But regardless, you have to tell Pearl about your plan. That's the only way forward from this point."

"Let me worry about Pearl." I point at Cole. "And no telling Savannah any of this."

He snorts. "I'll give you a couple of weeks to figure out how you're going to tell her. After that, all bets are off. I hate lying to my fiancée."

Rex elbows him. "You should give River some pointers on how to be honest with his woman."

"I doubt he'd listen."

Rex squints off into the distance. "You know, something occurred to me just now."

"They're called thoughts. And they're perfectly natural," I volley back.

He frowns. "Do you wanna hear my idea or not? I'm not the one getting caught with his pants on fire."

"Sorry." I duck my head. "Go on."

"We should approach the owner of the Atlanta Kings about investing in the project. He has a construction company that could replace Coastal Construction. If we took this to him, and made the offer sweet enough, he would probably take it. And you could make it worth Bishop's while to stay quiet." He gives me a sly grin. "Everybody has their price."

I sit up, my eyes widening. "Holy shit. I would love to be in business with Ray Kendrick."

Rex pulls out his phone, nodding. "He's a rain maker, that's for sure. It seems like an easy lay-up to ask him to be involved in the resort."

Cole chips in, "He'd be mad if we didn't at least ask, wouldn't he?"

Rex nods. "I'll make some phone calls."

Cole pins me in place with his gaze. "And you. Talk to Pearl. This offer is a ticking time bomb. It'll have to get resolved one way or another in the next couple of weeks. You don't want her to be surprised."

Twenty-Eight

*E*verything is ready, Savannah texts me. *The players are starting to arrive, so it's about time for the birthday boy to make an appearance.*

I smile and put my phone in the pocket of my dress.

Across the diner booth at Gem's, I slide my gaze to the birthday boy in question. River is buried in his phone, sending a series of furious texts. I place one hand on his, gently pulling him from la-la-land. "Everything okay?"

He looks up, turns his phone over, and gives me a crooked smile.

"Yeah. Sorry. I got kind of distracted, but this birthday brunch has been awesome."

I refuse to be suspicious today. After all, it is his birthday, even though I only found out about it because Sarah texted me, asking what our plans for today were.

So I just gloss over his weird behavior.

Maybe his birthday makes him angsty and pouty.

I snake his hand from across the table, squeezing it gently.

"This is unrelated to your birthday. But I wanted you to know that I'm officially ovulating again."

River cocks his head, a little smirk on his mouth. "Oh yeah? Is that supposed to let me know that I am free to hold up my end of the baby bargain whenever I like?"

"In the next thirty-six hours." I bite my lip playfully. "I am trying to make this sexy as opposed to scheduled sex."

"It's sexy. Trust me."

"Good." I look him up and down. "So what's eating at you?"

He sighs. "A project at work. I accepted a construction bid from a company that has the right speed and blueprints. But unfortunately... the construction foreman is Bishop."

"Whoa!" I protest. I feel a twist in my heart at Bishop's name. But it's funny I feel the hurt less than I would have few months ago, before I met River.

Maybe the key to letting go really is moving on.

I try to be pragmatic. "The company must really have its ducks in a row if you are still choosing to work with them."

"They do." River screws up his face. "I'm trying to get out of the deal."

I rub my thumb against the palm of his hand. "You know, I admire that about you. Someone willing to throw down with Bishop isn't exactly the easiest thing to find in a..." I hesitate for a second. "A fake fiancé, I guess. I'm not sure what to call you."

He grins and stretches out his hand to emphasize his words. "I like to think I'm a partner in creating life."

"Sure." I laugh. "Anyway, I just thought that I would tell you that I love that about you."

His eyes narrow on my face. "Is that right?"

My face heats. I just came very close to telling River that I love *him*. Which is absolutely not part of the plan.

Sure, it's something I've been thinking about. Pondering. Musing. But not actually thinking of saying out loud, for god's sake.

Releasing his hand, I give him a stoic look. "Let's go. I have another surprise for you."

I start scooting out of the booth. River screws up his face and pulls out his wallet. As if I would actually let him pay at my place of work on his birthday.

"Don't," I say, pushing his hand with the wallet back under the table. "Seriously."

His eyes flash but he knows when to keep his mouth shut. He slides out of the booth and stands, stretching. I put a casual arm around his waist and walk him to the door. His hand rests on my shoulder.

To all the world, we probably look like a real couple in love.

We are the only ones that know the truth. We made our expectations perfectly clear.

Butterflies erupt in my stomach, nervously fluttering around. I'm pretty sure that I'm the only one who is struggling with our situation.

Gem rushes up to us as we leave. "Have a happy birthday, River!"

"Thanks, Gem." River squeezes me and smiles.

Gem looks at me. "You can have the day off tomorrow, if you want."

"Really? You've got someone in mind to cover my shift?"

She nods. "My niece Mariana has come to stay with me for a few months. She's always looking to make a little extra *dinero*."

I lean into River. "Great. I think I could use a few extra hours to celebrate this guy's birthday."

"You have fun. Don't do anything I wouldn't do." Gem beams.

"Thanks, Gem," River says again. He pulls me in close and kisses my head. "I'll use the time wisely."

The bell chimes as we push out the door. It's bright today, nearly blinding, and windy as hell. I put on my sunglasses and River does the same.

"Are you ready for your second surprise?"

He grins. "I guess? I'm not used to people making a fuss for my birthdays."

"What else is a fake fiancée for?" I quip.

River shakes his head and pulls me in for a long, steamy kiss with lots of tongue. His hands grip my hips. When he finally pulls back, I'm a little bit breathless and my pulse is racing. "You know, we could always celebrate the rest of my birthday in bed..."

"Oh, we're going to do plenty of that tonight. Don't you worry. I have something extra special in mind for you. But first..."

He groans. "You're going to make me do something on my birthday?"

"You'll want to see what I have planned. Trust me."

River peers down into my face for a second. Then he tucks a strand of my hair behind my ears as he murmurs to me. "I do trust you, Pearl. I wanted to tell you–"

Whatever River was about to say is ruined by the arrival of a black Jeep with lifted tires and loud punk rock blaring from the speakers. River's brother Rex is driving, Lucy is riding shotgun, and Brooks is in the backseat.

"Can I give you a lift to the party?" Rex shouts to be heard over the sound of the radio.

River raises his sunglasses and gives me a stern look. "Are they part of the surprise?"

"Rex!" Lucy says. She turns and punches Rex on the

upper arm. Then she turns the music down. "Sorry, Pearl. He's a caveman. He doesn't realize that he is ruining weeks of work."

River's jaw drops. "Weeks of work?"

I wave her concerns away. "I think we should accept the ride, River."

He stares at me hard for a second, before he lifts me up to give me better access to the backseat. I scramble in, saying a quick hi to Brooks, who salutes me stiffly.

Once River clambers in, he settles me in his lap. Rex takes off and drives straight down to the beach, whipping the Jeep left. River wraps his arms around me and whispers in my ear. "I hate surprises. You are so going to pay for this later."

I turn my head and press my lips to his ear. "Wait till you see what I got you. If you're still mad by the time we're alone, I promise that you can spank me."

He grits his teeth. "Don't get me all revved up while I'm in Rex's back seat. I'm begging you."

I laugh and his arms tighten around my waist as we race down the beach. We drive maybe ten minutes before Rex pulls up near the Bennett family home. Sam and Cole are pulling two coolers up to a village of large white beach tents covering long white tables and white chairs. Fifty feet away, someone has the grill fired up under another tent and the tangy scent of cooking meat wafts over to me.

We pile out of the Jeep, and Brooks points over to where Savannah and Sarah are handing out beer and soft drinks out of an oversized cooler.

"Is that... is that Zeke Porter?" he asks, referring to the enormous man hunching his shoulders while accepting a Coke from Sarah.

River straightens, his gaze on Zeke. His muscles seem to have locked up.

"That's Ben, Riker, and Grady." Rex swivels his head to look at me. "Did you invite the whole Atlanta Kings roster?"

"No." I smile at Rex. "Sam actually helped me pick out who to invite. It's my understanding that there is bad blood between you and a couple of your teammates. So we invited a select few who you get along with."

I turn to River, expecting excitement. But instead, he looks a little pale.

"Baby." I touch his hand. "Oh god. Don't tell me you hate this present?"

He shakes his head, looking at me, his deep blue gaze seeming to impale me. Shock of all shocks, I see a sheen of tears in his eyes. I open my mouth, my heart skipping a beat. "Oh my god. Do you want to leave?" I squeak.

River pulls me close and kisses me so damn hard that his lips nearly bruise mine. His hands grip my shirt, his lips move against mine, I feel the stubbled texture on his tongue.

It's funny, because for a second, I still can't tell if he's upset or mad or happy. I'm knotted up with cluelessness.

The kiss goes on for a second too long before River breaks it. He cups my cheek, looking at me. "You did this for me? Just to make me happy?"

I suck my lower lip into my mouth and nod.

"I love it," he grates out. "Seriously, Pearl. Just... wow. No one has ever done anything like this for my birthday."

Covering his hand with mine, I beam at him. "You deserve it, baby. Happy birthday."

He kisses me again and then releases me. It's only then that I realize that we were being watched by River's entire family.

Oh. Right. That's the whole point of any of this... isn't it?

River grabs me by the hand and starts heading into the closest tent. He hugs his mom. Then we are introduced to the baseball players, all of whom are pretty chill and nice.

A short man with a full head of silver hair, and a black suit with a black shirt pops his head into the tent. "Am I at the right place?"

"Ray!" Rex says, surprised. "Guys, this is Ray Kendrick. He's the owner of the Atlanta Kings."

"Rex!" Ray says, shaking Rex's hand. "How's everyone getting along here?"

I lean over to River, who seems to be gazing at Ray with some kind of awe.

"Is he a big deal?" I whisper.

River nods. "The biggest. I've wanted to be this guy since I was fifteen." He narrows his gaze. "Wait, if you didn't ask him to be here... who did?"

"I have no idea."

Rex claps River on the back. "Ray, this is my brother, River."

"Ah!" Ray turns to River, shaking his hand. "You must be the reason I'm here. Your dad Sam asked me to swing by. Rex said that you have quite a bit of property on your hands. He said that you have an idea to develop it as a resort to cater to the new training camp."

River blanches. "Uh, I do. But I don't really want to talk business today, if it's all the same to you, sir. I've... been... drinking?"

I whip my head around and give River a questioning look. But he ignores me.

The older man smiles. "Well, I know how that can be. And y'all can call me Ray." Ray smiles as if he has had this exact experience thousands of times. Hell, maybe he has. "Where the hell is Sam?"

Suppressing a grin, I think how awkward River is being right now. I don't think I've ever heard the word sir out of his mouth before and it *shows*.

Sam trundles into the tent. "Ray! You made it."

Ray puts a hand on River's shoulder. "Just meeting your son, here. He's got your height, that's for sure."

Sam smiles at Ray and River. "You're dead right, Ray. He's a chip off the old block."

River grimaces. Ray looks at River, then nods to Sam. "I'm going to steal your dad for a minute. We have a group fishing trip coming up and I want to nail down the details. I'll catch up with you before I leave, though."

"Of course." River bows his head. When Ray is out of earshot, he mutters, "That's my damn stepdad, not my dad."

I have to bite my inner cheek to keep from chuckling. "You did well, even though he got your relationship to Sam wrong several times. Well done," I say. "But what was with the drinking thing? You're not drunk."

"I'll explain it later," River whispers. "Just remind me."

I hug his arm and bat my eyes at him. "Fair enough."

Once Ray is gone, Sarah declares that the food is ready to be served. We grab plates and pile them high with steaks, ribs, potatoes with butter, cheese, and bacon pieces, corn, salad, and blueberry pie.

We sit at the long table and eat, talking with River's family.

Honestly? I'm a little sad that soon enough, these family dinners will be off-limits for me. Being a part of River's family, even in such a temporary way, has been really eye opening. The way his family values having fun is something I will miss.

My family wants to have fun. But only after absolutely everything else has been finished and some resources have been put toward the future for good measure. The differences between a billionaire's family and your regular old blue-collar family are more evident when seen in this light.

When we're finished eating, River tugs on my hand and

leads me away from the tents. I cuddle up to him, shivering as the day turns from mild weather to overcast.

He puts his arm around me and guides me away from the water, toward the big house that looms large in the distance.

"Are you already calling it a day?" I ask as we get closer to the house.

River's lips twitch. "Just ducking in the house to get you a jacket."

I grin. "That's a smart idea."

He laces his fingers through my own and kisses my knuckles. "I thought as much."

When we make it inside the big, white living room, he sits me on a couch. "Wait here."

I tug at his hand, my heart thumping a little wildly. "Come back soon."

He is gone for less than two minutes and when he reappears, he holds up a soft pink cardigan. "Will this work?"

I pat the seat beside me. "Anything will work."

He smirks and settles the cardigan around my shoulders, then takes a seat next to me. "Have I told you yet how amazing you are?"

I give my head a slow shake, hypnotized by his eyes. He leans back on the couch, slipping his arm around my shoulders, and tucks a piece of my hair behind my ear.

My stomach is in my throat. I can't look away from his crooked smile.

"Can I tell you something?" River murmurs. "It's a secret."

"Anything." The word comes out all breathy.

Those sapphire eyes of his, two pools of molten blue heat, spear me and draw me into their depths.

"I think I'm starting to have feelings for you."

It's not what I expected him to say. Like... at all. But my

heart sails up into the clouds. Could he be having the same thoughts that I've been having?

"Oh, River." I cup his cheek. "I've been trying not to have feelings for you for a while now. Trying and failing."

He kisses me then, tender and slow, like we have all the time in the universe.

TWENTY-NINE
RIVER

It's the electric charge of desire that turns the air in Pearl's bedroom into a living thing, pulsing and humming between us. It's so real I could almost touch it. My heart thuds against my ribcage.

The reminder is as real as the deal I closed just this morning. Still, I shove that thought right out of my head. Sex with Pearl is on the table now... and that crowds out all other thoughts.

"River," she breathes. Her voice is a siren song that always draws me in.

I take a step toward her, closing the space that separates our bodies and our futures. Every fiber of my being is attuned to the magnetism that pulls me to her. The scent of her perfume fills my senses. It's intoxicating.

She's intoxicating.

"Hey." My voice comes out steadier than I feel. I reach up, my hand betraying the slightest shake. I brush a rebellious strand of hair from her forehead. The strand slips through my fingers like silk, but the touch of her skin on my skin is what sends a shockwave through me.

Did I just fuck up? I wonder.

Pearl's eyes are brown pools of mystery and allure. They scan my face and lock onto mine.

"River?" Her whisper cracks the tension, turning my name into both a question and an answer.

"Yeah, darlin. I'm right here."

I kiss her hand. My thumb grazes the soft skin below her ear. Her eyelids flutter like she's fighting the urge to close her eyes and just feel.

"You're always so in control," she teases lightly.

I see her, though. Her cheeks are flushed with the same heat I'm burning with.

"Control is overrated," I admit. The truth, if I've ever known what that is.

"Is it now?" Her lips curve into a half-smile that suggests she knows exactly the kind of fire I'm talking about.

"Absolutely." I let my fingers trail down the side of her face, barely touching. But it's enough to make her lean ever so slightly into my touch. "Sometimes, you've got to let go to really hold on to something."

Pearl's eyes sparkle with a mix of challenge and desire. "And what are we holding on to, River?"

"Let's find out." Heat radiates from Pearl's body as I edge closer. Her chest rises and falls in a rapid tempo that syncs with the pounding in my own. My hand still lingers near her face from tucking away that rebellious strand of hair, burns with the need to explore further.

Her chest heaves, rising and falling in a rhythm that beckons me. It tempts me beyond reason. There's no more room for words. There's no need for them. I crave her with a possessiveness that's both primal and profound. So I act.

In one fluid motion, I bridge the gap between us. My lips find hers with a fervor that's been simmering since the moment our paths crossed. The kiss is an explosion, a super-nova, a world-ending event that binds my world to hers.

It's always this way with Pearl. If I'd known that from the beginning, maybe I would have chosen to stay away from her.

But just as likely is the scenario where I found another parcel of land to build my dream resort on. It's all moot at this point, anyway.

She gasps into the kiss. I seize the opportunity to deepen it, savoring the taste of her. Kissing Pearl is like diving into an ocean where the only thing that exists is the sensation of drowning. I want nothing more than to be submerged forever.

"River..." she pants when we break apart. "I need—"

"Shh," I soothe. I press a quick, soft kiss on her lips. "No more talking."

We dive back into the kiss. Each movement of our lips is a promise, every shared breath a vow. The kiss escalates. Our tongues are locked in a dance that's as old as time yet feels brand new with every twist and turn. The rhythm of our desire beats a drum inside my chest, urging me on.

My fingers trail down from the softness of her hair to the delicate slope of her shoulder. The path is marked by her delicate shivers and raised goosebumps at my touch. The contours of her body beckon me. I am promised secrets and pleasures with every whiplash curve.

She moans gently at my touch.

"River..." Her voice is a caress against my name. It stokes the fire that rages within me. I feel like a greedy child. No matter how much of her moans and desire she gives me, I will still take every chance to steal more from her.

"Let me..." I murmur back. My words are cut short by the urgency of her lips reclaiming mine.

I can't think straight. Has any woman ever wanted me so nakedly as Pearl clearly does right now?

I map her form with my hands, reverent and hungry all at once. There's an artistry to the way her waist cinches before flaring into hips. Her curves fill my palms with a warmth I can't get enough of. My touch dips lower. I skim the silk of her dress with my palms. The fabric does little to hide the heat of her skin.

"God, Pearl," I groan against the sweetness of her mouth. I can feel her body respond to every stroke. Every press of my fingertips results in an open-mouthed moan. She arches into my touch. There is a silent plea that I answer with a firmer grasp.

She begs me to explore her deeper. And I vow that I will. I'll find every nook and cranny on her body. I'll memorize her shape. I'll be able to recall her curves like a map that is seared into my brain forever.

"More," she whispers. Her breath is hot against my cheek. Flames ignite in places that only she can touch to dowse them.

"Always more," I promise. "I want to give you every-thing that I have, Pearl. My pleasure. My pain. My eternity."

Panting, we break apart. Pearl's gaze locks onto mine, a wildfire blazing in her eyes.

With one swift move, she reaches for the nightstand and opens the bottom drawer. She produces a small, unassuming box. It's black with a delicate white satin bow.

"I got us a present." She wrinkles her nose, excitement shining in her eyes. "Maybe it's more of a present to me? We'll see."

My eyes fix on the box. What could it be? My mind fills with possibilities.

She flicks the lid open. Nestled within is a sleek black

vibrator. Its contours reflect the dim glow of her bedroom. I press a small on-off switch on one side, turning it on and off as a test. It buzzes sharply.

Her eyes sparkle with mischief as she cradles it in her palm. She licks her lips. An unspoken challenge hangs in the air between us.

"God damn." It's not just the toy itself. It's the certainty in her movements, the boldness of her choice. "I'm pretty sure that this is actually a gift for me."

"Only the best for my man," she replies cheekily. "Lucky for you, I'm willing to share."

The hum of the vibrator fills the room. I swear I get turned on more by its sound than Pearl does. I press her back into the pillows.

"I can't wait to watch how you touch yourself, darlin."

Her gaze latches on my face as she hikes her dress up around her hips. She raises her knees and takes off her panties, exposing herself. I edge toward the end of the bed. Here I can see everything. Her pussy lips are already dripping with moisture.

I watch, absolutely transfixed, as Pearl lets the device dance across her skin. She flexes her legs and her toes curl. I bite my lip. Her skin is glorious, molten mahogany, and I'm thrilled I can be here in this private moment when she touches herself.

"Enjoying the view?" Her voice is a velvet caress against the tension that crackles between us.

"Immensely," I admit.

She runs the vibrator along her collarbone. It's a tease, a preview of what's yet to come. Damn if it doesn't make me want to upend every plan I've ever made.

Who cares about my business? I would give anything to actually belong right here where I am at this moment.

"River..." she murmurs. "Kiss me."

I move up to kiss her lips gently. There's a hitch in her breath as she presses the buzzing tip against her nipple. The soft pink peaks harden instantly. She throws her head back, lost in the wave of pleasure that visibly ripples through her body.

"Fuck, Pearl." My voice is a rasp. I'm strained with desire that I am rapidly losing interest in controlling. "You're absolutely stunning."

Her eyes meet mine. Hers are heavy-lidded and brimming with heat. I see a reflection of my own hunger in them.

Soon, I chide myself. *Be patient.*

"Only for you," she breathes out. Her voice is a promise wrapped in a whisper. It seals the fate of the evening. Her fingers move in slow circles down her chest, tracing a path of ecstasy across her tits.

I know that this woman is both my ecstasy and my undoing.

The vibrator's hum whispers against Pearl's silken skin as she drags it lower. Her thighs part and settle ever so slightly. It's an invitation I'm burning to accept.

I want nothing more than to plunge my cock inside her pussy and ruin this moment. Every instinct I have says that I would make Pearl feel better than some buzzing toy.

But I hold myself back. I am a silent observer to the ritual she lets me watch. It hurts to be respectful. But sometimes a little pain now will equal a lot of pleasure later. It's the quick addition and subtraction of being a man.

"River," she purrs. Her voice is laced with a command that has my pulse thrumming in my ears. "Watch me. Am I as fun to watch as I am in your imagination?"

"You're even hotter," I assure her. "I want to see you make yourself wet, darlin."

I can't tear my eyes away. Not that there's anywhere else I would look.

My girl is almost touching her pussy now. When she rubs her clit, I want to be right there to lick up the pool of moisture that leaks down her thighs and ass.

Each pass of the vibrator along her inner thigh kindles a fire that spreads through my veins. She's incinerating any last vestige of restraint I might have clung to. With every delicate sweep of vibration, her arousal mounts.

Her pussy is fucking juicy. My fingers curl, clinging to the comforter beneath me in an attempt to still them.

"God, yes," she gasps. My own breath hitches as she finally runs the vibrator between her legs. "Fuck!"

I sit up. My eyes fasten on her wet, ready pussy lips.

My name is a moan on her lips. The sight of her back arching like a bow pulled taut with pleasure makes my fucking cock jump. Her eyes, those deep pools of whiskey, lock with mine.

There's no mistaking the raw need reflected back at me. There's hunger there, too. Look at her makes me *ravenous*.

"Fuck, Pearl." The words sound rough around the edges. They match the deep well of desire churning within me. "You're breathtaking, darlin. Touch yourself again."

"You make me feel so good," she whispers. "You make me feel this good, River. This wet. This ready. You make me want you to stretch out my pussy with your thick cock."

"Fuck, Pearl," I grit out. "I love when you tell me how good you feel."

Pearl's gasps fill the air. Her pupils dilate slightly. Her hips rock in jerky movements.

"River," she breathes out.

I move in between her thighs, propelled by the urgency in her voice.

"Show me what you want, Pearl." My words are barely a

whisper. But they carry the weight of my desire. "Tell me how to please you, baby."

She turns off the vibrator and sets it aside. Then with a confidence that ignites something primal within me, she grabs my hand. She makes me move to the edge of the bed.

"Sit," she commands.

I obey without hesitation, the CEO in me swiftly replaced by the man who craves her commands. Anything she says right now will happen, no matter how impossible it might be.

Anything for Pearl.

Her fingers wrap around the length of my cock. I suck in a breath and close my eyes for a second. When her touch shapes my cock, firmly and with certainty, and a low growl escapes me. I open my eyes and search for her gaze. She strokes me with a hunger that mirrors my own, her touch both commanding and giving.

I watch, entranced, as she takes what she wants. What we both *need*. I thought I was going to blow my load when she touched her clit. But now, I'm weak and about to topple over the edge just from the look of hunger on her face.

"Stand up for me, River." Her voice is a sultry whisper that cuts through the haze of my desire.

I rise to my feet. I'm hovering on the precipice between restraint and surrender. Pearl positions herself just so, sitting on the edge of bed, knees wide.

"Like this?" I ask. I fist my cock and guide myself to the entrance of her hot, wet pussy.

"Exactly like this." She hisses as I thrust in shallowly.

I groan as I thrust in again, going inch by torturous inch, claiming her with a fierceness that leaves no room for doubt. *This* is where I belong. Buried in her pussy, at her mercy. *I have no other reason for living.*

Pearl moves her hips against mine with purpose. I groan.

Each shift of her hips sends waves of sensation crashing over me. It's raw and real. It feels like the kind of passion that will swallow us both whole.

She turns on the vibrator and lies back. "Use this, sweetheart," she instructs. She holds it up and I take it from her.

"Where do you want it, darlin?" My voice is strained. The effort of holding back is evident in every syllable.

"Everywhere," she hisses. I oblige, pressing the device against her nipples first. As I watch, her head tilts back in ecstasy.

"River..." Her voice is a siren call. It draws me deeper into the promise pleasure.

"Tell me what you need," I urge. I trail the vibrator down, seeking out the epicenter of her pleasure. "Tell me what feels good, Pearl."

I lift her pussy lips and swirl the vibrator over her engorged clit. She stiffens, crying out.

"Right there," she groans. I focus my attention on her clit. The vibrations mingle with the rhythm of our bodies clashing together.

Her pussy grows tighter, her muscles locking. I thrust in and out and concentrate the vibrator in the same spot. "Give me everything, darlin. Give me your words."

"Fuck, yes," she hisses. I feel her tighten around me, a testament to the force of her pleasure. "More, River. Give me more."

"Anything for you," I swear.

The world becomes nothing but the cadence of our bodies. Our relentless tempo has us both spiraling into delirium. I'm thrusting my cock with a ferocity that's borderline primal. Every movement is engineered to stoke the flames licking at Pearl's core.

"More," she breathes out. Her nails are digging crescent moons into my back as if she's holding on for dear life. And maybe she is holding on. This moment where pleasure obliterates all else.

"Fuck, River..." Her voice shatters against the onslaught of sensations. Her pussy spasms. But I don't slow down. And she just keeps urging me onward.

"Don't stop, don't you dare stop." There's a command in her plea that drives me wilder.

So I don't stop. I wouldn't if I knew how to stop.

I'm a machine in human form now. I'm calibrated to her desires. Each movement of mine is designed to elicit that sweet sound of surrender from her lips. Her breath catches. She comes undone beneath me.

Once, twice... I lose count of the litany of climaxes that leave her breathless and quivering. I come so hard that I lose consciousness for a moment. All that exists is pleasure.

I'm being carried away by a river of gratification, into an ocean of carnal satisfaction. Only Pearl's sweet voice can bring me back.

"River..." It's a caress that somehow steadies the torrent within me. I cling to her, making a shelter for her out of my arms.

"Shh, I've got you." I ride it out, letting it crash over me, through me. It is a few more moments until every last shudder wrings itself from my body.

Spent, we collapse into a tangle of limbs, too exhausted to do anything more than breathe. I pull her close. Our sweat-slicked skin sticks in the most intimate of embraces and the heat of the night doesn't do anything to hinder the situation.

My cock remains nestled inside Pearl. It's a silent vow of possession and surrender all at once.

"Stay," she whispers, half-asleep, her fingers tracing idle patterns across my chest.

"Wouldn't dream of leaving," I assure her.

Eventually, Pearl gets up and puts on her bathrobe. I mumble discontented sounds and she shushes me.

"I'm just going to get the mail. I'm waiting on a tax refund check. Just relax, I'll be right back."

She shoves her feet into her fluffy alien slippers and disappears. I hear the trailer door open. Less than a minute later, I hear her close it softly.

Pearl heads back into the bedroom, taking her bathrobe off while she studies a piece of mail. In the dim light, I watch carefully as she opens a cream-colored envelope.

She makes a strangled sound. "It's a wedding invitation from Bishop. That slimy mother*fucker*."

I sit up, motioning for her to hand me the invite. Scowling, I read the whole thing quickly. They have picked a Saturday a couple of months from now, and intend for everyone to wear formal black-tie.

"This sucks." I set the invite on the bed. "It's a pretty low blow to invite you."

"Like I would be caught dead at their wedding." She makes a face. "Ew, no way."

I can see the tension in her face. Casually reaching out to the invite, I sweep it off the bed. Pearl gives me a funny look. "You know what?" I tell her. "Forget them. Who cares? We're going to be too busy fucking to give two shits."

She snorts. "How eloquent."

"It's the truth, darlin'."

There is a moment of silence that stretches between us, and hangs like a spider's gossamer web. Then she purses her lips, picking at the duvet cover. "Do you think we'll still be... together... in two months?"

When she looks up, I can tell from the look on her face that I need to tread carefully. I wonder if she has any idea

"I hope so." I shrug. "I can't see the future. But if I have any say in the matter, we will."

If I have thing my way, we will be together indefinitely. Not really forever. Just... longer. I need more time with her, pregnant or not. I think my feelings for Pearl have grown into something stronger than just a fake fiancé fling.

Her face is disappointed though, as if I've said the wrong thing. I don't know exactly how to fix it. So I draw her closer, tip her head back, and kiss her.

THIRTY
PEARL

I wake up with the sun already slanting through the blinds and throwing crazy stripes across our sleeping forms. River is lying on his stomach beside me, feet hanging off of the bed, breathing so deeply that he's almost snoring.

I turn on my side and burrow under the covers. I watch the rise and fall of his broad, muscular back. River is a work of art. There's absolutely no denying it.

Even if I didn't have a single feeling for him, that much would still be true.

I watch him for a minute more. There is some far-off possibility that I could just go back to sleep.

I deserve a day off, right?

But then the never-ending list of chores pops into my head. There will be trailers and cabins to turn over, like always. And I've learned from past mistakes that neglecting my chores causes them to pile up so high that it takes me a week to dig myself out again.

Throwing back the covers, I sit up and rub my face.

One day of laziness will end up being more stress for me than it's worth.

I slip from the bed, grab my towel, and head for a quick shower. The hot water feels nice for two minutes, then the water heater starts to run low. After that, it's a mad dash to get out of the shower again.

Wrapping myself in a towel, I step into the kitchen to start perking some coffee in the ancient coffee maker that came with the trailer. Usually I skip caffeine early in the morning, but today seems like I will need some coffee to get through it.

When I head back into the bedroom, River is sitting up against the headboard. He's looking at something on his phone, and the blanket is draped very casually over his thighs.

I stop and allow myself a moment to stare at the carven marble statue that I'm sleeping with. Every inch of him is perfect, hardened muscle and jutting bone. There's nothing soft about this man.

He looks up, a perfect little smirk perched on his lips. "Come here."

My heart skips a beat. Grinning at his command, I walk around to his side of the bed. River grunts, strips off my towel, and slides a hand around my waist. I sputter a laugh. He sits on the side of the bed, his legs spread, and pulls me inexorably closer.

"Your nipples look so fucking delicious. I think I'll die if I don't devour them."

I bite my lip and press my thighs together as River bends his head and runs the tip of his tongue over one nipple. I groan as it pebbles under his attention. "More." I put a curve into my back, pressing my breast closer to his lips. "Suck it harder, baby."

River grabs me by the waist and pulls me down on top

of him, where he proceeds to lick and suck at my nipples while thrusting his hard cock between our bodies. I reach down and position his cock just outside my already damp pussy. He groans and thrusts, a shallow motion, and we both release guttural sounds.

"Fuck, baby." I grip his shoulders, holding myself up as he drives his cock deep into my pussy. He sucks on my nipples, biting them gently. My eyes roll up in my head, and for a moment I'm lost in the sensation. His thrusts grow frenzied as I moan. I'm already about to come and he's only been buried to the hilt for thirty seconds. Sitting on top of him, I feel every fucking inch of his cock stretching out my hot, wet pussy. That, combined with the feeling of his tongue as he laves my nipple, makes me lose control.

"Fuck, fuck, River!" I cry.

"Come for me, darlin'. I want to feel you come on my cock."

He speeds up his thrusts and my hips work hard to keep pace with him. He grabs my hips and hammers into me at a blinding pace. I have a moment where I'm not sure where I stop and he begins, where he is everywhere I desperately need him to be. My eyes close for a second as I peak. River is right behind me, his cock pumping in and out of my pussy. I seize up, my pussy clenching his cock with a death grip as I throw my head back and cry out.

I can feel his cock spurting deep inside my pussy, the jets of hot semen seeming to go on and on. I want to keep going but I can't because my arms are shaking from the effort to hold myself up. I collapse and River slows his thrusts, his arms wrapping around me to cradle me.

He kisses me tenderly, unable to do anything but pull in the next desperate gulp of air.

I have a moment of pure, clear vision.

I love this man.

Deeply, madly. I know it is a bad idea. I know that it will probably only bring me heartache. But fuck, I can't help it.

This moment is perfect. The fact that I could even now be getting pregnant just adds to my glowing, happy feelings of satisfaction. This feeling is intoxicating and the need to say my feelings aloud balloons in my chest.

River kisses me, then rolls to the side, carrying me with him. Grimacing a second, he pulls his cock from my body. Then he kisses my shoulder languidly.

"Can we start every morning like that?"

I chuckle. "Maybe. We'll have to see. I think some more practice is called for."

"Mmm, I like the sound of that." He props up his head with his hand. "I assume that we have more to do today than just lie around and fuck each other silly, though."

Wincing, I nod. "Yeah. I need to check my phone to find out how many guests checked out and which rooms I need to clean."

He grabs my hand and kisses my palm. "Whatever you want, darlin'."

Scrunching up my nose, I sigh. "It's not really something I want to do. It's something that I have to do."

He narrows his gaze on my face. I expect his next words to be either a crude suggestion about what else I should 'do', or another question about how I can hope to keep up with my workload while I'm pregnant. I tense, waiting.

But he surprises me. "I poked around on the real estate market on your behalf. Quietly, of course. There are a ton of options for selling this place if you ever feel like it's too much work. You could make a lot of money and take care of your family." He holds up a hand. "I'm just letting you know. I am not looking for a response."

Some snarled knot of emotions surrounding my heart

hiss and moan. I jerk my hand away from his grip. "River, I told you."

"You did." He looks guilty. "I'm sorry I even brought it up."

I consider him for a long moment. One loud voice inside my head tells me not to trust him. But another says that if I trust him with my body, I might as well just give him my heart, too.

He smooths back a strand of my hair and cups my jaw, pinning me with that million-dollar gaze that makes me melt.

I lift a shoulder and give him a tight-lipped smile. "I'll forget it if you make me a promise to forget about the land. Just pretend that it doesn't exist. Deal?"

River looks nervous for a second before he answers with a smile. "Your wish is my command, darlin'."

Darlin'. I can't help but shiver and kiss his lips. "You make it hard to be mad at you."

"That's the point," he says, winking.

I push myself upright, then reach over to grab my phone from my bedside table. River fondles my breast as I check my texts for a message from Delta.

No cleaning today, she texts. But I do have a surprise. Come down to the cabin when you're ready. Bring River.

I snort. "Delta says we don't have to clean today. That's almost funny, because I've had to clean every day since I got here, including when I had a severe case of COVID." I squint at my phone. "She also says that she has a surprise for both of us. What can that be?"

He looks mildly surprised. "I have no idea. I didn't think Delta liked me much."

"Well, whether nor not that is the case, we've been summoned." I put my phone down. "She texted me hours ago, so we should probably get going."

I grab the coffees I made. We get up and get dressed in our cleaning garb, because I would guess that Aunt Delta's surprise is something like another leak in a cabin. Or maybe there's an owl infestation. Something of that nature.

But once we make our way to the cabins, there is a lot of commotion around the cabin at the very end, set off a bit from the others. Malik and Crisanto are carrying a squeaky metal bed frame out. I wait for them to pass, waving at them.

"Who is that?" River asks, pointing out my brother's boyfriend.

"Crisanto. He's Malik's very serious boyfriend. They've been together for years."

I hear my mom and Aunt Delta squawking at each other from inside, and I steel myself. I don't know what I'm about to walk into.

River casually grabs my hand and I toss him a grateful look over my shoulder.

When I walk into the cabin, I am nearly whacked in the face with a flying pillow. I neatly dodge it and it hits my chest, falling to the ground.

My mom looks over at me, apologizing. "Sorry, baby. Oh! You brought River too."

I am too busy gaping at the cabin. It has been hollowed out like someone taking a spoon to an avocado and just leaving the peel. My aunt Delta and my mom are stuffing the last of the bedding into trash bags.

"Is there seriously an owl infestation in here again?" I eye the ceiling skeptically.

"No, baby," Aunt Delta sings out. "We are getting rid of the old furniture and we're going to clean this whole place from top to bottom. My hard-working niece and her husband-to-be deserve to live in more than three hundred square feet."

My jaw drops. "Wait, this is for us?"

"Yes indeed!" my aunt Glory says, marching in through the open sliding glass door in the rear. She is pulling on a pair of bright yellow rubber gloves. "We're going to regrout the bathroom tile and replace the kitchen counter, too."

I glance at River, trying to gauge his reaction. He plays it close to the vest, nodding quietly.

"Are you okay with this?" I ask him.

River gives me a rueful smile.

"I'm actually trying to figure out whether I can get a custom bed to put in here on short notice. I'll bet I can." He holds his phone up. "Ladies, say the word, and I'll have an entire construction and cleaning crew out here. It would be my pleasure to help with that."

Delta drops the pillow she's holding on the floor. "We're absolutely going to take you up on that. In fact, if I had realized that was an option, I wouldn't have even walked in this cabin."

I beam at River. "Are you sure?"

He yanks my arm and kisses me on the lips. "Absolutely."

Aunt Glory strips off her gloves and places them neatly on the kitchen counter. "We have other cabins that need turning over, I think."

River waves her down. "Let my crew do those too. You three look like you could use a day of pampering." He raises his eyebrows at me. "What do you think? There's a spa up by Jekyll Island. I'm sure that they have room to roll out the red carpets for your family."

"Uh, that sounds awesome!" I gasp.

"Now wait a second, here," Delta snaps. "I am coming around to liking you even though you're not what I envisioned for Pearl. But don't think for a second that we are gonna owe you anything just for a day of spa treatments. We are all firmly on Team Pearl, you hear?"

River nods his head solemnly. "I would never think otherwise, ma'am."

Delta looks at Glory. "You hear this kid? Ma'am. I never."

My mom smiles. "That's her way of saying thank you, River. I'd love to go to the spa."

Delta grunts. Glory walks over to Delta and offers her an arm to lean on. Delta hobbles out on her arm.

Mom touches River's cheek briefly. "You treat my daughter good. That's all we need from you."

"Oh Mom..." I start. But she just smiles at me and then heads out of the cabin.

I bite my lip, looking around. "It's a nice thought. Not much of an upgrade, though..."

He slides his arm around my neck and kisses my shoulder. "Just wait till you see what my crew does with the place. I promise, you'll be impressed."

I pick up his hand and kiss his knuckles. "I'm already impressed, River. You don't have to do anything special other than just being your own wonderful self."

THIRTY-ONE
RIVER

"Wow. You did an amazing job," I tell Gil, the lead construction worker on the cabin. They've completely overhauled the bathroom and kitchen. Plus they've added built-in bookcases near the sliding doors, and built thin walls to separate the bedroom from the rest of the space. I paid an interior designer to come in after the construction workers finished and deck the whole place out in teak wood and the lush green of numerous potted plants. He also added a huge bed, a sofa with a side table, and a cozy little dining room table built for two. The space doesn't even look the same.

"I'm glad you approve, Mr. Taylor," Gil says. "I know it took a few more days than you wanted, but I think it's worth it."

And a part of me also wants her to have something to remember me by. Someplace to raise the baby, for however long she's allowed to stay on the land.

"Definitely." I walk over to the ten-thousand-dollar telescope that is set up near the back window. Touching it, I smile. "I can't wait to show my fiancée."

"If she has eyes, she'll be impressed," he affirms.

"Good man." I turn to walk to the door. "Thanks for doing my job on such short notice."

"Of course." He bows his head, walking out with me.

We part ways. He gets in his truck, and I head through the light sprinkling of trees toward Pearl's trailer. I'm excited to show her the finished cabin. I can just imagine her excited smile, and how she'll throw her arms around my neck. Anticipation of her reaction drives my footsteps as I walk into her yard and up the steps to the trailer.

When I open the door to the trailer, though, I can immediately tell that the energy level inside is much lower and moodier. Pearl is sitting at the dining room table, frowning at a small paper box in front of her. She looks up at me when I enter and her face screws up.

"Hey." Pushing my hand through my hair, I take a seat across from her. "What's up, buttercup?"

Pearl gives me a shaky smile. "I'm late."

I spread my hands. "Late for what, darlin'? You're going to have to give me more to go on than that."

She gulps and pushes the box across the checked table-cloth. Using a single fingertip, I spin the box around. My eyes widen as I read it.

Home Pregnancy Test.

Glancing up at her, I take a moment to phrase my question. "You think you're pregnant?"

I leave off the word 'already', though it seems obvious enough to me. We've only been together for a few months. I just assumed that we would have way more time to spend in bed together before... this.

"I'm not sure," Pearl confesses. "My period is late, but it's not unheard of for me to skip a month. I'm not really on a schedule or anything."

I relax a fraction. "Oh. Well... don't you want to know

for sure? I would think that you would be excited to find out."

She looks at me for a long moment. "I am..."

"But..." I raise my eyebrows. "What?"

Pearl blushes and looks down at the table. "I just thought we would have more time. That's all."

My surprise must be apparent on my face, because she puts up a hand to stop me. "I know what we agreed. I also know that I'm having feelings that we didn't agree to from the get-go."

I reach out and catch her hand, squeezing it. "Slow down. We don't even know if we have to make that decision right now."

To say that I'm glad that we're on the same level is the understatement of the year.

She pushes out a breath. "You're right. I'm just having a crazy amount of anxiety and I haven't even taken the test."

I push the box back toward her. "No time like the present."

She swallows and nods. She scoots out of the booth, disappearing into the bathroom with the test.

While I wait for her, time slows. I try to figure out how I'm going to tell my fake fiancée that I want her to move into the cabin with me, no matter what. It seems like a crazy thing to ask, especially if I don't plan to have an actual relationship with her.

But the thought of waking up with no Pearl in the bed beside me every day isn't exactly pleasant. God, I don't want to face that today.

I just want Pearl to be there, wherever I go. Is that so wrong?

Hearing her laugh, seeing her eyes light up, having her sass me when I do things the wrong way... I want that.

Pearl doesn't even know how rare and valuable I find the pleasure of her company.

The door to the bathroom creaks open. I look up to see Pearl looking tearful.

My heart jumps into my throat.

Is she about to say that she's pregnant with my baby?

Pearl waves a stick wrapped in toilet paper at me.

"Not pregnant," she says. "Yesterday, I wished I would have more time with you. Now I guess I got what I wanted."

Her affect is flat and monotone. I watch as she throws the test away under the kitchen sink and then washes her hands.

Inside, I feel a well of relief. Thank god. I don't have to change anything just yet. That's the best news anyone could give me, personally.

But I know how much Pearl wants this baby, and I can't ignore the heartbreak in her eyes. My heart feels small and dark from rejoicing about news that breaks her heart.

Without saying a word, she walks back to the bedroom and flops down face first on the bed.

I stand up, uncertain if I should comfort her or if I should give her space.

I've never actually received this kind of news, period. Much less with a girl that I was... what? Dating seems like the wrong word. Fucking seems too casual.

What's the correct term to describe the intense rush I feel whenever I look in her eyes?

My stomach flip flops, and I push to my feet. Heading back into the bedroom, I sit on the bed and gently rub Pearl's back.

"What's going on in there?" I ask.

Pearl rolls onto her side with a sigh. Her eyes are dry, but she is clearly not happy.

"I don't know. I am happy that I still get to spend time with you. But I've always wanted to get pregnant. It's a lot to process."

I pick up her hand, raising her knuckles to my lips for a kiss. "I get that. But it's only been a few months. It takes a while for some people to conceive."

She covers her face with her hands, and mutters her complaints through them. "What if I can't conceive? Or what if your sperm and my egg just don't have like... chemistry?"

I squint. "That sounds made up. Did you read that on Facebook or something?"

She stiffens and then glares at me. Removing her hand from my grip, she huffs. "I don't think accusing me of being ill-informed is the right call right now." She picks at a loose thread on her skirt. "I'm allowed to feel whatever kind of way I want about the test results."

"I never said you couldn't." I shake my head. "I'm just saying that we should be rational about this."

She drops her head into her hands. "It just feels like the world is kind of imploding."

I roll my eyes. "The world is fine. You're being a teeny little bit dramatic."

Pearl's head snaps up and she glares at me. "You know, River. I think I need some space."

"Space?" I say, scoffing. "What does that mean?"

She draws her legs up to her chest and tosses her hair. "It means you should spend the night at your place. Give me room to grieve if I want to."

I'm speechless. Space is the last thing I want. My first impulse is to draw her into my arms and kiss her worries away.

"Pearl--"

"Please go." She sounds broken, on the cusp of tears. "I'm not asking for much."

I stand and put up my hands in surrender, backing out of the bedroom. "I'm going!"

"Good!" she fires back.

Huffing, I turn and head out of the trailer. Once I'm outside, I head straight for my truck, which is parked near the cabin that I just refinished for her.

Seeing the cabin only worsens the aching hole that has opened up in my chest.

I turn my gaze away, clamp my jaw shut, and climb in my truck. It's always been something of a refuge for me and today is absolutely no exception. It's like being wrapped in a layer of bubble wrap, insulating me from the very real feelings I'm having and blunting them ever so slightly.

I spend the drive home reminding myself that Pearl isn't really my fiancée. Her emotions are not my problem. I also need to remember the goal right in front of me, so close I can almost reach it.

Her land. Her distressed land. That's what this is all supposed to be about.

But it isn't about the land, god damn it.

I went and let my heart get involved in this. At least I can admit that.

I have feelings for Pearl. I care for her. For god's sake, I just custom built a fucking cabin for us to live in together, for god's sake.

Instead of loving a cosmopolitan and career focused woman, I ended up falling for an offbeat diner waitress who really wants a baby. And I'm the idiot who wants to give her everything I have.

I make it to my house and cut the engine, but I don't go inside just yet. Because I'm not sure about anything else except for this one fact. If I don't at least try to smooth over the fight we just had, I'm a giant bag of dicks.

Blowing out a breath, I start my truck again.

I have an errand to run.

Thirty-Two

River shows up at my door the morning of my family's barbeque with a black velvet box in his hand.

I stare him down for a second. He glances down and kicks the cement step he's standing on.

"I'm sorry, Pearl."

Folding my arms across my chest, I level him with a look.

"You are not coming in this house so easily, River. What exactly are you apologizing for?"

There is tension in the lines of his face. "For fucking things up. For being an ass. I honestly didn't mean to upset you. I hope that you realize that I always want you to be happy."

Pursing my lips, I step back and make room for him to enter the trailer. He steps into the kitchen and then offers the velvet box to me.

"What is this?" I ask. I take the box and look at him. It's impossible just to embrace him the way I normally would.

A teeny, tiny, almost unseen crack has formed in the icy pond we're walking on. And it remains to be seen whether that crack will widen into a dangerous fissure or eventually knit together and refreeze.

He looks like a kicked cat, his expression watchful, his eyes just a little bit guilty.

"An 'I'm sorry' gift." River sucks air in between his teeth. "I bought them because I think you'll look beautiful in them."

I sigh silently and then open the box. When I see what's inside, I gasp.

Nestled in folds of silk is a diamond pendant necklace and a matching pair of diamond earrings. My mouth opens and I touch the necklace disbelievingly. "Oh, River," I breathe. I glance up at him. "You really shouldn't have. This is pretty extravagant for an apology gift."

He arches a brow. "Well, that depends on whether or not you accept the gift and my apology, or not. I hate the idea that you're mad at me."

I press my lips into a thin line. "Do you understand why I reacted the way that I did?"

He scrunches up his face, "After I left, I felt bad for what I said. Maybe you were a little fast to kick me out. But you have every right to your feelings. There's no denying that."

That's what I wanted to hear. But his words don't ease the tension in my chest. Still, I have to suck it up and act like an adult.

My family is having a barbecue about now. Showing up to the party without my supposed fiancé is a no-go. I have to make a decision to forgive River.

"I don't like being mad at you either," I finally say. "In fact, it is really stressful. I would much rather go back to the way things were."

He looks at the box I'm holding and cants his head. "Am I forgiven, then?"

I can't help the small smile that sprouts on my lips. "Yes, River. You're forgiven."

He slides around to take the necklace from the box. Then he moves my hair out of the way and fastens it around my neck. It's heavier than I expected, the diamond pendant sparkling as it finds its home just above my cleavage.

I set the box on the kitchen counter and change my earrings out for the diamond ones. With the necklace and my huge engagement ring, I am certainly dressed like a wealthy fiancée that looks right hanging on River's arm.

He looks at me, his lips twitching with humor. "You're going to be the envy of every woman at the barbecue."

"Like I want that," I say.

He kisses me lightly on the mouth, a peck. I dig my fingers into his shirt and pull him forward, seeking a more substantial kiss. He responds by pressing my body against the kitchen counter. The breath catches in my throat as he kisses me deeply, passionately.

River and I may not see eye to eye on many things. But sharing passionate kisses and caresses has never been a problem for us.

Eventually, I break the kiss and look up at him. "We should get to the party. Everyone will already be there by the time we walk over."

River sighs. "I know you have seen the cabin. But I'd just like to point out that it has a fantastic bed... which I'm excited to test out. We could decide to be a little late..."

I smooth a hand over his muscular chest. "Yeah, I'm not going to explain to Aunt Delta how we decided that fucking each other's brains out means that we could be late to her event. You don't know Delta that well, but I can't imagine that you want to be in the doghouse with her so soon."

His eyes sparkle. "I would gladly do it for you."

Shaking my head, I glance down at the diamond necklace that I am wearing. "We will have to spend time at the new cabin after this barbecue. I have seen it, but I haven't explored it yet. I'm dying of curiosity. That's a promise."

River steps back with a sigh. "Your wish is my command, darlin'."

"We should probably go to the barbecue now before Anitta and Bishop start a rumor that we broke up."

Thirty-Three

River

Whew. That fight seems to have blown over more easily than I thought possible.

"Okay," I tell Pearl. "As we walk, tell me who I'm about to meet at this barbecue."

She pulls me outside and we begin the walk down to the party. By the time we actually arrive at a part of the resort that I haven't seen before, I have gotten the history of twenty different family units that I don't know.

There is a covered area of tables on one side of the park. Amazing smoky, umami odors waft over from the six full-sized barbecues and smokers sitting just beside that. A cluster of older relatives sit in chairs on the far side, clutching cold drinks and umbrellas. The grassy space between is set up with two distinct areas, one for kids to play tag, one for adults to play cornhole. As we pass by the cornhole area, a stray bean bag misses the board and comes tumbling end over end toward my feet.

I grab it and chuck it back to a man who waves his hands and calls for its return.

"That's my Uncle Buck," Pearl says. "And the guys he's

playing with are my nephews from across the Alabama border."

I nod. Flo waves from the covered patio and I point her out. Pearl takes my hand and makes her way over to her immediate family. Her Aunt Delta and Aunt Glory are sitting at a table with other various aunts and cousins.

"Where's Malik?" I whisper to Pearl.

"He's having a sickle cell flare up, so he's resting today," Pearl murmurs.

That's too bad. It would be nice to have another familiar face here

"Y'all come sit with us," Glory says, waving us over.

"Y'all haven't met Pearl's fiancée yet," Delta says to the women she's sitting with. "This is River. He is a lawyer."

The other women murmur, excited at the announcement that Pearl is getting married. For the next ten minutes, I am paraded around and looked at. Pearl's family are mostly Black, although there are a couple adopted cousins and spouses who don't have the same skin tone. For the most part, everyone is polite, but they are a bit distant.

Pearl's mom puts her arm around me protectively and brings me to sit at her table. "You stick with me," she whispers. "All the interesting people are at this table anyway."

Pearl is pulled away to socialize with her extended family. So I just sit and make small talk with Flo, Delta, and Glory.

"So, River," Glory says, jerking her head at Delta. "My aunt has a little cash flow issue. I figured since you are a real estate attorney, you would be the perfect person to advise us on the matter."

"Glory! That's private family business," Delta growls.

"He's going to be family. He might as well know the state of your property."

I smile placidly, trying not to let my excitement about

her words show. "I'm at your disposal, ladies. Any time, not just right now." I take a look around at all the cousins that are within hearing range. "But it might be better to talk about this in a more discreet location."

Flo puts her hand on mine and leans in. "He is trying to tell you not to put your business on blast, ladies."

I duck my head. "Suggesting, nothing more."

Delta's brown eyes probe my face. She seems to be weighing my worth as a source of information, which is fair enough, "We should sit down and talk sometime soon. Not now, though."

I bow my head again. "Of course."

Glory frowns and jerks her chin toward the park entrance. "I was hoping that Bishop and Anitta would sit this one out."

Pearl appears beside me, gripping my hand. Her eyes are glued on Bishop. I pull her down to perch on my lap and slide my arms around her. "I've got you," I murmur.

Pearl gives me a grateful smile and kisses my lips lightly. "Thank you," she whispers.

I hug her close to my body, feeling a weird need to possess her, to tell everyone that she's mine. She's not; I know it better than anybody. But still the feeling remains.

Delta climbs to her feet when Anitta and Bishop sail up to our table. Anitta looks like she just tasted something sour. But Bishop?

His eyes are locked on Pearl. On my girl.

I wish I could put out his eyes so he couldn't even look at her.

The way she shifts on my lap says that she's feeling the same.

"Aunt Delta," Bishop says, his smile smug. "How are we doing today?"

Delta crosses her arms. "I didn't know that Anitta was

bringing a guest. I thought we had already talked about the matter and decided that she wasn't bringing anyone."

"This is Pearl's home, after all," Flo pipes up.

Bishop smirks. "Anitta and I are a package deal. Her mom asked her to be here, so I'm here too."

He rubs Anitta's very pregnant stomach. Anitta gives him an irritated glare and flings his hand off of her stomach. Bishop gives her a hard stare.

"You know, Aunt Delta," Bishop says. He never breaks eye contact with Anitta. "We were thinking of naming Baby Jones after you."

Pearl's limbs stiffen. But before she can react, Anitta blurts out with a string of curses.

"Son of a bitch! You fucking kiss ass little dick fucking loser!" Anitta yells, looking at Bishop. "I've had it with you! First you begged me to be your fake fiancée. But now you're trying to get close to Aunt Delta? No fucking way!"

As we all sit watching, she rips off Velcro straps around her waist and flings her pregnancy belly to the ground. Then she yanks her ring off.

"Baby..." Bishop starts.

"Baby nothing. It's done. We're finished." She shows everyone the ring, which she drops to the ground and stomps on repeatedly. I gape until I hear the telltale pop crackle of something shattering beneath her foot. "It's a fake ass diamond, by the way. Fake like this fake ass belly you made me wear!"

"Anitta!" Bishop bellows. "What the fuck?"

I'm left gaping at Anitta. What the fuck, indeed! Bishop turns an angry shade of purple.

Anitta points her finger in his face. "I'm leaving. You had better do the same unless you want my uncles to whoop your sorry ass."

I can't help the tiny laugh that leaves my mouth as Anitta storms off, Bishop following right behind her.

"The trash took itself out," Glory announces, dusting off her hands. "I can't believe my little niece would even give that man the time of day."

An older woman drifts over, waving a paper fan in front of her face as she sneers. "I agree. But thank the Good Lord, she's free of him now. I still hold her partially accountable, but Bishop is the one who looks like a jackass right now. That man is insufferable."

"That's right," Flo agrees, nodding. "You tell 'em, Donna."

I look at Pearl, who seems shocked. Squeezing her waist, I prompt her. "You okay?"

Pearl swallows. I see a sheen of tears in her eyes.

She's about to have a legit breakdown. I give her a gentle shake to get her attention. I slide her off of my lap and look around at the women in Pearl's immediate family. "I have to borrow Pearl to... uh... help look for my contact lens. It's loose in my eye."

The lie sounds phony, but her Aunt Glory smiles at me. "Go ahead," she says, waving a hand to shoo us away.

I lead Pearl to the entrance and we get about fifteen steps beyond it when she hunches over and covers her face. "Oh god."

I wrap my arms around her and pull her into a more densely wooded area.

"Are you upset about Bishop?" I ask, confused.

She shakes her head, wiping at her eyes. "No. We're doing the same thing Bishop and Anitta were doing, River. I don't want to be anything like them."

My head rocks back. "That's what you're worried about?"

"Yes!" she cries. "My family is going to be so disappointed, River. They'll know that I tried to deceive them."

"That's not true," I say as gently as possible. Cupping her cheek, I force her to look at me. "They never have to know."

A cold laugh bursts from her lips. "You're an optimist."

"Funny, no one has ever accused me of that. I would say I'm a realist."

She stomps her foot and looks at me with dread in her eyes. "We're fooling ourselves if we think that this... this moment in time... can last. We are nothing but a flash in the pan."

She's right, of course. But I want so badly to soothe her aching heart. I shush her and pull her against my chest.

"Does this feel flimsy to you?" I ask as I hold her close.

"No..." She sniffles. "But it does feel like a heartache waiting to happen."

I let her words hang there in the air. A part of me wants to refute her statement, to shut her down.

Another part of me thinks that maybe I should just tell her that I have feelings for her. Just come clean with the fact that I think we should be together in a much more permanent way.

My heart thunders in my chest. The words are on the tip of my tongue. But I am too much of a goddamned coward to say them.

For a moment, I genuinely loathe myself.

Pearl eventually quiets against me and we stand for a long moment, soaking each other up. I know that I will have to tell her how I feel before I reveal that I'm taking her land...

But I don't have to do it at this exact moment. There will be time.

THIRTY-FOUR

I sit in the passenger seat of River's truck and absentmindedly watch the scenery as it flies by. My stomach is fluttery and nervous. Not because of the GCUFOs meet-up that River is taking me to, no. But because I decided A Big Thing last night when I was falling asleep next to his big, warm body.

I decided that I have to tell River how I feel, today. More explicitly, that I have to say those three little words that I've never said to a man that wasn't my dad or my brother.

I love you.

Just thinking about it makes my whole body clench. It shouldn't leave me feeling petrified. But it does.

What if he doesn't feel the same way?

I sneak a glance at River out of the corner of my eye. He catches me looking and smirks. "What?"

I snicker. "Nothing."

River snakes his hand out and puts it on my thigh with a wink.

"Thinking dirty thoughts about me?"

I flush. "No..."

"Yes, you were. I can tell. You were just wondering when the next time that I can bind your wrists, cover your eyes, and spend hours bringing you close to the edge with my fingers and tongue deep in your pussy. Admit it. You're getting wet for me right now."

His deep voice washes over me and heat flashes through my veins. I bite my lip and try not to grin. "God damn it, River. You know I love it when you talk dirty to me."

"I could pull over somewhere private and we could recreate our quickie in the car." He wiggles his eyebrows.

"Quickie? We spent an hour in here, if I remember correctly."

"You know that whenever I fuck, I like to make an event of it. An hour is nothing."

I grin. "I do know that about you. And on behalf of women everywhere, I thank you. We need more than a little drunk groping and then sticking it in."

River's eyes sparkle. "I've never heard any complaints."

I laugh at that. "No, not from me anyway."

He squeezes my thigh and bites his lip in a way that makes me flush all over. "I'm going to make you scream my name later. You know that, right?"

I shift in my seat, my pussy damp. Maybe we should pull over and...

But before I can say anything, River turns off into the dirt parking lot beside the bluff. "This is where you want to be, isn't it?"

I huff. "Yes. If you think for a second that I'm not going to remind you of what we just talked about when we're on the way home though, you're crazy."

"Oh, it's going to happen. I'm going to enjoy making you wait for a little while."

He turns off the truck and slips out of his seat. I roll my eyes and follow him.

I really want to tell him that I love him. But it seems like he has his mind in the gutter. And I will admit, it is easier to keep my mind on his body than to think about the words that are on the tip of my tongue.

The anticipation of an orgasm is already building as we unpack the back of the truck. The knowledge that we are definitely going to fuck into the wee hours of the night sticks with me as we haul all of our stuff up the bluff. I bite my lip as River sets up our collapsible camping chairs, and our cooler full of drinks and snacks. He keeps bending over, and I feel lecherous for noticing his ass in those tight jeans he wears. There are plenty of other people moving around, getting their telescopes set up and chatting about alien encounters. But I have eyes only for River.

My crush on him has escalated to a full-blown infatuation. I set up my precious, beloved telescope; it's not the fancy one River bought for me, as I'm far too nervous to even adjust that one, much less pack it up and lug it out here. I admit, I'm busy looking at River with a combination of lust and love, watching him flex his muscles as he casually sets up our picnic.

I am not paying much attention. Unintentionally, I almost recreate the last of these meetings I went to, wherein I almost lost my telescope down the steep slope under the bluff.

This time, River comes to my rescue again, snagging the telescope in one hand while bracing me against his body.

Fucking swoon city over here.

"Thanks," I say softly, looking up into his incredibly handsome face. I can't stop making heart eyes at him.

River chuckles. "Careful, darlin'."

But before I can respond, he turns me loose and heads

back down the rocky slope toward the parking lot. I'm dying to just tell him that I love him

But I can't just blurt it out here, in front of all my GCUFOE friends. That's way too much private information for the public to have about me. That, and the fact that as supposed fiancés, we probably ought to have declared our love for each other years ago.

I manage to peel my eyes off of River just in time to see a familiar face walk by. Birdie doesn't even see us, because she is looking down at a small notepad, scribbling furiously. She is wearing a short, blue mock-turtleneck dress and white tights; she looks kind of like a character from Scooby Doo.

I eye her proximity to the edge of the bluff and call out. "Stop! Birdie, look out!"

Birdie's blonde head snaps up. She stops on a dime, only now noticing how precariously close to the edge she'd come. Her eyes widen and she steps back with alarm. "Oh god. I almost fell off!" She laughs and looks at me. "Pearl! I didn't know you would be here. It's always nice to see you, but you really just saved my hide."

I beckon her closer. "Are you reporting on this?"

She nods. "Yup. My editor sent me here. I don't think he realizes what a klutz I am, though."

I turn to River. "You know River."

He waves, then trundles off to the truck again.

"The fiancé! Yes, of course." She waves her notepad at him. "So who is the alien expert here?"

I wave at my telescope. "I'm not an expert in anything. But I have a telescope and I'm hungry to learn."

Birdie grins. "I know you're engaged, but apparently there's a whole dating app just for people into UFOs. I just downloaded it today." She winces. "I want to say that it's just a part of my research for this piece, but honestly? Maybe I'll try it. At least the freaks and weirdos on AlienMeetup are open-minded.

My brows shoot up. "Oh really? I had no idea."

"Well, there's no need for you to worry about it. One, you're not a single mom. Dating guys as a single mom is the worst. But more importantly, you're already practically married to one of the Billion Dollar Bennetts."

She is so wrong. I'm actively trying to become a single mom. And my relationship with River is as fake as a dime store spray tan. But I can't tell her any of that. So instead, I smile and say, "The Bennett-Taylors actually hate that nickname."

She frowns. "Oh my god. I'm sorry. Did I put my foot in my mouth?"

"Nah." I wave my hand at my telescope. "Do you want to check out the skies tonight? Venus is supposed to be easy to see, according to my almanac."

Birdie grins at me. "Yes! I'll definitely take you up on that."

I show Birdie how the telescope operates and let her look around. But while she is oohing and ahhing, I have a belly full of sharp rocks.

Is what she says true? Am I setting myself up for misery by trying to become a single mom? More importantly, am I crazy to let this fake engagement go on? Without telling River how I really feel, I could be risking everything.

But what if I tell him and he doesn't feel the same way about me? It would be a heartbreaking end to this whole mess.

River comes back from the truck and chats with Birdie. But I am too caught up in my thoughts to follow the conversation.

Birdie smiles at me. "I have really enjoyed talking to y'all.

But I should move on and talk to someone else. I'm really trying to get a firsthand account of alien abduction."

"You should try Jim Mathers. He's right over there, in the priest getup." I point him out. "He's eager to tell anybody that will listen about his multiple experiences being abducted."

"That's what mama wants to hear." Birdie gives a little wave. "See y'all later!"

River sits down in a camping chair and pulls the other seat up next to him. He pats the chair. I sit down beside him, full of nervous, jittery energy.

He puts his arm around mine and tugs my shoulders close, kissing the top of my head. He's hitting all the right buttons and I shiver pleasurably.

"It's a nice night out," River says. He sweeps his gaze around the clearing. "A good turnout for the meeting, too."

I look at him, trying like hell not to let my anxiety show. "Yeah."

He arches a brow. "You okay? You seem... weird."

I can't stop myself from blurting it out. "I love you!" I say, my voice a squeak.

His eyes grow dark and wide as takes my hand.

"You love me?" he repeats. "Seriously?"

I nod, feeling my face flame.

He kisses the back of my hand and smiles at me. "I love you too, Pearl. I just wasn't sure if I should say it or not."

My heart seizes. "Really?"

He nods, somber for once.

"Yes, darlin'. I'm not sure where that leaves us. I never planned..." He shakes his head, sucking in a breath. "I don't know."

I screw up my face. "Does this change anything for us? I know you have a future envisioned that takes place in Atlanta... and I still want to have your baby..."

"Slow down. Can we just kind of live in the moment? I know that I love you. That's all I know."

My heart thuds painfully against my ribs. "We can't live in this bubble for very long..."

He leans in and places a searing kiss against my lips. His touch is so knowing, so confident.

I can trust that, I think.

THIRTY-FIVE
RIVER

I wake to the feel of Pearl's ass pressing against my cock. Turning over, I drift my fingers over her sleeping face. Her eyelids flutter and I kiss her.

She's sleepy, but her hand slips down my ribs and to the waistband of my boxer briefs. I thrust into her touch and those big brown eyes of her open a scant inch.

I kiss her again, more insistently this time. She's just wearing a t-shirt and no panties, so I pull the t-shirt up over her head and kick my boxers off. Twilight seeps in through the blinds and plays faintly across the bed as we kiss and grope each other. My lips work against hers. She strokes my cock a few times before she heaves herself up and straddles me.

I fist my cock and stroke the tip up and down her slit, gathering her juicy wetness. It makes me groan as I fit my cock to her.

"God, River," she whimpers. She soon eases herself down my length, her hot pussy clenching my cock.

This early in the morning, I'm already primed and on the edge.

"Fuck, darlin', you'd better hurry," I warn her. "I'm already close."

Pearl gasps and rides my cock, her movements slow. I slide my hand between our bodies, rubbing her swollen clit. She picks up the pace and I thrust along, my hips meeting hers.

I'm fucking starving for her. Here she is riding my cock and I'm already planning the next time I can be under her, inside her, breathe her in.

Her breaths quicken. "Just like that, baby. I'm going to come."

Her innermost muscles clench once, twice. She's not lying.

While I keep fucking her, I rub her clit with a steady hand as she rides my cock. She shatters, trembling, moaning, coming apart at the seams.

I follow her over the edge, letting go, careening so fast that I'm not fully in control of myself. Her pussy clutches at me, destroying me, milking my semen. I fill her with hot lashes of my seed, thrusting until there is nothing left.

When we collapse, unable to breathe, she lets out a chuckle. I reach out and pull her into my arms.

"What?" I ask.

"Nothing. That was just some amazing morning sex, that's all."

I brush back her hair from her forehead. "If you want to sleep a little more, I understand. It's still very early."

She kisses my lips and then settles in my arms with a sigh.

While we're lying in bed drowsing, my phone buzzes. I groan at having to hunt around on the floor and root through my clothing to find it. When I see that it's Wesley calling, my eyebrows rise.

It's early in the morning. The sun has only barely begun

to rise, just a slim crack of light on the horizon. I've never known my assistant to arrive at work so early.

"Hello?" I say.

Pearl stirs in bed and I pad buck-ass naked out of the bedroom, closing the room divider behind me.

"Hey, boss man. I came in early to redo the whole filing system. I figured you wouldn't mind, but you aren't per se interested in my schedule, either."

I try to string together a thought. "Uh huh..."

"Right. Anyway, that's not the point. The point is that Ray Kendrick's on the other line. His office has apparently been trying to reach you for a couple of days."

My heart rate rises. This is totally news to me. "Ray Kendrick? It's insanely early. He knows that, right?"

"I didn't think I should point that out to his staff. Will you accept the call?"

I look down at my nudity and shrug. "Yeah. Of course."

"Okay, I'll connect you. Hang on."

A few seconds later, Ray comes on the line. "Hello?"

"Ray! It's a surprise to hear from you."

He chuckles. "Sorry, I know it's early. I don't sleep for more than a few hours a night and I am an early riser. Hope it's not a deal breaker."

I clear my throat. "No, not at all. What's going on?"

"Well, I'm just excited about what you presented me with. I'm tantalized, you could say."

My heart jumps into my throat. "I'd be glad to have you on board, Ray." I lean against the kitchen counter, sneaking a glance toward the bedroom. "Especially if you are willing to take the place of the construction company I just signed a placeholder contract with."

"Ahh, that's not a problem. As Rex may have informed you, I own a whole construction firm. So that's taken care of. Plus, I would love to be involved in this project because it's based off of all the tourism that the new baseball training complex is going to bring in."

"Absolutely makes sense for you and your brand." I try to think of what to say now. "I am really energized to get this project moving."

"Now, you probably know I'm going to ask this question. Do you have the rights to the entire property sewed up? I mean the whole frigging shebang."

"Uh, well..."

"That's not really encouraging, son."

"It's a little complicated. But with you on board, I am ready to pull the trigger. It can be wrapped up in a week. Two, tops."

There is silence as Ray considers my words.

"That could work. We'd have to close the deal and cement it shut, though. I don't want any uncertainty. That's not how I do business."

"No, sir." I feel beads of sweat across my brow. "I completely understand that."

He chuckles. "Well, all right. If you get bogged down with the seller talking about numbers, you can call me. I'm open to a lot of options. Just as long as we get the rights free and clear."

"Understood. I will reach out to the seller immediately." My eyes travel to the flimsy partition. The woman I love is sleeping on the other side, not knowing that I'm right here in her trailer, making a deal that will sell her down the river.

God, I am a worthless, trash human being. I feel like the lowest of the low.

"All right, River. Let's stay in touch about this. I'd like a daily update until we get a contract in place."

"You got it. Thanks for reaching out, Mr. Kendrick."

"It's like I said before. Call me Ray. And have a good day, River. Give my best to your dad."

The line beeps and goes dead. I sag against the counter.

Fuckkkkk. I really have to talk to Delta and make her an offer now. God willing, she trusts me enough that we can execute the deal without a lot of fuss.

Pearl will be blindsided, though. There's no avoiding that.

Pearl hasn't even known me for six months. And she's not my fiancée, either. In real life, she doesn't have to forgive me when I tell her about selling her inheritance.

She may very well never speak to me again once I tell her. But

Walking back to the bedroom, I slip into bed beside her. Pearl murmurs something, rustling in her sleep, and resettles herself with her hand on my heart and her leg thrown across mine.

I turn my head, burying my nose against her scalp. I take long, deep lungfuls of air. As if I can get enough of Pearl just by breathing her scent in.

Pearl's eyelids flutter open. "River? Are you okay?"

Her voice is sleepy. I gulp. "I don't know," I whisper.

"Shhh. It's just a dream." She lays her head on my shoulder, her eyes drifting closed. "Go to sleep, baby."

THIRTY-SIX
PEARL

When I step out of the helicopter, my eyes are wide as I clutch my sunhat to my head and take in the scene.

Just a two-hour drive from home is this amazing estate, with rolling green hills, shadowy vales, and rows upon rows of grapevines as far as I can see. To our immediate right is a winding white gravel path that rises to a majestic fairytale castle straight out of childhood storybooks. There is a white-uniformed driver waiting for us beside a golf cart.

I turn my wide-eyed gaze to River and he grins, spreading his hands. "What do you think?"

"It's incredible. Is this the surprise you promised?"

The winery itself is great, but of course I'm not drinking because I'm trying to get knocked up. So I'm a little confused as to why River would bring me here.

"My folks asked us to meet them here," he says. He gives me a side hug and hurries me toward the golf cart.

"What? Why?" As we sit on the golf cart and are whisked up toward the castle, I'm stumped.

"That's part of the surprise." He grips my hand. "I promise, all will be revealed soon."

The golf cart comes to a stop in the gravel turnabout in front of the castle. Up close, the white limestone walls of the castle are pristine, the flower boxes in every window overflowing with trailing red roses, and the castle's ornately carved wooden front door is open. Beckoning us to enter.

"There are no cars allowed up here," River says. "Everything is brought up by golf cart."

I am too busy staring up at the castle's spires, trying to count them. It's one of the most astonishing buildings I've ever seen.

"Pearl!"

I blink and see Sarah rushing out of the castle's open front door, looking absolutely radiant in a peach silk dress. Seeing her, I'm glad that River made me dress up in a spring-green pantsuit.

"Sarah," I say, walking over to hug her. "It's nice to see you. River refuses to tell me why we are here."

I'm only half-joking and Sarah laughs. "Sorry, that was my fault. I thought that you could check this winery out as a venue."

"A venue..." I say, squinting. "Wait, as a place to host a wedding??"

I spin, pinning River with a look. He is smiling with his hands stuffed in his pants pockets. As if he were a real fiancé surprising his bride-to-be.

But he's not my fiancé. And surprising me with a wedding venue is something we should've agreed on ahead of time. If this is for real, my family should be here. And if it's not...

I struggle to keep my expression pleasant when all I really want to do is throttle him.

Smug bastard.

I force a smile to my lips. "We're just researching, right?"

Sarah squeezes my arm. "I'm here to help you. No pressure. The last thing I want is to be a pushy mother-in-law." She pinches her lips together and grimaces. "The castle does have an opening in September, though."

I look at River, in search of rescue. He eases himself between us, giving his mom a hug.

"Let's just enjoy the day. We can talk about dates some other time."

"Now River, if we need to put the brakes on this wedding--" She starts lecturing.

He is fast to reassure her. "Mom, chill. We're at a beautiful place, which we may or may not use as a venue later. Can we agree on that?"

I suppress my rage and bob my head. Inside, though, I'm seething. River doesn't even seem to care that it crosses the line between misleading his parents and outright lying.

"Fine," Sarah says. She makes this funny little indignant expression. Which is basically what I feel, too.

My stomach feels off as I realize that I am really starting to warm up to Sarah. A sigh escapes my lips, unbidden.

Sarah pushes her son aside, takes my arm, and steers me toward the castle entrance.

"Come on. Us girls have to stick together," she says.

I give her a weak smile and let her pull me inside.

The foyer of the castle makes me feel like an actual princess. The impressively high ceilings are a crisp white. A massive gold and crystal chandelier draws the eye as we step under it. There are two uniformed footmen on each side of the red carpet leading up a set of grand stairs.

"Oh my god," I say. "This place really is fancy."

"So fancy," Sarah says. "There are accommodations for

two-hundred people to stay the night here. An incredible Michelin-starred restaurant. A huge tasting room and an impressive wine cellar. Plus, they have the most gorgeous indoor and outdoor spaces for events. Oh, and a full-service spa."

River's stepdad waits at the top of the stairs, dressed in khakis and a canary yellow golf shirt. He holds a glass of red wine as he smiles at us.

"Welcome to the Castle Vineyard. I just got done taking a tour of the golf course that's on the property next door." He looks at Sarah. "We might just have to move in here, honey."

I'm so used to seeing Sam scowling at River that his good mood takes me by surprise.

"That's nice, dear." Sarah glances behind us to where River is standing. "Maybe you could practice your swing with River later."

Sam doesn't skip a beat. "I'll take any reason to get out there again. I tell you what, that's a thinking man's heaven."

River's lips twitch but he doesn't say anything. He just bows his head.

Great. First he drags me here without a simple heads up. And now he's going to make me do all the heavy lifting of socializing with his mom.

River is a dead man once I get him alone.

I glance at Sarah. "Do you have a suggestion for where you would like to start the tour?"

She links her arm with mine and bumps my hip with hers. "You bet I do. First things first. Let's go to the tasting room, get a glass of wine, and then have a little tasting menu from the chef."

A real smile blooms on my face. Okay, this isn't SO bad. But I'm still gonna kick River's ass when we get home.

"A tasting menu?" I ask.

She pulls me toward a large set of oak doors.

"It is technically a bride and groom's tasting. But I'm not about to let you have all the fun by yourself! We'll pick the hors d'oeuvres and they'll serve a sampler of what might be served for a dinner service. And then every kind of cake and dessert option that you've ever thought of. Trust me, it's the best part of wedding planning."

We walk into the tasting room. One wall is a bar, set up with a number of oak casks and countless bottles of wine stacked on thin wire shelves. The other side of the room has a window that looks off into the woods. There are tables made of old wine casks dappling the floor of the tasting room. I settle into a seat across from River, trying to keep my attention on Sarah as she seats herself and chats about the possibilities for throwing parties at the castle.

I'm mostly trying to focus on his mom instead of blowing up at River.

Sam and Sarah carry most of the conversation as we are served wine and an appetizer sampler. I lean over to catch the waiter's attention.

"Can I please have a glass of ice water?"

He bows and fetches it for me without complaint. Sarah pauses as she's about to take a sip of red wine.

"Everything to your liking, Pearl? You can ask for a different type of wine if you don't like red, you know."

I flush and shake my head. "I have a little bit of a headache," I lie. "I don't think that adding red wine to that is a good mix."

"Ah." She smiles, but I can see that she's just a bit crestfallen. "I see."

"These crab dumplings are nice," River says, pulling the conversation away from me. "But I don't like the little pancakes with caviar."

"I love 'em," comments Sam. "I don't care for the pate crostini, though. Too rich for me."

I sip my water and try the burrata, a smooth white lump of cheese with grilled grapes and basil leaves. It's quite nice; all of the food is excellent.

But by the time the dessert course arrives, I can't have more than a couple nibbles of the huge slices of red velvet and traditional vanilla cakes. There are easily twenty thousand calories on the table: key lime pie, berry galette, bananas foster, apple crumble with cinnamon streusel. Usually I would be at least tempted to sample a few more.

But I push my plate away early, my stomach feeling as though it has been wrung out. I listen to River talking to his parents for a little while before I eventually get up.

"I'm going to head outside. I need some air," I say, fanning myself.

River shoots to his feet. "Let me walk you around. We were going to tour the event space outside next anyway."

"I'd love some company." I turn to Sam and Sarah. "But please, feel free to try all the desserts. I want a full report when I get back."

Sam looks at me with a devious smile and hooks a finger on plate full of peach cobbler to pull it closer. "It's a tough job, but I will serve faithfully," he jokes.

I turn to River, waiting expectantly. He offers me his elbow and swans me out of the room.

As soon as we are far enough down the hall to be well out of eyesight and earshot, I drop my hand and glare at River. "You're a dead man," I say, not mincing words. "Deeply, incredibly dead."

"What?" He appears genuinely surprised. "Hold on, let's go outside."

After trying a few doorways, we finally find the one that leads into the event space out back. I stop and stare around at the whole scene. Like earlier, I gawp at the bluff we are standing on. It eventually drops off into verdant rolling hills covered with rows of grapes. At the edge of the bluff is a woven wicker arch. All this stands against the backdrop of the castle. I can easily imagine rows of folding chairs and a white piece of fabric stretched across the ground to form an aisle for the bride to walk down.

The view is such a perfect picture that it makes me a bit speechless. River catches my eye and waves a hand at the beautiful surroundings. "Like what you see?"

I pin him with a hard look. "River, this place is breathtaking."

"It is, isn't it?" He asks, grinning as he scans the area.

Pulling at his arm, I bring the attention back to me. "Yeah. And if I were actually getting married, I would love this place. And then I would probably die when I found out how much it cost."

"Cost is not an issue." River gives me a little smile. "My parents are nuts about this venue."

"Do you even listen to yourself when you speak?" I snap.

He pauses, confused. "Yeah...?"

"Then why are you acting like we are going to actually get hitched?" I smack his arm. "You're making me feel crazy, River."

"Ah." He shoves his hands in his pants pockets and kicks a clod of dirt on the ground. "Yeah. About that."

I look at him, fundamentally not understanding what's going on. "What in the hell are you talking about?"

His smile vanishes and he bites his lip. "Hear me out. What if we just get married?"

I blink rapidly, feeling a bit lightheaded. "I'm sorry. I think I misheard you."

He catches my hands and looks down into my face, his eyes beseeching.

"I think we should get married. We love each other, after all. And it would give our kid a leg up, for sure. He'd be a Billion Dollar Bennett instead of... you know, not."

I swallow. "What about your future living in Atlanta, married to some career-obsessed woman?"

River rolls his eyes and stretches out his arms.

"Look, I'm... I'm changing my mind. Is that allowed? What if we get married and make an honest attempt at being a couple?"

I shake my head. "You're asking me to give up all of my independence for a maybe? A 'hey let's try it, see if it works out?' No thanks."

"Don't be so dramatic. What I'm asking for makes sense."

"Maybe it does to you. But to me, it just sounds like a nice daydream. Meanwhile you're always planning to leave me to chase some dream woman who I can't possibly compare with."

"That's crazy. You're the one I'm with. I want us to give this a chance."

I stare at him for several seconds, feeling the blood pounding in my head. River is not listening to me. I need to be sure that I'm the only woman he wants, not a trial run. And I'm tired of shouting to make myself heard.

"I can't be here anymore." I massage my temples. "I have to go."

"Look... It's just marriage. Just some gobbledygook said before our families to make things between us 'official'. Nothing more than that. All that we need to know is that we love each other, right?""

I turn abruptly. River catches my arm, making me whip my head around and glare at him. "You're just leaving? Come on, we can talk this through."

My lip curls. "I don't know if we can. You don't want to

marry me for the right reasons. You just don't want your parents to find out that you are full of crap."

"That's not true," he says, sounding aggravated. "Give me a chance to explain, Pearl."

I pry my wrist from his grip and move toward the exit, tears already building in the corners of my eyes.

THIRTY-SEVEN

RIVER

It's been a tense few days since Pearl left me standing at the castle. She said she probably just needed some time to '*think about things*', whatever that means. She's talking to me all right.

But she seems to have so little to say. When I offered her a ride to work, I was honestly slightly amazed that she took it. But now that I have her in the close confines of my truck cab, I don't know quite what to say.

I'm sorry?

Why don't you want to get married?

Is it something about me?

None of those things seem like enough. I pull my truck to a stop in the parking lot of Gem's. Pearl flashes me a quick smile and opens her passenger side door. "Thanks. I'll get a ride home from Gem."

Sucking in a breath, I try again. "Are you sure you won't let my parents put down a deposit on the castle? Like I already explained before, we can get married without it being a big deal. I promise that if you hate it, we can get it annulled. It's just a piece of paper, nothing more."

I want to clutch at her shoulders and yell, "Pearl! Just let me love you!!" But somehow, I'm pretty sure that would only make things worse.

Pearl pauses, then pulls her door closed and looks at me. "I don't think that's a good idea, River. You and I just see marriage differently. What you're offering..." She hesitates. "I might be showing my small-town roots. But I won't be talked into signing a marriage certificate just because you don't want to tell your parents the truth."

That stings. I heave a sigh. "That's not why I'm proposing marriage."

"No?"

"No! I think we could make each other happy."

"If you think that, then let us date for a while and see. You're putting a lot of pressure on me by suddenly deciding that you want our fake relationship to be real."

"You're already wearing my ring, Pearl. I'm just asking you to attend a very fancy party and sign a piece of paper. Everything else will continue just as it has been."

Pearl's eyes scan my face. For a second, I think I might have just said the magic words. But then she slowly shakes her head. "I don't want to talk about this anymore. And I'm going to be late for my shift."

"You're going to be late for a job you wouldn't need if you just said yes to my proposal."

She leans over, kisses me on the cheek, and opens the car door again. "I'll see you back at home."

As she closes the door, I call to her. "I'll be at the cabin tonight!"

She waves and heads toward the diner's front door. Grumbling as I start my truck, I head down to park on the side street.

If I were to tell the me from three months ago that I was trying to talk Pearl into marrying me, what would he think?

He would laugh at me. Frustrated, I slam the door to my truck and hurry toward the office.

When I get inside, I see Wesley. He is in the middle of a giant tornado of file folders spread across the floor. He looks up calmly, as if he hasn't strewn just about every folder in the office around.

"I know what you're going to say. You don't like the mess. But when I get the folders into chronological order, it'll be a snap to find files when I need them."

"O-kay..." I walk around the mess, heading for my office. "Can you make a coffee run?"

Wesley nods. "Already did. There's a coffee with cream on your desk. And you have a surprise visitor waiting in your office."

I slow. "Who?"

"Your dad."

I grimace. "He's my step-dad. And you should've led with that information."

He nods, his eyes drifting back to the chaos on the floor in front of him. "I'll keep that in mind, boss."

Shaking my head, I open the door to my office. Sam stands by the front window, peering down the street toward the lighthouse. He turns and frowns at me as I close the door to my office behind me. "You're starting the work day pretty late, wouldn't you say?"

I feel my neck heat. I just go with, "Pearl needed a ride to work, so I took a few hours off. Is that okay with you?"

He spreads his hands. "I didn't mean anything by it."

I give him a sharp glance and stride over to my desk. "Do you want to sit down?" I motion to the chair across from me and Sam sidles over to it, giving it an imperious look before sitting down heavily. "What's on your mind, Sam?"

He sighs and studies me for a moment before replying. "I came by to tell you that I was wrong."

Among the hundreds of things I thought I'd hear Sam say, that wasn't one of them. It's not often that he admits something like that. I raise an eyebrow and fold my hands in my lap. "What were you wrong about?"

He picks an invisible piece of lint from his dark slacks. "About you and Pearl. I thought you were full of shit when you told me that you two had dated for long enough to want to get married." He hesitates. "Actually, I thought you were trying to game the system and get your inheritance early. But I saw the way you act around Pearl up close when we were at the Castle Vineyard. She was upset. You left the table to make sure she was okay. That's when I knew that your relationship was real."

I'm too stunned to say more than, "Uh... yeah. Okay..."

Sam leans forward, narrowing his eyes on my face. "I just wanted to make sure I came and apologized in person. I'm sorry that I had doubts about your intentions. I know that we haven't exactly had the easiest relationship, River, But I do love you. I only want what is best for you, son."

I duck my head. "Thanks, Sam. I... uh... I love you, too."

Now I feel like a complete fraud. Sam eyes me, nods once, and stands up.

"Okay, then. You should let us know if you want to rent the vineyard out. I'm not your mom, so I don't need your marriage to be right this damn second. If you want to set your wedding a year or two in the future and make it a long engagement, be my guest. Whatever makes you happy."

I stand up, feeling the beads of sweat break out across my brow. "Uh, thanks."

Sam stands there, waiting. I realize that he probably wants some sign of affection. I walk over and give his arm a squeeze. He seems okay with that and smiles at me. "I'm going to get out of your hair now. Have a good rest of your day."

He ambles out of my office and I'm left drawing in deep breaths. Jesus Christ.

I was not expecting Sam to get emotional like that. Sam is pretty amiable, but he's always been sort of standoffish with me. This change in his demeanor makes me feel really guilty all the sudden,

Have I been wrong in misleading my family about my engagement?

My hand trembles as I reach out for the cup of coffee that Wesley left for me. I heave a sigh of resignation the second I touch the paper cup.

I can't see the coffee because it has a lid on it, but I know that it's gone cold.

Swallowing, I stare at my cup for a full ten seconds before making up my mind to just walk the block down to the market and replace it. Maybe when I get back, I'll have my shit together.

Walking in the shadow of the building awnings, I head down the pier toward the market. The lighthouse rises up and blocks the midday sun. I keep my head down, half-lost in thought.

Have I really fucked up? My parents are going to be crushed when I tell them the engagement's off. And it will be off, because Pearl is eventually going to find out about me selling her property.

Part of me is willing to admit that by trying to talk Pearl into marrying me, I am attempting to bind her to me forever.

"River!"

I glance across the street to where the voice came from. There is Bishop, sidling up to me like the cat that ate the fucking canary.

Damn, I hate this guy so much. I am in no kind of mood to want to talk to him today.

I wave him off. "Not now, Bishop."

He grabs my arm, which automatically makes me jerk back. Bishop glares at me and tries to grab my arm again. "You and I need to talk."

My very short fuse blows when he grips my wrist, I struggle with him, grimacing. When I wrench myself free, his eyes narrow into slits. "I need to talk to you now," he growls.

"Fuck off."

I'm turning on my heel to keep walking when he stops me with his words.

"I'll tell Pearl that you are planning to sell her family land if you don't pay me not to."

My steps slow. I hesitate, scowling, and look back at him. "I'll sue you so fast you'll wish you'd never heard of me."

He grins. "You're fucked if Pearl finds out about your plan. From what I can figure, Pearl was probably a target for you before you even started dating."

I give him a blank look. "I don't know what you're talking about."

"I think you do. I think you're willing to pay me a cool five million dollars to cover up the truth, too."

My eyes narrow to slits. "You signed an NDA to protect me against just such a thing."

He spreads his hands. "And now I'm telling you that if you don't agree to pay me, I'll go to Pearl's Aunt Delta and tell her the whole plan."

I curl my lip. "That shows how little you know about Pearl. She would rather die than pay blackmail to you." I spit on the ground. "You don't deserve her. Just leave her and her family alone."

Bishop's face contorts. "You're going to be sorry about this, River."

Shaking my head and giving him the middle finger, I start toward the market once more. "Fuck off and die, Bishop," I call over my shoulder.

But inside, a voice screams at me.

I'm definitely out of time to come clean with Pearl about her family's lands.

Thirty-Eight
Pearl

I'm sitting in the living area of my new cabin, surrounded by luxury everywhere I look: a white leather couch, a cashmere throw blanket over my feet, a water feature gurgling faintly in the background., I'm surrounded by vibrant flowers and plants. You would think that I would be rolling around in it, luxuriating in the details that River chose for our home.

But instead, I am staring at a box that contains a pregnancy test. It's unopened and sitting on the dark wood coffee table, seeming to stare right back at me.

I try to tell myself that it doesn't matter what the test says. Either way is fine with me. Things with River are going well enough. But soon, we will reach a natural conclusion.

I don't want to marry River. I mean, I love him, but his reason for proposing is all wrong.

Perhaps I will take this test today and the results will tell me that I'm pregnant. It will be everything I have wanted for the last few months.

And yet...

It's going to spell the end of the road for me and River.

So even though I should be vibrating with excitement over peeing on a stick, I'm not.

I exhale a big breath that I didn't know I'd been holding and crack my neck. Somehow, I cannot bring myself to do it right this second.

I get up off the couch and carry the test back to the bathroom, hiding it in the chic new mirrored medicine cabinet. Just as I stow it away, a knock comes on the door.

It's obviously not my fake fiancé, because he has the code to the new keypad beside the door. I check the security camera screen and see my Aunt Delta standing outside the door. Her expression is pinched.

What on earth is that expression? My stomach flip-flops when I wonder if it has to do with the IRS calling. Could my aunt have received bad news?

Swinging the door open, I greet her. "Hey, hey. Look who it is."

Delta's lips thin. "Can I come in?"

"Of course." I step back and wave her inside. "I was wondering when you would come by for a tour."

"I'm not here to view the property, baby. I'm here because I got a text message asking me to meet here."

I look at her curiously. "Who asked you to meet them here?"

She shakes her head. "I didn't know the number. It just told me to be at your door two minutes ago."

"Huh. That's super suspicious." I squint. "Is it possible that whoever sent you that message doesn't know that I've moved? It's not exactly common knowledge outside our immediate family."

Aunt Delta checks her phone and shrugs. "Could be. Should we walk over to the trailer?"

"I don't really have any idea who is sending secret

messages. If I did, I'd send them a text telling them where to meet me." I shrug. "Let's go outside and check."

I open the door and follow Delta out onto the porch. The sound of gravel crunching under tires makes me look left. I see an ostentatiously lifted white truck coming down the lane.

My stomach drops. I can tell from here that it's Bishop driving his truck. What the hell is he doing here?

Grabbing Delta's arm, I still her and jerk my chin toward the truck. She raises her eyebrows, but says nothing.

Bishop pulls to stop before the cabin and gets out. Delta scowls at him, one hand going to her hip in a gesture that I know all too well. She's pissed.

Bishop smiles at Delta as he strolls into the yard. He avoids my gaze, which only makes my queasiness increase.

"Miss Delta," he says, stopping when he's just a few feet away. He cuts a look at me. "Pearl. I heard you moved from a friend at my construction company."

"What are you doing, young man?" Delta pops off. "I thought I was clear as day when I asked you to leave my property. There's no call for you to be running around, hiding who you are just to get an invitation."

"I did it for you. For both of you. I can't just sit by and watch you be taken in by that con man," he says, spreading his hands.

"Who?" I ask, my tone frigid. "Give us a name, Bishop. Nobody here is interested in your made-up hooey."

Bishop puts his hands behind his back and smiles. "You should know by now, Pearl. You've been shacked up with the man for months."

Delta licks her lips and looks at me. "You mean River?" she asks.

"The very same," Bishop says, solemn as a grave. "It's

time you two knew what River has been up to. See, he targeted you, Pearl."

"What are you talking about?"

He grins like a gator sizing up his prey. "Your man has sold you down the river. He's been scheming to get your land before he even started dating you. Bragged about how you were going to inherit it. And then he told me and my boss that the property was about to fall into arrears with the government. He's been scheming on this since the first day you met, probably."

My mouth opens to defend River, but Bishop's words are still reverberating through my skull. I open and close my mouth a few times, trying to figure out if what he's saying could possibly be true.

It doesn't sound like something River would do. Then again, I don't really know River, do I? I only met him a few months ago...

Delta lifts her chin and eyes Bishop. "And what do you want, Bishop?"

The smile slips from his face. "What do you mean, what do I want? It's life changing stuff!"

"Why are you telling us about this?" I ask, finding my voice. "What do you get out of it?"

"Just the pleasure of ruining your boyfriend's life." He grins.

My stomach flip-flops. This is way worse than I imagined when I first saw my aunt frowning.

Delta lurches forward, sweeping both hands at Bishop. "Get off of my land. Pearl doesn't want you back. She can do better." She flicks her hands again. "Go on."

Bishop's whole face darkens. His smile is nowhere to be found. "Y'all just going to let River Taylor swindle you? Because if that's the case, I wasted my damn time."

He swings his gaze to me. I am devastated by the news

Bishop brings, but I don't want to give him the satisfaction of knowing that. I point to his car. "You heard Aunt Delta. Get out of here, Bish."

His lip curls. "Can't believe you would pick him over me. He's trash, but because you think he's pretty, you keep him around. Disgusting."

He spits on the ground and then stalks off to his truck. I stare at it as it backs out of the narrow lane. Bishop revs his engine and takes off in a squeal of tires.

I glance at Aunt Delta, who looks at the horizon in intense concentration. She doesn't like many people. But she has an affinity with River. I hope that Bishop is really full of shit, because if not, I'm not the only one whose life is going to be ruined.

"Auntie." I tug at her hand. "Bishop is a liar and a cheater. You can't believe a word he says."

She fixes her gaze on me. "Pearl Mae, you had better get to the bottom of this. If River is really the shark that Bishop makes him out to be, you have some decisions to make." Her mouth pulls down in a frown. "If River was sly enough to target you in order to steal my land, I think he needs to get the hell off my land. I don't even know what else to say because I'm so damn mad."

Worry claws at my heart. Is that the case? God, if Bishop's aim was to sow seeds of discontent between River and me, he succeeded with a flourish.

"I'm sure that's not the case. But I'll ask River about it the second he gets home."

My aunt studies me for a second before slowly nodding. "I think that's for the best, pet."

I swallow, nodding. My head feels like it's full of thick cotton batting and my senses are dull.

Delta reaches out to me, giving me a quick hug, before she steps off the porch and walks toward her trailer.

I sit down on one of the wicker chairs on the porch, thinking over whether or not Bishop could possibly be telling the truth. Have there been any signs that River was too curious? I try to think back and my head starts aching.

Sighing, I shake my head. I would never have thought that easygoing River could be so two-faced.

I drift back inside and take a shower, hoping to clear my head. But it still feels like I'm in a fog.

When River finally arrives home, I am curled up on the couch again. This time I'm not thinking about pregnancy tests, though. I'm brooding over one question.

Did River betray me?

When he comes into the cabin, he tosses his keys on the kitchen counter and unbuttons the top button of his dress shirt. He groans and collapses on the couch beside me, burying his head against my shoulder.

It's a familiar move and an invitation to snuggle. But I stiffen and he quickly realizes that something is off. River sits up, his eyes scanning my face. "What's wrong?" He cups my cheek.

I pull away. "Bishop stopped by."

River's eyebrows jump up. "Are you okay?"

I pin him with a hard gaze. "He said that you were a con man. That you targeted me because I'm going to inherit Delta's property one day."

His eyes flash. "That's not true."

"No?" I cock my head. "So you are not trying to steal my family's land and sell it out from under us?"

He pauses for several moments, pursing his lips. His hesitation tells me everything I need to know.

"Oh my god," I whisper. Tears prick the corner of my eyes. "It's true, isn't it? Bishop was right!"

"Hold on a second." River puts his hand on my arm,

squeezing it. "Slow down for a second. Bishop has muddied the waters here."

"So you're not a con man? You didn't start a relationship with me in order to meet Aunt Delta and make her an offer?"

He licks his lips. "I did, but..."

"Oh my god!" I shake off his touch, repulsed. "You seduced me, knowing that you already had a plan to steal the land I was supposed to inherit. That's... that's awful."

"Pearl--"

I put up a hand to stop his words. "I thought you loved me, River. I thought we were going to have a baby together. But it was all just lies." I shake my head, disbelieving.

"I do love you, Pearl."

"Bullshit! That's just total bullshit."

An aggravated expression passes over his features. "Don't tell me what I feel."

I stand up, pacing away from the couch.

"How can I believe that you love me when almost everything you've ever said to me was a lie?"

River cuts his eyes at me. "Don't be dramatic."

"Don't be a traitor!" I yell. I feel flushed and unhinged.

"So, what? You're breaking up with me?" he demands.

"Yeah, River. I am breaking up with you. God, you know, you really had me fooled. Turns out I am just incredibly naive to think that someone like you would deign to be with someone like me."

"That's not fair," he growls.

"Well, neither is life. But there you have it." I cross my arms. "I think you should leave before you disappoint me again. That's the worst thing you could ever do."

He flinches. "Pearl, I think we should keep talking."

I point to the front door. "I want you out."

He stands up and studies me for half a minute. I'm shaking, full of emotions. He opens his mouth, starts to say something. Then thinks better of it and shakes his head. "I'll go to my place for the night," he says. "When you've cooled off, call me. It's not as bad as Bishop made it out to be. I swear."

I stalk to the front door, swing it open, and motion for him to leave. I am barely keeping it together and if he doesn't go right now, he's going to see me break down and cry.

He doesn't deserve to see me be vulnerable.

Tensing his jaw, he picks up his keys and walks out of the cabin. I slam the door shut after him and run to my bed.

The tears start pouring down my face the second I sink into the mattress and press my face against River's pillow.

It smells clean and masculine, just like River himself.

THIRTY-NINE
RIVER

My house is as quiet as a morgue at midnight. The housekeeper came by every week to dust and gather the mail, so at least the place is spic and span. But after living with Pearl in that tiny trailer and fixing up the cabin for her, my house seems empty and depressing.

I lie on my bed, arms flopped out wide, trying to think of what to do. How can I prove that I really love Pearl when I am actively trying to sell her Aunt Delta's land and profit wildly?

I don't know. The ceiling fan turns above my head and I try to count its lazy revolutions. I lose count after fifteen and close my eyes with a sigh.

Pearl seemed very done with me yesterday. Will she still be angry and disappointed in me today?

The doorbell chimes and I sit up. My heart begins to pound. There's no time like the present to figure out if I've completely fucked up my life or not.

When I open the door, Pearl is standing there, looking vexed. Seeing her feels like taking a Valium. It's near immediate relief and relaxation, even though that's not really appropriate for the circumstances.

Pearl thrusts a small duffel bag at me and it hits me squarely in the solar plexus. I grunt; the wind is knocked out of me and for a few seconds, I breathe funny.

"The T-shirt you insisted you need is in the bag. So is everything else you left at my place." Pearl crosses her arms.

Leaning out the door, I look both ways, checking for my neighbors. No one is hanging around, but I still beckon her inside.

"Come in. Let's not give the neighbors anything to gossip about."

Pearl rolls her eyes but steps in the door. "What more is there to say?" she asks, her tone aggravated.

Closing the door, I head to the kitchen. There's no food in the fridge, but at least I can have coffee. "Let's just sit down and talk this through."

I grab a stool and the kitchen bar and pull it out for her. She looks at me with an unreadable expression and crosses her arms. "You're awfully calm about all of this."

"I'm a problem solver, not one to dwell on things." I sit down and push a coffee mug toward her. She shakes her head.

"I'm not staying that long."

"Pearl. Come on, please."

Her mahogany eyes pin me in place. "No. You lost the right to ask me for things when you fucked me over."

Pushing out my cheek with my tongue, I heave a sigh. "I'm sorry that you're caught up in this. Okay? I am. I love you more than I've ever loved anyone."

"And yet you're still going to try to sell our land out from underneath us!"

I wince. "It's not my fault that Aunt Delta hasn't paid

her property taxes in years. At least I care what happens to your family. Most land developers don't."

"Most land developers don't cook up a lame excuse to try to date the beneficiary and agree to give her a baby, either." She tenses her jaw. "I can't believe I fell for you, River Taylor. You're going to destroy me."

"Pearl..." I reach out for her.

Fire sparks in her eyes as she steps back. Rage flares on her face. "You don't get it, do you? I don't want you. I could never want someone who lied to me like you did for months and months about something so big. It's unforgivable."

Her words echo in my head. Unforgivable. Is that true?

"I'm sorry that I deceived you. Really, Pearl. I can't change the fact that you eventually will be forced to move, one way or another. But I love you. I need you in my life. I'm begging."

Pearl's eyes mist up.

"How can I forgive you? How can I trust you ever again?"

The emotion in her voice skewers me. I can't give her up. I won't.

"It would take some time to rebuild trust. I'm not saying that it'll be easy. But you have already taken risks. It's almost crazy to think that we could just sign a contract and bring a baby into this world with no repercussions. That's a risk in itself."

She swallows hard. "It was risky. I don't know what the hell I was thinking. But I do know that you can't build a relationship off of sex. And without trust? That's the only thing between us."

"Pearl..." Her words are breaking my damn heart. "Don't leave. Please."

She shakes her head slowly. She turns on her heel and marches out of the room.

I watch her leave in silence. When the front door slams, I feel a gnawing emptiness in the middle of my being, threatening to eat me alive.

FORTY

PEARL

Looking at the pregnancy test stick, I purse my lips. I already know what it is about to reveal to me.

Because what could be more perfect than finding out I am pregnant when I have spent the whole day in bed, crying over River's betrayal? It feels fated, in a way.

When the test shows two lines, indicating that I am indeed pregnant, I have to steady myself on the bathroom sink because it feels like my legs are suddenly made of soft rubber.

Is this getting what I have always wanted? Or is my body betraying me as surely as River did?

I guess it's a bit of both.

After washing my hands and disposing of the test, I head right back to my bed and flop down face first. Curling up and pulling the comforter over my head feels essential right now.

God damn. How did my life get so fucked up so fast? Three days ago, I didn't know anything was even wrong. I still probably wouldn't know if River hadn't made a lasting enemy in Bishop.

Is it wrong that a small part of me just wishes that Bishop had kept his trap shut? Instead, he had to snitch on River. Which unleashed hell on me.

What the fuck is going on in my life right now?

After crying all morning, my tear ducts are completely dry now. I'm just miserable.

Miserable and pregnant. What a great way to start my baby-having journey.

My phone vibrates. I sigh heavily and reach for it. It's a text from Sav.

Cole says that you broke up with River. Is there any truth to that wild rumor?

I pause, uncertain what to say. I end up with, *Yes. But only because he's a backstabbing son of a bitch.*

What? is her response. *Then, where are you?*

At my cabin.

Can I come over? Or do you want to come to our house on the beach?

I think about that for a second. The whole cabin is heavy with my grief and I'm pretty sure that the air is ripe with depression. I wouldn't want cheerful, sunny Savannah to catch my depression, somehow. Plus, a change of scenery might be nice. I've cried on all the pillows and blankets here already, so it might be nice to sniffle at the beach for a couple of hours.

I'll come to your place, if that's cool.

She answers almost immediately.

Totally. Birdie is here too, FYI. But she promises to take her journalist hat off and don her friend hat instead.

Totally fine. I could use some advice from her, actually. I'll be there soon.

Twenty minutes later, I am clomping up the back stairs to the street entrance to Sav's house. The door swings open and Sav welcomes me into her house with a huge hug. I take it because I desperately need the support right this second.

"Let's grab a glass of wine and then settle down in the living room," she says. Her tone is sweet as pie but there is a distinct air of steely authority underneath that.

"Sure," I say, following her. Once we get into the kitchen, Birdie greets us.

"Hey, Pearl." She wrinkles her nose. "Did you really break up with River?"

I nod. "I had to."

She offers me a hug. I accept it, smiling at how much Sav and Birdie are alike. There may be slight differences between the two sisters: Sav dresses sweet and summery in a lacy white dress, while Birdie looks sassy in her smart green mini dress and winged eyeliner, looking for all the world like a 60s airline stewardess.

"Thanks. And yeah, I'm definitely more than a little heartbroken. I feel so betrayed."

Sav whisks a bottle of sparkling rosé out of the fridge and pops the bottle. "A little bubbly?"

I shake my head slowly. "I can't."

Sav looks up. "Can't? Or just don't want any right now?"

I exhale a long breath. "Can't. I'm pregnant. River and I were actively trying to conceive when all of this happened."

Sav sets the bottle down. "Holy shit. Okay. Back the train up."

"I'll tell you the whole story when we sit down. Go ahead and pour yourself a glass."

Sav gives me a rueful smile. "I actually can't have any either. Cole and I are waiting to tell people, but I'm pregnant too." She winces. "Sorry, was I raining on your parade?"

"No way," I say, shaking my head. "Any good news is more than welcome right now. And that means that my baby will know its best friend from birth!"

Sav squeals and hugs me. "Besties from birth!"

I smile, but my happiness feels like it's weighed down with a ship's anchor. There is nothing buoyant in me today.

"Well, I'll have the bottle, then," Birdie says crisply. "It's been that kind of week, you know?"

"I do, unfortunately," I sigh.

"Let's get comfortable by the bay window and talk it out," Sav suggests. "When you said River and the word betrayed, my stomach turned sour."

She pours us a couple of fuchsia-colored herbal iced teas and we all settle into the couch beneath the big bay window in Sav's living room with our drinks.

I nervously pick at my skirt. "Since I'm dumb enough to tell someone I barely know my problems, I told him at your engagement party that my family was struggling to pay property taxes on the land." I pull a face. "Looking back, it must have driven River wild knowing that all he had to do was sweet talk me into asking him for help."

Birdie cocks her head. "Why would you ask him for help? I know his family has money, but..."

I nod. "He's the CEO of a real estate firm."

Birdie sucks in a breath and wrinkles up her face. "That's really awful."

"Yes." I hesitate. "At least I didn't let him get me pregnant. We were, you know, *trying*."

Birdie chokes on her glass of wine. There is a minute of Sav pounding on her back and Birdie coughing loudly before they settle back. Then the attention is all on me.

"How could you think that was a good idea, Pearl?" Sav scolds me gently. "It sounds like a plan destined to end up with broken hearts."

I shrug my shoulders. "Well, hormones might have played a part. River suggested this plan, and all I had to do was say yes to it and I would get guaranteed orgasms. It seemed like a no brainer."

Birdie groans. "I know that feeling."

"I have to admit that did play a big role in my secret hookups with Cole. He does this thing with his tongue..." Sav says, staring off. After a second, she shakes herself. "What were we talking about?"

"About how River betrayed Pearl, I think," Birdie supplies.

"The thing is, I knew that River wasn't husband material. I kept trying to remind myself of that. We were supposed to each get what we needed from one another and get out." My lips twist. "I feel like such an idiot."

Birdie makes a sympathetic expression. "We all make mistakes where guys are concerned. I mean, I ended up with Dex in almost the same way. I was just snowed by his dick-hole of a father."

I wince. "I just knew that River would let me down eventually. Men always disappoint me in the end. But I was like... hypnotized. Dick-matized."

Sav balls up her mouth. "And you fell for him too, it sounds like."

Nodding, I feel my face heat. "Yep. I made some really stupid ass decisions this time."

Birdie rubs my knee. "Well, you came to the right single mom. Let's make a plan. I can tell you the main things you need to be worried about and we can go from there."

Tears prick the corner of my eyes. I thought I was all cried out, but apparently not. I look between the sisters. "Can I have a hug?" I croak.

Before I know it, I am being hugged from both sides.

"Well get through this. I promise," Sav whispers to me.

I feel the first tear begin to fall and I don't resist it in the least.

FORTY-ONE

RIVER

I sit in my truck, staring up the driveway at my parents' house. A familiar feeling of panic washes over me. I know that I have to tell my mom and Sam that my engagement is off. But damn, I don't want to see the disappointment in their eyes.

Still, I've been putting off my mom's insistence of a family dinner for almost a week now. I have to face reality.

I fucked around with Pearl and her family and now I'm firmly in the finding out phase. The sad, lonely part of this journey.

I fell in love with her. *I* messed it all up.

I have to get her back. But to do so, I think I must eat crow.

There is a rap on my window and I nearly jump out of my skin. It's Rex. He opens the door to the truck. "How long are you going to sit here?" he asks.

I slide out of my truck and hit the lock on my keychain. "Just gathering my thoughts."

"Uh huh." He gives me a skeptical look and leans against my truck. "I hear you and Pearl called off the wedding."

I make a face. "You could say that. She dumped me like a sack of potatoes."

He winces. "Ah. I assume that she found out about your plans for the Jackson land?"

I look down at my feet and kick a little gravel pile. The rocks scatter everywhere. "She did. Bishop told her about my plan. I'm going to sue him into the next century, but that won't undo what has already been done. Pearl knows everything now."

Rex folds his arms across his chest. His eyes scan my face. "Be honest with me. Did you two date in secret for two years before you got engaged? Or was that just a lie to fool Sarah and Dad?"

I rub the back of my neck. "It was for show. At least, it started that way... but I caught feelings for Pearl almost right away." I'm quiet for a beat. "I really fucked up, Rex."

His expression tightens for a moment and then he steps closer, pulling me into a one-armed hug. "Sorry, little brother." He turns me loose and sighs. "I have your back when we get inside. Telling Sarah and Dad about all of this won't be easy. But it has to be done. Just get through it."

He squeezes my arm brusquely and pulls an Atlanta Kings hat from his back pocket. My heart feels leaden as I watch him put it on. I nod.

"Thanks," I say. I start trudging toward the house. "Let's get this over with."

When we get inside, we find the family already at the dining room table, waiting for dinner to be served. They were clearly talking about me because they all fall silent when I step into the room.

I sweep my gaze around, taking in all the faces; evidently my mom has called everyone to be here, since all my siblings and their various partners are present. That can't be a good sign.

My mom looks at me, not smiling at all or even getting up to greet us. That's totally unlike her and I cringe internally.

Rex claps me on the back as we say our hellos and sit down in the last two available seats.

My mom looks down at her empty plate, her expression pinched. Sam glares at me from the other end of the long dining room table.

"River, you have some explaining to do," he says. "I had to hear about your breakup from Savannah."

Savannah looks annoyed. "I am here to give you a piece of my mind, River. What the hell were you thinking? You're a complete idiot for messing thing up to this level."

Cole puts his arm around her shoulders, wordlessly letting us all know that he has her back. It's sweet, but ultimately works against me.

Clearing my throat, I look at my mother. "I was processing what happened. But I should have called you and talked to you about it." I cut my eyes at Cole and Savannah. "I didn't realize that word of my broken engagement would spread so fast."

Cole grunts. "News flash, River. You're not the only person in the universe. Your little break up affected a lot of people. Savannah cried about Pearl being hurt. I don't like it when you make my fiancée cry."

My brows rise and my neck gets hot. "I'm sorry if the end of my relationship had a profound effect on you," I say, my tone dripping with sarcasm.

"River, be serious," my mom growls. Everyone looks at her with shock. But her eyes are narrowed on my face. "You have really screwed up this time. How could you break up with Pearl? She's perfect for you!"

Her words knock the breath out of me. "Mom, I didn't break up with Pearl. She dumped me."

"And why did she do that? Hm? She doesn't seem like she does things just because she has a whim."

"I'll tell you what I reckon," Sam says. He glares at me. "I think River wasn't honest with Pearl about his scheme to buy her family's land and she found out. Am I close?"

My face contorts. He's dead on the money, which irks me. I hate when Sam is right about any damn thing. So I change the subject very slightly.

"Look, Pearl and I want different things from life. It happens to everyone."

Cole shakes his head, glowering at me. Savannah's shoulders tense up. It was a low blow mentioning Cole's first wife Holly, but I feel like everyone is making a mountain out of a molehill over here.

Am I devastated about Pearl's decision to end things? Yes. Absolutely. But I know when I've been rejected.

I need to lick my wounds and bide my time while I figure out a new way to approach Pearl.

FORTY-TWO
PEARL

Malik looks at me as I come out of cleaning the bathroom in cabin two. I toss a roll of paper towels at him and he catches them.

"Are you sure you're okay?" he asks again. "You haven't been this quiet since that time when you were sixteen and you had mono, but you had to clean the cabins because everyone else came down with really severe cases of the flu."

I lean against the kitchen counter, trying to decide how much to tell my little brother. Malik stares at me.

"What's wrong? Something worse than your breakup with River?"

I hesitate, not knowing if being pregnant counts. It's not even in the same realm as River's knife in my back.

It's something else entirely.

"There is something, yes. But if it's okay, I'm not ready to tell you just yet." I ball up my mouth. "When I do tell you, you'll understand. I promise."

Malik's brown eyes study me for the barest moment before he shrugs. "I trust you. And I'm cheering for you, too."

I smile at him, but there is an almost palpable air of sadness. Yes, I'm pregnant... but what kind of a life will this baby actually have if I just move back into my trailer? Everything is up in the air right now, especially if the family gets kicked off the land by the IRS. There's always a spot in my mom's condo, of course. But that's not a long-term solution for raising a child.

The decisions I'm going to have to make soon have been making me lose sleep, tossing and turning at night.

Malik waves a hand in front of me.

"Anybody in there?"

My cheeks warm. "Yeah, of course. Just... thinking about what I have to do next."

Malik nods. "Okay. Well, I picked up the mail for the Vintages already. It's on the counter behind you. I'm going to run into town to meet some friends. Can you take the mail to Delta's trailer on your way to drop off the mop and scrub brushes?"

"I can do that." I bite my lip, staring at Malik. On impulse, I give him a quick, hard hug. When I let him go, he looks at me funny.

"You're making me worried that you have a terminal diagnosis or something."

I shake my head. "No such luck. You'll have to put in the work to make me leave if that's what you're hinting at."

He pins me with a searching gaze. "You're real weird today." He sighs and checks his phone. "I'm going to be late to meet my friends if I don't hurry. Are you sure you're good?"

Grabbing the mop, I give him a stiff faux salute. "I'll be fine. Run along now."

He gives me a quick kiss on the cheek and then heads out. I grab everything and pull it to the front door, locking it tight. Then I remember Delta's mail. I go back inside and grab it. It looks like a few letters and a bunch of direct mail ads for getting your AC repaired or a local pizza delivered. I shift the pile and a large manila envelope falls out. Curious, I put the letters aside and examine the envelope.

I gulp when I see that it's from the Internal Revenue Service and it's stamped 'IMPORTANT DOCUMENTS INSIDE'.

God, what could this be? I feel like there's almost no answer that's good.

My heart beats as I flip the envelope over, toying with the sealed flap. Should I open it? Aunt Delta would have a fit if I do. But then I would be in the loop with whatever the IRS is telling her.

My fingers hover over the seal. I feel like I have the devil on one shoulder, egging me on. And on the other shoulder is just a rather untalkative angel.

At the last moment, I roll the manila envelope up and stuff it in my pocket. Then I head outside again, head bowed as I fidget with the keys.

"Pearl?" comes the soft voice from behind me.

Nearly jumping out of my skin, I whirl and flatten myself against the door. Sarah Taylor is standing on the path, her arms wrapped around herself. She gives me a plaintive look. "Sorry. I didn't mean to scare you. I... I just wanted to talk. I hope that it's okay that I came here."

I feel sweat breaking out over my brow. "You came to talk to me?" I ask.

Sarah nods, clasping her hands in front of her body. "If you don't mind."

Pushing my hair back, I brush off my stretchy black leggings. Her presence here is making me anxious. After all, I've seen the luxury she lives in. I don't for a second believe she's not judging me, even if she is soft-spoken and kind.

"Why don't we sit over there at the picnic tables?"

Her smile is instant. "That would be great. I'm not going to take up too much of your time. Honestly. I just want to chat for a minute."

I force a smile to my lips and head over to the picnic tables. But my mind is going a million miles an hour.

What does River's mom want to talk to me about? I can't fathom why she thinks it would be a good idea.

When I reach the old wrought iron table, I take a seat. Sarah does too, after she brushes a spot clean. Then she looks at me.

"You know, Pearl, you're pretty special. River has never brought another woman home to introduce to the family."

My stomach sinks just a bit. "Mrs. Bennett..." I'm not sure what River has told them. Does Sarah even know that our whole relationship was fake?

"I know that River isn't the easiest man to love." She smiles sadly. "Sometimes, a tragic event that happens to a young person shapes them so much that they begin to grow around it, rather than actually healing. I don't know how much River has told you about his father..."

I sit up, interested. "Nothing at all."

She nods. "I thought so. He was pretty young when his father passed away. To my knowledge, he doesn't remember much. But when I met Sam and decided to blend our families... I think River felt a bit lost in the shuffle. He's been secretive since then, especially about his dating life."

"That tracks." I trace my finger across the whorl of wrought iron on the table in front of me. "I'm not sure what it has to do with me, though."

"I watched you two together. He has never seemed very happy or open at family gatherings. But when he was with you, he was... I don't quite know. Happier? More vibrant?"

Sarah shakes her head to herself.

"I'm not making much sense, but I guess what I'm

asking is... is there any way that you two can forgive each other? He won't explain anything except for some kind of property dispute between you two."

I want to yell that River is a no good con-man, but of course that isn't Sarah's fault. He's a big boy who makes his own terrible decisions.

How much should I tell Sarah? When she finds out that I'm pregnant in a few months, she will probably put two and two together. Is it worth hiding the pregnancy from her?

How about the fact that my engagement wasn't ever real?

I push out a long breath. River and I spent so much time lying to this woman. It's time for some honesty.

"River and I only ever had a casual relationship. The engagement was something he lied about to get his trust fund early."

Sarah's hand flies to her heart. She looks stunned. "You lied?"

I flinch. "Sort of. I never wanted to make a big deal out of things like he did. River proposed publicly without telling me beforehand. He invited my family to your house for the engagement celebration when I was trying to keep my family from knowing about the scheme. He... has a way of doing things that he knows might upset people first and asking forgiveness later, rather than just asking permission in the first place." I pause. "But we were sleeping together. And now I am pregnant."

Sarah looks shocked. For half a minute, she is silent. Taking it all in, I guess.

"You're pregnant?" she asks.

I nod slowly. "Yes. I broke things off with River after I found out that he targeted me because of the land I'll inherit one day. But I'm definitely carrying his baby."

"Good lord." She reaches across the table to me and I grasp her hand. "That is a lot. I don't know if I could overcome all of that."

I nod. "Yeah. It's not great."

She licks her lips. "Can I ask how far along you are?"

I screw my face up. "Not very. I haven't even been to my official first doctor's appointment. I am not telling anybody because it's so damn early."

"But you've told River, right?"

I shake my head. "No. I don't know how to talk to him right now without screaming at him."

That draws an unexpected chuckle from her lips. "I know just what you mean." She rolls her eyes. "You will have to talk to him eventually, though. You two are connected for life, now."

I squint. "Actually, we're not. I signed a contract freeing River from his obligation to this baby. The plan was always to raise it on my own."

Her brows descend. "You're not serious. You can't think that I will let you struggle with single motherhood like that? No way. That baby you're carrying is my grandkid."

"I'm not asking or expecting anything."

"You should be expecting a lot." She pauses. "Honestly, once River knows about the pregnancy, he's probably going to throw himself at your mercy and beg for you to take him back."

I snort. "River has a ton of dreams for his future. And I don't play into them at all. From the beginning, he told me that he plans to settle down a decade from now in a big city with someone career-minded. I don't see myself fitting anywhere in there."

Sarah leans forward and pins me with her gaze. "Plans change. Especially when there are kids involved. River is lighter around you, less self-conscious. You might have been faking an engagement, but he can't fake happiness."

I wave the idea away. "He might have feelings for me. But he isn't willing to give up his future to live here. Besides, how can I trust him again, knowing what he did?"

Sarah stares at me for half a minute and then stands up. "I'm going to tell him to apologize."

"He has apologized. It's just not enough."

"When he finds out about the baby--"

I interrupt her with a sharp reprimand. "Don't tell him that I'm pregnant. It'll only complicate matters."

She arches her brow. "When are you planning on telling him?"

"I'm not sure yet. Soon, I guess. But I would rather do it on my own terms."

Sarah sighs. "Very well. I won't tell my son that you're carrying his baby. But he will still try to beg for forgiveness, I think. Because like it or not, he loves you. I don't think he'll be foolish enough to throw that away."

I shrug my shoulders. "That's nice, but I'm afraid you're dreaming."

Her smile hardens. "We'll see about that. I won't take up any more of your time. I'll see you soon, though. I can feel it."

"Bye," I say. I watch her walk back to her SUV and drive away.

"What was that?" I murmur to myself, shaking my head.

I have no idea how I should feel after that. If anything, I'm more confused!

I shift and the IRS letter that I stuffed into the pocket of my leggings pokes me in the leg. Withdrawing it, I look at the envelope.

Not giving myself time to hesitate, I rip it open and pull out the thin stack of papers inside.

. . .

THIS IS YOUR 90 DAY NOTICE OF INTENT TO SUE. IF YOU DO NOT REMIT THE OVERDUE BALANCE OF $67,368.49, WE WILL BE FORCED TO FILE CRIMINAL AND CIVIL CHARGES PURSUANT TO MONIES OWED. WE WILL ALSO BE FORCED TO PUT THE PROPERTY UP FOR A SHERIFF'S AUCTION; YOUR FAMILY WILL HAVE TO LEAVE AS SOON AS THE PROPERTY FALLS INTO DISTRESS.

I gape at the top two lines, printed in red ink.

I have no access to funds to help her out. But if I don't do anything, it sounds like the government can take our land and Aunt Delta will go to jail. What the hell am I supposed to do with that information?

FORTY-THREE
RIVER

I'm in my office, toying with a pen while staring off into the distance, when Sam knocks on my open office door. I look up with some surprise and straighten from my slumped posture.

"Knock knock," Sam says. Without waiting for me to invite him in, he steps into the room and closes the door behind him. He waves toward the reception area. "There was no one at the front desk, so I just came on back."

I clear my throat, waving to the chairs. "Have a seat. I figured that Mom would send you or one of my brothers to scold me sooner or later."

Sam sits, his expression grave. Not a particularly good sign, if I'm being honest.

"I did come to talk to you. Your mother didn't send me, though." He presses his lips together in a thin line. "We need to have a talk about how you've been behaving lately."

I can barely repress an eye roll. "Great. Sounds like a good use of my time."

Sam rocks back in his chair. His bright blue eyes burn

into my face. "You've been an outsider since I met you, River."

Confusion snarls my guts. "That's not what I expected you to say."

He gives me a prim smile. "Ever since you first walked into my house, you were skittish as a new colt. I always felt like I was at a loss for how to reach out to you. I guess... I could've tried more. But it always seemed like you were fine. You had good grades, you had friends. It was easier to focus on my kids who outwardly needed things. Rex with his baseball games, Lucy wanting to learn how to ride a bike. But with you... you and I never had anything in common."

I narrow my eyes at Sam. "No, we didn't."

Sam frowns and steeples his fingers. "I have a lot of things I would do differently if I could do them again. But not connecting with you was a big oversight. As adults, we have a lot in common."

I cant my head curiously. "Where are you going with this, Sam?"

"Bear with me for a minute." He waves me down. "We are both cunning. We share a certain ruthlessness that makes other people nervous. But most of all, ambition burns bright in both of us. Wouldn't you agree?"

"Yeah..." I nod my head slowly, trying to guess what his point is. "We both see the world the same way, I think."

Sam appears thoughtful. "I think a lot of that comes from the same place with you as it did with me. I always felt like I didn't quite belong. Like I was outside, looking in at all the people in my life. I felt like no one cared about me. And I wondered if it might not be the case that there was just something unlovable about me. Like I was just broken."

I swallow tightly. "That's not the Sam I know."

"No." He smiles a bit sadly. "I felt that way before I met

my first wife. She was really the change in me. She helped me see that I wasn't broken. I was just an oddball."

I look down at my desk. I often feel that I am broken, or that I'm an outsider. It's a little like Sam telling me my own story. I clear my throat.

"I appreciate you telling me all of this, but what does it have to do with me?"

"We're getting there," Sam says. "Since the moment that your mom and your family moved in, I knew something was off about you. I should have taken more time to investigate. But if you remember, it was a pretty chaotic time for all of us. My attention was pulled in a lot of different directions. But that doesn't change the fact that the second I married your mom, we became family."

I tap my fingers on the smooth wood surface of my desk. "You did a great job stepping into a fatherly role for Brooks. You went to all his debates and all his swim meets. But it was obvious enough that I wasn't a Bennett. Not really."

"Your mom wouldn't let me adopt you kids. I wanted to give you my last name."

I snort. "That wouldn't have made me fit into the family any more."

He sighs. "It would have showed you that you belong here, River. You always have. I should have pushed for adoption more. It would have been a way to signify that you were one of my kids." He picks a speck of lint off of his shirt. "Because you are one of my kids, River. I know I don't say it enough, but I love you. I care about whether or not you are about to burn your whole life to the ground."

I roll my eyes. "My current predicament has nothing to do with you not paying enough attention to me as a child."

"I think it does." Sam stabs his finger into my desk. "You needed to know that you belonged to my tribe. I let you down. And now you're seriously about to screw up your chances at having a happy ending with a girl you love." He raises a brow. "You love Pearl, don't you?"

My face grows hot. "Desperately."

"Well, then you're going to have to do something to try to fix this situation before it is too late. But first..."

Sam unzips his jacket and pulls an innocuous file folder from his jacket. He slides it across the desk to me.

I look at him, a little confused, and open the file folder.

PETITION FOR ADOPTION is splayed across the top. I look back at Sam, my brow furrowing. "What is this?"

"A first step. River, I know there is no going back in time to correct my mistakes. But going forward, I'm going to treat you as though you were my son from birth. Brooks, too. That should start with you getting all the benefits of being a Bennett. And continue with me helping you work out favorable terms with Ray Kendrick to give Pearl's family a big chunk of money as part of their agreement to sell their lands. It's not the best outcome, but it's the most favorable to Pearl's family, now that we are this far down the rabbit hole."

I don't quite know what to say. "You don't have to do any of this," is what I come up with.

"I do. You're my son, River. I want what's best for you."

I suck in a deep breath and look down at the form because it's easier than enduring Sam's gaze. If I signed this form, I would finally be one of the Billion Dollar Bennetts.

I stare at it for several seconds before I look at Sam. "Can I think about it?"

Sam's lips twist with a flash of humor. "Of course. It's there for you to think about forever, if you want." He exhales. "I think we have bigger problems to deal with at the moment."

I can't stop staring at the contract, so I close the folder and break my gaze.

"You're worried about Pearl?"

He bobs his head. "I am."

I stand up and walk over to the window, peering out at the lighthouse in the distance.

"Do you think I have pushed her away?" I ask, my voice going to gravel.

"Hard to say, son. I don't really know her like you do. But I know some information about the property tax lien."

My head snaps around. "What kind of information?"

He smiles. "I heard that Delta Jackson owes less than seventy-five thousand dollars. So if I were a romantic guy, I would find a way to gift that amount to my beloved. The only string I would attach to the gift is that Delta has to sell the land. She obviously struggles to pay the taxes."

"And the property is in disrepair." I purse my lips. "I wonder if Ray will work out a deal that affords them a ton of money."

"Ray will be more than fair. But I was thinking about what I would want if the deal were being made on my behalf."

I arch a brow. "And?"

"I would push for a minority ownership stake in whatever is being developed. Even one percent would probably be tens of millions per year."

My heart starts beating fast. "Would Ray go for that?"

"I think he'd love it. You just paint a picture of him as a benefactor that allowed a Black family that's owned the land here for a hundred years to continue on owning a piece for a hundred years to come. Between that and offering to lend Pearl the money to pay the IRS--"

I hold up both my hands to stop him." I think we're way beyond that. I'll cover it and if Pearl takes me back, that'll be money well spent."

Sam scratches his chin. "Are you planning on using the money in your trust fund to cover that?"

I shrug my shoulders. "Yeah. It's the only money I can get my hands on right now. Unless you say otherwise, I guess..."

"No, no. The money is yours. I just wondered if that wasn't going to put a dent in the money you were going to personally invest in this project."

I make a face. "There will always be more projects. But I only have one shot to get Pearl back."

"Atta boy." Sam nods. "I'll fill in any gaps in funding. You just have to sweet talk Ray."

My stomach fills with lead. "Right."

"It'll be fine. Just use an upbeat tone and keep emphasizing that he'll save a piece of historic property from falling into the hands of outside developers. That's Ray's soft spot." He pauses, then zeroes in his gaze on my face. "I wouldn't encourage you to talk to him if I didn't believe in you."

I push out a breath and nod. I believe him, but the prospect of talking to Ray Kendrick and asking him for a favor has me rattled. I pull myself together. "Okay."

"Okay." Sam stands up, a tight-lipped smile on his face. "Just remember. You're my son. Bennetts can do anything they put their minds to."

I nod. "Uh... yeah. Thanks."

Sam eyes me for a long minute. "You've got this, son."

And with that, he lumbers out of my office. I sag into my chair, rocked by all the things that have just been revealed.

Forty-Four

Pearl

The bell above the diner door jangles, slicing through the sizzle of the grill and the soft burble of conversations. I glance up, my hand halfway to pouring coffee into a chipped mug.

When I spot him, I freeze. River stands there, six feet three inches of pure trouble, wrapped in an expensive blue button down and dark slacks that probably cost more than most peoples' weddings.

"Hey," he says. His voice sounds as smooth as the top-shelf whiskey he prefers.

It's been days since we last spoke. Yet his presence still sends a shockwave through me and rattles my composure.

"River, what are you doing here?" The words tumble out, sounding more bitter than I intend. This man knows how to unravel me, but I can't afford to let him see that.

Not now. Not after everything that's happened.

He steps forward, his gaze locked with mine, a strange vulnerability flickering in those ocean-blue eyes. "I need to talk to you."

I look to my left, where there are restaurant patrons occupying the booths and the countertop. The restaurant isn't slammed right now, but neither is it dead in here. River probably didn't even think about that before he strode in here. "I'm working," I say. "I still have bills to pay."

I expect River to give me a petulant look. But instead, he glances around me. His gaze lands on Gem, who is just coming out of the kitchen. "Gem, do you mind if I borrow Pearl for a few minutes? It's important."

Gem looks between us and nods. "Of course you can."

Putting my hand on my hip, I toss River a mulish expression. "River, I swear. You have no concern for anyone who isn't you."

He swallows hard, ducking his head. "Please, Pearl. Come with me. If you don't like what I have to say, it'll be the last time I bother you." His plea is almost a whisper, rough and gravelly. It makes me shiver.

I set the coffee pot down with a clatter, my heart pounding against my ribs. Every instinct screams at me to say no. I should tell him to leave me alone. But there's this aching curiosity in my heart. This hope that maybe, just maybe, he's got something worth hearing.

Even saying yes to this tiny demand of his prickles across my skin. It feels like I'm already giving in to him. But I can't say no. "Fine," I murmur. I slip my order pad into my apron pocket. "But this better be good."

We weave through the tables and I catch the curious glances from regulars. They know River; everyone in town does. The wealthy bad boy who swept me off my feet only to drop me into a mess of heartache and secrets. He leaves lively gossip in his wake wherever he goes.

My hands tremble slightly as I push open the back door and step outside. The cool air is a welcome relief from the diner's warmth and buzz. River follows, shutting the door behind us with a soft click that feels oddly final.

The last time we stood here, things were entirely different. There was a lot I didn't know.

It was a sweeter time.

"Talk," I demand, crossing my arms. As if such a gesture can build up a barrier against whatever River's about to say.

He takes in a deep breath and runs a hand through his perfectly styled hair, making it stand on end in a way that would be comical if my stomach wasn't tying itself into knots. "All right, Pearl." He shakes his head. "God, I think I'm nervous. That's what you do to me."

River pulls out a picnic table bench with a scrape against the gravel and gestures for me to sit. My fingers trace the rough edges of the wood, focusing on the table in front of me to keep myself grounded.

"First off," he starts, still standing. His voice strained, as if the words are being dragged out of him, "I owe you an apology, Pearl. A big one. I am so sorry. I didn't mean for you to find out this way."

My expression contorts and he is quick to add, "I shouldn't have done it at all. I have more regrets about it than you know."

"Uh huh. What way would you have preferred I find out that you were selling me out for thirty pieces of silver?"

River frowns. "When you told me about the IRS and your family's land, I should've offered my help right away. Again, Pearl. I am so sorry."

I stare at him. I study the tension in his jaw. The way his hands clench and unclench. The apology hangs between us, heavy and unexpected, but somehow it doesn't soothe the tightness in my chest.

It doesn't change the past. And honestly, I'm not sure it changes the future either.

He stops pacing and meets my eyes, his own filled with a turmoil that echoes the churn of emotions inside me. "There's more. You deserve the whole truth." He takes a hesitant step closer. "Part of me, a selfish part, was afraid you wouldn't agree to let me help."

A bitter laugh escapes me before I can stop it.

"And..." River continues, hesitating as he searches my face, "I liked the idea of you being my fake fiancée too much. It was thrilling. Having everyone believe we were deeply in love made my life more interesting."

"Even though we weren't?" I can't help the edge in my voice, or the way my hands ball into fists on my lap. Games of pretend might be fun for people like River. He has everything he could ever want already. But for people like me, these games can be dangerous. They can threaten everything.

"*Especially* because we weren't in love," he admits. There's a raw honesty to his words that stops me cold. "It felt like... control, I guess. I was tricking everyone into believing that I'd found love. The one thing they never stopped bugging me about. And when you said you'd do it, under one condition..." He trails off, looking at me with an intensity that makes my heart skip a beat.

"Getting pregnant," I say softly, filling in the silence. "That's what I needed from you."

"Right." River nods, his throat working with a swallow. "You are incredible. You make me feel so damn wanted, too. How could I refuse?" He thrusts a hand through his hair roughly. "It felt too damn *good* to be so fake. I didn't even realize that I had messed up until it was all slipping through my fingers. And then I fell for you... and ruined the whole plan."

His confession hits me like a storm deep in the heat of summer. It's sudden and overwhelming and makes me gape.

I stare at him, trying to decipher the emotions swirling behind his sapphire blue gaze. Is this just another tactic, another play in his bad boy handbook to get what he wants?

"Please, Pearl," he pleads, pinning me in place with his eyes. "Hear me out. I have a plan to fix this mess. For your family and for *us*."

Us. The word hangs in the air, fragile and potent. For a moment, I let myself imagine that it could mean something real. I can't let him know that I'm feeling this way, so I fold my arms across my chest.

"You have until Gem comes out to fetch me," I say with a sigh.

River leans against the picnic table, his hands braced as if he's holding himself steady. The late afternoon sun filters through the leaves above us, casting a mottled pattern of light and shadow across his face. I can tell this isn't easy for him. But there's a determination set in his jaw that tells me he's not backing down.

Not yet. Not this time.

"Addicted," he breathes out, the word hanging heavy between us. His gaze pierces me through and makes my breath come in shallow pants. "I've been addicted to you since the first time we slept together, Pearl. I can't stop thinking about you. And the worst part is, I don't even want to try."

My stomach knots at his admission. The spicy memory of our first encounter sends a wave of heat through me despite my resolve to stay angry. Anger has its place.

And right now? That place is firmly between us. It's a dense barrier of hurt and betrayal.

"Your feelings are intense, River," I say, keeping my voice steady. "But intensity doesn't erase what's happened. My Aunt Delta will lose the property, River. That's on you."

He flinches at that, his expression twisting with regret.

"I know," he says. It almost sounds like he's choking on the words. "I was wrong. I was so damn wrong, Pearl. I was selfish. I got caught up in having you any way I could. Even if it meant stretching out our game of pretend. I think I figured that if I had you for another month or two, I'd finally get you out of my damn system. But I think it's actually had the opposite effect."

I want to believe him. Falling into the familiar comfort of his arms and forgetting the world sounds so blissful. But the real-life consequences of his not being honest with me will affect more than just me.

"Nice words don't pay off debts or mend trust," I remind him. My heart twists with the urge to give in. "You might be feeling crazy, River. But I'm the one left picking up the shattered pieces of my life."

He steps closer, close enough that I can smell the cologne that clings to his skin. It's a scent that's become painfully, heart-wrenchingly familiar. "Let me help pick them up," he urges, his voice low and persuasive. "I can fix this, Pearl. Just let me try."

I consider the man before me. River seems flawed and desperate. And yet somehow, he is more honest than he's ever been. River may be used to getting his way, but right now he looks like someone who knows he's gambled everything and might have lost more than he ever could have bargained for.

The practical side of me wants to shut him down. My instinct is to protect the remnants of my wrecked trust.

But still...

There's something in the way he stands before me, raw and open, that chips away at my defenses.

"Actions."

He raises a brow. "What?"

"Not words. Actions." I fix him with my gaze. "If you're

serious, then prove it. Until then..." I leave the sentence unfinished, turning away from the intensity of his gaze, though every fiber of my being screams to look back.

My hand is on the diner's back door, ready to push it open. I can already see myself escaping back to the chaos of my shift.

But River's words stop me. "I didn't just come here to say sorry, Pearl."

"No?"

I freeze, fingers curling around the cool metal handle. The hum of the diner fades into a distant murmur as I turn to face him.

His eyes are earnest, pleading. "I came with a plan."

"Plans don't pay bills," I retort, but curiosity gnaws at me. The idea that River Bennett, with all his power and wealth, might actually have something up his sleeve that could help is both infuriating and intoxicating.

He leans against the diner's brick wall, arms folded as if he's preparing for a siege. "Your family's debt—"

"Is none of your business," I cut in, but he's relentless. "I never should have told you about it in the first place. Especially since I know now that you were just looking for a way into my family."

Bitterness makes me grimace.

He takes a deep breath.

"Seventy-five thousand dollars. I know that's the figure hanging over you all."

I snort. "And? Like I said, it's for us to figure out."

"What if I want to clear your debt?"

My breath hitches. Seventy-five grand might as well be seventy-five million to us. But there's a catch; there's always a catch with River.

That's how I got into this damned situation in the first place.

"Before you snap at me, just hear me out," he continues. "All I need is for Aunt Delta to agree to sell the land."

Anger flares hot and bright in my chest.

"You think throwing money at the problem is going to make everything okay?" I spit the words out.

River steps forward, blocking my path with his presence alone. "No, I don't. But it's a start, isn't it? It gives your family a fighting chance."

His proximity is disarming. His scent wraps around me and evokes so many memories. Happy memories at that. My resolve wavers as I look up into his searching eyes. He's not just offering an apology.

He's laying down his weapons.

"Let me do this, Pearl. Please."

The word hangs between us, heavy with implications and unspoken promises. I want to march right past him. I need to put distance between his desperation and my aching heart. But the Pearl who would've walked away doesn't seem to exist anymore. Not after everything that's happened between us.

"Fine," I relent. My voice is barely a whisper. "But this changes nothing between us. Understand?"

"Understood," he says. Relief softens the hard lines of his face.

River leans across the table, his fingers stretched out toward me but not quite touching. His gaze is intense, urging me to listen, to really hear him this time.

"I've been talking with Ray Kendrick."

My eyebrows shoot up. "Ray Kendrick? The same Ray Kendrick who owns the Atlanta Kings?"

"Yeah, that one," River confirms. "If Aunt Delta agrees to sell the land to him, she won't just be walking away with a check. She'll retain a one percent ownership stake in the land. And not just the land, Pearl. Anything that gets built there."

I'm momentarily speechless, which is a rarity for me. "You mean...like, if they build a..."

"A resort, yes. She'll have a stake in that too. Perpetual income. That's a piece of the pie forever."

"She wants it to be wild forever," I say slowly.

"I don't have control over that. I can lend you money to pay her debt off, but I can't make her pay in the future. You could be back in this spot in two years. What I'm offering is so much money that you'll never have to even think of how much anything costs for the rest of your life. For your kids' lives. For your kids' kids' lives."

He spreads his hands wide to encompass just what he's offering.

It's a lot to process. A part of me wants to dismiss it as another one of River's grand gestures. Is this just his privilege talking? But the sincerity in his voice is hard to deny.

"There's more." He pauses, making sure he has my full attention. "I've made sure that a portion of land will be set aside. For your family to build new houses on."

"New houses?" I echo. "River Taylor... are you telling me you've thought of everything?"

His brow furrows.

"Everything but how to make you believe I'm serious about this," he admits. A half-smile that doesn't quite reach his eyes appears on his face.

The audacity of his plan is staggering. It's not just money. It's security. It's stability. It's a future for my family that doesn't involve renting out aged cabins or waiting tables. It's almost enough to make me forget why I was mad at him in the first place.

"Show me the paperwork," I demand. That's my practicality kicking back in.

River doesn't hesitate. He pulls folded documents from the inner pocket of his tailored jacket. He smooths them out in front of me, pointing out where Aunt Delta's signature would need to go.

"Right there," he says softly. "With one signature, this whole nightmare would be over."

I scan the pages. Each line of legalese screaming promises and potential betrayals. But as I look closer, I see River's influence all over it. There is the clause about the 1% ownership. On the next page, there is the allotment of land for housing. It's all there, in black and white.

"River..." My voice trails off, the weight of his offer leaving me breathless.

I lean back, trying to take it all in.

"This plan is quite generous. But what's in it for you? Where's your cut?"

He shakes his head. The corners of his lips turn up in a wry smile that doesn't quite mask the pain in his eyes. "Pearl, the only cut I want goes to Delta. There's nothing else I'm taking away from this deal."

"Nothing?" I ask. I'm not willing to let him off the hook that easily.

"Absolutely nothing," he affirms, stepping closer. His presence is like a live wire that sends a jolt through the air between us. "Except maybe a second chance with you."

"River, you can't be serious." My voice barely rises above a whisper. "After everything..."

"Look at me, darlin'." He reaches out and squeezes my hand. His hand is warm against my cool skin, grounding me. "I love you. I need you. You are the only thing that matters. You're my safe harbor in any storm."

"River..."

"Say you believe me, Pearl." His plea is soft. But it seems to thunder loudly in the quiet of the evening.

"But River," I start, my voice trembling with the weight of uncertainty. "What about all those things you said? About not wanting to tie yourself down? You always talked about marrying some high-powered executive, someone who matched your ambition. I'm just... I'm just not her. Never will be."

River shifts, leaning his hip against the weathered wood of the picnic table, and there's a vulnerability in his eyes that I've never seen before. It's like he's pulling back a curtain, giving me a glimpse into a private room where his deepest fears are on display.

"Pearl," he says, his voice lower now, intimate and laced with something that sounds a lot like pain. "My whole anti-marriage spiel? It was a front, a defense mechanism. I was scared of being left behind. I was a coward because I thought that no one in their right mind would choose to be with me. It was easier to pretend I didn't want it than to admit that maybe I'd never be loved like that."

"Oh, River..."

"Let me get it all out," he says. "I was terrified that if I let myself want anything too much, I'd end up alone. So I convinced myself I didn't need love. It was a faraway idea, always on the horizon. But that was before you. You've changed everything, Pearl." His hand finds mine across the table, warm and solid. "You make me want to be brave."

His touch sends a shiver skittering across my skin. The River before me is a far cry from the polished, untouchable billionaire. He's human, he's flawed, and he is reaching out for connection.

"River..." I start, my voice softer than I intend.

He squints and winces. "I don't like the sound of that."

It's hard not to crack a smile.

"You have to know how sweet you can be. When you're not being bossy, that is." I reach across the table, mirroring his earlier gesture. I enjoy the texture of his skin against mine. "You are lovable. You are loved."

His gaze is fixed on mine. "My family doesn't count. Hell, no one else really does." He brings my knuckles to his lips and kisses them briefly. "I want you to love me."

"I do love you. But—" She looks torn. "I was already taken for a fool once."

River stills my lips with a fingertip. He looks at me, a storm brewing in those deep blue eyes.

"Give me another chance, darlin'. I swear on everything I am, I will not let you down again. I will be relentlessly honest and the one you can always count on." His voice is fervent, a solemn vow spoken from the depths of his being.

The intensity in his gaze anchors me. For a moment, all the noise of the world fades away until there's just the two of us. I breathe out, feeling the air being sucked from my lungs.

Is that enough for me to take a chance on him? I will have to take the risk of a lifetime.

"River," I whisper. My throat tightens as tears well up in the corners of my eyes. My vision blurs, but I see him clearly. "To hear you say that..." I blink, tears beginning to fall. "That's all I ever wanted."

River shuffles back from the bench and lowers himself to one knee. The gravel crunches under his weight, a stark, grounding sound that jolts me back to reality.

"River, what are you—"

"Shhh," he silences me with a gentle intensity. His hand reaches out to take mine. His touch is warm and certain. His eyes don't waver from mine. "Pearl, I want to do this right."

He takes a deep breath, almost as if he's drawing strength from the earth beneath him. "Will you marry me? This time, I want you to say yes to me for real. We can marry with just our mothers present. No fanfare. No pretense. Just us."

My heart races, pounding against my ribcage like it's trying to break free. This is what I've yearned for, isn't it? The real deal, not a game or a strategy. But the hesitation coils in my stomach, tight and insistent.

"River, I..." I start. The words seem to stick in my throat. A million thoughts crash through my mind.

Can I trust this feeling? Can I trust him?

"Take your time," River urges softly. He stays on one knee, his gaze never leaving mine. There's a vulnerability there I've never seen before, a raw hope that makes him look more approachable, less like the unattainable bad boy and more like... well, just *River*.

"River, before I say yes, there's something you need to know," I whisper. My pulse thrums in my ears. Every beat of my heart reminds me that I could be throwing away everything by springing this on River right now.

But he needs to know.

"Anything," he says. His thumb rubs small, comforting circles into the soft flesh on the back of my hand.

I take a shaky breath. "I'm pregnant."

His hand tightens around mine. But he doesn't stand. He's steady as he promised he'd be.

There, in that quiet space behind the diner where life seems to stand still, I see something in River that I recognize from the stories my mom told me about my dad. That charm, that intensity. But I see something else looking in River's eyes.

Commitment. The promise of steadfastness that I've never known, but I've always *needed*.

"Really?" His voice is a mix of wonder and awe, like I've handed him the most precious gift imaginable. "You're pregnant?"

I nod my head.

"Really."

River's eyes widen and he takes a deep breath. Is he trying to steady himself? Or is he already backing out of his promise?

He cups my face and gives me the biggest, most unexpected grin.

"I really hope you're telling me so that I can get excited. Because I am so fucking excited, darlin'. Just think about it. A little kid with your eyes and my cheekbones running around here."

He says it with such awe. I swallow, unbidden. "You mean it, River?"

"I can't wait," he stammers out, his voice thick with emotion. "I can't wait to be a real dad to our baby."

Tears well up, unbidden, and spill down my cheeks. This is everything I never knew I needed. My heart swells so much it hurts, the ache of years without this kind of pure affection bursting at the seams. The love I missed as a kid seems to flood into this single moment and it fills every hollow space left by my departed father.

"River," I choke out. My voice cracks. "You don't know how much that means to me."

He reaches up and brushes away my tears with the pad of his thumb. His touch is gentle, almost worshipful. "I mean it, Pearl. I swear. I mean every word."

I sniffle. I had my life planned out. But I have to laugh at myself for thinking I could've ever parented this kid alone. It was a crazy idea, wanting to skip the partner part of having a baby. A piece of the puzzle I thought I could just leave out.

I never let my missing father matter. So why should a father be needed in my own baby's life? It makes sense after a fashion. But looking at River now, I see how selfish that decision would have been. It would have affected me, him, and most importantly, our child.

"God, I was being foolish," I admit, the realization

washing over me like a cold shower. "It's a day of admitting we were wrong, I guess."

"We're doing this together now." River squeezes my hand. "You're not alone anymore. That is, if you'll say yes to my marriage proposal."

I take a deep, stuttering breath. The weight of his gaze anchors me to the spot. The intensity in those sparkling blue eyes screams something that words can't capture. It's raw and it's real. And it's so much more than I ever thought that handsome River Taylor would bring to my doorstep.

"River," I start. My voice is gritty with emotions. "I've tried to picture my life without you. Believe me, I've tried." I pause, my heart hammering against my ribcage as if trying to meet his halfway. "I don't just want you in my life, babe. I *need* you. And not just because of the baby but..."

I falter, searching for the right words.

"Because you love me?" he finishes for me.

"Because I love you," I confirm. "Because you're my soulmate. And I can't bear the thought of facing the rest of my life without you."

River does not disappoint me.

His smile widens like he's just won the biggest gamble of his life. But despite his work, this isn't about contracts or properties. It's about us, messy and imperfect and fucking beautiful. He takes my hands in his as if he's holding something precious.

"Then marry me, Pearl. For real this time. No pretenses. No conditions. Just us. Together, building a life, and having a family. What do you say?"

My heart skips a beat. I'll remember this moment for eternity.

"Yes," I breathe out.

The word is a promise.

A vow.

An anchor.

"Yes, I will marry you, River Taylor."

He kisses me, his lips claiming mine with a passion that sets my soul ablaze. Every kiss we've shared before pales in comparison to this one. His arms wrap around me, pulling me closer. I melt into him, surrendering to the pure energy that courses between us.

FORTY-FIVE
RIVER

The aroma of steeping tea does little to calm the nerves bouncing around my stomach. Across from me, Pearl's eyes are wide and searching. Her great aunt Delta's are narrowed with skepticism. The weight of the family's future rests on the shoulders of this moment.

And despite my usual confidence, it feels like a crushing boulder pressing down on me.

"Delta," Pearl starts. Her voice is steady but I can hear the ripple of anxiety beneath it. "I know you're worried about what will happen next time the taxes come due."

The old woman snorts, a sound that somehow carries both derision and sadness. "Do you have a way to solve that little problem?"

My hand slides across the table, pushing the contract towards her. It's thick because it is packed with legal jargon designed to protect and serve.

"Read this," I say. "We've structured a deal with Ray Kendrick. It's more than generous."

"A deal? What kind of deal?"

"Aunt Delta," Pearl says. There is a pleading undertone

to her words. "You can't afford to keep the property as it is. We all know it. This deal is your one way out that doesn't make you homeless." She taps the contract. "This is an offer from Mr. Kendrick for at least fifty million dollars."

Delta's jaw drops. "My land is worth that much?"

"Yes, auntie. You would know that if you ever so much as talked to any of the people that have offered to buy it."

Delta picks up the document, glaring at me. She sniffs and then pulls out her reading glasses. Her fingers are surprisingly nimble as they flip through pages. She reads, "Fifty million now, plus an annuity? What's the catch?"

Pearl leans forward, her hand resting on her stomach. The secret is still an unspoken promise between the two of us.

"There's no catch," she says. "We will need to make some changes, though."

Delta's gaze sharpens. "Like what?"

"The cabins and trailers... Auntie, they will have to go. But this land here..." She spreads her hand over the map I lay out for her. "These acres stay with us. We can build, start fresh. Our family will have a place... a place to belong."

"New beginnings without losing our roots," Delta murmurs, nodding slowly. She touches the paper, almost reverently, tracing the lines that mark the Jackson family legacy.

"Exactly," Pearl says, her smile blooming like a promise. "We hold onto the heart of it all. The current structures on the land can't stay. Mr. Kendrick wants to buy the land and build a resort on it."

Delta snorts. "I can't believe you think our family's land should be a goddamned resort."

"Delta, the thing is," I start. Pearl cuts me off with a sharp look.

"Let me do the talking." She turns to her great aunt and

folds her hands neatly on the table. "This isn't just about River or me. It's about our future. Our family's future. You have to see that. You can't leave me or anybody else owing thousands of dollars on this property. It simply isn't *fair*."

Delta leans back in her chair, the lines on her face deepening. It makes her appear like one of those wise trees you see in storybooks. "And how can you even sit next to that man after what he pulled? If it were up to him, I think he'd take the land and leave you behind, honey."

I flinch at the accusation, but Pearl remains calm. She spreads her hands out on the table. "I won't lie, Aunt Delta. I'm still mad as a hornet at times," she admits. In the space her admission leaves, I feel a fresh pang of guilt. She shakes her head. "But anger's a luxury we don't have right now. And he's not just River, the man who made a mistake. He's also the father of my child. I think some space can be made for him at the table, regardless of whether or not he messed up."

Delta stares off into the distance for a minute. "Your child?" she repeats.

I nod, feeling the weight of responsibility settle heavier over my shoulders.

Pearl reaches across the table, taking Delta's weathered hand in hers. "Yes, our baby. A little baby carrying your DNA. And we need to think about what kind of world we want to bring that baby into."

Delta's eyes shift between us. For a moment, there's silence except for the creaking of the old house settling. I can almost hear the gears turning in her head as she weighs her options. It's her legacy against the raw deal life has handed her.

Delta nods slowly. The lines etched deep in her face seem to soften just a fraction. There's a flicker of something like understanding in her eyes. "I see," she murmurs.

It takes everything in me not to react. I just nod once.

Pearl clears her throat. Her eyes lock with mine for a brief second. She bites her lip for a second before saying more. "We would like our future children to know that they will always have a home here."

Delta lets out a long breath, the fight in her gaze softening. "I never had children of my own," she murmurs, almost to herself. "But I suppose it's time for the next generation to take the lead."

Tears glisten in Pearl's eyes as she stands and moves around the table. She wraps her arms around Delta in a fierce hug. "I love you, Auntie."

I watch the two women. Feeling like an intruder on a private moment, yet also part of something much larger than myself.

Pearl turns to her great aunt with a plea shining in her eyes. "River has a plan, Auntie. He's willing to clear the property tax debt. The whole seventy-five grand of it."

"Seventy-five thousand dollars..." Delta repeats the sum like she's tasting each syllable, bitter and sweet at the same time. "All right," she finally says, her voice carrying the weight of generations. "Let's do this."

Relief floods through me, swift and sweet, but I mask it with a nod, playing it cool. "I'll take care of the payment right away. You'll have the IRS off your back by sundown."

"Thank you, River," Delta says, and there's no mistaking the gratitude in her tone. It's a new chord in the symphony of our complicated relationship, one I hope to nurture.

"Always," I swear. "We're family now."

"And always take care of Pearl," Delta commands, her gaze piercing into mine.

"Nothing is more important to me," I swear, my voice unwavering. "Delta, I know you have every reason not to trust me. But I love Pearl. You can always trust that I will do whatever I can do to make her happy. Listen, I messed up *royally* here. You have my permission to kick my ass every other Thursday for the next five years because of it. "

Delta picks up the check, her fingers brushing against mine. Her eyes linger on my face for a heartbeat longer than necessary. "You're a good man, River Taylor," she acknowledges. The corners of her mouth lift into a semblance of a smile. It's not quite warmth that passes between us, but it's close enough to respect.

"Now, what are y'all planning on naming this little one?" Her eyes flicker to Pearl's still-flat belly, where our future kid sleeps.

"We haven't decided yet," I admit. The words come tumbling from my lips as my hand instinctively moves pat Pearl's stomach.

Pearl shoots me a look and I ease my hand away from her stomach, sliding it around her waist instead. She flashes me a quick smile of appreciation.

"Delta's a strong name," Delta suggests, a mischievous twinkle lighting her eyes. "Just saying."

A chuckle escapes me, warm and genuine, as I glance at Pearl.

"Maybe."

She leans in to kiss me and all thoughts of naming the baby vanish in a puff of smoke.

FORTY-SIX
RIVER

My heels dig into the cool sand, anchoring me as if I'm bracing against a storm that's yet to come. The ocean breeze tugs the hem of my slacks. The scent of salt is heavy in the air. My pulse thrums through my veins. It's a relentless beat that wars with the restless shushing of the ocean.

"Easy, River," I mutter to myself. I scan the horizon where blue sky meets a deeper blue sea. The families from our two worlds are about to collide. A billionaire playboy turned hopeless romantic, waiting for a very practical diner waitress.

Is it a match made in heaven? For most people, it would not work. But I love Pearl so much that if I think about her for too long, I get short of breath. So in our case? *Yes*.

A car door slams and my head whips around. The first of the guests appears. She's a lone figure shuffling across the sand, eyebrows knitted together in confusion. It's Aunt Glory, her usually tense expression giving way to bewilderment. She spots me and waves a hand.

"River! Where is Pearl? And what's all this?" Her voice

carries over the sound of the waves with a touch of irritation lacing her words.

I stride over to her, clasping her hand with both of mine. Pleading with my eyes for her to approve. "Trust me, Aunt Glory. You're going to want to be here for this." Pasting on a nervous smile, I try to appease her. She is Pearl's family, after all, and she affects how Pearl will feel about today.

"Aunt Glory?" She narrows her eyes at me. "Today's the wedding, then?"

She looks at me, searching my face for a hint of today's events. But she finds only earnest excitement. With a resigned huff, she claps me on the shoulder and heads toward the makeshift gathering area.

One by one, our families arrive. They trickle onto the beach, each face a reel of the same emotions. Confusion softening into surprise, speculation turning into curiosity. Lucy and Savannah arrive, their eyes as wide as can be. Cole follows them and stops briefly to shake my hand. He moves on quickly because more of my family begins to turn up.

"River, you sly dog," my brother Rex says. He gives me a quick one-armed hug. As he pulls away, a smirk appears on his face. "What's the big secret?"

"All will be revealed." I tap the side of my nose. The conspiratorial gesture has him chuckling and shaking his head. Then I move on.

"I never thought I'd see the day when River Taylor got us all riled up for anything other than a wild party," Eden teases, her laughter ringing clear and bright.

Her dickwad boyfriend is nowhere to be seen. *Hallelujah.*

"Today we redefine 'wild', Eden," I reply. My palms are sweaty.

I hug my mom and clap Sam on the back, ushering

them into the party. Rhett jogs in right after them. Brooks shows up a little late and goes to hang near Eden, whispering something in her ear that makes her snort. Malik and Crisanto show up next holding hands.

But before I can focus on that, Pearl's mom arrives. I make sure to greet her, and walk her over to the small confluence of people that mill around, chatting. Pearl's mom is the final guest that must be here for a surprise wedding.

As I watch both of our families assemble here on this stretch of sand, something settles within me. The playboy, the pragmatist, the boy with a faraway dream of what someday could be like. They're all me, different chapters of my own book. Today, I will write a new chapter.

One that's been waiting to be written since the day Pearl walked into my life. God, I can't wait until she arrives.

"Welcome everyone," I finally call. My gaze sweeps over the gathered crowd. "Thanks for coming. Especially under such mysterious circumstances. I think you'll be glad you came."

The sun dips lower, casting a golden sheen over the beach. My mom seems to spot Pearl first, because she turns with a gasp.

Every muscle in me tightens. I turn my head.

That's when I catch sight of her. Pearl glides across the sand like she's walking on clouds. Her blush rose, off-the-shoulder lace dress makes my jaw drop. It has a loosely fitted top and midsection that stops just below her bellybutton and flows outward in layers of sheer pink and lace. It emphasizes her curves and trails behind her, lifted by a gentle breeze.

I have an odd moment where time seems to slow down. She's drifting toward me, her black hair pinned up quite elegantly. Then she lifts her eyes, looking at me with a knowing smile.

My hand goes to my heart. It seems to have exploded in my chest. I'm fairly certain that I'm now dead and somehow being rewarded in the afterlife.

"Wow," is all I can muster as she reaches me. Her smile is brighter than the glints of diamond light shimmering off the ocean behind us.

"Hey," she whispers, coming to a stop before me. Her eyes skate over my suit jacket and up to my face. Her smile widens.

God damn, it feels good that she approves of me. All ego aside, it's nice to be looked at as an object of desire by the one woman that makes my world keep spinning.

I catch her hand, my fingers rough against her soft touch. Her fingers are so delicate. They slip neatly between mine. "Are you ready for this?"

Pearl's eyes meet mine, her gaze steady, brimming with certainty.

"With you by my side, I feel ready," she responds. Her words wrap around me like a promise.

It's my turn to smile now. I let it spread across my face, unguarded and full of love. I clear my throat. My heart pounds like a drum against my ribs. When I speak, my voice is strong and clear.

"All right, everyone!" I call out. I clap my hands.

The attention of the crowd has been pinned squarely on us this whole time, but now they fall silent. I give them a sarcastic little bow. "If you'll all follow us, we have a little surprise in store."

There's a communal shuffling of feet. A symphony of murmurs and rustling fabric sounds as they exchange looks. Aunt Glory's eyebrows hitch up like she's just been offered a front-row seat to the greatest show on earth.

Rex tilts his head, the smirk still playing on his lips. "Surprise, huh?" he says, rubbing his hands together. "Lead the way, River."

With Pearl by my side, I guide our procession across the sand. A trail of Bennett-Taylors and Jacksons are in tow. Each step feels deliberate, significant.

"Ready to shock them?" I lean in. My lips brush the shell of Pearl's ear.

The grains of sand shift beneath our feet as Pearl and I weave a path down the beach to the waiting reverend. The rhythmic crash and hiss of waves is loud in my ears. I sneak glances at Pearl, noting how the sunlight plays off her dress. She's an ethereal figure, a goddess held down to the ground only by the touch of my hand.

"Look at you," I murmur. "You're so damn gorgeous."

Pearl's laughter is light, like the sea breeze that toys with strands of her hair. "Speak for yourself, River."

The reverend stands waiting against the backdrop of the restless ocean. A prettier picture could not be bought.

"Here goes nothing," I whisper. I say it more to myself than to Pearl, though she hears me. Her lips turn up and she gives my hand a reassuring squeeze.

"Welcome, everyone." I turn to face our families, my voice carrying over the shore. "Thanks for coming this far. I plan to make it worth your while."

Aunt Glory's eyes dance with curiosity. Rex's smirk has bloomed into a full-fledged grin. Sam's gaze is heavy with something like pride. My mom is fully weeping already.

"River, what's all this?" Aunt Delta's voice is tinged with trepidation.

"Trust me. You're going to love it."

I turn and take Pearl's hands. They are cool and steady in mine, a stark contrast to the warm rush of blood pulsing through my veins. I glance down at our interlocked fingers briefly before I lift my gaze. When I meet her eyes, I feel like I'm freefalling into a warm pool of hazelnut chocolate.

Diving, willingly. I just have to say the words. I open my mouth and somehow, the vow begins to pour out of me.

"From the day you walked into my life, you challenged every idea I had about what it meant to be happy. I had never really thought of what it meant to be truly... *fulfilled*."

Her smile is subtle, but it shines brighter than the sun overhead. The guests lean in, listening closely to catch my voice over the waves.

"The first time we met, I didn't even know that I was looking for you." My voice cracks a little. It sounds raw and real. "I am so glad that you gave me a chance. I know... I know that we had a rough start. That's my fault. But from here on out, I'm going to be everything you need."

A murmur ripples through the crowd. But I'm looking at those mesmerizing pools of mahogany. It's the squeeze of Pearl's hands that lets me know that I've hit the right chord.

She takes a deep breath and gives me a smile.

"Today, I'm vowing to be your partner. Through thick and thin. For better or for worse. Together, we'll stand the test of time."

She says through a sheen of tears, "Today, I take you as my husband. My one and only dance partner for the rest of our lives. Together, we'll be the happiest couple on earth."

The reverend steps forward, his presence gentle but firm. "Now, by the power vested in me, I pronounce you husband and wife. You may kiss the bride."

Time stutters to a stop as I lower my lips to hers. The taste of her is electric and it surges through the both of us. Someone whistles enthusiastically. When we break apart, our families on the beach burst to life with cheers and applause. I see my mom out of the corner of my eye, her face the very picture of elation. Tears stream down her cheeks unchecked as she holds onto Sam for dear life.

Yeah, she didn't get to plan the wedding. But the look of radiant happiness on her face right now means a lot to me. When Mom finally leaves Sam's side, it's to come straight to me, cupping my face tenderly.

"River!" She sniffles. "You really did it. You got married."

I wrap an arm around Pearl, pulling her close. "Yeah, Mom, I really did."

My mother offers Pearl a hug and Pearl takes it with a pleased grin.

This is perfect. Better than I could've dreamed.

Pearl grips my mom's hand and squeezes it. "There's more."

"More?" My mom looks like she's going to faint. "What more is there?"

She turns slowly to our assembled families. I watch the soft sweep of her hand as it finds its way to her stomach. It's flat as a board still. But Pearl rests it there like a whisper of things to come.

"We have one more surprise!" Pearl calls out.

The chatter ceases, the air charged with anticipation. Every eye is fixed upon us. More specifically, everyone looks at Pearl.

"We're expecting a baby," she announces. Then she blushes and beams at the same time.

God, I do love her.

A collective intake of breath ripples through the crowd. Then it turns, erupting into exclamations of sheer astonishment and joy. My heart swells beyond the confines of my chest. Pearl's gaze meets mine. I see nothing shining there but love and excitement.

The family crowds in, ready for hugs and well-wishes. Aunt Glory muscles her way up to us with her boisterous laugh. She opens her arms and drowns us both in a hug. "Congratulations, you two!" she bellows loudly.

"Thanks, Aunt Glory." I chuckle, squeezing back just as fiercely. "We're pretty excited."

I cup my hands around my mouth and shout to be heard over the crowd. "If you will all join us at the Cape Bistro, we'll have a little feast."

Leading Pearl from the beach is something special. For the first time, I hold my wife's hand.

My wife.

I'm drunk on that idea for whatever reason.

After we settle in on the patio of the bistro, I can finally relax a little bit. It feels unreal to me still. The buzz of conversation is a gentle hum in my ears. The salty tang of ocean air on my lips. Sam's hand lands on my shoulder, heavy and reassuring.

"You've made me proud, son," he says, his smile broad.

"Thanks, Sam." My voice is thick with emotion. I have to work to keep it steady. "It means a lot coming from you."

His grip tightens for a moment, a silent echo of the sentiment. Then he releases me and steps back. The pride in his eyes doesn't wane.

If anything, it burns brighter. Sam isn't a man of many words. But his few words carry the weight of entire conversations.

"You know, your mother and I are always here for you both," he says. He nods toward Pearl, who's laughing at something Savannah has just said.

"Wouldn't want it any other way," I reply. He nods and moves back to my mom. I'm left thinking that I'm still getting used to hearing compliments from Sam, but it's starting to grow on me.

There's a soft touch on my arm. I turn to see Aunt Delta. Her silvering hair is caught in a loose bun, wisps escaping to frame her face. It is etched with lines of a life well-lived. She's always been like another grandmother to Pearl.

Now, by extension, she will be one to me. At least, I hope so.

"River," she begins. She takes my hand between her trembling ones. Her eyes shimmer with unshed tears. "Take care of my grandniece and that little one." Her voice cracks, but it's strong with conviction. "You've proven yourself to be a good man."

"Thank you, Aunt Delta." I squeeze her hands gently. "I promise, they're my world. Nothing comes before them."

"Good." She nods, satisfied. She pulls me into a hug that smells faintly of lavender. "Keep that promise and you'll live a good life."

"I plan to," I assure her.

When she steps back, there's a twinkle in her eye that tells me she believes me. "Go on, then," she says, releasing me. "Your bride looks like she needs a dance."

I chuckle. I catch Pearl's eye, signaling with a tilt of my head toward the makeshift dance floor we've set up on the sand. Her grin is all the confirmation I need.

"Careful," she teases. I draw her close, our bodies aligning with ease. "Don't drop me now, my bad boy billionaire."

"Never," I promise. I spin her out, then back into my arms.

"Ready to show everyone just what we're made of?" I ask. "I mean, dancing-wise."

"Always," she replies.

FORTY-SEVEN

PEARL

FIVE MONTHS LATER

The first sliver of morning light creeps through the curtains of the house we finally settled on and bought together. Stretching like a contented cat, I can barely keep a grin from my lips. I'm already basking in warmth that has nothing to do with the sun. River's arm drapes over my waist like a living band of heat securing me to him.

River Taylor is *mine*. My heart flutters in my chest. It's not from the lingering traces of last night's passion. No, it's but the simple, overwhelming joy of his presence.

If it's possible, I think I might be drunk on love.

"Good morning, darlin'," River murmurs without opening his eyes. His voice, hoarse with sleep, sends shivers down my spine. It's crazy how even half-awake he can make me feel like I'm the only woman in the world.

"Morning," I whisper back. I wiggle in his embrace so we are face to face. The stubble on his jaw is just heavy enough to be enticing, not scratchy. It matches the tousled look of his hair. He's as perfect as a picture.

Also, to go back to what I was thinking only a moment ago, River Taylor is my husband. *Mine.*

"Did you sleep well?" His eyes flutter open now. His open eyes revealing pools of such intense blue they rival the most beautiful gemstone.

"Like a dead thing," I admit. "And you?"

"Never better," he says. He pulls me closer until our bodies touch. "I dreamt about you, actually."

"You lie like a dog." I playfully tap his chest, but my heart swells with affection. "I look like I've swallowed a volleyball."

He laughs and his touch wanders down to my belly. He rubs gentle circles into it.

"I promised you that I would never lie to you again. And I've held to that promise." His thumb traces the line of my jaw. "I love waking up beside you. That's another true thing."

His fingers dance along my spine, drawing lazy circles that send sparks across my skin. In these quiet moments, before the world demands our attention, we exist in a bubble of contented bliss.

"Let's stay like this a little longer," he whispers against my lips before claiming them with his own. And really, who am I to argue with such a persuasive argument?

The gentle nudge against my palm pulls me from the cocoon of River's embrace. I ease out of bed. Stretching my arms with a peculiar feeling of laziness that comes from a night wrapped up River's arms. The slight kick from within my growing belly elicits a gasp from my lips.

"Whoa!" I press my hand over the top of my swollen stomach. "Easy there, karate kid."

In response, our daughter kicks me two more times in the left kidney. My face contorts and I stifle a curse.

"Well, good morning to you too," I whisper to the baby. I shuffle to the full-length mirror. The woman staring back at me is transformed so much that I don't fully recognize her. Every curve is more pronounced. Her belly seems to shift although she stands still.

The swell of my belly is *mesmerizing* to me.

"Have you been busy while we were sleeping?" I ask the baby. "Or dozing, I guess. You don't really let me sleep anymore."

I direct my words to the gymnast performing flips inside my body. My hand smooths over the fabric of my nightgown

The creak of the door heralds River's arrival. I turn around and give a start of surprise. I hadn't even heard him get up. His silhouette framed by the strong shafts of morning light that shoot across the bedroom floor. He carries a tray laden with breakfast. The scent of fresh jasmine tea rises to greet me. Setting it down on the bed, River sidles up behind me, wrapping his arms high up on my expanded waist.

"Hope you're hungry," he murmurs. His lips tracing the shell of my ear, sending shivers down my spine despite the warm air.

"Starving," I admit. Whether my craving is for the food or his touch, I'm not entirely sure.

He guides me back to the bed and the plush mattress welcomes us back. I sit, my legs splayed out wide. River sits beside me and his thigh presses against mine. He picks up a slice of toast, butter glistening under a veil of strawberry jam, and holds it to my lips.

"Open wide," he teases.

I roll my eyes and oblige, taking a bite. It's extremely

sweet followed by the buttery flavor that bursts across my tongue. As I chew, he pops a piece of melon into his own mouth. He seems a bit restless and watches me with eyes that are a late-night sky.

"Delicious," I sigh, reaching for a strawberry. But instead of eating it, I bring it to his lips. "Your turn."

He accepts the offering, his teeth grazing my fingertips in a fleeting kiss that promises more. We continue this dance of feeding each other, laughter mingling with the clink of cutlery, each bite an unspoken vow.

"River, this is..." I start. Then I pause and shake my head. "I wish you could know what I'm feeling right now."

"Darlin'." He leans in, giving me a brief kiss. "Your emotions are really apparent. You are too easy to read."

"For you, maybe. Other people seem to find it hard."

"They obviously aren't trying." He cants his head with a wiggle of his eyebrows.

I lean back against the pillows and a contented sigh escapes me. River's hand finds mine, his thumb drawing idle circles on my skin.

"So, what's the game plan for today?" he asks.

"Let's tackle the nursery," I say, excitement bubbling up inside me. "I can't wait to see the crib that my family made for me in there. Plus, we need to find the perfect spot for Sarah's quilt."

"Ah, yes, the infamous crib. I can't believe that they just gave that behemoth to your Aunt Delta. It must've taken five people to build it," River says with a playful grin.

I fold my arms across my chest. "It was made by my relatives. It's definitely going in the nursery."

"I'm just teasing you, darlin'. It'll be the centerpiece of the nursery, no doubt. My mom said that having someone buy or build a crib for you is actually a huge honor."

I eye him. "It is. Not to mention it's insanely beautiful. I know that it's all wrapped up in protective bubble wrap right now. But I can't wait to put in in the nursery."

"Well, we'd better get to it, then."

He squeezes my hand. I smile and get up. We make our way to the nursery, a room that just screams *potential*. The walls are a blank canvas, awaiting my personal touch. Flat-packed boxes of unassembled furniture beckon us. I roll up my sleeves, ready to dive in. But before I can even consider one of the boxes, River halts me with a gentle tug on my elbow.

"Wait, Pearl. I've got something for you first." The corners of his mouth twitch. He's excited.

He strides over to one of the big square boxes. With a flourish, River lifts out an assortment of baby items. And not just any items, either. Each toy and decoration is adorned with images of adorable aliens and tiny UFOs.

"River!" My hand flies to my mouth. Tears prick at the corners of my eyes. "This is…" I shake my head. "It's perfect. You know how much I love this stuff."

"I know, I know," he says softly. He wraps an arm around me and pulls me into his chest. "I wanted our baby to have an interesting hobby, just like her mom."

"Thank you," I whisper, leaning into him.

"Anything for you and our mini cosmonaut," he murmurs, kissing the top of my head. Together, we begin arranging the furniture. Soon, the nursery slowly transforms from a room into a realm of starry-eyed adventures.

I'm standing on my tiptoes, pressing a decal of a shooting star onto the pale blue wall. River sidles up behind me, his hands finding my waist.

"Imagine," he whispers, his breath tickling my ear. "A baby with both of our features gazing up at these stars. She'll be dreaming of galaxies far, far away."

"Easy there, Han Solo." I can't help but giggle, leaning

back into his solid chest. "Maybe she'll be an astronaut. Maybe she'll chart a whole new world."

"Speaking of that..."

River steps back, reaching for a hefty book that's been sitting on the edge of the crib. It's bound in soft baby blue leather. He hands it over.

"Before you thank me, I want you to know that my mom suggested this. She'll probably ask if I took credit for her idea." He sticks his tongue out.

"I'll let her know that you gave her credit." I leaf through it. Each page is full of information, references, and credentials of a different potential nanny. I arch a brow at River. He forestalls me with a hand.

"My mom suggested that we'd need some help," he says, watching me closely. "Someone who can step in when you need to catch your breath or close your eyes for just a moment. Moms are great, but these nannies are reliable too. Plus, you might eventually decide to go back to work somewhere."

"River, this is..." The word *thoughtful* seems too small, too simple for the man who stands before me, always thinking ten steps ahead. "I don't even know where to start."

"We have time," he assures me, his voice steady and sure. "We'll find someone perfect, someone who will love our baby almost as much as we do. Perhaps several someones."

"Several? There's only one baby!"

He shrugs and gives me a sly smile. "We'll see about that."

"You're crazy."

"I take it as a personal challenge to make it happen." There's a wicked glint in his eyes and he rubs his hands like a cartoon villain.

I can only shake my head.

I thumb through the glossy pages, each nanny's smiling

face blurring into the next. Credentials in fine print swim before my eyes. Degrees in early childhood education, mastery of three languages, proficiency in infant CPR. I'm awash in a sea of qualifications, feeling the swell of decision fatigue.

"Look at this one," River says, pointing to a page. "She speaks Italian. Think of the lullabies."

"Maybe," I muse. "Do you think it matters more that they can cook or that they have a gentle soul?"

"Both." He grins, brushing his thumb over my swollen fingers. "But the soul part is non-negotiable."

"Your mom will want someone with a sterling silver résumé," I say, half-joking. But I also know the weight her opinion carries.

"True, she's got high standards," he admits. His tone is light but carrying a shadow of old expectations. "But she's just excited. So is your mom. They're going to spoil this little girl rotten."

"An army of grandmothers at the ready," I chuckle, closing the book with a

"Let's take a break, yeah?" he suggests.

I wrinkle my nose. "I needed a break as soon as we got in here."

He tilts his head and stares at me dubiously. "Is this too much? I told you I would bring in a decorator to do all of this."

"No way. I want to be able to tell our daughter that I did everything in her nursery." I push some stray hairs back out of my face. "I do want to go sit down, though."

We step out onto the porch and I grab a seat. My aching feet and the twinge in my back lessen as I sit back in the rocker. The salty breeze immediately kisses my skin. I inhale deeply and let peace begin to seep into my bones. My eyelids threaten to slide shut.

"Close your eyes," River's voice is a whisper.

"Already way ahead of you, baby." I shut my eyes and the world goes dark.

I hear the soft clink of metal first. What is he up to? Then I feel the cool slide of a chain around my neck. My heart trips over itself, anticipation coiling tight. "You can open your eyes now."

I look down and gasp with delight. Dangling from the silver chain is a tiny flying saucer pendant that is studded with diamonds. I touch the pendant with a finger.

"River!" It's a breath, a laugh, and a sob. "It's perfect!!"

"Thought you'd like it," he says. He leans close and his words are a warm buzz against my ear. "A little bit of the extraterrestrial for my starry-eyed wife."

"Why today?"

"Today is the eleven month anniversary of you agreeing to be my fake fiancée."

"Really?" I squint, doing quick math. "No, it can't be."

River throws up his hands. "Okay, you got me. The real story is that I saw it in a shop's window and I thought you would love it."

I chuckle.

"I do love it," I turn, wrapping my arms around him. "For this. For everything."

"Always, Pearl." His arms encircle me, strong and sure. "You're my world."

My lips find his with an urgency that speaks of raw, unbridled emotion. Our kiss is a dance. A push and pull of need and affection that leaves us both breathless. His hands roam over my back. He pulls me closer until there's no space left between us, only the heat we generate together.

"Can you believe we're going to be parents?" My voice is thready. The enormity of it is all making my heart race with anticipation.

River's hand finds mine. Our fingers intertwine with a comforting squeeze.

"Every time I think about it, it feels more surreal," he admits. Then he chuckles lightly. "But then I feel a kick, and it's like, 'Yeah, this is happening.'"

"You should switch places with me. One day, she was still. The next day, she's like... ready for me to know she's a whole ass living human being."

River smiles. "God, I hope that our baby doesn't get your mouth. It'll only cause us trouble."

I stick my tongue out at him. "We're ready for her, though. We'll handle whatever chaos she throws our way."

"More than ready." His thumb strokes the back of my hand.

"What about midnight diaper changes and lullabies off-key?" I tease, remembering how he'd once confessed his fear of not getting the hang of those dad duties.

"Especially those," he grins, leaning in to press a kiss to my forehead. "I'm imagining teaching her to negotiate her bedtime. Or to close her first real estate deal before the age of ten."

"Let's aim for potty training first, Mr. CEO." I can't help but laugh, picturing our daughter as a mini mogul in diapers. "But honestly, I just want her to know she's loved. No matter what."

"Hey," River's voice turns serious. He props himself on one elbow, looking down at me with an intensity that heats my cheeks. "You didn't have the best examples of men in your life. But that's in the past. We're going to shower this kid with so much love that she won't know what to do with it all."

"Promise?" My question is half-playful, half-plea.

"Cross my heart." He draws an invisible X over his chest.

We fall into silence again and let the stillness of the room envelop us. The quilt Sarah made whispers tales of heritage and warmth from the rocking chair. The alien-themed mobile above us whispers of adventure.

"Think she'll dream of space travel?" I muse out loud. My gaze fixes on the tiny UFOs dangling from the mobile over the crib.

"Definitely. With a mom who has her head among the stars, how could they not?" River jokes, nuzzling into my neck, sending a cascade of goosebumps down my arms.

Thank you so much for being a part of this romance! I'm so grateful to have a romance reader like you! As a special token of my gratitude, I've written a bonus epilogue with your favorite characters – River and Pearl. Read it here.

I must admit, I have really enjoyed writing this series. Billionaire romance is my number one love, but forbidden is a close second. I'm over the moon to write some tropes and stories that I've been longing to write for years. Get ready for me to weave a web about baby bargains, fake fiancés, best friend's little sisters, and more!

The Bennett-Taylor siblings each deserve a happily ever after... and Rex and Birdie are next! Keep your eyes peeled for their spicy romance! Turn the page for a taste.

Epilogue
Pearl

After the baby is born

"Where are we?" I ask.

River gives me a grin that would stop traffic. It almost knocks the breath out of my chest.

I glance at River out of the corner of my eye. He's full of surprises. His hand is warm in mine, his grip reassuring, as if he can sense the swarm of butterflies doing somersaults in my stomach.

"And here we are." he says, half-turning to flash me that heart-stopping smile. The one that promises mischief and something slightly more meaningful, all at once. "Surprise! I know it's been a while since we have done anything but play with the new baby. Tonight, real life is on pause. Mom has our daughter. All we have to do is relax."

"Just for the night?" I ask. "I don't want to leave the baby for long."

He kisses my knuckles. "We'll be back at our house in the morning."

My lips twitch, but my eyes also fill with tears. I dash away my tears. "You spoil me, River."

He squeezes my arm. "You deserve every penny I spend on you, darlin'."

I give a little shiver. It's automatic; River has trained me to practically pant when he uses my pet name. I lick my lips.

"Let's enjoy the view first. We can explore later," he suggests.

I raise my brows and shrug. "Fine by me."

He lets go of my hand for a moment, leaving me adrift. Soon, he returns with a pair of blankets tucked under his arm. "Thought it might get chilly," he says.

River walks me through the house. Everything is gleaming, marble and chrome and warm wood. I stifle a laugh.

"You unpacked!" I say.

He nods. "I wanted everything to be perfect for my darlin' wife."

My heart squeezes at the pet name.

"You did great," I assure him. "Just having furniture is a big step up."

"That's a solid burn." His lips twitch with amusement. "Come outside. There's more I want to show you."

He stops at a pair of French doors and throws them open. I stop and stare at the beach just a few hundred yards beyond where we stand.

Talk about a million-dollar view! I step out onto the back porch. I'm too consumed by the sunset on the water to really think of much else.

River spreads the blankets across the wooden planks of the deck beneath our feet. One blanket lies smooth and inviting, while the other gets bunched up at the corners, forming a makeshift pillow.

"You are always prepared," I note, impressed despite myself.

"Comes with the territory," he replies. He smirks and a hint of that CEO authority seeps into his tone. I love that about him. There's a playfulness there too. He issues a challenge as he pats the blanket next to him. "Join me?"

I would go anywhere this man leads me.

I settle onto the soft fabric, my eyes on him. The warmth of the day still lingers as the setting sun paints the sky in streaks of orange and purple. River sits beside me, close enough that I can feel the heat from his body. My chest constricts when I see the way his eyes darken when they meet mine. It's attraction, sure. But it's also something rawer.

Something like the vows he said to me at our little beach wedding. My mouth kicks up at the corner.

"Nice view," I say. I'm not looking at the ocean, though. My gaze is only focused on him.

"Best in the house," he agrees.

I know he's not talking about the water either.

River's gaze locks onto mine, a cool sapphire tone that threatens to drown me here and now. My heart is a hummingbird trapped within the cage of my ribs. Its frantic beat feels like a drumroll. Building to the moment unfolding between us.

"Beautiful," he murmurs. He hooks a wisp of my hair with two fingers and tucks it behind my ear.

River is a magician and I'm desperate to watch his next trick.

He leans in closer, the air charged with electricity. With every tiny shift, every breath he takes, the anticipation builds.

"River..." His name is a prayer on my lips. It's a plea for something I can't quite define.

"Shh," he soothes. He cups my cheek, rubbing his

thumb lightly over my lips. My mouth opens and I have the damnedest time keeping my eyes open.

Between my legs, a thrill of excitement makes me press my thighs together.

A kiss, hot and searing, lands on my lips. I kiss River back as the world tilts on its axis. Our mouths move together. Every brush of his lips feels like magic against my ever so sensitive, bee-stung lips.

My hands roam across the broad expanse of his back. They trace the muscles that ripple beneath his shirt. I can feel River; his solid presence presses against the softness of my own form. He groans, opening his mouth more. He only kisses me with a greater fervor.

His touch ignites lines of flame as he strokes his hands along my waist. I suspect the fires will never fully be extinguished.

Not while we are both alive and sucking each other in with every breath.

"God, Pearl," he groans against my mouth. "My little wife."

I revel in the sound of the word, roughened by desire from his throat. *My little wife.* His words give me chills and tear a demand from my lips.

We tear each other's clothing off, clawing, unable to stop kissing for long enough to properly undress. His touch slows at my bra and panties. He takes them off with careful, respectful grace.

I don't want that, though. I'm not just the mother of River's child. I'm his wife. I want to embody that, to take that meaty bone and suck it down to the marrow.

"You won't break me, baby," I tell him. I take one of his hands and grab my right breast hard. "I promise that I'll say something if I can't handle anything you give me."

River's sapphire gaze studies me. "Are you sure?"

"Trust me. Trust yourself," I whisper back.

He nods silently. "I'll try."

That makes me kiss him again. The salt air is thick with tension and the moon bears silent witness to our naked lust. It's been too long since we have touched with the actual intention of making each other burn. The most we have done in this vein is to masturbate next to each other before collapsing in a pile of exhausted limbs.

But not today. This moment is all about reconnecting and rekindling the fire that always lays smoldering between us, ready to burst into full-fledged flames at any second.

He pushes me down on my knees with no gentleness. I suck in a breath.

"River, I'm always so hungry for you. Do you think it will always be this way?"

His face creases in a faint smile. "I think it will be, darlin."

My knees sink into the blankets River has spread out, their texture rough against my skin, grounding me in this moment of surrender. He stands before me. He looks like an Adonis backlit by the dim lights spilling out from the beach house. His chest heaves with anticipation and his burning eyes lock onto mine.

"Show me what you can do, Pearl," River's voice is a low growl. It is laced with the husky timbre of lust that sends ripples of pleasure down my spine.

His words aren't just a request. They're a gauntlet that he lies down before me.

Eager to rise to the challenge, I reach for him. My fingers curl around his heat. The power I wield in this act sends a thrill spiraling through me. I look up at him, seeking permission in his gaze. In it, find nothing but dark, unbridled yearning staring back at me.

God *damn*, he's fucking sexy. And he's only interested in *me*.

How did I ever get so lucky?

"Please, Pearl," he utters.

Nothing more, nothing less. His words sink into my soul and brand me.

I take his thick cock into my mouth. The taste of him is still as intoxicating as the finest wine. Or cinnamon whiskey, if you're an afficionado.

I explore, experiment, and tease. My tongue laves his length and my body aches faintly. Sucking his dick is the prelude to pleasure for me. Doing it well is a particular point of pride.

It's a skill I have kept on call for the last few weeks when I have felt too tired from staying up with our newborn to want to be touched. River is still every bit as horny as he was before the baby came and sometimes I feel like rewarding him for trying to keep things romantic between us.

River's hands find purchase in my hair. He guides my head with gentle pressure. I love feeling his excitement. I let him know that I am enjoying myself by gripping his ass and moaning around his cock.

His breath hitches. It's a sign that I'm sucking his cock well. I get lost for a minute in the rhythm we create. Giving everything I have, taking everything he has for me. It's intoxicating.

"Fuck, Pearl... just like that," River's voice breaks. I love it when he is about to lose it.

But he soon stops my ministrations. He pulls out of my mouth and draws me up to stand.

Our roles reverse as quickly as the ocean tide.

"My turn," he murmurs. "Be a good girl for me and be still."

A rivulet of anticipation drips down my spine and

pools somewhere low in my body. His lips trace a searing path down my neck. He sucks and marks me with bites kisses that feel like a branding. With every caress, he worships my body as if it's sacred ground. I'm lost to the sensation.

I'm in awe of being adored like this, without reservations.

"River," I gasp. I barely recognize my own voice. It's laced with an urgency that borders on desperation. He answers with a hum against my skin. The vibration sends another surge of pleasure rippling through me.

Heat builds within me. A fire is being built, sparked by River's relentless tongue and teeth touching my every sensitive spot.

Suddenly, I have to have River inside me. Pressing him back gently, I guide him down onto the bed. He goes without resistance or us having to communicate anything out loud. We both know where the ultimate goal lies. How we get there is more or less beside the point.

I mount him, fisting his thick cock and bringing to my wet, hot pussy entrance. He gasps as I begin to impale myself inch by torturously slow inch. His cock stretches me out, filling me to the brim. I feel like I'm worshipping him, taking my time and being surrounded and filled by him at the same time. Fucking him, rocking my hips back and forth slowly, is almost a religious experience.

"You feel so good, darlin," he purrs. "So fucking wet for me."

"I need to feel you move inside me," I breathe out. "Please, baby. Give me everything. Don't hold back."

He grips my hips and starts to move beneath me, driving his cock up into my desperately needy pussy. My eyes roll up in my head briefly.

But I force them to remain open so I can see the pleasure

on my man's face. His expression is open and raw. His eyes bore into mine.

My hips move with a fervency that matches the pounding of my heart. Each thrust pushing me closer to the edge of reason. His hands grip my hips, guiding me, encouraging me to abandon all restraint. I comply willingly. I'm driven by a hunger that only he can satisfy.

"River," I pant. "Tell me what you feel, sweetheart."

He gazes up at me, his eyes dark pools of desire. I see reflected in them the depth of our connection. It's not just our bodies that are entwined

Our very souls are enmeshed in a way that is concrete and permanent.

"God, yes, Pearl. I love when your greedy little pussy takes what it needs like that," he rasps out from below me. "Fuck me like it's the last thing you'll ever do, darlin."

His praise spurs me on. I ride him harder.

I'm lost in the moment, lost in him. I honestly forget that we're in a physical space and time for about half of our sex session. But when a flicker of movement catches my eye, I start. Strangers are strolling along the shoreline and their laughter carries faintly on the breeze.

I freeze. Should I try to cover myself?

What if they see? What if they laugh? My body doesn't look the same as it did before my pregnancy and I've definitely got some insecurity about it.

"Hey, hey..." River's voice is a steady anchor amidst the swirling eddy of my fears. "Look at me, sweetheart."

I look at him, swallowing. I don't have to speak my fears aloud. River knows. He always knows.

"Don't mind them. They don't matter. It's just you and me here, Pearl. Only us." He runs his hands through my hair and then down to my breasts. He shapes the flare of my hips.

"Look at yourself. So fucking beautiful," he murmurs. "And all mine."

His hands move to my hips. His touch isn't restricting but it's reassuring, as if he's grounding me to this place.

I want to believe him.

"Are you sure?" My voice is a fragile whisper.

"Absolutely." There's no hesitation in his reply, only certainty.

God, the love burning bright in his eyes right this moment takes my breath away.

With that thought, my anxieties wane. I move again, slowly rocking my hips at first. He meets each rock with a thrust of his own.

"Let them watch," I pant, a rebellious spark igniting within me.

River's response is a low chuckle and is rich with approval. "That's my girl."

River slips his fingers down between our bodies and finds my clit. He moves his fingertips in quick circles, sending rivulets of heat spiraling through my core. His eyes lock onto mine, a mischievous glint playing within their depths. It's as if he knows exactly which strings to pull to orchestrate the melody of my arousal.

"Let go, Pearl," he murmurs, his voice a velvet command that vibrates through me. "Give it to me."

I surrender to the crescendo building within me. It's fueled by River's knowing touch. He knows me. He knows how to give my body pleasure. The edge blurs. There's just my silted breath, just his touch, just the pulse of need throbbing between us.

The pleasure peaks, crashing over me like the waves against the shore. A cry escapes my lips, uninhibited and raw. River smirks. It's a testament to the ecstasy that he draws out of me with such ease. Then he bites his lip and lets go. He thrusts a few final times before his breath catches. I grip his waist as he comes. I feel his cock pulse inside of me, no doubt releasing thick streams of milky white cum deep inside my pussy.

I groan with satisfaction at the feel of everything ending as it should. We belong together. I rock my hips gently, keeping River seated inside my pussy.

As the intensity of my release ebbs, the figures drift away, mere ghosts against the vast canvas of the beach. River and I, still entwined on our blanket-covered sanctuary, share a knowing smile. It's one of those smiles that speaks volumes, a shared secret that wraps around us, reinforcing the bond that has grown stronger with each stolen moment.

"Seems we've gone unnoticed," he teases, his chest rumbling with laughter against mine.

"Good," I reply, my breath still catching in my throat. "Because I wasn't quite ready to share you with the world."

River's arms wrap around me, pulling me flush against the solid wall of his chest. The warmth of his bare skin radiates through the thin fabric of my dress, sending a wave of comfort and desire coursing through me.

"You," he murmurs, his lips brushing against the crown of my head. "Are absolutely perfect, darlin'."

I laugh. It's a light, airy sound that floats on the air. "Perfect, huh? That's a dangerous word."

"Only if it isn't true." His hands glide down my back, tracing the curve of my spine with gentle reverence. "I know that you are. If we had an audience, they would know it, too."

"River!" I swat at him playfully. The absurdity of the idea sends another ripple of laughter between us.

"Only kidding. I mean, unless you're into that." His voice is thick with amusement. I can feel his stubble against my cheek when he laughs.

"Let's stick to our own private world for now."

"I would complain, but that means I still get to fuck you, so..." He pulls a face. "You won't hear a word out of me."

"Oh, is that right?" I laugh and kiss him.

"Let's stay like this forever," he murmurs.

"Forever sounds perfect," I agree.

Forty-Eight

Birdie

I stroll into Savage Pizza, my heartbeat already pounding. See, I'm going to ask famous baseball player Rex Bennett for an exclusive, in-depth article where I shadow him for a few weeks.

And if he says yes, I have a shot at replacing the editor at the newspaper I work for. Can you imagine? Me, in the coveted editor's chair! It's been my dream for years.

All I have to do is get Rex to say yes to the article. I scan the restaurant, which is pretty packed, until I find a familiar set of faces.

"And that's why they call him Buzz Saw!" Cole Bennett crows.

The twelve people at the table break into a raucous laughter. His brother Brooks, the man in question, is red as a beet but laughing harder than anyone. "That's not fair! What if I tell everyone how you peed down the slide in fifth grade?"

"I consider that a show of dominance," Cole jokes.

The crowd laughs again.

I walk up to the group, feeling a bit nervous. My sister Savannah only got engaged to Cole a few months ago and we have been slowly introducing our groups of friends to each other. The Billion Dollar Bennetts don't truly need any friends because there are so many of them that it's hard to keep them straight sometimes.

"Birdie! Over here!" My sister stands up and waves me over to where she has an empty chair saved for me.

I give the group a quick smile and hurry to sit next to Sav. She usually dresses very feminine and romantic in swishy little sundresses and big bows in her hair. At the moment, she is insanely pregnant and wearing a white maternity dress sprinkled with flowers. She looks radiant and also exhausted.

"Do you want a margarita?" she asks. "We have a pitcher."

That's Sav; always doing everything in her power to make everyone around her comfortable.

"Yeah. But for god's sake, let me grab it. Just relax."

The group around us breaks up into small conversations. I pour myself a lukewarm margarita from a pitcher. I take a sip and instantly set it down.

I don't want to insult anyone that likes this sugary drink. But it's absolutely disgusting. Pushing it away, I eye the half-full pitcher. I should've known better.

I look around the enormous table at the other people assembled. Aside from Sav and Cole, there's Cole's brother River, River's wife Pearl, and then the other Bennett Brothers. Brooks and Rhett, if I recall their names correctly.

Where is Rex? He's the reason I got a babysitter for my son Dex tonight.

The names are certainly in the brown leather spiral bound notebook in my purse. I'd have to go back through my copious notes and check. The second I had the idea to do a focus feature about someone from the Billion Dollar Bennetts, I started keeping meticulous track of every interaction I've ever had with the family members.

Other than the Bennetts, there are several handsome men and a few insanely beautiful women. I don't know these women from Adam. But using my reporter's eye, I notice that they are all very dressed up. Short, expensive dresses. Long fake nails and heavy fake lashes. They are all immaculately made up, as if they are going out to a club.

When in fact, they are here at the only vaguely cool bar in South Shore. It's mainly a pizza restaurant and it doesn't even serve shots. Just pre-made margaritas, wine, and a lot of beer.

My gut tells me that these women are single and this group has a lot of handsome, single men. I cast a jaundiced eye over the offerings. Yeah, I can see that each man is handsome in his way. Rhett is hot in a studious, glasses wearing sort of way. Brooks looks handsome in his red plaid shirt and jeans. The other man at the table that I don't know is wearing a light blue polo and khakis. And he is downright smoldering.

I lean over to Sav. "Who is that in the blue shirt?"

Sav looks and then nods. "That's Walker. He's best friends with Rex and Rhett."

I raise a brow and make a note. The more I learn about the Bennetts, the more fascinating they become.

Savannah links her arm through mine, her radiant smile looking at home anywhere – even if it's a scuzzy pizza joint with a bunch of pool tables in the back room. Cole moves chairs and sits by us, his hands casually tucked in his pockets.

"What's up, Birdie?" he asks. He lifts a light-colored beer toward me and then takes a sip.

"Not much." I force a smile to my lips. "Thanks for inviting me out."

Cole slides a long look at Sav. Sav ignores him and leans forward to change the conversation.

I would guess, then, that Sav invited me out. Whatever. It's not the first time I got a pity invite because I'm her sister.

"Have you been working on a new story, Birdie?" Savannah chirps, squeezing my arm.

"Maybe. I'm chasing down some leads. Trying to decide on which story I want to pursue." A total lie. I've been working this Bennett story for a couple of weeks and loosely following up on other leads just to make my boss, Herman, happy. "But tonight's about cheap drinks, cheaper jokes, and catching up."

"Speak for yourself," Cole interjects. He leans over toward me a boyish smirk. It makes him look like he's planning something mischievous. "I brought the good stuff. A bottle of red that's older than you."

"Ha! As if anything could be older than me," I quip back, playfulness lacing my voice. "Haven't you heard? I'm twenty-six *and* I've got a kid. I'm in bed at nine p.m."

Sav shakes her head. "Don't let him lie to you. We go to bed when the sun goes down. Charlie would rather die than let us sleep in."

Charlie is Cole's son. I thought that my son Dex was his Aunt Savannah's number one love. But her priorities have shifted since she met Cole.

Now, I'm pretty sure Charlie is her favorite human being alive. Followed by Cole, her unborn baby, and then Dex is somewhere after that. It's been a harder transition for me to accept than Dex because he loves having a kid his age in the family.

Chuckling, I accept that I just have to deflate my ego a little.

I'm mid-laugh when the atmosphere shifts. The room's energy tilts on its axis, as if realigning to a new north star.

My mouth goes dry.

He sucks all the attention from everyone. *He* is why the young women are all dolled up.

He's why I'm here, too. I don't even have to turn to know he's arrived.

Rex Bennett, the enigmatic and charismatic pro baseball player for the Atlanta Kings. He's built like an oak tree, tall and thick, with too long dark hair that flops into his eyes and has to be pushed back regularly. He's ridiculously, unspeakably handsome. He's been famous forever and is considered something of a hometown hero.

As for the women... He is notorious for being a huge player. Somehow, none of his conquests seem to mind that he flits from girl to girl, never settling.

And did I mention that he's Cole's big brother?

My pulse picks up a staccato rhythm that I can't quite keep in check. I'm just excited about the possibility of getting closer to my... uh... story. Yep, that's it.

"Speak of the devil..." Savannah murmurs, her gaze slicing through the sea of bodies to where Rex holds court at the entrance. He is every inch the athlete; broad shoulders set in an effortless stance, his smile easy but with a hint of arrogance that comes from being chased by both fame and fans. His eyes, a striking shade of blue, scan the room until they find us.

God, is he looking at me? I'm older than the other girls at the table. I'm wearing a simple green dress with a Peter Pan collar instead of a barely there gold tube dress. And I have a frigging kid.

Actually, that probably makes me the perfect target for a player like Rex. Wine me, dine me, never call me again. I would say I get it...

If I weren't a naturally curvy girl. I'm more of Penelope Featherington from Bridgerton and less of a skinny Minnie. I'm not sure where that puts me as far Rex is concerned.

Not that I really need to worry about that. Rex is my ticket to getting a promotion. If I sleep with him and someone finds out, my objectivity in reporting on him could be called into question.

Which is fine. Rex may be pretty to look at, and a good athlete, but that's as far as it goes. I'm not interested in him.

Actually, I'm not interested in anyone until my six-year-old is out of the house.

"Time to charm the snake out of his den," I whisper to myself. I smooth down my dress. I've got a story to chase. While Rex might be notorious for playing the field, I'm about to show him I'm not one to be outmatched.

I wait while Rex works his way around the table. He spends a few minutes talking to the women, who are here for him. Their flirtations are so obvious that it's actually pretty hard to watch.

Just when I think Rex is free, another random girl comes up to him from the restaurant and starts talking to him.

Ugh. Will I be forced to endure watching fans heap their adoring attentions on Rex's head? But then he breaks away from the strange woman and comes closer.

"Cole," he says. His tone turns flirty. "And Savannah. How are you feeling, sugar?"

My sister smiles, but doesn't engage with him head-on. "I'm feeling well, thanks for asking."

Cole glares at his brother. "Watch your tone."

Rex rolls his eyes. The threat rolls right off his back, like a duck shedding water. He turns to me. "Hey. How's it going, Birdie?"

I blush and smile. *Rex Bennet knows my fucking name.*

Of course he does. After all, I followed him on assignment before. And his family is about to become permanently linked with mine.

But that knowledge still thrills through my bones.

"Pretty good. Just working, the usual. Um—"

"Right. It's nice to see you again." He looks away.

Already, I am losing his attention. I need it.

I need him to pay attention to me for an hour or two.

I take a step toward him, my mind already spinning questions I want to ask. I think of the stories I need to coax from those all-too-knowing eyes. But first, I need an 'in', something beyond the formalities of mutual acquaintances.

"Didn't think you'd make it. The season keeping you busy?"

He turns fully, attention honed in on me like a spotlight. "It has its ups and downs. But I never miss an opportunity for good company... and great drinks."

"Ah, then you're in luck. Cole's been bragging about the vintage of his wine." I flash him a conspiratorial grin and sashay closer, close enough to breathe in his cologne, a mix of cedarwood and something else, distinctly him. "Though, between you and me, I think he's just showing off."

"Wouldn't put it past him," Rex laughs, the sound rich and inviting. A lock of hair falls over his forehead, and he flicks it back with a practiced charm. "You know, I could use a guide. Someone to navigate me through the perilous waters of Cole's wine selection."

"Perilous waters? Please, consider me your personal lifeguard." I offer a hand with mock solemnity, my fingers brushing against his. Electricity sparks—unexpected, thrilling.

"Is that so?" His eyes twinkle with amusement, and he takes a step closer, entering my personal space as if he belongs there. "Hope you're certified."

"Only the best for the Bennett-Taylors." I keep the tone light, playful. I'm threading a needle here, weaving between flirtation and professional curiosity.

I interviewed Rex for a brief piece about the trades his team made earlier this year. But I need to go deeper on him.

Rex is a treasure trove, just waiting to happen. This is the longform story I've been waiting for. It's a chance to prove I can handle more than the fluffy stuff I've been writing lately. But damn if Rex isn't making it hard to focus.

"Good to know." He leans in, lowering his voice, and the crowd fades into a blur. "Because, Birdie, when it comes to navigating uncharted territory, I prefer someone who's not afraid to dive into deep waters."

Oh, this man is trouble with a capital T. But as I meet his gaze, feeling the magnetic pull of his presence, I can't deny it—I'm tempted to swim in those depths, reporter or not.

"Oh! I— t-that's nice." I stutter.

Rex's response is a lopsided grin, one that tells me he's game for the banter. "I've been told I have that effect on people," he says, leaning against the mahogany bar with an ease that speaks of countless hours spent in gyms and on fields. "Can't say I mind it when the outcome looks like you."

"Flattery will get you everywhere—or nowhere fast," I retort. He's good, I'll give him that. And not just on the field.

"Let's aim for somewhere in the middle then." His eyes, a deep shade of brown, lock onto mine, and there's a challenge there, something that goes beyond casual flirting. It's like he's trying to read the plays before they're called, and I wonder if this is how he sizes up his opponents.

"Middle ground sounds safe," I concede, feeling like we are two players assessing each other at the start of a game. "You never know what you might find there."

"Exactly," he nods, and the conversation shifts, like we've silently agreed to drop the pretense and actually talk.

"Tell me, Rex, aside from dodging overzealous fans and hitting home runs, what gets you out of bed in the morning?" The question is bold, maybe too personal, but I want to see beneath the exterior—the man behind the stats.

"Sunrises," he answers without missing a beat. "There's nothing quite like the silence of the world before it wakes up. Plus, it reminds me that I've got another day to do something great."

"Sunrises," I echo, surprised by the poetic note in his voice. My mom would call that a sign of a soul that appreciates the calm before the storm, a sharp contrast to my dad's all-consuming blaze that left us more than once in the ashes.

"Ever tried capturing one on camera?" I ask, intrigued despite myself.

"Every chance I get." Rex pulls out his phone, swiping through photos until he finds a collection of dawn's early light captured in hues of gold and pink. "Not bad, huh?"

"Definitely not what I expected from the Atlanta Kings' notorious slugger," I admit, my voice softening. There's a vulnerability in sharing this side of himself, and it's as disarming as it is endearing.

"Life's more than baseball," he says, pocketing his phone. "What about you, Birdie? What drives you when the alarm goes off?"

"Stories," I reply, the word slipping out with a certainty that roots me to the spot. "There's something about unraveling the threads of someone's narrative, finding the truth amidst the noise."

"Ah, the intrepid reporter," he teases gently, though his gaze is thoughtful. "Seeking out the stories that need to be told."

"Something like that. Though, I'm starting to think some stories are more complex than others."

"Like mine?" His eyebrow quirks up, and it's clear he's not just talking about his career statistics or latest game highlights.

"Yours could fill a book, I bet," I say, half-joking, half-serious. The layers of Rex Bennett-Taylor are proving to be more intricate than I'd anticipated.

"Only if you're the one writing it," he counters smoothly, and the air between us crackles with something unspoken, a current that's pulling us closer with every word exchanged.

"Maybe I will," I muse, the idea taking root. "But only if you promise to give me more than just sunrises and baseball."

"Deal," he says, and extends his hand. I take it, feeling the solid warmth of his grip, a silent pact between us.

As our hands slowly part, I realize that this isn't just about landing a story anymore. With Rex, it's about discovering the unexpected.

The laughter from our group fades into the background as I lean closer to Rex, his guarded eyes holding stories untold.

"So, Mr. Mysterious," I start, my voice low and teasing. "What's off-limits in the Rex Bennett-Taylor exposé?"

He leans back, a half-smile playing on his lips, yet there's a barrier there that wasn't before. "Birdie, every man has to have his secrets."

"Even from a charming reporter who's dying to know more?" I bat my lashes at him, playful but persistent.

"Especially from them," he replies, his tone light but firm. The challenge in his eyes stirs something inside me, a mix of frustration and intrigue. There's a story behind those blue depths, one I'm determined to uncover.

"Fair enough," I concede with a mock sigh, though I'm far from giving up. "But you've piqued my curiosity now."

"Good," he says, his hand finding mine under the bar, sending a jolt of electricity through me. His touch is warm, inviting, and I can't help but wonder what it would be like to delve deeper into the enigma that is Rex.

Our fingers entwine. The world narrows down to the two of us. I feel the heat of his skin seep into mine, branding me with a desire to break through his defenses.

"Curiosity can be dangerous," he murmurs, his thumb brushing over the back of my hand in slow, deliberate strokes. It's a simple gesture, but it's laced with promise, a tantalizing hint of what could be.

"Isn't that what makes life interesting?" I counter, a flirtatious smile curving my lips as I meet his gaze head-on. "Taking risks, chasing the thrill..."

"Perhaps," he concedes, his eyes locked onto mine with an intensity that makes my breath catch. "But some risks are more rewarding than others."

"Guess we'll just have to find out which ones are worth it," I whisper, the words hanging between us like a challenge.

"Guess we will," he agrees, and there's an edge to his voice that sends a shiver down my spine.

For a moment, we're lost in each other, the tension palpable. Then Savannah's laughter breaks the spell, reminding us that we aren't alone. We pull apart, but the connection lingers, a thread stretched tight with anticipation.

I glance around to make sure no one noticed our intimate exchange. Everyone is wrapped up in their own conversations, oblivious to the silent dance happening right under their noses. And I can't help but feel grateful for the distraction.

Because right now? All I want is to explore this magnetic pull that keeps drawing me back to Rex.

Thank you to Theresa, Patricia, and Angela. I owe you all a million fancy daiquiris the next time I see you! Don't let me forget.

About Vivian Wood

Vivian likes to write about troubled, deeply flawed alpha males and the fiery, kick-ass women who bring them to their knees.

Vivian's lasting motto in romance is a quote from a favorite song: "Soulmates never die."

Be sure to join her email list to keep up with all the awesome giveaways, author videos, ARC opportunities, and more!

Vivian's Works

Cape Simon Billionaires
Small Town Billionaire Romance
The Grumpy Boss Agreement
The Fake Fiancée Proposition
The Playboy Rival Arrangement

Hush Hush Club
Forbidden Billionaire Romantic Suspense
Such A Good Girl
Such A Spoiled Brat

Married At Midnight
Forbidden Billionaire Romance
Deal With The Devil
Wed to the Devil
Vow to the Devil

Ruined Castle Trilogy
Forbidden Billionaire Romance
The Single Dad
The Nanny
The Caress

Broken Slipper Trilogy
Forbidden Billionaire Romance
The Patron
The Dancer
The Embrace
Possessive

Dirty Royals
Forbidden Royal Romance
Cruel Heir
Sinful Princess
Pretend Princess

King's Capture Duet
Dark Billionaire Romance
King's Capture
Queen's Sacrifice

Sinfully Rich
Steamy Billionaire Romance
Sinful Fling
Sinful Enemy
Sinful Boss
Sinful Chance

Billionaires Ever After
Steamy Bad Boy Romance
His Best Friend's Little Sister
Claiming Her Innocence
His Fiancé To Keep
His Lovely Virgin

Addiction Duet
Angsty Dark Romance
Addiction
Obsession

Other books
Wild Hearts

For more information....
vivian-wood.com
info@vivian-wood.com